THE GREATER ENGLISH NOVEL

L K CLARKE

ISBN 978-0-9575103-2-6

This edition © Botty Publishing Ltd 2014
Botty Publishing Ltd is a registered company founded by
Richard Goodall in 2012
www.bottypublishing.co.uk
email: hello@bottypublishing.co.uk

<u>Thank you:</u>

Katja Ammala, Camille Clarke, Kevin Clarke, Yvette Clarke, Rowena Gregory, Helen Macpherson, Dima Martynenko, Gerd Pichler, Michaela Renner, Philip Roth, Polina Veselkova and the enlightened being that is Richard Goodall.

Introduction

Deep within the bowels of Yorkshire, which any proud Yorkshire man, woman or child will tell you, is the largest, and therefore most important county in England, lies the small town of Skipperton. It is a town full of folk who, if you were to ask them where they came from, would reply 'Skipperton, Yorkshire' with both names sharing an equal importance, as if one could not exist without the other. Some of them might allow you to call them English, even less British. Label them European, however, and the best you'd come away with is an angry glare and a few choice words.

Skipperton was founded in 1090 by an errant town crier, who, having wandered the streets of Hull for over ten years, one day decided he was bored of being the voice of other people and wanted to live somewhere where people would listen to him, the real him. He proclaimed himself a new messiah who, having been struck by a bolt of lightning straight from the heavens, had obviously been chosen as a vessel by God. The voice of whom was now inside his head.

'What does the voice say?' asked those people who stopped to listen to him.

'Why it says to head west to settle on a patch of earth that will be the gateway to the universe,' the crier announced, his voice bellowing throughout the cobbled streets of the square. And so, without further ado, he checked to see where the sun was in the sky, called out to those who wanted to be saved (fifteen souls; eight men, seven women, plus thirteen sheep, five goats, three pigs - and a chicken, which unfortunately never made it to the sacred destination, so the chroniclers of the journey say.)

The settlement's rise wasn't quite as stratospheric as Henry Skipperton had expected, but it did grow in each of the seven years he presided over it as chief, and on his death bed, looking out at the carved piece of stone that read *Iauna est enim universum*, he still believed that one day the town would live up to its motto.

Unbeknownst to him, as soon as his soul had departed, those of the fifteen who had originally moved with him, downgraded the sign to read *Gateway to the World* as they felt embarrassed at leaving their homes in Hull, which though admittedly had been rather dull, at least had a port where people passed through.

It was only to save face that they didn't downgrade further, but sure enough, future generations, concluding that anyone would mock them for such illusions of grandeur, kept reducing the motto in scale, until now, in this present day, it is simply engraved on a small stone that reads *Gateway to our Homes* and is dwarfed by a colossal white rose that bares the town's name inside it.

This is not to say that the 10,000 inhabitants of the village that is nearing its 1,000th birthday are not proud of where they come from. Indeed those readers who thought, when reading the opening salvos of this introduction, that the "Bowels of Yorkshire" was a slight, have been thoroughly mistaken. Such a moniker was actually bestowed upon the town by the people itself, as was recently told in: **Skipperton. Yorkshire. History.** by The Mayor himself:

'By 'eck lass, what ya tryin' 't say? 'T bowels are 't gut. Withart gut fulla food 'n drink thy 'eart, lungs 'nt noggin can't work. 'S right in centre of ys, all 't rest works round it. Take it away 'n thow'd b nothin'. Way to a lad's 'eart is through 'is stomach. Way to Yorkshire b through Skipperton.'

NB: Individuals in the account that follows have had their speech, for the most part, translated into "Modern English" for the sake of coherence.

The Vicar

Cuthbert Johnson had always been a vicar. Well, not always: once upon a time he had been a small boy who went to school like the rest, but whilst there he had known he wasn't meant to follow his classmates into the world of work. It had been his dad who had pointed it out to him, sometime around his ninth birthday.

'Son,' he said, placing a hand on Cuthbert's slender shoulder. 'What do you want from life?'

'What do you mean?' Cuthbert had replied, not really knowing what to make of the question. He'd wanted mashed potato for dinner and hoped there would be chocolate ice-cream for dessert, but that had been all that was on his mind.

'I mean what do you want to be when you grow up? You know most boys your age long to be firemen or astronauts or sports stars.'

'None of those,' Cuthbert said, almost with a judder, which his dad felt rising through his bones.

'No son, that doesn't surprise me in the slightest. I've seen you in the playground. What position were you playing in the game today?'

'Referee.'

'Referee,' his dad said, sighing with shame, turning to try and hide the look of disappointment from his son. 'Did they make you take that position?' he asked, though he already knew the answer.

'No.'

'No,' he sighed. 'Son, nobody chooses to be the referee. Everyone wants to be scoring goals, winning the game, taking the glory.'

'But the game needs a referee. If there wasn't one, it would never be fair,' Cuthbert said, though in truth it was a role he had no strong feelings about either way.

'You're right of course,' his dad admitted, steering them down the street towards home, a pleasant piece of suburbia. 'Okay, well why don't you tell me about the girls instead,' he added.

The 'g' word caused Cuthbert to turn the colour of his school jumper. It made him look like a giant tomato, his dad thought.

'I mean I was your age once too, believe it or not,' he continued, 'and by golly I know they can be intimidating at times. Why the first time I saw your mum, my tongue felt like it was a loose slab of ham sloshing around in my mouth, but you know that's another story. What I'm trying to say is that boys are naturally nervous of girls, but not to the extent that they faint in their presence.'

'I told you, like I told Miss Stevens, I hadn't had any breakfast the first time, and the second time it was really very hot. It was just a coincidence that Stephanie happened to be standing beside me on both occasions,' Cuthbert said, his legs momentarily giving way as he thought of Stephanie, who in his mind resembled an earthly angel.

'Well son,' his dad replied, wiping his feet on the welcome mat, 'maybe what all this is trying to tell you is that you have a calling in some other direction.'

Cuthbert might not have thought about his father's final statement too much had it not been for the assembly in school the following morning. It wasn't as if his parents were churchgoers, and his one surviving grandma only visited church on Christmas Eve to sing a few hymns and see who, out of her old acquaintances, had made it round another 365 days. That Friday morning, however, Cuthbert had, theologically speaking, been shown the light.

The local vicar had been invited to deliver an assembly to talk about God, about being good and doing the right thing, basically what every other adult in the school ever told him. But finally, in summary, the small, unassuming, bald-headed man, who had kept his hands piously close together throughout his morning sermon, told them that: "God gives *direction* to us all. He calls to us, but sadly only some of us hear. Please make sure you have your ears open all the time."

Cuthbert could hardly believe it when he heard this

voice telling him to be a vicar. He stuck his finger in one ear, then the other, thinking he may have misheard, but when he removed his digit, he found the words still resonating. His path had been chosen: a vicar he was to be.

It had been easy studying for his role in the church at a theological college in the Home Counties. Everyone had been very nice and he had shown great dedication in applying himself to learning all the theory and rhetoric involved in being one of God's teachers.

It helped that there were no girls there to distract him. Being placed next to Cindy Walker during his French O level exam had been the reason he had dropped from his expected B to a D. How had it been remotely possible to concentrate when she sat there chewing her pencil, rubbing one bare ankle with her other foot and leaning forward to write with the top button of her blouse undone?

Cuthbert thought about her often during his years of training, and Stephanie, and Keri, and a host of other girls, but the fact that they weren't around to smile a pleasant hello, or possibly even want to converse, made life much simpler and easier.

In fact, when Cuthbert secured a post as a curate in a Home Counties village, some of his superiors began to suspect that he was finding life all too easy. The local parish where he served was quaint and twee. The pews were always full, as were the coffers. Those who visited every weekend were families who ate their evening meals round the table together, wore ties for work and school, baked buns for sales and had floral dresses that matched their wallpaper. They tried to outdo each other in their quest to help their parish and heaped so much praise on Cuthbert that he was almost buried underneath it, was unable to see reality any more. What he required was a dose of the real world, his bishop concluded, after bestowing upon him the title of vicar.

Birmingham. Cuthbert had liked the sound of it. Burr-Ming-Ham. He'd broken it into its three syllables, rolling them off his tongue. It was a place he'd never visited, much like the rest of England. His parents had taken him to Brighton a few times, but with no real friends or relatives north of the Watford gap, they'd barely felt the need to head outside of the M25 at all.

When Cuthbert arrived in The Midlands, it was as if he'd entered another country altogether, one with a strange new language, its own array of beliefs, and a slight drop in temperature. After four cosy years, it was not what he had foreseen, but if that was the Lord's way, then so it was to be. At theological college, they had warned him that he would face many tests in his life, but they had reassured him that God would see him through it. His first came quite quickly, succeeded by the second, third, fourth, fifth...

Slogans had been an area Cuthbert had excelled in. His parish in Surrey had always asked him to come up with the new pun for the billboard outside the church. The board's purpose had been to make the regulars chuckle and there was always the hope of attracting into the church those who were easily lured into consumerism by fancy adverts.

Seeing it as the church's calling card, Cuthbert had a naïve faith in the efficacy of the slogan and so was dismayed, when he reached his new home, to discover that the billboard was empty. However, at the same time, it presented the perfect opportunity for him to immediately stamp his authority on the parish. His young rector tried to warn him, as he set about slapping the large sheets of A1 upon the naked wooden boards, that the billboard had been left vacant for a reason, but Cuthbert laughed him off, insisting things would be different now he was there with his own witticisms.

Four months later, however, the billboard was regretfully once again decommissioned, as every poster met a similar tragic end at the hands of vandals within days of being rolled up - *Jesus saves* became *Jesus enslaves*, while *God is Great* was treated with a materialistic sliver of an *I*. The final straw came with *God Loves All* given a star suffix and a footnote that read *Except Jews, Blacks and*

Homosexuals, with a photoshopped picture of Jesus at the Last Supper as dark as a man of Middle Eastern origin would be, surrounded by the disciples, who for some reason were all naked and frowning.

Cuthbert's superiors, having heard about his battle with the billboard, hoped that the vandalism had succeeded in sheering away his naïvety. However, no one could have foreseen the torrent of abuse and blasphemy, which not only completely dispelled his innocence, but also meant that he feared sneaking out from underneath his blanket for fear of what awaited him.

Firstly his offer to pray for God's intercession on behalf of his parishioners led to some unexpected requests: for God to give out that week's lottery numbers; for God to make a girlfriend more attractive; for God to induce weight loss; for God to not kill, but possibly maim an ex.

Then there was Janice, a parishioner who had seemed harmless enough. She had visited him on a weekly basis with items collected from nature which, she insisted, bore the face of Christ. Encouraged by Cuthbert's reception of these items, she eventually brought in more exotic objects, including her own faeces, through which she appeared to have scraped her own fingernail.

Next was a poster pushed underneath his door designed by high school boys titled - *God Touched Me* - below which was a drawing of a naked man with an arrow pointing to an erect penis, which had to have been drawn on a far larger scale to the rest of the body, Cuthbert concluded.

The defining moment that ended his reign in the parish, however, came when Britney, one of his regulars, visited him in her purple velour tracksuit, with the word "Pimp" stitched in pink sequins on her back.

'Your honour,' she began, which was just the latest term for him to be addressed by. He'd been greeted with father, highness, penguin, Lord, magician, fraud, sir, master and grandmaster.

'Yes,' Cuthbert replied, with the same trepidation that filled his voice whenever he was approached.

'Well you know I've been coming for a few months now about the welfare of my father.'

'Yes,' Cuthbert said, his reply dragged out, his gaze drawn, despite himself, down at her large breasts, which jiggled in her white Versace vest. All too often he'd found himself thinking about women's breasts in the hope of escaping the reality of work: not only their breasts, but other parts as well. It had come to the point where, when out in his casual daywear on a Tuesday afternoon, in an unfamiliar part of town, he'd actually made it half-way to the till with a magazine covered in foil so only its title was on show.

'And I've been doing the praying that you told me to morning, noon and night, saying them with my meals so as I don't forget.'

Cuthbert nodded his approval, hoping it would make Britney wobble a bit, but she was too focused.

'And as you know through my reports, it hasn't really been working. In fact if anything it seems to have made the lung cancer worse, and you know I have no doubt that you've been praying for him also, because that's your job and all, but I guessed that since you don't really know him, well, you haven't been putting everything into it.'

Cuthbert tried to assure her that this was not the case, but Britney powered on, waving away anything he might have had to say.

'So, I realised what I need to do. You see when Trevor wants to persuade me to do something I usually don't want to,' she looked at Cuthbert, and guessing he wasn't on the same wavelength, spelled it out to him, 'you know, up the bum and that. Well he brings me a gift, butters me up, so I was going to bring you a bottle of whiskey, but then I was reading up in The Sun the other day and I discovered what you really like.'

'That means,' at this point she reached into her jacket pocket and removed a passport sized photo of a young blonde child, staring quizzically back at the camera as if he had never seen one before, 'if you produce the results, I promise I'll bring my young nephew Billy over to stay the night.'

'So, I believe you're here to make a request for a transfer to another parish,' Bishop Henry said, his brand new robes shining in the light from the stained glass windows of his residence, an apparently accidental effect which it had taken him hours to achieve. His jowls hung, thick and meaty, and his eyes sparkled. He was a man to whom the Lord had been very kind indeed.

'Err, well, kind of,' Cuthbert replied, his reasoning escaping him, certain the Bishop was going to send him off packing back to his borough with the news that, surprise, surprise, the Lord was testing his faith. 'You see it's just that, well I was thinking that I would like to see somewhere different, take on a new challenge.'

'Hmmm,' the Bishop said, surprised the young vicar had lasted as long as he had. It had been a real shock when he'd discovered, just over two years previously, that he was being sent someone vibrant and fresh faced, for the parish had seen the demise of far tougher, more seasoned men, some of whom had turned into successful sinners, deserting the church completely in order to lead a life with whiskey and women. At least Cuthbert hadn't been snapped by photographers in his cassock with his hands down a stripper's knickers.

'I agree. I think it's important to tend to a new flock too, helps keep you on your toes.'

Cuthbert nodded enthusiastically.

'How would somewhere with a slower pace of life fit you?' the Bishop asked, a recent death having just opened up a quaint spot a couple of hours north.

'That would be excellent!' Cuthbert blurted, before controlling himself. 'I mean if that is where you think I should spread the word of the Lord, then I shall endeavour to work all hours of the day to do so,' he said, sensing that the Lord was a fairer man than he had begun to give him credit for.

'Well then, pack your suitcase and take the next bus north, you're ascending higher on the Lord's ladder as it were, up to Skipperton.'

'Sorry, where?' Cuthbert replied.

'Skipperton. Lovely little place. You'll need to stop over in Leeds, then take a smaller bus from there. I do believe some people still travel up by horse and cart though.'

'Horse and cart!' Cuthbert exclaimed, starting to think he was being bamboozled, but the Bishop nodded sagely.

'They're becoming rarer, admittedly,' he said, standing to let Cuthbert out of his residence. 'Anyway, don't worry yourself about that, Lucy will provide you with all the fine print, and I am certain that you shall find your new home far more becoming than your present one. Oh and Cuthbert,' he said, as Cuthbert made his way out, even more shakily than he had entered, 'I don't say this to many of our congregation, but do try and get yourself a...' he paused on the brink of 'wife', swallowed and, lowering to such a hush he could barely hear himself, whispered, 'girl.'

Upon entering Skipperton's crumbling town walls, Cuthbert was struck by the feeling that he'd set foot in a village built to resemble something out of history. He'd visited a "Roman" village when he was at primary school, a place where everyone had dressed up in an attempt to bring to life what it would have been like to live thousands of years ago. Since then Cuthbert had come to realise that the people who worked in such places were probably even lonelier than he was. At least when he walked round the supermarket in his "costume" most people greeted him with a respectful nod of their head.

What he also realised, as the Bishop's final words resonated through his mind, more so than anything that had come from the New Testament or *Psalms*, was that for him, his work attire acted as a sort of force field. Within it he could speak to women, because he knew that all they wanted was to share their problems. It was a completely professional relationship that didn't require him to think of small talk that could lead him anywhere. It brought him close to the opposite sex, but at the same time kept him at a distance. He was both Clark Kent and Superman; it was just a question of how to mould those two people into one, because he'd always assumed, that like God, the right woman would just happen to find him and it would feel as easy being in her company, as being in the Lord's. What he didn't expect was to find her waiting outside his new church for him.

She was an oasis in the desert, a diamond in the rough, for after half an hour in Skipperton, Cuthbert had begun to think he would prefer the mockery of Birmingham, where at least he'd been able to understand what people had said. Here when he'd asked for directions, having become lost down a maze of cobbled alleys, he'd thought the first man had quoted Shakespeare and the second a jumble of foreign obscenities. It had only been the fact that they had both pointed in the same direction that had eventually led him to the church, which was where she stood in all her splendour. From what he'd viewed of the town thus far, she was as much of an oddity as he was. She was tall for a start, 5'8" possibly, give or take an inch or two for her heels, which gave extra definition to her sculpted calves. The rest of her legs lay hidden under a black pencil skirt.

'Oh father, I've been waiting for you,' she said, her pronunciation suggesting a lack of higher education, but at least he could understand each word and wasn't thinking about where he could buy a dictionary. He even ignored the use of the word "father" because he was too busy staring into her chocolaty eyes. He doubted he'd have to stare down too deep to reach her soul, but brains weren't everything were they? There had to be a balance, and he'd cover that end of the relationship for them. She had high cheek bones, luscious eyelashes, glossy hair and pouting, plump lips. He wasn't aware of the perfume she was using, but it was drifting through his nostrils and wrapping itself round his heart. Would it be too creepy to reply that it was strange, but he'd been waiting for her too? Such a sentence may have flowed from him and swept her off her feet, but instead Cuthbert almost choked on his words and a whole stream of phlegm caught in his throat.

'Oh Jesus,' the woman said, reaching forward to help, before recoiling at her own words. 'Oh God…oh no not again,' she almost cried in horror, her fingers going into her mouth, as Cuthbert tried as delicately as possible to hack up what was turning him purple. 'I mean oh darn,' she finally said, clicking her fingers, 'another list of things to add to my confessions,' she continued. 'Hey, are you okay?'

Still bent double, Cuthbert raised a hand to show that he just needed a minute, taking the time, through a stream of tears, to admire her legs again. So smooth, like breasts, breasts were smooth. He bet hers were the silkiest, smoothest, milkiest ever…hang on, had she just mentioned confession? He looked at the building. It did seem rather more ornate and grandiose than he was used to. The stained glass windows were double the size of his previous work place and the spire rose into the sky, reaching up to honour and touch the Lord, rather than piously and humbly bowing before him.

'I'm sorry,' he muttered, the woman having returned to standing straight, a silk scarf hanging loose around her neck. She looked at him longingly, like some film noire actress: 'but is there another church in town?'

She shook her head, her hair swishing slowly, black as coal.

'This is the only one in town, father.'

Cuthbert would have just been happy to stare at her lips all day. What kisses they would give! He shook his head and shrugged, took out his large, old-fashioned iron key from his briefcase and placed it inside the lock. The door into his new abode opened with a creak.

It was Catholic, there was no doubt about it. There were two confession booths and a cardboard box standing on the altar which had been marked "wafers", only to have had "Body of Christ's" scrawled over it in red marker. He looked around for someone to help him out, but only the woman, who had followed close behind him, was there for answers.

'What…'

Cuthbert allowed his voice to drift off across the dusty pews. It looked like the place had simply been abandoned. There was no light switch, only candles of various stubby sizes, standing mid drip around the vast hall.

'Who...'

It was like a freezer. The woman shuddered behind him, stamping her feet, the sound of which echoed off the walls. He would have no doubt felt the icy air to a greater degree if he hadn't been full of bewilderment.

'When...'

What was the saying, if the key fits? Had the tenancy agreement come to an end? Was it someone else's turn to have a go? Maybe the news Henry VIII had become head of the church had only just reached them?

'Can we get into the confession boxes?' the woman asked, through chattering teeth.

Cuthbert looked at her. Would it hurt just this once? Of course he knew what to do; anyone who'd watched more than ten hours of TV did. He already had his three Hail Marys ready to hand out. In his head he ran through all the tones in which he could say: 'go on my child,' but it became apparent he wouldn't have to provoke her into more detail. Their seats had barely finished groaning before she started.

'So it's been two weeks since my last confession because nobody's been here. But it's really the same thing as always. I don't know if the other father left any notes?'

Cuthbert shook his head, then, when no reply came, realised the reason was because he couldn't be seen.

'No,' he replied, rather more deeply than was necessary.

'Well father, it's like this, I can't stop thinking about sex.'

Inside his box Cuthbert gulped, and almost instantly found himself erect. Trying to hide it with his hands did nothing to aid its deflation.

'I don't know what to do. I mean it's not like Harold doesn't service me, but it's always so monotonous and perfunctory, and what I think about is exciting things; masks,

15

whips, doing it outside, with people watching, with people joining in...'

Cuthbert was no longer listening to the words. If this was what confessions were like, how was anyone surprised priests were going around sticking it into the nearest person they could lay their hands on? When he realised she'd come to a pause, he asked the only question that seemed relevant.

'Is Harold your husband, boyfriend or err, just a casual thing?'

The Skipper

If Cuthbert Johnson had required hardly any thought regarding his choice of occupation, Harold Baker had needed none at all. Born the only son of the great Geoffrey Baker, he had been raised with the understanding that it was his divine right to take control of the Skipperton Tea Empire. As soon as he had been able to put one foot in front of the other without toppling over, his father had guided him round the factory, introducing him as his heir to the workers, who, in admiration of their employer and his genial ways, stopped to salute the young Harold as though he were a future emperor, rather than the next in line to the biggest company in their small, northern village.

But to the people of Skipperton, Skipperton Tea was an empire. A household could consume a box of twenty in a day. It was known that in some houses they considered it such a sacrilege to discard anything that bore the name and famous logo of Skipperton Tea that they used the cardboard packages to wallpaper their houses. On these precious boxes, Emperor Geoffrey held a hot mug of Skipperton tea in his hand, with the words: 'A great start, middle and end to the day' inscribed above his beaming face.

A doctor had once found, when up from London conducting research, that there wasn't a single human in the village that didn't have an abnormal level of the tea in them. It was practically what women breastfed their children. If only he had been a veterinarian, he would have discovered it was what flowed around the veins and arteries of the animals too. Cats enjoyed theirs especially milky, dogs drank theirs watered down, whilst pigs and cattle supped theirs from troughs as a nightcap. Was it any wonder that their meat tasted so good? And of course that wasn't taking into account the crops, for which the farmers of Skipperton used the finished bags, squeezed to a thread of their life from ripping, as fertiliser.

In the first, fresh days of spring, after the crops had

been planted and new born lambs frolicked in the fields, residents stopped on the side of the lanes to stare in awe, drooling at the sight of what looked like one giant tea bag on the horizon, giving its final drops of goodness to enrich the soil.

Needless to say, Geoffrey had been granted the keys to the town midway through his twenties, when he was still the same debonair, suit-wearing gentleman who adorned the tea boxes. This honour had allowed him to herd his small flock of sheep through the middle of the town's cobbled paths, where he would greet those shops and people he passed with a raising of his crooked cane to their bows and curtsies. He would proclaim to the townsfolk that the future of Skipperton Tea, and therefore Skipperton itself, was in safe hands, because Harold, his son and heir, was accompanying him in order to become accustomed to the duties of his role.

That mantle eventually passed to Harold on his twentieth birthday, when his father had decided, at the ripe old age of thirty-six, that he could no longer give the company the energy it truly deserved.

In many ways it was the end of him. The following decade led to his slow decay, where his time was mainly spent in his rocking chair, listening to the wireless, reading the Skipperton Gazette, gradually becoming thinner, until one day he eventually went as he would have wished, drowning in his morning bowl of tea. The news was met with widespread mourning. His coffin was laid open in the town square for the thousands of residents to pay homage to, each filling his coffin with a priceless tea bag, until his face was barely afloat. His obituary ran on the front page of the 20 November, 2010 edition. There were even suggestions that the village should erect a statue of him in the town centre, but The Mayor settled on a plaque beneath their beloved founder, Henry Skipperton, his famous town crier bell held aloft. *Geoffrey Baker, Mr. Skipperton Tea* it read. *1964-2010. Beloved son and father to all.*

All this might have seemed too much of an act to follow, but thanks to the years of constant preparation, of hearing every grain of wisdom passed down to him first hand, Harold never once batted an eyelid at the prospect of leading the empire on his own.

The most important discovery he had made during his ten years leading the company though, had not been given to him. It had come during his wanderings through the factory and his time spent analysing the books, sitting in the receptionist's office, and it had been this: if he employed people with a high level of aptitude in senior management positions, if they knew their roles and the jobs of their subordinates, then it meant he hardly had to lift a finger at all. The place literally ran itself. He tried his theory out one week, kept away from it all, slept in late and spent his time at the market and taking walks around the abbey instead. When he returned from his leave, he was pleased to find everything running as he had envisioned. Judith, his father's secretary, who at fifty-four, still moved in the same clockwork fashion she had done thirty years earlier, had even made the decision to hire a new girl to take her place, for the time when she eventually expired over her large, chunky typewriter. And why shouldn't she have done? After all, she knew more about the ins and outs of the position than Harold did. So, with the business in not just one pair of safe hands, but a multitude of them, Harold decided that he could start up another venture, one even closer to his heart.

It was a photo that had sparked his obsession, one that rivalled the rest of the town's fixation with Skipperton Tea. Slap bang centre on the gilded mantelpiece, between a photograph of his parents' wedding day and one of his mother aged fifteen, reclining on a chaise lounge her head held high, was the image of his granddad, Fred Baker, standing shoulder to shoulder with the greatest Yorkshireman to ever have existed, his namesake Fred Trueman (God bless him), shining corky in hand.

Even on the day before his death at the hands of his own tea, Geoffrey Skipperton had raised a crooked finger, barely more than a piece of bone and started, proudly, on his favourite story.

'Hit a pair of sixes off him that day did your granddad,' he said, his eyes sparkling as he relived that moment he'd borne witness to, and savoured more than any other.

'Both of them struck plum with the middle of the bat, straight down the wicket into the crowd. Almost identical they were, as beautiful strokes as you'll ever see. A short step down the crease and it was like the ball was carried off by angels. If only you could have seen Trueman's face (God bless him). Stunned isn't the right word. His jaw fell agape. This man, not an Aussie, nor an Indian nor a Lancastrian (at that Harold and his father both leaned forward and spat into the fire), but a Yorkshireman, slogging him in such fashion. Of course the next ball Trueman did him, a slippery in-swinger clipping the bails of middle and off, the type only geniuses can produce, but by then your granddad had already sealed himself into the Skipperton cricket club's history books.'

Harold had heard the tale so many times he'd started to believe he too had been in the crowd that day to witness the historic feat. What he was certain of, however, was that, despite all his father had planned for him to do with Skipperton Tea, it was his greater destiny to follow in the footsteps of his granddad.

Having explained to Judith and the others in management positions that he wasn't disregarding his duties, but merely delegating further power to them, as they were the ones who had to make split second decisions on the shop floor, he made his way down to the dilapidated cricket club with the aim of transforming it, so that it would attain the same level of prestige that belonged to Skipperton Tea.

Despite his granddad's performances, Skipperton had not been a great side that had seen itself fall from grace; they had merely always been ordinary. It seemed they were happy to languish mid-table, win a fraction more than they lost and be in the bar by five 'o' clock for a round or three of Skipperton Black Ale. They were a set of men who played the game for their leisure, not for greatness, and if there was one thing Harold's dad had always made sure he aimed for, it was greatness. Tea leaves hand sifted and checked under magnifying glasses, the font on the boxes hand stencilled, each of the tea tasters aged below ten so their taste buds hadn't been tainted by Woodbines and ale. Details were important: they were the difference between defining a town's drinking habits and being merely a nice brew; the few runs that marked a fist pumping win from a heart breaking loss.

In terms of his own ability, Harold didn't doubt himself either as a player or a leader, though he hadn't actually played a game since leaving school at fourteen. He'd had enough practice with the factory workers though, who, on their breaks, would appease him with a couple of overs each, their ability (what with them being men of North Yorkshire) of a fine standard, since being able to bowl a tight line and length was treated with an equal importance as numbers and writing at school. The narrow spaces of the factory hadn't allowed much scope for sweeps down to third man or slogs out onto the leg side, but his forward defensive was incomparable, and now and then he would shuffle forward for a glorious drive straight back down past the bowler, his body finishing in a sculpted line, a warrior brandishing his mighty long sword as if he was about to bring it down through an enemy's body.

On the evening of his momentous decision to transform the fortunes of the Skipperton team, Harold walked into the club's function room, The Arms, after the team had concluded a light, early evening's session in the nets. Harold's appearance brought both the players and those ardent diehard fans, who only ever drank in that pub so their money went straight to the team, to a standstill. Some of the players stood from their chairs, while those that were already standing bowed as if Arthur Scargill had entered. A few, who were totally overawed by his presence, merely sat with their mouths agape, nudging one another, following his every step across the room.

Since this was business, Harold desisted from his

usual wave of acknowledgement and made a beeline straight for the manager, also a Harold, but one whose parents had often joked that they had been too poor to afford the final r of the surname Baker, and had to make do with the abridged Bake instead. He was now nearing his sixtieth birthday and had been in charge of the team for over forty years; the job, like most in town, a role for life. How much life he had left in him, however, was debatable. Any decisions he made came from instinct and noise alone, since his cataracts were so bad he thought that a great fog had descended on the world two years ago, but had been delighted that cricket had decided to battle on through it.

'Harold,' Harold said, his shout, not moving the manager from his stool. Harold Bake simply continued staring to the side of Harold, with his hand wrapped tightly around his own tankard, decorated with a white rose on one side and a willow bat on the other, half full of Skipperton Black and distinguishable from other tankards only by a small chip in the handle. 'I've come to take over the team,' Harold added, his mind made up that this was the only option.

'Oh you have, have you? And just who do you think you are?' Harold yelled, pointing at Harold, who stood in front of a signed picture of Michael Vaughn and The Ashes, hanging on the whitewashed wall. The picture had been ripped in half to eradicate it of the alleged hero of the hour, fat Lancastrian Freddie Flintstone or whatever they called him, leaving the former England captain without his left arm, making him an even more godly character in Harold Bake's eyes.

'Harold Baker.'

'Harold Baker the cobbler?' Harold Bake asked, with more than a little confusion.

'Nope, not that one.'

'Young Harold Baker that runs the paper round and who, when he was a little nipper, was bent over my knee a fair few times to be spanked into shape?'

'Nope, not him either.'

'In that case, the only other Harold Baker I know of

is…'

Realising whom he was addressing, Harold Bake fell silent and, bowing low, made the profoundest of apologies: 'You'll have to excuse me, my eyes aren't what they used to be, sir. By all means, it would be the greatest honour for me to hand over this team to you.'

Harold gave his predecessor a pat on the back and turned to face his audience, who awaited his conference with the same anticipation as those who had been present when Moses returned from the mountain.

'The reason I'm here is simple,' Harold said, his gaze crossing to the replica picture of the one that stood on his mantelpiece, hanging, a little dusty and skewed on the bar's wall: 'to make Skipperton Cricket Club as successful as Skipperton Tea.'

A rapid upward trajectory of the team's fortunes wasn't too difficult to implement. Along with the manager, out went half the players in a retirement testimonial, since they were either as old as Harold Bake, as infirm as him, or both. Towards the end of an innings it had often been nigh on impossible for an umpire to tell if the ball had taken a nick off a pad or if it was simply the bones of one of the old brigade creaking under the stress of raising the bat higher than their waists.

All those players whose time had been adjudged to have run out, took it well, acknowledging that they had begun to hope deep down, whilst batting or fielding second, that the other players would just get it over with so they could be inside next to the fire with a pint of Skipperton's finest.

The next simple step, alongside recruiting younger players through trials, rather than simply bringing in players' sons, was to construct a proper training regime that ran for an hour after work every Monday, Wednesday and Friday. Since the edict had come from the owner of Skipperton Tea, not one of the players' bosses had a problem with letting them leave a quarter of an hour early if that was what was required.

The third step was to transform singles into doubles

and cut down on opposition boundaries by implementing a smoking post-match only rule, which was met by a few grumbled, or rather coughed, complaints, but which on the whole was complied with immediately. It was then, around two months later, when Harold had licked them into some sort of shape, that he began the smaller tactical refinements of batting order, fielding positions and bowler rotation, all of which had been unheard of under the previous manager, who simply let whoever had their pads on first go out and open up.

The ultimate stroke of genius from the new Skipper, however, was promising each player a free box of Skipperton Tea for every victory.

The results flourished. There was no need for a settling in period. They started pre-season with a win and the victories kept rolling in from there. Seven wicket maulings; tons scored all the way down the order to ninth; a different bowler taking five wicket hauls each game; spinners bowling maiden after maiden on pitches that were flatter than their caps, and all of it for the pyramid of tea boxes that awaited them on the dressing room table post match.

They proved most adapt at the 50 over game, regularly posting scores of 300+, a target so intimidating that they could tell as they walked into the dressing room for lunch that most of their opponents had already thrown the towel in. The North and East Yorkshire league was pretty much wrapped up with half the season still to go, but it was the National Cup where they found themselves truly surprising other teams. Their confidence was so high that, though no one said it for fear of jinxing their form, they honestly believed they could go all the way and put to the sword any of the goliaths two or three divisions above them.

If anyone had known what they were running on, there would have been calls for drug tests and for the tea to be placed on the banned substance list. Yet it wasn't the tea itself, but love and lust for those little filtered bags that drove the players on, made them give all they could, and more, for it wasn't just for them, but their wives and children, aunties and uncles, who stood and watched, cheering them on, knowing what prize was in store.

Then, one day in August, across the dreaded Pennines, the quarter-final draw of the One Day National Cup pitted them away against the Redillian Lancashire Cricket Club. This club shared a similar record that season to themselves, albeit in the respective division above. This wasn't just a game. This was revenge. Always was. Not a personal revenge: the two teams had never met, had never even heard of each other until the draw; nor was it anything to do with their fathers or grandfathers. The revenge was for something that hadn't even occurred during the lifetime of their respective clubs: it was for August 22nd 1485, the Battle of Bosworth Field.

Duly, the Skipperton team approached the match in the frame of mind that they were going to war rather than for a place in the last four. The pride of the White Rose was at stake, and though the load was heavy, the team knew that they had the ability to bear it. When they reached the ground they found that on paper the odds were in their favour, just as they had been for Richard III and his ten thousand Yorkist men on that fateful day over five hundred years ago.

Redillian's lead strike bowler, who had a strike average of 8.32 that season and had amassed five wicket hauls in each of the previous rounds, including a stunning 9-9 in the prior one, had been side-lined through illness from a suspected tainted hotpot. Still stony faced, and spitting each time they saw the board that announced the county where they were playing, Harold warned his players to take no notice of this news and treat the game as they had prepared for it that week.

He won the toss, and on what was a flat pitch with a nice sunny sky, elected to bat first. It proved a wise decision, for at 6.44 runs an over, they posted a very formidable 322, and with the ball in hand, they did what appeared to be irreparable damage in the first ten overs, reducing the hosts to 40-4.

Maybe it was because they thought they had the

game sewn up and had turned their minds to the boxes of tea. Perhaps it was because after seven hours they had exhausted their adrenaline reserves, but whatever the reason, despite a continued tenacious bowling attack, the fifth wicket would not fall to let them in at the tail end. The partnership didn't race at the 7.05 an over it required to win the game, it gnawed and nibbled at the runs in the form of singles and doubles, frustrating the Skipperton players. The bowling, growing more determined, began to lose shape in its line and length, which the pair of Lancastrians duly dealt with in a controlled fashion, so that with five overs remaining, they required 63 runs off 30 balls.

Sweat poured not just off the players, but also the spectators, who knew and would always say that this was the most fantastic thing about cricket, how in the space of a couple of overs - one or two incidents - a match could be turned. And so one or two incidents proved to be correct. It came down to the final over. 11 to win. It had swung this way and that, a boundary in favour of the Lancastrians, a wicket for the Yorkshiremen.

In stepped Richard Egbert. He already had four wickets to his name, and there was just one more to collect. He was a giant of a man, imposing in every sense; his 6'4" height, his 15 and 1/2 stone of weight. From beneath a thick black moustache, his lips never moved. His stare could stop any man in his tracks. He wasn't one of words, he was one of actions. Skittling stumps, breaking bails, bruising bouncers and match-winning maidens were what he specialised in. His thick forearm was the length of his size fourteen shoes from crook to wrist, his hand another foot on to the tip of his middle finger. In it the ball looked like a berry ready to be crushed. When he gripped it a certain way, it was almost impossible for the batter to see it until it had left his palm and was rocketing at 80mph+ towards them.

The first two deliveries went to plan, yorkers the batter could only manage to block. Egbert had it in him to produce another four, and indeed with the next ball went one better, knocking out middle, but before his teammates had the chance to leap from their positions and run over to congratulate him, the umpire signalled a no ball. Richard walked very slowly back to the crease and stared down at it, not saying a word. He looked into the eyes of the umpire, who did his best not to immediately avert his gaze.

Without any show of emotion, ball back in hand, four balls still to bowl, and the wickets back standing, Richard once again launched himself into his run up and found himself being nicked down to third man for two runs. Redillian now required 9 from 3. The next ball met a similar fate, struck this time, quite cleanly back behind him to leave Redillian 7 adrift. A dot ball and the tie was beyond them. Egbert steamed in and this time, though the batter got nothing on it, the umpire stretched out his hands to signal a wide - an extra run and still 2 deliveries to bowl.

Harold, from his position at second slip, watched Richard carefully, rocked on his heels at the thought of going across to speak to him, adjust the field, take the pressure off him, but this was a man who didn't feel pressure, who set his own fields, who had a rhythm that was distracted by consultation, not helped by it. All season he had only given away six runs in extras, four wides and two leg byes, and now two in a single over, he had to be enraged. He was, he raced in with a bouncer and was top edged over the wicket keeper for 4, leaving Harold no other option than to stride over to him, whilst the ball was retrieved from behind a bush.

'Remember those first two,' he said, maintaining a respectable distance, 'another one like that.'

'The third and sixth were exactly like that,' Richard remarked, catching the ball he had been tossed. He rubbed it down the length of his red marked right thigh.

'I know. They weren't good calls. Just keep it tight,' Harold replied, his trust in his bowler implicit. He wouldn't have traded anyone else to take his place that minute, not Goughy, not Bresnan, not even the great Fred (God Bless Him) himself.

A collective hush fell across the venue as Richard took the liberty of re-pacing his run-up, striding out twenty long paces, twisting his hips slightly to lengthen his stride and mark a run-up that had served him precisely for seventeen years and over 480 wickets. He stopped when he reached his plot and spun on his heel, turning to face the batsman who'd taken a couple of small steps down the crease, prodding at the ground with his bat, trying to keep calm, blocking out all the outside interference, while his partner stood crouched at the other end in a sprinter's stance, ready to burst from his blocks as soon as the ball had been released, regardless of where it went.

Like an arrow sent true to its target by that legendary figure Robin Hood (who those in Yorkshire claim to have been a Yorkshireman and not from Nottinghamshire, for had he been born in Nottingham he surely wouldn't have been brave and bold enough to commit such acts), Richard sped down the worn run-up and bowled another yorker, which the batsman, like he had done with the first couple of balls, blocked with the tip of his bat. This time, however, rather than remaining stationary, he sprinted forward, his partner already half way down the pitch, a race on between him and Paul Baker, the wicketkeeper, to reach the crease and ball respectively.

Meanwhile, amongst the bedlam, the umpire had once again raised his arm vertically to signal a no ball. This time, rather than continue with his duties and back up behind the wicket for the throw that would be hurled his way once the ball was in Paul's hands, Richard walked calmly over to the umpire, and waiting until he was inches away, his moustache bristling as his upper lip trembled, growled: 'You're a bloody cheat.' And without another word, he walked from the field, as the two Lancastrian batsmen dived safely over their respective creases to secure a heroic victory.

'Cheat.'

It was repeated another ten times as the Skipperton players walked from the field without shaking hands, without acknowledging anyone that wasn't wearing the White Rose. They didn't stay for the obligatory round of sandwiches, refused to stand and listen to the Redillian chairman and the other officials, just collected their suit bags and brogues, stepped onto their fleet of cars, and without saying a word, took a collective telepathic vow never to cross west of the Pennines again. It was an utter disgrace. They could whip out the inkwell and quill to write a formal complaint, but what good would that do? The cricket board at Lords wouldn't pay attention to them; the bigwigs had always been on the side of the Red Rose since that defining moment of English history five hundred years ago. All you had to do to look for proof of such favouritism was take the slightest interest in football, dominated for the past fifty years by Liverpool and Manchester United, whilst the Yorkshire teams languished in the lower leagues. And when one of them did finally win a title in 1991 (Leeds United) look what those within the game had done to conspire in their embarrassing downfall.

But the biggest piece of evidence, the one that put the bias beyond all doubt, was all those on the wireless reporting for the BBC, claiming that it had been fat, old Freddie Flintoff who had inspired England to reclaim The Ashes for the first time in eighteen years and not the genius of the skipper Michael Vaughn. Well just look what had happened during the following series with the leader out injured: a five-nil whitewash with the team coming home, their tails firmly between their legs.

Thus the result against Redillian wasn't a blotch on the copybook of the Skipperton players, it was the blood on their hands. But rather than lead to despair, desperation and a dizzying demise, it had the opposite effect. The team became an impenetrable force; they swept aside every club that crossed their path, all of it in the vain hope of cleansing themselves of the injustice that had befallen them.

The Plan

Four years to that very day, Harold sat at Judith's desk going over the monthly books; page after page of crumpled, blue lined paper with her spider-like handwriting scrawled neatly between each line; every paper clip and pencil accounted for. Without that day's newspaper folded beside him, he could have been fooled into thinking he was staring at a copy of their files from last month, last year, the last decade. Give or take ten bob here or there, and taking into account the steady rise of inflation, the monthly balance remained the same, a nice healthy five digit sum that had the ability to simply flow, without him lifting a finger, into his bank account, which he never bothered so much to glance at. He could make a pretty good estimate as to the seven digit number stored within it, but since he was safe in the knowledge he had the brass to pay his bills and the shillings to buy his Skipperton Black, why bother to check how rich he was? It had never made any difference before.

It was true that he would have had a damn sight more if he hadn't found himself a wife, but though her tastes in clothes exceeded his, there wasn't much Dorothy, the town's finest seamstress, couldn't rustle up for a couple of ten pound notes. Plus, it wasn't as if Rachel had fallen for his money.

They'd been playing Ramsgate Old Boys of Derbyshire in the preliminary round of the National Cup, and having won comfortably, had made their way to the bar with a collective swagger, carrying their own case of Skipperton Black and the dripping to add to their complimentary sandwiches. As soon as Harold had entered the room, it was like she was the only thing in it. Her face was in profile, all sharp and precise, not like the girls that were the wives, daughters, nieces and aunties in Skipperton. It wasn't that Harold didn't like that sort of girl; it was just that none of them had ever made his heart swell at the same time as his trousers. Now though, shuffling his briefs, he made his way

31

immediately to the bar on which she was leaning, and subtly sniffed the air she fragranced with her perfume. It was like delving deep inside a newly opened box of the finest tea leaves. He wanted to bury his face into her and never let go. The easiest way to make her acquaintance would have been to buy her a drink, but she was already ordering.

'...and just a tea for myself please. Ta.'

Harold's heart almost burst at the enormity of the situation. This was the type of scenario you heard about on the wireless or were forced to read about in books at school. It was pure Mandy Dingle and Paddy Kirk. He cleared his throat and shuffled a little closer. It was just a business proposal, that's how he needed to see it; that would keep him calm when thoughts of what sort of business he was after flashed into his mind. The waiter brought over a gin and tonic, a Coke, and an empty cup.

'Were you after the Darjeeling or the English Breakfast, duck?'

Harold stepped in before she had the chance to answer.

'It's alright my good fellow, she's having the finest cuppa in the world. Just bring the kettle over here,' he said, removing a bag from his top pocket, the orange background and large S of the tiny square cardboard tab pinched between his thumb and forefinger, as he lowered it into the empty white china mug. Rachel looked at him, her head cocked on the side.

'You're the opposition captain. 46 off 55 balls,' she said. 'You should have made more too, but you played at that silly one swinging away from off stump.'

'I could see my fifty coming up in style,' Harold said, casually. 'Are you some kind of reporter?' he asked, glancing past her to see the rest of his players, who would have been making all sorts of mocking gestures had it been one of the younger players in the presence of a lady and not himself.

'No, a sister of the spinner,' she said, her words showing no sign of shame, though the chap had gone at almost 8 an over.

The waiter interrupted them to pour water into the cup, milk coming in a jug, a lump of sugar already on the saucer.

'That'll be seven pounds ten,' the waiter said, looking from Rachel to Harold, almost exactly at the same time as Harold proclaimed: 'Let me get this,' meaning of course the tea, which he began to stir gently with a silver spoon, as both Rachel and the waiter stood in anticipation for him to reach inside his pocket. But then, remembering where the team originated from, and seeing that they'd brought their own drinks, Rachel paid whilst Harold remained oblivious, dribbling in a drop of milk and scraping off just a tiny fragment of the sugar. He gave the bag a final squeeze against the side for good luck and stepped away in admiration, as the rich swirl of treacle coloured essence seeped from its side into the pure golden colour at the centre of the cup.

'It's ready,' he said, watching her fingers curl around the handle, her nails long and painted with a brilliant white tip. She put it to her lips, a red mark staining the outside of the cup as she took a large gulp. Harold could see in her eyes it was like no tea she'd ever tasted; in the moment that the liquid ran down her throat: she'd glimpsed heaven.

She tried to remain casual. She replaced the cup on the saucer, but kept hold of it.

'So,' she said, 'apart from tea and a spectacular forward defensive, have you anything else you'd like to impress me with?'

Harold returned to the numbers from his daydream. The young heiress to Judith was scrutinising each line, listening intently to her, but then that was her job, and it was easy compared to his.

Four years and not a day went by that he didn't think about the injustice of the cup result, and he knew the rest of the team were the same. No matter what they did, they couldn't shake it from their systems. He'd thought reaching the Premier Yorkshire League would be enough. They'd exacted revenge on home soil against another Lancashire side in the cup and were on a 122 game winning streak, but nothing would lay the ghost to rest. The only time they'd lost since the dubious defeat against Redillian was on a technicality the season before when they'd refused to travel to Bolton to play their scheduled third round National Cup game, giving up their right in the process to be the first team to win the trophy three years on the bounce.

At every game, home and away, the team played under the gaze of county scouts, who had poached a couple of his starlets only to see the backs of them months later as they wandered home to Skipperton, claiming they were homesick. Harold suspected it wasn't just the smell of the town, the taste of their mum's stew and the sound of a yard of Black being poured that brought them back, but also the sense that they couldn't move on before righting that wrong.

'Everything looks in order to me Judith. I don't know what I'd do without you, and Deborah, you're going to make a fine replacement when the time comes,' Harold said, standing from his wooden stool. 'It's the dedication of you two that keeps Skipperton Tea running,' he added, his praise filling them with a sense of satisfaction that made them glow. 'So unless either of you calls, I'll pop by in a week's time. For now I've got to go and see Father Johnson.'

'Oh, you've no need to go see him,' Judith said, removing her spectacles to give the lenses a good clean against her cardigan. 'He should be atoning his sins to you, not the other way round.'

Harold laughed at such a statement, tipped his virgin wool flat cap in their direction and bid them a good day, thinking it was only fair that next month he considered giving them a raise.

He walked down the cobbled paths, his hands constantly out of his pockets to wave at traders on the market stalls or the boys and girls playing hop scotch or catch, the excitement of glimpsing him never waning even if they had spotted him five minutes previously.

As he reached the church, the bell rung from the top of its tower to announce the hour. It was a pleasing sound

34

that Father Johnson had revitalised. He had done so much to spruce the church up and make it welcoming that it had become something of a Mecca in the first six months of his tenancy. The stained glass had been cleaned so the images of the brightly clothed saints shone, the pews had been reupholstered, and his sermons were kept to bite size chunks that everyone could digest. All of this had earned the people's trust, with a few quietly muttering that maybe those from outside weren't so bad after all. Most importantly he always kept the doors open, and since Harold had decided there was nothing left for him to do personally in order to rid himself of the anguish that constantly plagued him and his team, it was time to take his problem to the big man upstairs. Plus Rachel would be down there. She was forever going in to help organise charity events and make daily confessions of her sins (though what they were Harold couldn't fathom. She never cursed and she couldn't even swat a fly, preferring to shoo them out of the window with the newspaper instead). It was rather a good job he wasn't a paranoid man, because since Father Johnson had arrived, she'd spent as much time at church as she did at home. It was only the fact that Harold knew (thanks to knowledge gleaned from The Skipperton Gazette) that men of the cloth only liked pre-adolescent boys, and couldn't do anything with women, that kept him from becoming suspicious. With all that in mind, he not only had a lot of time for Father Johnson, but thoroughly respected his views.

'Father.'
        'Rachel.'
        Every time he heard that voice, Cuthbert was certain the Devil was lurking nearby to claim his soul, and a small part of him wanted Methuselah to do so. It would have been easier to justify his feelings if Harold had been a hideous character, a womaniser, wife beater, a general misogynist, but he was the most genial man in the town, always smiling, forever willing to add a few coppers to the collection plate, and adored by anyone who had ever tasted a Skipperton

brew.

Thou Shall Not Covet Thy Neighbour's Wife.

Why was that the one commandment everyone knew even if they'd never laid eyes on a Bible? Surely it was confirmation of a man's good taste to have someone entertain such untoward thoughts about their wife?

Oh it was no use! Every excuse he tried was pathetic, unreasonable, a crime against the Lord's wishes, and yet there was no way Cuthbert could stop himself. He did everything he could to lure her down to the church, felt wretched if he went a day without seeing her, was physically sick if she was out of sight for a whole weekend. Just what was God doing testing him in such fashion? Hadn't he done enough to prove himself in Birmingham? One evening Cuthbert had done his best to argue that this was actually the Lord rewarding him. The Bishop had said for him to 'get himself a girl' after all, and for all his impure thoughts and sinful actions, Cuthbert found himself receiving no penalty; rather the inverse in fact, as the bond between him and Rachel grew closer.

'We'll have to finish this some other time,' Rachel whispered, through her side of the booth, her neck red, her breathing rushed as she cut short her latest fantasy.

Cuthbert told himself it wasn't just for her that he had kept the two booths installed, but because they allowed him to become closer to the whole community through the thin veil. It was as if they poured their hearts out not to him, but God himself, like they would do of an evening, kneeling before their beds. And wasn't it true that a problem shared was a problem halved?

'I look forward to our next meeting my lamb. Make sure the duration is not too long, for the Devil is keen to uncleanse.'

'Oh, don't worry, I'll be back tomorrow. I'm sure I'll have dreamed up something else by then. Do you think the Devil will ever leave me father?'

Cuthbert sincerely hoped not.

'We can but yearn that it will be so. Now go and say

err…seven Hallelujah Josephs and be merry,' he said, adjusting his robe, as Rachel stepped out of the booth to greet her husband, who stood staring at the altar with his hands loosely held behind his back. The place certainly had a more feminine touch. The thick candles were vanilla scented and the polish used on the pews wasn't just there to do the job. If Harold closed his eyes he could well have been at home.

'Hi darling!' Rachel exclaimed, shimmying over to him in a dress she must have picked up from Dorothy that morning. It was blue and it looked like it had been crafted out of crepe paper. Harold stared at her cleavage; he fancied it could hold up his bat, and then remembered where he was.

'Hello my beautiful,' he replied, leaning down for a peck on the cheek, only to have his lips assaulted and his tongue molested as she wrapped a bare leg round his.

'You know nobody could see us if we lay on one of the pews,' she purred, running her tongue around his ear lobe.

'No, that's true,' Harold whispered, hoping that God was momentarily busy with another part of the world, as he attempted to wrestle himself free from his wife's grasp. 'But Father Johnson might hear, and it's him I need to see.'

'I'll be quiet, I promise,' she replied, in a hush, curling her bottom lip.

'No doubt you would be darling, but can it not wait until we're home in the bedroom?'

'In the garden.'

'In the spare bedroom.'

'On the kitchen table.'

'On the lounge sofa.'

Doing her best to hide her disappointment, Rachel acquiesced.

'I'll be ready and waiting for you,' she said, practically skipping through the heavy oak doors. 'Don't be long.'

From his confession box, Cuthbert leaned back from the microscopic peep hole that had allowed him to witness the tryst and clenched his fists in frustration. Perhaps it would be better if he and Harold switched jobs? Maybe the Skipper was a homosexual? They had been married for four years and they still didn't have any children. He crossed himself and begged for the Lord's forgiveness.

'I need a sign my Lord, please give me a sign,' he prayed, bringing his hands together, while he stared at the top of his confession box, newly painted black. It was strange to think The Almighty had so many super powers; x-ray vision, supersonic hearing, telepathy. It was like he was the original superhero. Cuthbert managed a smile; he could use that as a slogan, there was no need to fear what would happen to it up here in Skipperton, and Rachel would know where to buy all the utensils. An image of her naked, with her legs spread apart on a plush cream sofa flashed into his mind. It sure wasn't easy knowing which the real signs were.

'Tell me my child,' he said, in his deepest baritone, thinking that the way these Catholics phrased things certainly didn't do them any favours, as Harold pulled the door behind him, 'what is on your mind?'

'Err...exactly, right this second?' Harold asked, shuffling uncomfortably on the wooden bench.

'I mean, what did you come to see me for?' Cuthbert replied, the Rachel in his head now kneeling and looking over her shoulder, beckoning him closer. Great minds really did think alike.

'Oh right. Yes, well you see the problem is to do with the cricket team father.'

'A problem with the team?' Cuthbert exclaimed, for like anyone within the town walls, he was kept updated with all the happenings, and the team's good fortunes escaped no one. 'But I thought that you've been unbeaten for four years!'

Inside his box, Harold nodded sagely.

'Four years to the day,' he said, 'but it's that defeat. Unjust it was, and no matter what we do, no matter how many games the lads win, no matter in how much style, we can't seem to erase it. There isn't a gesture grand enough, no matter how many championships and cups we win. I mean I think revenge in the National Cup final would do it, but the chance of that happening is slim, and what if we were to be beaten again? That'd finish off the lads once and for all.'

Cuthbert let out a low hum. He had always been fond of cricket, had enjoyed those summer months at school when he could pretend he was actually involved in a sport by standing thirty metres from the play with only a slender chance of being called into action. He followed the national team too, it was a sport that could be on in the background and not interrupt his reading or work. They were currently out on tour in India, one all in the series with two tests still to play, and if he'd been a gambling man, he'd have placed a few quid on them to nick it. Remarkable to think how good they were now, when during his years as a teenager they'd have been thoroughly beaten before even stepping off the plane, their middle order collapses laughable even to the man who built his house on sand.

'You know,' he began, ready to start as always with an analogy from the Bible, not because it was what came to him first, but because it was what people expected. 'It is not only us who sometimes find ourselves at a crossroads and aren't quite sure of what our calling is or what will serve to make us happy. Jesus himself set forth into the desert for forty days and nights to see if he could...' Cuthbert's voice trailed off. Like a revelation of Moses, the idea was there fully formed in his mind, as if it had always been there and had simply required the right combination to unlock it.

'Father?' Harold enquired, as the silence lingered.

'Yes,' Cuthbert said, though not in reply. His eyes had glazed over, as the plan unravelled in his mind, not of his own device, but handed to him, delivered from above. 'He knows what you must do,' he continued, almost in a trance. 'You are to be just like the son in many ways. You must go into the wilderness with your flock and show the people the true way.'

'The true way?' Harold asked, a little spooked by the way it sounded, as though someone was speaking through Father Johnson rather than the man himself.

'Cricket. The game. It needs an ambassador, a knight to take it to corners unknown, just like those brave people who once, with Bibles tucked underneath their robes, left to spread the word of the Lord, so must you travel the globe bringing the game to those who are unaccustomed to its form.'

'The globe? I don't think so Father. We've vowed never to head west of the Pennines.'

'But your path is east.'

'Oh.'

'You shall head into the sun and make pilgrimage to Darjeeling, India.'

'Hey, that's where the tea leaves for Skipperton Tea come from!' Harold exclaimed.

'It is?' Cuthbert said, sounding genuinely surprised. 'Well did you know that there they too have a team which has been undefeated for the past four years?'

'I didn't, no. Don't know too much about them except they send me tea and they're brown,' Harold said, honestly, racking his brain as to any more information he could pull up on the area or the country. They loved their cricket, that was for sure. It was a bloody big place with bloody loads of people. Hot too. That was about it. Judith sorted out all the accounts and spoke to them, but the relationship was a pretty simple one; they shipped over crates of tea leaves, he sent money into their bank account.

'Well I suppose we could sort of make a holiday of it. Rachel's been pestering me to go some place hot.'

'Oh no,' Cuthbert said, hoping the two words hadn't been filled with as much panic as he'd felt. 'No,' he added, gravely, 'this is not a holiday. This isn't about families and loved ones. It's about the team, being together as a unit and putting to bed the demons that have been haunting you. This will be your quest, your trial, your redemption!'

The words echoed, filling the church as they bounced off the stone walls, rattling through Harold's body.

'Suppose it sounds like it could work. How would we get there, fly from Leeds and Bradford?'

40

'No. This is not a short term fix. This isn't a two week holiday to make yourself feel better. This is a tour, and not one of these recent three tests, couple of one dayers, pretend we're playing baseball 20-20 games to end it so we're back home in time for tea and biscuits tours, this is going to be the real deal. The long trek, visit every nook and cranny provincial site, build up for six months until the showpiece final tour of the golden era.'

'Bloody hell!' Harold exclaimed. 'Six months? Are you sure?'

'Just one second, let me confer?' "Uh-huh. Ummmm. Okay." 'Absolutely positive.'

'Well...' Harold said, all that he could manage at such news. He'd just expected to be told to keep his chipper up and carry on believing.

'I want you to know that He wants me to help you,' Cuthbert said, in a hushed, reverential tone, as if speaking any louder would cause him to mishear the information he was being passed. 'I shall arrange the itinerary and set you on your chosen path. You must gather up your team, like Moses did, and lead them out of the pain of this purgatory and into the salvation of the promised land.'

Harold had begun to lose track of what was being said.

'Err, just to clarify. You're going to organise some games for us in some countries along the way to India, and I need to go and tell my players that they have to take six months off work?'

'Harold. The Lord has blessed you in a certain department.'

Had he as well? Cuthbert thought back to the huge image of the penis posted under his door in Birmingham. Was his own adequate? Would Rachel point and laugh, and would he, in that moment, receive his comeuppance for siding with the Devil? Only time would tell, for their paths had been chosen.

'Remember what He said,' he continued, his heart fluttering like a humming bird. 'Use your talent, don't let it go

41

to waste.'

The Team

Dumbstruck, Harold strode forward on automatic down the tight, winding cobbled alleys, away from his home and to that of his teammates. He had completely forgotten his promise to Rachel, her name not being one of the twelve he held in his mind on a team sheet, listed in batting order. Questions kept coming to him, plenty of them, but questions were what he paid others to answer for him, and he was positive that once he had rounded up his team and returned to Cuthbert, The Vicar would have a great many more details that would fill in the rising number of blanks.

He took a right down Boycott Lane, past the post office on the high street, so busy concentrating on what was inside his head that he didn't notice the first drops of spitting rain dripping onto it, which meant that by the time he'd unfurled his flat cap from his pocket, his greying hair was already coated with a light, greasy sheen. He checked up into the sky, like an umpire would, for signs of whether the rain was there to stay or if it was going to pass over, and saw a huge bulking bank of black cloud rolling in on the horizon towards the church. Harold shook his head, The Lord had a strange way of showing his pleasure sometimes.

The door he came to a halt beside first was that of his opening batter, the only yellow door in a town of blacks and browns. It had been painted with gloss and shone like a golden chicken nugget in a bucket of burnt wings. The owner was a genius with the bat. It wasn't an understatement to admit that if he hadn't been discovered to occupy the crease, the team would have been mid-table at best. How and why he had stayed in Skipperton when he had been offered contracts so lucrative that they made people spit out their tea! in shock, was baffling. With his ability he could have easily made as much money as Harold in the previous four years, if not more, what with his chiselled jaw and a pair of eyes that everyone found themselves staring dreamily into no matter what their gender.

Harold just made sure he thanked the Lord and continued to grease the collection plate when it was passed round, though it wouldn't have surprised him to learn another member of the team was using voodoo, because that kind of loyalty (some may have chosen to label stupidity) only came from dogs, not genii.

He was such an enigma that there was both an air of intimidation and a whole host of myths surrounding him. His name, for one, had been changed in an attempt to make him less otherworldly. John Smith he'd been dubbed, for three reasons; firstly because his batting was so smooth, secondly because he was foreign, not like Skipperton Black, and finally (the public perception of the moniker), as a term of endearment to fit in with a team that shared three surnames between them and a town that claimed double that. Larson, his family name, the one he scrawled as his signature, big, bold and angular, there was no reference to in any of the Skipperton births, marriages and deaths books. Nor could anyone recall a family moving to the town and raising a bone white, straw haired, 6'2" athlete, who belonged in the pages of a child's Viking history book, minus the long hair and beard.

One conspiracy theory accounting for his existence was that he had been a Nordic invader in 800, but had fallen down a crevice into water and been frozen into a 1200-year coma.

Another, more plausible suggestion, was that he was actually the reincarnation of the legendary Australian Donald Bradman. The evidence that made this a more likely actuality than the iced Viking theory was that he carried a framed picture of the batter with him at all times and, even more bizarrely, his run average after every ten innings stood at 99.93, 0.01 below Bradman's score at retirement.

The frustrating fact about this (yes frustrating, not astounding), was that it was obviously calculated, as if attaining a higher average (and 150 was by no means beyond Erik) would be considered sacrilege. Addressing such an issue with a man who basically won the game and averaged 45 runs per innings more than the next batsman, however, seemed out of the question.

Harold's hand came out to knock, but in line with his uncanny knack of predicting the future, Erik opened the door.

'Come in,' he said, moving into the lounge, letting Harold close the door behind him. 'Tea?' he asked, a fresh pot residing on the rickety wooden table beside his armchair.

'No, I'm just popping in. Have to see the whole team,' Harold said, distracted by the bat that was held on plinths above the mantelpiece. Weathered, worn, without a grip, it was a bat from another era, one that could well have belonged to Bradman. There was as much intrigue surrounding it as there were to the origins of Erik's own bat, which some claimed had been pulled from the earth *Sword in the Stone* style. Harold had never enquired about either, lest his star disappear like a genie.

'Sounds important,' Erik said, topping up his mug.

'It is. Very. Well, I'm organising a six month tour to India, where we'll play against another team who have been unbeaten for the past four years. I've to finalise the details. Obviously everything will be...'

While his captain and manager spoke, Erik stared at him over the lip of his golden mug, the liquid flowing down his throat like the river had poured down Thor's gullet from the endless horn. Now he lowered it.

'I'm in,' he said.

Harold couldn't contain his delight. He extended his hand.

'Wouldn't have wanted to do it without you,' he said. 'There'll be more details at training, be sure to pack yourself a big bag, but don't worry about the tea, I'll take care of that,' Harold added with a wink, a large mental tick at the top of his sheet. Beneath it was the swashbuckling left hander, Stuart Barker the butcher.

The butcher's was at the top end of the hill on the high street. Most of the façade had once been painted red, but three-quarters of the way through the job, Stuart's grandfather had run out of the colour and found the only other tin he had was brown. This paint had been of a watery consistency and once applied, appeared as though a heavy rain had carried it down to the ground in streaks. They could have recoated it in the thirty years since, but it was all part of the establishment's charm.

Stuart had once told Harold: 'People expect to see it as much as they expect to see a Barker behind the counter. Plus it looks like bacon, and people end up ordering a few rashers even if they hadn't been thinking about it on the way up.'

Without removing his flat cap, Harold pushed through the door, which rattled the bell, announcing his custom.

'Oh, Mr. Baker!' was the call that greeted him from Stuart's wife, Susan, who stood behind the counter, a woman who more than matched her husband in stature. She curtsied, wiping her bloodied hands on her red and white striped apron, looking more like she was preparing to head up a scrum than daintily welcome his presence. Their little boy, four years old and learning the family trade, was down by her knees weighing a couple of joints. He also stood to attention, as his mother dragged him to his feet, and not sure what was expected of him, threw in a salute instead of a bow.

'Are you here for your usual kilo of mince and pair of trotters?' Susan enquired, stepping across to the grinding machine, no discernible point as to where her neck ended and her shoulders began.

'I will take my usual yes, though I was wondering if I might have a quick word with Stuart too,' Harold said, wondering if he should tell Stephen he could now stand at ease.

'Oh certainly Mr. Baker, he's downstairs practising as we speak,' Susan said, grabbing half a cow from the display shelf in her left hand, a meat cleaver the size of a bat in her right.

Careful not to slip on any blood or entrails that had been discarded and missed the bin, Harold ducked as he

46

descended down the stone stairs into the basement, shivering a little as the temperature dropped. He was met by the distinct sound of meat and bone coming into contact with a hefty implement, after which came the sound of it making contact with another object and either a hearty cheer or a disgruntled muttering. Harold remained on the bottom step, not wanting to make his presence known so that he could view his boundary smashing batsman's practice routine in all its glory.

At the far end of the wall hung carcasses (mainly bovine), that were attached to a pulley. Directly opposite, twenty-two yards away, stood Stuart, feet shoulder width apart, wielding a large meat cleaver. He held it down, tapping it against the outside of his left knee, the thick middle of the blade facing the body of the dead animal.

'One more from the over,' Stuart said to himself, coming fully upright in pretence that he was being distracted by something in the crowd. He gave a small wave to an imaginary groundsman signalling he wanted the side screen moving, before resuming his position, his chest so large it was a surprise his hands came together to grip the makeshift bat. Releasing his left hand for a second, he reached out and prodded a button, which sent a carcass tearing down, faster than a horse at the races. Attacking it with a step forward, Stuart raised the cleaver chest high and swung it across his body, slogging midway through the meat, which opened in the same fashion Harold's jaw had the first time he'd witnessed the regime. If it had been a ball, the object would have sailed out of the car park. Stuart's record for windows smashed in a season was twelve, balls lost seven, cats killed in trees one. Yes, he was prone to going for a duck after swinging at a ball heading out towards third slip, but he was just as likely to leave a bowler strategically going off injured after being clouted for 25+ in an over. His strike rate was 250.6. More than once in a season was he liable to club half a century off 10 balls.

'Think that one would have gone down the throat of the man on the boundary,' Harold teased, as Stuart wrestled the cleaver free from what remained of the cow.

'Taken his throat out more like don't you mean Skipper?' Stuart said, his voice deeper than a foghorn. He removed his glove to shake Harold's hand, which became encased, like he'd offered it out to a cave. 'What brings you down here?'

'Well, I wanted to talk to you about a tour to India.'

'Don't like killing cows in India,' Stuart said, shaking his head sadly.

'I didn't know,' Harold replied, hoping that wasn't going to be a sticking point. 'What I do know is that there's a team in Darjeeling that have also been on a four year unbeaten run, and The Vicar, well The Lord himself, wants us to embark on a tour as ambassadors of the game.'

'Hmmm, well no point discussing the subject without the missus,' Stuart pointed out, leading the way back to the shop floor, where his wife had wrapped Harold's meat in newspaper and tied the bundle with a piece of string.

'Love, Harold here is organising a tour to India for the team,' Stuart said, turning to face Harold to allow him to take over.

'Yes, a rather long tour, six months in total, but everything will be paid for and I can supply extra so that you can hire a replacement to work here in the meantime,' Harold said, to the couple standing shoulder to shoulder. Their bed had to have a stone base. 'I mean I don't expect an answer right this very minute,' he added, but Susan had already made up her mind.

'Mr. Baker, for you Stuart would happily take a tour to the North Pole and it's about time Stephen pulled his finger out around here instead of having mummy and daddy doing everything for him, so I think everyone involved will be a winner.'

Standing next to his wife, Stuart beamed and ruffled his son's hair, of which there was hardly any left.

'Looks like I'll be needing to go and put in a few more hours practice then Skipper,' he said, planting a kiss on his wife's rosy red cheek, before grabbing Stephen's hand.

'Come on son, time to go downstairs to see how daddy deals with the moo cows.'

Swinging the bundle of meat, Harold stepped out of the butchers whistling his favourite tune, *Greensleeves*, (which was still doing the rounds on the local radio station even though it had been out when he was a young nipper), to find the sun was beaming and a rainbow was arching across the Skipperton sky. Fifteen minutes in and he had his three top order batsmen. He beamed with delight, as he took a turn away from the high street, determined to collect his players in batting order rather than in convenience of location. Should he have chosen to do it in terms of importance, however, the school would have been his second stop after Erik's, for it housed the headmaster, all rounder, and catalyst for the whole tour, Richard Egbert.

The noise from the children, who had been sent to school on that day, rather than being out at work, could be heard as soon as Harold left the high street and headed down towards the fields. He could see the boys playing in the yard with their quoits, wooden hula hoops and jacks, and the girls with their skipping ropes. It was strange to think that twenty years previously someone had stood upon the lip of the hill and watched him performing the same games. The uniform was still the same, a grey jumper and trouser combination with the Skipperton emblem sewed, usually in the left hand corner, though since each one was done individually by the child's mother, the tendency was for the rich to show off and take up the whole front of the garment with the white rose.

Since they were too embroiled in their own activities, none of the children stopped to pay Harold their usual respects as he walked down the path and past Marilyn, the receptionist, who was catching forty winks with her thick spectacles lying on top of her breasts, which were covered, as they had been for the past twenty, thirty, forty years? by a thick pink cardigan with a greying Georgian neck ruffle. Out of courtesy, Harold crept down the corridor, which was

49

coated with the latest pieces of neatly written work. He stopped to admire a couple of sheets and found there wasn't an ink blot in sight. Most of the writing had to have been done by girls; it was joined and cursive, a style he'd always found difficult to emulate. The only reason his palm hadn't been rapped with the cane during those handwriting lessons was down to his parentage, since each finished sheet would be covered in blotches and bleeds.

The first display piece was simply columns and columns of animal names neatly written. It was strange how after you'd read the word "dog" ten times in a row you weren't sure if it actually meant anything. The paper beside it was again another expertly crafted sheet, though it too would have been more impressive if he'd walked past and admired it from a distance rather than actually attempting to read it. They both made him feel a bit better that none of his work had ever been deemed good enough for display.

'Excuse me there duck, coming through,' a female voice said, from behind him, making him turn to the side to see the school cook waddling towards him, clutching a large silver pan.

'Oh Mr.Baker! My apologies!' she exclaimed, almost spilling the contents of the pan in her desperation to curtsey. Harold reached out to steady it, the white entrails slipping and sliding across each other, as the cook continued to speak, expressing her gratitude for such a fine cups of tea and offering warm words about his father.

'See the kids are still being given the best Yorkshire has to offer,' Harold said, breaking into her monologue.

'Oh yes sir! Nothing but the finest ingredients, and they have a choice for lunch too since Mr. Egbert's been in charge, tripe or black pudding for their main and then for dessert they can have either cream or gravy with a giant Yorkshire and their cuppa Skipperton,' the cook beamed, a little black moustache running the length of her top lip.

'Well, then I expect many more excellent cricketers in the mould of Mr. Egbert coming through,' Harold said, allowing the cook to move past, her back never turned to him, as she bowed her way to the kitchen.

Harold watched her disappear, then knocked on Richard's door and let himself in.

'Morning,' he said, finding the Headmaster not alone in his office, but in debate with his seventeen year old son, Richard II, a teacher at the school. They were discussing a new set of slates.

'They are better than the last ones because they wipe clean far easier,' Richard II, was saying, rubbing his finger over a line of chalk, which vanished underneath. His dad, meanwhile, from his leather throne, was turning each slate over, holding it close to check for flaws. Harold picked up one from out of the box, the stone definitely thicker than he remembered. He let it balance in his outstretched hand.

'Must be 25 ounces,' he chipped in.

'Which means they won't crack as easily,' Richard II added with a nod, the spitting image of his dad, except without the moustache and that extra weight that gave his old man an extra yard of pace and clout of bat. There was no doubt the kid was talented; another year or two and he'd be pushing his dad for the all-rounder spot, but it seemed for now, like with the rest of the team, Pa Egbert wasn't about to budge.

'You'll have to leave them with me,' Richard said, keeping one out on his oak table, next to his ledger and telephone, the brass earpiece hanging in its cradle. 'For now,' he continued, twisting slightly so as to address Harold, 'I have to see what Mr. Baker wants.'

Taking this as his cue to exit, Richard II gave Harold both a smile and a nod, trying hard not to display any frustration, and closed the door quietly behind him.

'Always keen to impress and improve,' Harold remarked, often finding it strange how different a father could treat a son.

'Hmmm,' Richard muttered, wiggling his lips so his moustache squirmed like a giant caterpillar. 'Anyway,' he added, pushing himself out of his chair, his forearms oars, his brown hobnail boots canoes, 'what is it you came to see

51

me about?'

'Cricket, what else?' Harold replied. 'But in particular a chance to right wrongs and put to bed ill feelings.'

'Go on,' Richard said, his cheeks and chin totally bald, never showing a glimpse of even the tiniest hair, as if every one of them had congregated to the promised fertile land above his top lip.

'I'm organising a tour to India. A six month tour like they used to go on in the good old days.'

To this news Richard didn't react for a good twenty seconds, just stared straight ahead. Finally his hands twitched inside his pockets, he rolled onto his heels and then up onto his toes.

'I'm out.'

'You're out? But I haven't given you any details yet!' Harold exclaimed, his pulse quickening, knowing full well that there was no point in arguing with him, because there wasn't a more stubborn bugger in the land.

'Heard enough Harold. It's not going to happen. It's no reflection on you, I think you've done wonders for the team, but if you think we have to leave home to go in search of redemption, if you think this trip will erase the memory of the game against those bloody Lancastrians... (they paused to wipe their mouths on the back of their hands) ...then I think you're mistaken.'

'And what if I'm not? What if this is what we need? What if we go away without you and you're left to stew for the rest of your life?' Harold asked, a headache forming at where he went from here. Did he go for an extra batter or bowler? Neither of whom would match his stalwart's standard. It'd be like replacing the milkman with a milkwoman.

Richard took a step back towards his chair, contemplated sitting and then decided against it, swivelling on the spot instead.

'After Carol and I were married,' he said, loud and clear, 'we went to her Auntie Jane's caravan in Scarborough for our honeymoon. And do you know how long I lasted?'

'Three days.'

'Exactly, three bloody days. Headaches and nosebleeds is what leaving here got me. Oh don't get me wrong, I can stay overnight when we're playing a cup game, but past that my body starts craving the air here too much, the Black, the tea.'

'So what if I promised you a six month supply of Black and tea? And because you'll be with your team all the time, it'll smell, look and feel like you're at home. Your body will be tricked.'

'And what about Carol?'

'Oh, she'll be fine,' Harold said, wanting to point out she probably saw herself as a widow anyway what with the amount of time he spent in this office and down at the cricket club. 'There'll be all the other wives to spend her time with. People go off and serve their country for months at a time and when they return it's as if they were never away in the first place.'

'And here, this school,' Richard added, ignorant of just how complete an argument Harold was putting across. 'Am I supposed to close it down for half a year?'

'The school was here before you arrived, it'll be standing when we return, and Gerald's your deputy! What's the point of having a deputy if you're not going to use him?'

'Well there you go Harold, you've said it yourself. Have someone deputise for me.'

'But...' They won't be as good? You can't be replaced? We won't be the same without you? There was no way for him to win. He gave a shrug, as Richard picked up the slate board from his desk.

'Good luck Harold,' he said, plonking himself into his chair, neither of them attempting to make eye contact. 'Give me a shout once you're back.'

Good luck? They'd bloody well need a lot more of it now.

'Mr. Baker.'

It shouldn't have surprised him. When Father Johnson had delivered the news he'd expected to return to him with a rather sheepish explanation that all he'd been able

53

to muster was a lot of strange looks and uncertainty, but with Erik and Stuart coming on board as quickly as he had done, it had begun to seem like a mere formality, like he was ticking off a grocery list.

'Mr. Baker, Harold, sir.'

Harold lifted his head to find the wiry frame of Richard II standing before him. He stared up at him, his thin body making him appear an inch or two taller than his father.

'I'm the man to replace him.'

Harold said nothing.

'Listen, I know exactly what you're thinking. Groves can make a solid 35 plus each game, but put a ball in his hand and he's more likely to think it's an apple and try to eat it. On the other hand there's Ed. He'll keep it tight, he's good for long spells and he'll pick up the odd wicket here and there, especially on a flat pitch, but shove a bat in his hands and you might as well stick a bollard on the crease.'

The lad was a touch harsh, but unfortunately he wasn't far off with his assessment.

'Mr. Baker, you just said it yourself: what's the point in having a deputy if you're not going to use them? I mightn't be proven at the top level, but I've more runs and wickets than anyone else in the reserves.'

'Richard II,' Harold said softly, 'I have no doubting your ability, but to be honest with you lad I fear you might snap in two. There's more meat on my wife.' (Oh bollocks he thought, Rachel had probably worn her fingers down to the knuckles by now).

'Then I'll start eating more. I'll have five spuds a night instead of three.'

Versatility, it was what you needed when you didn't have any idea of the conditions, and young Richard II was right, without him they'd be a batter or bowler short. Harold tossed over the mince and trotters to him.

'Get yourself started immediately lad. Next time I see you I don't want to be mistaking you for a whippet prancing around on its hind legs.'

Three and a half players, three and three-quarters if he was being generous. Harold walked as if in a trance, torn between taking a hard line approach to bully the rest of his team into submission and being soft and sympathetic, though neither would help to bring Egbert Snr on board now. What did you expect from a man who still refused to have a privy installed inside his house?

Harold picked up his step as he exited the school, his presence in the corridor causing a sudden hushed reverence from the pupils, who stood to the side forming a second inner corridor through which he walked. He passed them without any gesture of acknowledgment and carried on at pace out onto the street, ready to walk back up the hill and down the high street, before he realised batting at number five was not Dereck "Del Boy" Smith of the post office, but the practically mute right hander, Alan Smith.

The Gnome was his nickname; not because he was short or had a beard or wore a red hat or enjoyed fishing or loitered in other people's gardens, but because at the faded, dusty crease, he stood as if rooted there, an almost immovable object. He was a player from the old era where time spent batting was considered as precious as runs scored. Not once had he played at a ball he didn't need to, with the willow bat he had carved himself. A carpenter by trade, there wasn't a house in the town that didn't own a piece of furniture crafted by his sturdy hands. Harold's mahogany dining table, with cricket bat legs, was one of his finest products, but like all men of trade, when it came to how they treated themselves, the quality differed vastly from what clients received. His was the house with a door two inches shorter than the rest of the street.

Harold spied him through his front room window whittling away at a structure as tall as himself. If it hadn't have been for the single light pine colouring, and the fact the piece didn't move under his touch, Harold would have thought The Gnome was about to embark upon a moment that would best be committed in privacy. However, since it was a well known fact he had neither a wife nor girlfriend,

Harold simply pushed open the front door and shouted his greetings.

Stepping straight into the lounge, he found himself drawn into a spot the difference competition between Alan and the wooden statue. His batter and silly mid-wicket catching expert had frozen, his hands by his sides like a guard standing duty, ready to bark singular answers to questions from a visiting superior. Harold took a step closer to the statue and marvelled at the craftmanship. It was uncanny. It wasn't life-like, it was though someone had coated Erik in timber.

'Bloody hell!' Harold exclaimed, touching the high cheek bone, expecting it to feel fleshy, for the lips to respond. 'Just planed this bit?' he enquired, the area around the lips coated with a touch of moisture.

'I had to get really close for the hair, lots of detail there, I'm creating the team, in batting order,' came the reply.

Harold didn't think he'd ever heard Alan speak a sentence with a comma in it. He laughed and slapped Erik on the back.

'Just imagine if we had two of him playing with us hey?' he said. 'One that could bowl though, an Erik at both ends, sandwiching us.'

Alan's mouth flapped open and shut.

'Would be nice,' he managed.

'Nice? It would be a dream come true!' Harold exclaimed. 'Though I'd get no credit as manager and captain. It'd be like spotting a Lancastrian in a tea market,' he added, pulling the pose of a teapot, a gesture that usually brought about a heartier laugh than the one Alan responded with. 'Anyway,' Harold continued, folding his arms, keeping his wrists sturdy, 'I'm also sorting out the team in batting order for a tour to India. Six months, expenses paid. Don't know all the details yet, have to discuss them with Father Johnson. This man's in though,' he said, giving wooden Erik a soft jab on the shoulder.

'So am I,' Alan said, without hesitation.

'Good lad,' Harold replied, his hand out to confirm it

was a deal. 'Well then, I'll leave you to finish Erik off. Oh and when you come to do me, let me know because I'll give you the wood, some right solid wood,' he added, immediately back on track, with just an added thought aside, as he broke into an amble, heading towards the post office, with one more player to collect before he stopped for lunch - who was there in the town that was single and would treat The Gnome right?

Up above the town hall, the larger of the two iron hands took an edge closer to XII. Around him, shopkeepers were idling to their doors to check if there were customers lurking down the streets or alleys, before they flipped the signs on the inside of their doors to indicate they were taking the next hour off for some well earned grub. When Harold reached the post office, with three more notches of the big hand to run before the brass bell chimed midday, the closed sign was already showing, with only the short line of customers inside being allowed to complete their transactions. Dereck's assistant, a second cousin of his, a sixteen year old called Julie, whose father owned an allotment to the side of Harold's slender patch and produced the greatest carrots in the world, ones so huge a single stick made a hearty portion for four, at first waved her hand to signal he would have to come back later, until she realised who it was, and glowing corky red, fumbled for her set of keys to undo the lock.

'Ever so sorry, I didn't look properly,' she said, bowing so low her head was closer to his waist than his neck.

'Don't be a silly sausage,' Harold remarked, waving at Dereck, who had been forced to halt the transaction he was midway through, due to the fact that Mister Shepherd had dropped the pen he was using to write the cheque in order to turn and inform Harold the last cup of tea he'd drunk was the best he'd ever bloody well had and if her highness had any sense, instead of handing out awards to a bunch of rich southerners, who were most likely queer or who had ties to Bosworth Field, she should give him a knighthood, which of course he should then reject, because acceptance would only lead to people thinking he was queer or secretly southern or worse.

'I'll bear that in mind if the time comes,' Harold responded, in earnest.

'When the time comes,' Mister Shepherd repeated, finally turning back to complete his transaction, leaving Harold to take a break on the chair underneath the notice board, which was filled with white scraps of paper announcing new deals, ninety percent of which were written in the same handwriting.

'*Too knew skooters 4 sale, £7.35 ONO*' read one, '*Looking for a nice knew ketle? Call in at post office*', said another. Harold didn't have a clue where Dereck sourced the products from. If anyone ever asked he would just wink and tell them: 'never you mind', and in the next sentence try to flog them something new. Harold had seen people pay in their weekly pay cheque one minute and leave with half of it already spent, struggling beneath the weight of goods they didn't even need. Mister Shepherd, right that very moment exited with a nod, carrying a brand new pair of tartan slippers, ones that big Stuart Barker would have struggled to fill. He noticed the look of confusion on Harold's face and waved away any concerns.

'Don't worry Mr. Baker, sir, Dereck tells me that I'll grow into them in no time,' he said, happy with his purchase, as behind his desk, Dereck appeared to produce a sheepskin jacket from his crotch, which he dangled enticingly in front of Miss "Littlest" Louise Smith. In its own special way Harold wouldn't have been embarrassed to call Dereck's ability genius. It had seen numerous lbw calls overturned and awarded. If it was required he'd had bad light stop play, and on the other hand he'd talked his way into them playing the final overs in a blanket of darkness to sew up a game. His most momentous occasion had come two years ago when they'd been under the cosh at home to Newer New York on the afternoon of day two in a four day match. Erik had been too ill to bat in the first innings and facing a follow-on with him still bedridden and the pitch doing all sorts for the opposition spinners, it had started to look ominous. That was when Dereck had spotted a rain cloud approaching cautiously in the distance and proceeded to argue with the umpire and bowlers for a whole twenty minutes on how goats were a superior species to sheep, until the rain began to fall, washing out the rest of the day's play. Suffice to say Erik recovered, Stuart was magic, and the winning streak was retained with a final session of spellbinding reverse swing.

'Afternoon Gaffa,' Dereck said, grinning as the final patron left the premise. 'What can I do you for?' he added, his moustache a neat, thin pencil line.

'I need your services for a tour I'm arranging to India,' Harold said.

'Hot there, need something called sun lotion, I can get my hands on a few bottles,' Dereck said, removing a pencil from behind his ear and a pad of paper from his top pocket. 'Might require some hats and sunglasses too. Buy them in bulk I can work a discount. How long is the tour?' he enquired, mid-scribble.

'Six months.'

'Six months!' Dereck's body remained straight as his feet jogged of their own accord and pound signs glazed his eyeballs.

'Well we're going to want all sorts then aren't we Gaffa? Supplies of Brylcreem, razors, shoe polish...' his hand began to blur as it streaked across the page.

'I take it that you're in then,' Harold said. '...rolling tobacco, talcum powder, Old Spice,' Dereck nodded, flicking over the page. 'Aye, Julie here knows the ropes and our Kenneth can cover me. Now have you thought about a nice new pair of leather gloves? Man in your position has to keep his hands fresh and smooth...'

As he exited the post office, stomach rumbling, Harold knew it would be better to head home for a spot of pie and chips immediately, because the longer he left Rachel, the madder she would become.

'You don't care for my needs.' 'You're always doing

59

your own thing.' 'Where are you when I need you?' And then to top it all off he'd have to break the news he was leaving for another six months. If it was possible, he'd have put off going home until after they returned from tour: 'are you sure I didn't tell you? Blimey,' but at least he could muster another few hours without his ears being attacked.

He stretched his fingers against the leather gloves, forced to admit that they felt bloody good indeed, and made his way down to The Caf. The establishment was the oldest business in the town. It had been founded along with the town itself and had always been in the possession of the Smiths (nothing to do with Alan or Dereck), handed down from father to eldest son, unless of course there was no son, in which case a daughter assumed control, about once every four generations, like now with Mrs. Melinda Smith (just a coincidence her husband happened to share her surname.)

"The Caf" it read, in black paint on the facade, above the two window blinds that were forever half drawn. The menus, written on lined paper, were stuck to the inside of the glass. Most of the writing was faded, but the top line was still easily readable - *All meals served with a pot of Skipperton's finest*. Last time Harold had gone through two, a different coloured knitted cosy on each. When most families ate, it looked like a huge rainbow running down the middle of the table.

'Afternoon Mel, noon Jonesy,' Harold said, greeting the pair behind the counter, who stood in their matching green aprons. In front of them was an array of pastries and other delicacies: pork pies, Yorkshire pasties, steak and kidney / meat and potato / liver and onion / tripe and turnip pies, black puddings, white puddings, all of which glistened under the glass, glazed with so much whisked egg they almost looked fake. On the bottom shelf stood the dessert products, stuffed with cream substitute to keep them from going off, sprinkled with so much sugar they looked like gems pulled from a diamond mine.

'The usual?' Mel enquired, reaching for the lard to re-coat the frying pan.

'Aye love,' Harold said, finding that despite all the tables having been filled when he first entered, there was now one available in the corner. 'Cheers,' he said to the room, scanning it to find not one, but three of his players hunched over their portions of Toad in the Hole.

'Lads,' he said, with a nod, taking a step in their direction.

'Skipper,' they chorused, their Yorkshire puddings floating in gravy, the remnants of sausage filled with just the right amount of fat and gristle. Three Barker's they were, Paul, the candlestick maker, Fred, the baker and his son John, the joint youngest player on the team at fourteen. Their shops were side by side on the high street, their abodes above them. Their wives took it in turn to cook the evening meal, and since they didn't consider being anything but the best of pals, they'd knocked through the wall separating them.

'Need to speak to you lot about something important,' Harold said, his pair of eggs being cracked against the side of the frying pan that already housed bacon and sausage, which together with a handful of mushrooms, would soon be nestling inside his crispy suet pudding to give him his Full Yorkshire Breakfast.

'About a tour?' Paul asked, the slenderest of the trio, raising Harold's eyebrows. 'Heard rumours Skipper,' he added, touching up the last remaining hairs on his head that rose into a wispy point. 'We were just in the process of discussing it.'

'Discussing what?' Harold enquired, defensively. 'You don't know any details yet,' he added, bringing across his plastic seat to squeeze himself between them. 'I was about to have a spot of lunch and then make my way to see you three about it. Doing the rounds in batting order,' he concluded.

'Oh we know. That's why we gave you your own table instead of inviting you over. Thought you might want to eat in peace,' Fred said, his face round and doughy, a part of him forever covered in flour, whether it be a light dusting on his clothes or a dry crusting on his skin. There was many an opposition player who had refused to shake hands with him before play, suspecting it was a sign of leprosy. They would then later stand at the opposite end of the wicket facing him, expecting not only the ball, but also his arm to fly down towards them.

'Well, might as well kill two birds with one stone and all that,' Harold replied, as his plate and brew were placed before him. 'Cheers Mel love, looks delicious as usual,' he said, clutching his knife and fork, before turning back to his players. 'So, what is there to discuss about a six month paid tour out to India spreading the goodwill message of the gentleman's game along the way?'

'Business Harold. Easy enough for some of the players, like Alan, he works for himself and Stuart has Susan, who, if we're being honest, knows more about butchery than he does. Blonde John Smith, well Lord knows what he does, but whatever it is he can probably do it on his head in the middle of the sea. But what about us?'

'Dereck's having his niece and brother cover for him,' Harold pointed out.

'My niece's three years old and my brother died in the mining accident of '93,' Paul said, not afraid to let Harold know by his tone how aggrieved he was at such a suggestion. He made a point of staring straight at his Skipper, who chewed thoughtfully on a piece of bacon rind. For Harold it was the best food they produced in The Caf, apart from on a late Sunday afternoon when all the roasts had been finished and they would take the tins they'd been cooked in back into the kitchen and mop up the leftover goodness that had congealed at the bottom of them with what remained of the sliced white bread.

'How many candles do you sell a day?' he asked.

'Depends,' his wicket keeper replied.

'On what?'

'Seasons mostly. Summer I look at about ten packs of five, but in the winter I'll do quadruple that, maybe more if it's biting cold; snowing and such.'

'So in six months you'd be looking at?'

'Just under twenty-five thousand.'

'Right, and how many can you produce a day?' Harold asked, gesturing over to Mel for another pot of tea.

'If I've no distractions, five hundred, although once I managed six,' Paul said, the only one at the table who found this an achievement.

'And it's not like they go off is it?' Harold said, thinking that depending on what mood Rachel was in when he finally returned home, there was every chance he'd be back in The Caf for a spot of beef and tatters for his dinner. 'So if I could supply you with a couple of helpful elves who could carry on your work through the night, and say loaned you the cash for the supply of wax required, then I figure by your calculations that you could have a stock ready in around a fortnight so that all your missus would have to do is hand out the candles in one hand and accept the money in the other'.

'Could work,' Paul admitted, wiping his hands on his trousers, picturing Margery in her rocking chair bobbing back and forth, a pile of candles to her left disappearing, a stack of coins to her right building into a tower.

It was an unknown fact that it was because of her that he'd found his position as wicket keeper on the team. As soon as they'd been married on her fifteenth birthday, she'd started making radical changes to the house, and to the lesser extent his workspace. Her biggest contribution had been to insist that, because she had once splintered her foot so badly the doctor had almost been forced to amputate when she was a child, *all* their floors were to be carpeted. Paul had tried to point out that wax and carpet were not the best of pals, but Margery had told him that since they weren't children, they could be expected to take care of their surroundings properly. The demands had instantly, and unwittingly, put him into practice; diving, rolling, performing back flips across the rooms in order to keep drips from ruining the decor. Nothing escaped his palms. One second he'd lurch forward into the kitchen, the very next he'd be somersaulting backwards through the lounge, the aubergine shag pile carpet resembling a minefield with all the indentations from his knees and elbows.

'Right, that's him sorted,' Fred said, 'but what about me and my boy? Are we supposed to start filling the ovens to bursting and have my missus sell green rock buns for five and a half months?' he asked, John nodding at every word, their relationship practically telepathical, since the only time they weren't in each other's company was when they were sleeping.

On the pitch they worked in tandem, bowling from opposite ends of the ground, sussing out batsmen's weak spots, conferring at the end of every ball, tenacious, relentless, a pair of wolves attacking from either side, moving in on their prey until the only way out was down their gullets. Ever since the day John had been able to stand, Fred had had him bowling and catching, the baker's dozen a redundant term in Skipperton due to the fact every thirteenth ball of dough was used to find line and length; the yorker and full toss being their primary deliveries, though when they were inclined, the beamer was slung in for good measure to rattle those sturdier batters. As if that wasn't enough, their capabilities out in the field were possibly even superior, run outs a speciality thanks to the workplace ethic of one of them tossing across a random handful of dough squeezed spherical for the other to hurl towards a single stump that stood underneath the oven, with the first to make five hits entitled to the best cut of meat for that evening's meal.

'Bit of a tougher one to solve that,' Harold admitted, resting his knife and fork together on his empty plate. 'But I do believe Father Johnson might be able to help us out with that this coming weekend. Your Donna does all the cake baking right?'

'Aye, she's in charge of the sweet stuff, but I'm telling you now she doesn't have a clue about the savoury side. It would be as beneficial to stick our cat in charge of the bread business, bless her.'

'As long as she's responsible for the jam roly poly, lemon curds and spotted dick, I think we shall be fine,' Harold said, casting a quick glance down at his watch. 'Anyway chaps it's been a pleasure as always,' he added, standing, confident he could place a tick by all three players, 'but since I've only a few minutes before my day resumes, I'm going to have to grab my cream scone to go.'

Usually when he visited somewhere that wasn't in walking distance, Harold would take the car, a vehicle that never failed to impress all those it passed, but since that meant returning home to collect it, he decided to take the bus instead and strolled down to the nearest stop, which was marked by a framed timetable covered by Perspex that had been nailed to the stone wall.

Right on cue, the red double decker trundled into view, the conductor hanging off the back step to welcome him aboard.

'Well let The Lord strike me down, if it isn't Mr. Baker himself,' the conductor announced, his words causing the two women sitting at the front chatting to rise out of their seats.

'Oh I do say you're looking very dashing today,' Deborah Egbert said, her hair a shade bluer than her friend's, the pair of them wearing cardigans they'd knitted each other last Christmas, thick and chunky enough so they didn't have to put the fire on of an evening.

'You're too kind,' Harold said, digging into his pockets for some change. 'But shouldn't the pair of you still be in your lessons? I'm sure school doesn't finish until three.'

'He's as charming as his tea is tasty,' Sue Smith gushed, seating herself, pushing her tongue against the roof of her mouth to make sure her teeth weren't about to drop, as Harold handed over twenty-five pence to the conductor, Simon Egbert, a man who had been in the same year as him at school, but who had dropped out at twelve when his father had died, to step into his clothes (literally), and become a conductor. Where once the jacket and trousers had hung loose, been tied with pieces of string to stop them falling off, now they nipped at his forearms and shins.

'Oh, been a while since you rode with us Mr. Baker? Prices have gone up in the past ten years you know? It's thirty-five pence to the East End now,' Simon announced, typing the numbers into the ticketing machine that was held around his neck by a thick white band.

'Bloody inflation,' Harold muttered, delving into his pockets again, finding he had no more copper or silver coins, just a large gold and silver one.

'Whoa, steady on there Bank of England! You paying my wage for the day? You must have something smaller,' Simon balked.

Harold turned out his pockets to show they were absent of anything except fluff and lint.

'Well in that case, between me, you, Steve, Sue and Deborah, since it's you and all, I guess we can let you ride at the old fare.'

'Oh your secret's safe with us,' Deborah nodded.

'Well thank you very much,' Harold said, taking a seat. 'I'll make sure Judith sends you all a couple of free bags of tea as a thank you,' he added, looking past the ladies at the road, which he was certain they'd already driven up once.

The bus slowed as a man emerged from the door of a terrace on the right, holding a briefcase in one hand and his cap secure to his head in the other. Steve, the driver, swivelled in his seat as the man came aboard, puffing and panting as though a couple of zeroes had been added to the yardage they'd just witnessed him jog.

'Thought I'd have missed you,' he wheezed, taking a seat, Simon not even asking to see his weekly pass, as Steve put the bus in motion again.

'Well you know George I went past and I said to myself, bloody strange George not being at the bus stop at this time, so I went round in a loop thinking that something must have delayed you,' the driver said.

'Aye, you're not wrong, you know your stuff. I'd left a piece of paper up in the bedroom,' George managed, his breathing still not settled.

'All part of the job,' Steve said. 'People just think it's

about steering the wheel this way and that, but you've to be a thinker too,' he added, tapping his forehead, applying the brakes in plenty of time when he saw Jenny Smith standing ready to cross the road.

The service dropped Harold on the doorstep of his spinner's house, the one he resided in with his father since he was still only fourteen. The sky around the rows of terraced houses was black, with constant plumes of smoke rising from the chimneys, so that no sooner had Harold stepped off the bus than he was sneezing and his face was filmed by a thin layer of soot. Such was the extent of the dark dust in the neighbourhood not one household contained a set of curtains, since it provided an impenetrable barrier to the sun's rays.

Kevin Smith, the window cleaner, had long since given up on the area, due to the fact he'd barely broken even, what with the amount of equipment he'd ended up using. That was the official line anyway, though everyone knew he simply wasn't welcome in the area after making the flippant suggestion that it would be better if they burnt wood instead of coal.

Harold tried the front door and found it was locked, forcing him to knock instead. It brought slow, suspicious footsteps on the other side.

'It's me, Harold,' Harold said, replaying the team's last match in his mind and the special performance from his young protégé. He had made it known on numerous occasions that this was the kid to take over the captaincy when he retired. Not only could he make the ball turn on a pitch as flat as postage stamp, but he was canny too. He was a reader of the game, never unfazed by anything, and whether or not it would catch up with him in later years, by God the kid had stamina. He could hold down one end for a whole day if you needed him to, the 1st to the 100th ball tossed onto a threepenny bit. He hadn't actually taken any wickets in the game Harold was reliving, but he'd bowled eight consecutive maidens, which had left the batters so frustrated, that when they'd sought to take out their aggression on the seamers, they'd ended up cutting and hacking their way back to the pavilion.

First one bolt was withdrawn and then another, and finally the door was pulled back an inch to reveal Jamie Baker's dad, David. He was short, small even for a man of Skipperton, where the average height was 5' 8". He wasn't pleased to see Harold, but then he possibly hadn't smiled since '93, same as most of the folk from the east side of town.

'What do you want?' he said, his face smudged, his clothes always black, as if he was constantly in mourning.

'I've come to talk cricket,' Harold said, forcing his way into the house, which consisted of three rooms, all of them with fireplaces that were burning heartily, despite it appearing that only David was home. 'Yes, I'm organising a tour around Europe and Asia you see, gathering a team to teach the heathens the sport of cricket and defeat a team of Indians who also have a four year unblemished record, and of course your lad is an integral part of my plans.'

David didn't say anything. He stood with his arms hanging by his sides, though not loosely. His shoulders were hunched, so it looked like he had an invisible coat hook inside his jacket. That was what happened when you spent your days hauling bags of coal from the minute you could crawl; you developed muscle upon muscles, though now it was sagging and turning to fat.

'You know there's no need to worry about his safety, I'll treat him like he was my own for the whole time,' Harold said, ready to remove his jacket and gloves what with the heat.

'Aye, I bet you will,' David grunted.

Harold stared at the man (the dwarf if he was being anatomically correct), with a look of confusion.

'Oh don't give me that look. I know full well what you're trying to do to my boy. You don't have an heir and you want to steal him from me.'

'I don't know what you're...'

68

'You do though, don't you,' David said, taking steps forward. 'Because he thinks he's better than his old man already. He comes home from school and wants to do his homework, starts using all these long fancy words, like unblemished, yeah that's the type of word he's picked up from you, whatever it bloody means.' He was within a couple of feet now, his dust covered face purpling. 'But he isn't going anywhere, because I've built a mine in the back garden so that he can get himself down there ten hours a day and put in some proper graft. See what it's like to earn a real living like his old man did.'

Harold was glad this was happening behind closed doors, because if anyone had been privy to witness such a statement he'd have had no choice but to offer a duel. As it was, he remained as calm as he could, but took a step forward, so they were almost toe to toe.

'You are going to ruin your lad's future.'

'Pfft. I am going to make my lad's future! Not let some Thatcher in disguise destroy it.'

Harold stormed down the road clenching and unclenching his fist. His reaction to the comment seemed like a dream, but the facts were that David was lying face down in his house and there was blood smeared across his new leather gloves. He could feel a headache brewing. His bowling attack had been decimated by two people living in the past. Now he was going to have to go and ask for the services of his back up spinner, and though he wasn't a poor second choice in terms of quality, there were other large hurdles that were going to have to be overcome in order to persuade him to join.

Al Smith was the founding member, the director, the treasurer, the vice-president...basically any position ever created, of the SNP. He was a one man tirade of leafleting and a constant bane on some secretary's life down at Westminster, since his letters and calls demanding complete autonomy for Skipperton were as relentless as his derogatory comments about foreigners of all descriptions. When Harold had announced in The Skipperton Gazette that he was to marry Rachel, Al had stood outside the tea factory with a picket sign demanding a boycott of the product, until he realised that since it was the only tea produced in Skipperton, and because he'd already picketed the shops that had once sold other brands of tea a few years ago - forcing them to sell only home grown brands - he would be without tea at all. So he had made his way back to his house and office to produce a pamphlet on the disasters of inter-racial dating, proud of the fact his own family tree closely resembled a stick of bamboo.

His house had been passed down from the very first generation of Skipperton settlers and was on a small mound that used to be surrounded by a moat, which had since dried and was now a muddy circle you were forced to skip over if the sun hadn't been out all day baking the ground dry. Directly in front of the house, on an eight foot pole, a flag billowed, one which Al had designed himself for when they gained nationhood, and looked a lot like the school logo. He'd been working on lyrics for the national anthem for a good few years too now, but he had yet to release them into the public domain, a surprise since everything else that went on in his head either came out in oration of an evening at The Arms or in his pamphlets. These were pushed through every letterbox in the town once printed, an event that was sporadic in nature and could vary from daily to fortnightly.

His latest distribution had claimed that the recent outbreak of swine flu was part of a larger conspiracy that took in mad cow disease and aviation flu and that would in the future include a mutton virus, with the aim of the Nigger/Jew/Arab league to turn white folk into a bunch of vegetarians so that they could take over the world. It was therefore up to every Yorkshire man, woman and child to make sure they went down to the butchers.

According to Stuart it had done little to increase business overall, but the sale of lamb had risen.

Harold used the white rose door knocker to draw his spinner's attention away from his latest article that promoted the reconstruction of Hadrian's Wall.

'Skipper.'

'Al, lovely to see you,' Harold said, wiping his feet on half a Union Jack, with the word **shit** scrawled on it.

'I'm actually in the middle of something important at the moment,' Al said, pointing to his sheet of A4, which had the title *Too Many Cock Jocks*. 'So can we make it quick?'

'Try to, Al,' Harold said, seating himself. 'Basically, what it boils down to, is that I need you for some games of cricket.'

'I am one of your players.'

'A vital one.'

'Goes without saying,' Al said, suspicious, but then when wasn't he suspicious?

Harold drummed his fingers against the table.

'Listen Al, I'll get straight to the point. It's a sixth month tour through Europe and Asia.'

A look of confusion passed over Al's face, as if those names didn't mean anything to him, but the man wasn't an imbecile, and the next second it appeared he was on the verge of choking, until he managed to splutter: 'Harold, I've been down as far as Bailey Abbey (ten miles from Skipperton) in the summer, and I had to stop going because of them flocks of nigger wogs all clogging up the place in their fancy schmanzy cars with four wheels and five gears, talking in their bloody posh tones - no offence to you and your missus - and so there isn't a chance in Hell that I'm going to go somewhere for six months where I'm going to see and hear complete bollocks in a load of bloody different voices. My ears'll be constantly bleeding and I'll be sick because of the stench.'

'But Al, this is about redemption, about what happened against the Lancastrians.'

'Harold, listen, I've let it be known enough times how we can gain proper redemption over those Lancastrians, but everyone's too bloody soft around here nowadays. Honestly, sometimes I wander through town and I don't recognise the place anymore.'

Harold drummed his fingers against the table once more. There would be pitches out in the east as dry as a bone, ones that could use a pair of spinners, let alone one, but it was no use trying to reason with a man who relied on *Book of Herbs and Remedies* circa 1743 for any ailments, because the nearest hospital was thirty miles away and he might as well go and speak to a dog since they'd make as much sense as foreign doctors.

'Tell me about it,' Harold said, instead. 'Price of Black's gone up in The Arms.'

'Three whole bloody pence! Oh don't think there isn't a piece on that in my latest edition. Basically it's bloody robbery is what it amounts to.'

'Can you imagine if you could, say,' Harold paused, lowering his voice, 'have your next couple of pints for free?'

'Well,' Al replied, sniffing, 'they wouldn't really be free would they? There'd be some sort of catch, which means it probably wouldn't be worth my while unless by "a couple", it meant my next ten rounds.'

'Six.'

'Seven.'

'Deal.'

Seven pints. Dereck would be fuming if he knew how bad his bargaining skills had been, but if the truth were told, he had to have hid his desperation well or Al could have held out for the ten, which was now how many players he had on board. The tour was going ahead, one last pre-dusk stop and he would have bagged himself a dozen, which was going to have to rely heavily on the top order.

His eleventh choice was Edward Egbert, who, without the prodigal talent of Jamie Baker, would be the team's youngest player. Since his dad was the twelfth man, 'The Wise Owl', William Egbert, a player who could be trusted to bowl a few creaky overs and prod the ball around with the bat to put his partner on strike, Harold didn't see this meeting being met with any problems.

The house they lived in, with Mrs Wilma Egbert and three other children (girls all older than Edward), was a vast property out on a farm. Such was the size of the building, it was the one accommodation in town that acted as a boarding lodge for foreign guests. William's compliance in such an issue did not lead to as much disgust as would have been expected by other Skippertonites, since at the rate he charged the foreigners, he had more than enough to put on a large spread every Saturday night at The Arms.

The nickname "Wise Owl" came from the fact he was the only person in the town who spoke another language. A child of one of his guests had left behind a picture dictionary with French to English translations and he had studied it long and hard enough to become fluent. Most people had mocked it as a waste of time, but now it was going to prove a mighty useful tool for the road. Plus, he was a person Harold could trust with big decisions. He watched the game, saw it from a different angle than those who became embroiled in the thick of it all. He was calm, and though his best playing days were behind him, they weren't so far gone that he couldn't be trusted to step in and deliver some of the old craft and guile he had been famed for in his youth.

His son on the other hand was a bundle of energy. There was never an opposition ball struck to the boundary he wouldn't chase down, and more often than not he would reduce what seemed like a lost cause to a mere two runs, his whites forever tainted green.

As a bowler he still had a lot to learn: his out swingers and in swingers were rare, leaving him a tidy bowler, reliable, not dynamic, but Harold was hopeful that the tour would be the making of him. It went without saying that as a batter there wasn't anyone else who could scarper through for a quick single like him. He had the pace and energy to run all day, and though his efficiency meant he averaged a meagre 8.65 per innings, throw him in as a night watchman with Erik or Richard II (players who could also cover the ground), and they could run comfortable twos all day long.

Harold was met at the door by Wilma, who had her apron on from her duties in the kitchen. She beamed as she welcomed him inside. She really was a scrumptious piece of crumpet, one of those woman that rather than deteriorating with age, seemed to grow even tastier, like a pot of tea left next to an open hearth. She asked immediately if he would be staying for dinner, and though it was something he would have enjoyed immensely, he turned down the proposal, since he guessed taking Rachel out might go some way to sweetening his absence.

He explained such reasoning, as he allowed her to lead him through to the study, where her husband was sitting reading under candlelight.

'Skipper,' William said, standing and removing his reading glasses in order to shake his captain's hand. 'What brings you here at this time of the evening?' he asked, sliding his bookmark in firmly.

'Thought word might have already reached you,' Harold said, admiring the bookcase - Alan really was one of the finest craftsmen the town had ever produced, no doubt about it. 'Been asked to go on a tour to Asia by God himself, as some sort of way to banish those demons we picked up four years ago.'

There was no need to remind William what position he'd batted that day or what his statistics looked like from the game, it was embedded in every one of those eleven players like their birthdays.

'Might be a bit late for me don't you think?' William asked, his last start coming more than two years ago.

'It's you and your lad that I'm after. Going to need a second opinion out there, an assistant who knows the ins and the outs of the game, but one who can still roll with the punches when needed. Also, your lad's been in good form, we'll need energy like his to get us through six months.'

'And who else would be joining us?' William enquired, going across for his pipe, though since Harold didn't appear to have his, he reached into his pocket and offered out a woodbine.

74

'Everyone except Richard and Jamie,' Harold said, such news making William wince. 'I know, big blows, but that's why I can't have any more of my first choice refusing me.'

'Oh, don't you worry Skipper, wouldn't dream of it,' William said, with a shake of his head, blowing the thick smoke towards the ceiling. 'And I can tell you now that Edward's going to love it when I tell him. He's upstairs reading at the moment, and you know geography's his favourite subject. Even if I wasn't coming he'd jump at the chance to join you, so you are sure that you want me there, it's not just a gesture?'

'Wise Owl,' Harold said, shaking his head. 'When I was too ill to make it to that game up at Carlisle last year, who did I put in charge? It might never have been stated, but you're my second in command,' he added, their moment broken into by the call of Wilma from the kitchen, demanding her husband's services when he had the chance.

'Bit like in this house then,' William said, laughing with Harold all the way to the front door. He patted him on the back, still chuckling as he made his way to the kitchen. Harold's smile, on the other hand, quickly vanished, because now he'd finished recruiting, he had to go and face Rachel.

Harold opened the back door, keeping hold of the handle as if that would help reduce the noise it made. If they owned a dog, he reckoned he would have sneaked inside its kennel and camped out for the night, sending it inside to take the flak for him instead. Perhaps buying a puppy would be a good gesture to make, give her someone to keep her company while he was away? She had to have something to keep her occupied; the phrase 'The Devil makes work for idle hands' had never been more appropriate.

The kettle had just finished boiling. Faint wisps of steam rose from its iron spout. Harold contemplated pouring himself a cup, but this wasn't the time to act casually. It was then that he realised Rachel wasn't alone in the house. He could hear her in conversation, not an angry conversation, but a calm, almost whispered one, and so concluding that since there was company she would have to act in a somewhat reasonable manner, Harold dropped his stealthy approach and walked into the lounge, announcing he was home in the jovial manner he had felt upon parting from William's company.

The two set of eyes followed him into the room.

'Father Johnson!' Harold exclaimed, 'what a pleasant surprise,' he added, so delighted by the man's presence that he didn't consider how The Vicar might have found his wife when he arrived at the house. 'And of course you're a sight for sore eyes darling,' Harold continued, going across to hug Rachel, whose first instinct had been to discreetly grab at, and tweak hard, the end of his penis. However, since that might have put it out of use for the rest of the day, she satisfied herself with deftly gripping one of his balls between thumb and forefinger, her hands more nimble than a thief's. She stared into his eyes and announced that he should have called.

'I should have done,' Harold admitted hoarsely, the image of a Brazil nut inside a set of crackers in his mind, the shell splitting into tiny fragments. 'So we can do whatever you want for the rest of the day and tomorrow,' he added, a comment that seemed to appease her for now, as he gingerly made his way over to his armchair.

'Well at least we won't have to waste any time on explanations as to what you've been out doing all day, because Father Johnson has been telling me all about the tour you've been chosen for,' she said.

'I've managed to collect together a team for it,' Harold said, 'it's a little short on bowling options but...'

'Does this mean that in your absence you'll be leaving me in charge of Skipperton Tea? As I've heard that's what's happening with most of the other players,' Rachel said, her question a rhetorical one.

'Of course darling,' Harold replied, 'who else?' he continued, suddenly reminded of what he was required to do in order to secure the services of Fred and John, 'and we can talk about that if you so wish, but I've really got to have a conversation with Father Johnson first if that's okay?'

'I suppose so,' Rachel said, standing, 'but as soon as you're done, you come and meet me outside in the garden, ready. Is that clear?'

The Dream

Cuthbert stood on the pulpit looking out at the largest congregation he'd ever seen. It was the size of congregation they'd had when people truly believed in Heaven and Hell, and treasured The Bible rather than using it to press flowers and keep out draughts. They were squeezed shoulder to shoulder, staring at him in silence, awaiting not just his words, but the words of The Lord, who had decided it was best to send their cricket team, their husbands and sons, baker and butcher, candlestick maker and carpenter, half way around the world. There were people standing, people he'd never laid eyes on before through all his work and walks around the town. Some looked as though they'd been living underground for years, others kept checking their surroundings as though they'd turned up in the wrong place by accident. He cleared his throat, checking down into his Bible, which had inside it the sermon Harold had helped co-write. Cuthbert had almost tried to persuade the tea Tsar to do the reading instead of him, or at least share the stage rather than sit there in the front row, conversing amiably with those around him about the weather and the afternoon market.

Cuthbert squeezed the silver cross that usually hung around his neck, but which was now on the verge of delivering a dose of stigmata to his right palm. He might not have felt so nervous were it not for the fact *The Wicker Man* had been on television late last night and the end scene was playing in a loop in his head.

'Good morning,' he began, his gaze roving everywhere except to the spot where Rachel sat, next to Harold (though they weren't holding hands, or kissing. In fact they hadn't shown any signs of affection to each other at all since they'd arrived come to think of it). She was dressed as if she had come for a funeral. Not his, he hoped.

Before his stint in Birmingham, Cuthbert had always felt his formal attire worked in the same fashion as Batman's costume and would help him walk through the world unharmed, protected by a force field, but since then, and especially now, his robes felt flimsy and certainly not fireproof.

'Today's sermon is from *Luke, Chapter Four*, where we find Jesus heading out into the desert for two-hundred and forty days and nights.'

There were some in the congregation who thought they'd misheard The Vicar, were certain he'd made a rather large mistake in terms of the time table, but when a couple of them slyly opened The Bible that was stored on the rear of the pew in front of them, they found that it was indeed 240.

Cuthbert had paused to allow dissenters time to heckle an interjection or for God to send down a lightning bolt through the roof, but everyone seemed fine with the details he'd given.

'Now the reason Jesus went out into the wilderness was because he was looking to prove to himself and others just how far he could stretch his capabilities. Not only that, but he wandered across the heathen land to gain more followers, to convert more people to His Father's ways.'

There came nods from a few of the regulars; others hadn't changed their expressions, still unsure as to where all this was going and what it had to do with them.

'At one stage, halfway into his journey, when he was on the brink of starvation, for he hadn't eaten in days, The Devil appeared before him and said: 'if you truly are the son of God, then why do you starve? Why not transform these rocks that lie before us into loaves of bread?' And Jesus looked at him and said: 'man cannot live on bread alone, but he could on cakes.''

Harold had directed him in their practice runs to really emphasize that part, but Cuthbert just couldn't bring himself to do it, certain this was where the violence would erupt, where someone would label him a fake, a sinner, and he would be beaten to death like the brave apostle James the Lesser. Here came the first dissenter, raising their hand as if they were in the classroom.

'Err...yes?' Cuthbert managed, the idea of relinquishing his position and applying for a normal, everyday job, after running away with Rachel, occurring to him only then. If only he wasn't in so deep.

'Does that go for women as well?' the woman asked; her name was Judith, if Cuthbert remembered correctly.

'Does what go for women as well?' he asked, unable to recall what he'd been talking about.

'The eating of cake instead of bread,' came the reply forthwith.

'Oh,' Cuthbert said, his eyes roving the church once more, this time for a camera. He was probably being viewed live on Channel 5 or else the police were ready outside. Was it fraud he was committing? Would it be more painful to be burnt or stoned? He'd heard all about the runaway thief of '66. What had happened to the body exactly?

'Well yes,' he continued, 'men, women, children, everyone for the whole two hundred and forty day period,' he said, ignoring how ridiculous he sounded. 'It's a special lent, one that only comes round every two hundred and forty years as part of a special celebration of Jesus' victory over Satan,' he added, the accuracy of the maths bothering him as much as the rest of the story - the same went for the congregation apparently.

Down in the front pews Harold turned and winked at Fred and John, who both gave him a solid thumbs up. Everyone, it seemed, was happy, everyone that was except for Keith, the town's Mayor for the past twenty-five years, who now stood, near the middle of the fourth row.

'Okay, lovely bloody story and all that, and I don't think you'll find anyone who doesn't enjoy cake around here, but why don't you tell us about what's happening with twelve of our finest!' he demanded, wagging his finger, his hair and beard white, his body slender. Now that he was angry, he resembled a down on his luck Santa Claus.

'Well, what I was trying to do through the story of Jesus was present an analogy of...' Cuthbert stopped. What had they told him at college? Reach as many people as possible. He had to think lowest common denominator and start digging.

'They are going to go across the globe teaching the game of cricket, as well as putting Skipperton on the map.'

Harold and a couple of others winced. Cuthbert was sure he could see the glint of pitchforks, as more than three dozen people rose from their seats.

'Put Skipperton on the map! What the bloody hell's that supposed to mean?' The Mayor cried, almost choking on his bile, as jeers went up around him, an early bonfire night on the horizon.

Cuthbert's Adam's apple bobbed like it was being dunked.

'What it means,' he rasped, taking a small step back from the pulpit, 'is that this town used to have the motto 'Gateway for the Universe' in the square and what does it have now?'

Those that had stood, sat in shame. There were mutterings of how it hadn't been their idea to degrade it or anyone of their lineage, as they passed the blame down the pew. Keith, however, remained on his feet.

'We've been waiting on funds to rebuild that sign for the past couple of years. Do you know how much it'll cost? Bloody fortune. But don't think we don't believe those words here,' he said, patting his stomach roughly. 'That's not the point though is it? What I want to know is what gives you, a foreigner, the right to send these men out? These men belong within the great boundaries of this town.'

The whole room appeared to nod as one. A young girl shook her head in disgust as her mum leant across and whispered: 'it's true, he's not even from Yorkshire you know.'

'God told me,' Cuthbert said, truly believing it now, his voice firm.

'How can you be sure it was him?'

'Because there was no one else in the room. I heard it in my head. It was deep and sounded as though it had come through a large, white beard,' Cuthbert replied, feeling like he was in a circus rather than his own church.

'Yeah? Well I once heard it in my head that there were no more Yorkshires,' Keith remarked, pausing for the gasped shocks. 'Very upsetting dream it was, but that doesn't mean it was real does it?'

'Listen, this voice was so deep I had to listen very hard to understand it, but I told Harold exactly what He said and now I, He and the players know that the new twelve apostles are ready!'

The team, whose attention had been shared between Cuthbert and their player-manager, now stood at a nodded signal from Harold, who stared up at Cuthbert as though he were ready to be knighted. Was that it? Was that who they were, a reincarnation of Pope Urban II and his knights? Those of the round table more like it. In which case did that make Cuthbert Lancelot to Harold's Arthur?

Cuthbert had once overheard some boys in Birmingham telling a joke about those fabled knights, crass it was, but he recalled it word for word.

Arthur wanted to know which of his knights he could truly trust in order to name them heir, so he pretended to receive a letter calling him away on a week's journey. Before he went, he fitted Guinevere with a chastity belt, except this belt had a hole where her fanny was and when you put anything inside this hole, it triggered a blade to snap down and slice the object off.

Returning seven days later, Arthur immediately called all his knights into the banqueting hall and told them to drop their trousers. He walked down the line to find that every one of them no longer had a dick, until he reached the end and there was Lancelot, still intact.

'Lancelot, you have passed my test and proven that you are the only knight who is truly loyal to me. Therefore it is you whom I will bequeath my kingdom.'

Lancelot was speechless.

Cuthbert touched his tongue, whilst the congregation, not quite sure what was expected of them, gave the twelve men a light smattering of applause, which Cuthbert broke into, keen to have them out of the church while they were still accepting of the situation.

'I would like to let it be known that all proceeds to the collection plate this week will be put towards the cost of the trip. Now let us lower our heads and pray.

'Dear Father who art in Heaven, please watch over both the team and this glorious town for the duration of the tour. Amen.'

'Amen.'

The collection plate found its way back to him twenty minutes later with a record amount of £3.33 in copper, two buttons, one of his own candles and a heavy dusting of coal.

The Coach

'Right, let's go over this one more time,' Harold said, his lounge currently looking like a travel agency.

'Okay,' Cuthbert replied, not knowing how Harold wasn't able to see through him. He hadn't made eye contact with him or Rachel for the past three weeks and the three of them had spent so much time together they resembled a family. Each night, before he went to sleep in his hard single bed, having said his prayers and kissed the cross that hung above him, and most importantly turned off the light so the images of Jesus couldn't see what he was up to, Cuthbert had practised the lines that let her know his real feelings.

'There's no need to feel lonely, the church is open twenty-four hours a day.'

'I'm here for you and not just as a vicar.'

'You're so beautiful, I think being inside you would match an eternity in Heaven.'

'So,' he continued, bending at the waist. 'These are your passports.'

They could have been done express in one day, but since that meant a trip to Liverpool, Cuthbert hadn't even suggested it.

'They have visas inside them for most of the countries, but I've written down what you have to do for a couple of others because of the time frame. At the borders of some of the other countries they'll simply stamp a page when you enter and exit. You cannot, under any circumstances, lose them.'

'Passports, right, sorted with them,' Harold said confidently, Cuthbert already having answered his question as to why it didn't say anywhere on the front: Skipperton. Yorkshire.

'This here is your medical bag. These tablets are particularly important as they prevent malaria. You have to start taking them two weeks before you reach Indonesia.'

'Indonesia?' Harold interjected. 'I thought you said that

was a new fangled way of keeping in touch with you?'

'No, that's the internet,' Cuthbert replied, shoving the bottle of Doxycycline back into the bulging hold all.

'And this is...?'

'My bank card,' Harold said, taking the small piece of plastic from Cuthbert's hand. 'Put it in machines called ATM's to withdraw money,' he continued. 'You know, I can pay for you to come with us, kind of as a tour manager,' he added, a suggestion he'd already raised before.

'You know I can't,' came the reply, at the same time as a surreptitious glance was made in the direction of Rachel, who was busy making dinner, her nimble hands stroking along a cucumber of all objects, caressing it as though it were The Lord's finest creation.

Internally Cuthbert prayed for himself. He'd considered buying a Dictaphone to hold down the play button so it repeated his repentance every ten seconds. Now he no longer saw himself as Pope Urban II or Arthur/Lancelot, he was General Haig, sending cannon fodder out into the trenches.

'No, I know,' Harold said, moving over to the map, which he'd loaned from the school. 'Just thought you'd enjoy the holiday, it's not that we can't manage,' he added, still amazed by all the corrections Cuthbert had made in an indelible black pen. No USSR, Hong Kong handed back to the Chinese, Germany as one.

'So this is a photocopied list of all the clothing you'll need,' Cuthbert continued, watching Rachel now work an aubergine between her palms.

'Oh that's all sorted, Dorothy is taking care of all that. Had each of the lads down and measured,' Harold replied, his own three-quarter length pea coat already packed at the bottom of his kit bag. Talking of peas.

'Love, how's dinner coming along?' he enquired.

'Almost there, the chicken'll just be another few minutes. I assume Father Johnson will be joining us?' Rachel said, stroking her hair from her eyes, her gaze meeting Cuthbert's for a fraction of a second, making his heart swell.

He was certain that it was beating with such might that it was thumping out of his chest in a cartoon fashion.

'He will be won't you Father? We've this itinerary to run through, which'll take a bloody age.'

'Err, well I don't want to intrude and what are you having exactly?'

'Chicken, chips and mushy peas,' Harold said, arching his back to push his stomach out.

Naked, Cuthbert reckoned he would look better, especially since he'd started a training regime. He could now do twenty-five press-ups in a row, and if he tensed really hard, to the extent he feared he was on the brink of soiling himself, he could feel stomach muscles he'd thought only existed in films.

'Chicken, chips and peas? But what about the cucumber and the aubergine?' he asked.

'The what and the what?' Harold said, shuffling the set of papers that held all the important details of the teams, places and times they were due to play.

'The vegetables.'

'Oh! I let her do what she wants with them, as long as they don't find their way onto my plate,' Harold said, leading them into the side of the kitchen that constituted the dining room. At its centre was a large table which had a stack of Yorkshire puddings on it and a pot of tea, which was actually two pots that had been welded together. Were it not for their long spouts, they would have resembled a grand pair of mammaries, Cuthbert thought. Harold was forced to stand to lift the pot(s) above the necks of the three yard tall mugs in order to pour. A guest, possibly the one visit Rachel's parents had paid to see them come to think of it, had queried whether it wouldn't be better to simply install a trough or gutter round the outside of the table, and on each first pour, Harold thought it sounded like a wise idea.

Cuthbert sat down to his left. His stay had been pre-empted for there were three dollies laid out as place mats, one of those sweet female touches he'd never been privilege to.

'Don't be shy, tuck in,' Harold said, trying not to show the strain he was under, as he half lifted, half shuffled his chair, which more closely resembled a throne, round to Father Johnson's stool.

Cuthbert, meanwhile, dipped the ladle into the steaming gravy, poured a dollop of the sludge into the bottom of a couple of Yorkshires and handed one to Harold as the Skipper plonked himself down, his legs level with Cuthbert's chest.

'Ta Father,' Harold said, gripping his yorkshire by the crispy, browned edges, the soft bottom sagging under the gravy's weight.

It didn't look elegant, but Cuthbert had found the only way to eat them like this, when they were offered as an oversized hors d'oeuvre, was to pinch the sides so it resembled a mini canoe and shove it all in, in one single go. No sooner was his mouth bulging, than Rachel walked over with their plates laden with a mountain of food.

'Oh now that's hardly fair is it?' she breathed, bending to lay their dinner before them, the view down her top enough to make Cuthbert start choking.

'Looks like someone's not used to having their mouth full,' she added, cheekily, her attempt to hit Cuthbert's back and dislodge the food, coming across more like a massage, her fingers working the tension, softening his shoulder muscles, but hardening another to such an extent that he feared, as it strained against the fabric of his trousers, it was about to snap. He'd return to his bedroom and find himself in two pieces, like a decapitated snake. It would be a just punishment, the cruellest blow, but if there was ever proof needed that He was watching them, it would be one to end all debates.

Cuthbert clutched at the lip of the table to stop his flailing and, concentrating solely on the pudding, managed to swallow enough of it to allow him a gasp of air.

'Sorry, it went down the wrong way,' he wheezed, wriggling in his chair, wiping away the tears with a tissue.

'I hate it when that happens,' Rachel concurred, giving

her husband's shoulders a rub on the way to grabbing her plate.

Harold showed no signs of being perturbed by the action at all.

'So, our opening game's in Bruges,' he said, giving his fork, covered in a deep green mush a wiggle, pronouncing the city Brug-ez.

'That's the first one yes, on the seventh of September. They're a brand new team. They sounded very keen to learn the game,' Cuthbert said, watching Rachel walk past the opposite side of the table to come to the head of it at his end. 'And from there you head to Amsterdam for a day/night match before three in Germany if I remember correctly,' he added, shuffling through the itinerary, hearing Harold mutter something about a failed European tour of Hitler's. Even if he had won, Cuthbert somehow doubted it would have had any effect on Skipperton, the town would have resembled *Asterix and Obelix*.

Underneath the table, Rachel stretched her legs and caught Cuthbert on the ankle with her toes, which were covered by a thin layer of nylon. Cuthbert tried to pretend that it was a cat stroking against his legs, a pussy cat. There was a slight trembling in his voice as he reminded Harold they were playing a total of sixty-five dates, as the toes, the pussy, brushed against him again, nuzzled up, yearning for the tips of his fingers to stroke its fine hairs.

Cuthbert juddered, almost bursting into a flood of tears, as his body throbbed in ecstasy, life pulsating from him. He felt as though his soul was bursting out.

'Forgive me.'

'For what?' Harold asked, the internal message intended for The Lord only, blurted out loud instead.

'I…I forgot I have a meeting this evening a rather important one that I really must be rushing along to now very nice dinner I'll be around tomorrow,' Cuthbert blurted, hoping it all made sense, as he shovelled up a mound of mushy peas and, as accidentally as possible, whilst moving to stand, dropped it on his spillage.

'Oh, let me get a cloth to wipe that,' Rachel said, Cuthbert not daring to look at himself, ordering her to remain where she was, muttering: 'excuse me' repeatedly as he stumbled and fumbled his way out of the kitchen and through the front door, a hand covering his crotch all the way as if he was auditioning for a role as a Michael Jackson impersonator.

Rachel and Harold, without breaking from eating, shared a look.

'Sometimes I do wonder about him,' Harold remarked.

'He does seem very nervous a lot of the time,' Rachel said, their conversation stopped by the ringing of the doorbell, which had them both glancing at Cuthbert's vacated space.

'Must have forgotten something,' Rachel said, dunking a couple of chips to take with her to the front door, which she was surprised to find wasn't hiding Father Johnson, but a rather pleased looking Dereck.

'Good evening Rachel love, is The Gaffa in?' he sang, unable to keep still on the welcome mat, which was cut into the shape of a rose.

Having heard his player's voice, Harold was already behind his wife.

'Now then Gaffa, wouldn't trouble you at your humble abode like this usually, and may I say Rachel dear dinner smells delicious, but if you ever need a little more seasoning I've this perfect little grinding machine, operates on batteries too so you don't have to worry about the elbow grease, can try it before you buy since it's you, but anyway I'm off on a side track there. What I came for is to show you this,' he said, extending his arm behind him, out onto the road.

'Bloody hell,' Harold remarked, wiping his greasy hands on his trousers. 'What have you gone and done now?' he asked, full of glee, taking the lead out to the vehicle, which was parked, rather haphazardly, on the curb.

'I had to promise a couple of favours, worked a couple of deals here and there, let a little sideline slide, but I thought it's exactly what we were wanting,' Dereck said, jittering like

89

his clothes were full of mites.

'It's a beauty,' Harold admitted, stretching out his hand to touch the freshly painted bodywork, 'but it must have cost a fortune. How the bloody hell did you find the money for a double decker coach?' he asked, stepping aboard, feeling like the admiral of a ship.

'That's the beauty of it,' Dereck replied, pointing out the modification at the front, where the cigarette lighter had been exchanged for a plug and kettle. 'This isn't a coach, it's a double decker that's undergone numerous tweaks to look like a coach. Did me some reading of the highway code see and found buses aren't allowed on motorways, and if you think this is nice, just wait till we go upstairs,' he added, as Harold took his time to survey the layout. Chairs had been ripped out to make way for small tables, which had ashtrays and beer mats on top and cool boxes underneath, and the windows had proper curtains with the white rose as a perpetual pattern.

'We'll be able to have some right card games on these,' Harold said, pretending to deal a couple, feeling like he was in a dream, his words drawing a nod from Dereck, who withdrew his notepad and made a scrawl. 'Maybe we could ask for a couple of the framed pictures from The Arms too,' he continued, heading up the stairs, safe, cocooned by the musty smell of Albert's carpets, which lined every part of the floor, well not every part, because the old bugger never had been the most deft with a Stanley knife when it came to the fiddly corner sections. To his credit though, he knew his colour schemes. It was impossible to tell if the carpet wasn't already riddled with cigarette burns, ale spills and patches of vomit.

Harold came to a halt on the top step. He didn't know what he'd expected, but this trumped it. Six single beds with matching Skipperton duvets. He stared down at the welcome mat, which had Skipperton emblazoned in the middle and the town's original motto stitched round the outside.

'I know you said we'd be staying in hotels and the like, but I thought if anyone needs a quick nap then they can come up here for forty winks,' Dereck said, squeezing his way alongside Harold to marvel at the ambience he'd created; Brut sprayed into the pillow cases, smoke blown onto the curtains, candle holders screwed into the wall.

'It could be any of the lads' bedrooms and it's on wheels. It'll be like we've never left home,' Harold said, excusing himself as he turned away from Dereck to wipe away a tear caused by a speck of dust. Speaking of which, he'd have to blow the thick layer off his chequebook for this one. He patted Dereck on the shoulder twice.

'Don't worry,' his batter said, 'you can pay in instalments for this. Paintwork of them white roses on the outside's going to cost you a little extra though.'

'But I didn't ask for them,' Harold blurted.

'You rather have them painted over? Red's going cheap.'

'No.'

'Knew you'd want them. Now, what with the dust and all, have you thought about a new handkerchief? 75% cotton, and there's a discount in it since it's you.'

The Escape

The town hadn't been as quiet since the death of Geoffrey Skipperton. In fact it hadn't been that quiet then, what with the tears and gasps of mourners. What had taken hold of the centre now was a stunned silence, as if, even though they were all aware of it, had heard about the set date on the wireless or read it in T' Gazette, they hadn't really expected it to happen, like the moment England finally won The Ashes back to back again or The Second Coming.

None of the players knew quite what to say to such a turnout, and they weren't about to show their feelings in public by hugging and kissing their wives. A simple peck on the cheek and: 'I'll see you soon love' sufficed, as if they were embarking on a day trip to Leicester and would be home that evening for supper, their slippers warming by the hearth. They tried not to show their nerves, and when they found their guard was on the brink of slipping, they climbed aboard the coach, Stuart first, after almost decapitating his son with a hair ruffle, then Paul, Fred and John, their heads bowed, contemplating whether this was the correct decision, their livelihoods in the hands of their wives.

Paul had woken to the same reoccurring nightmare for the past week; electric bulbs, flashing disco lights, electricians and all because he hadn't built a large enough stockpile. Ruined for the sake of six months of cricket to a list of places he hadn't previously known existed. He hesitated on the top step, but Richard II, having waited as long as he could in the hope of his dad coming to wave him off, ploughed into the back of him.

'Sorry.' 'No, my mistake.' They said, glimpsing the identical emotion in each other's eyes.

'You...' Paul started, his gaze roving past the all rounder to those watching them, a thousand statues staring at the coach, 'looking forward to this?' he added, giving himself an internal slap.

'Oh aye,' Richard II replied, trying hard not to think of

all those hours spent practising in the back garden with his dad, who this morning hadn't even joined him at breakfast for a final Yorkshire, but remained in his chair reading a book. 'It's all I've been thinking about. That's why I bumped into you, because I'm in such a rush to be going,' he continued, his words cracked like a seventy over ball.

From the street, one foot on the pavement, one on the cobbles, Harold observed his players and knew it was best they set off without loitering any longer, because it would only take one of them to quit and they'd all become renegades. It was only Erik he hadn't any worries about: the man appeared as nonplussed as usual, one of those old Roman gods chiselled out of stone. If the lad's house was on fire, Harold doubted anyone would be concerned, they'd expect him to douse the flames with a single puff from his lungs and stroll out the front door unblemished.

Standing by the talisman's side, Alan looked not relaxed exactly, but his usual self. Maybe it helped on these occasions having no loved ones to wave you off?

'Right love,' Harold said, placing his hands on Rachel's shoulders, 'I bought fifty first class stamps from Dereck so I'll make sure that I write to you once a week. Make sure you keep yourself busy, remember you're in charge of an empire while I'm gone, but I'll be back in no time,' he added, forced to wince as she laid her hands on his hips, his body sore from the waist down after what she'd done to him last night. It was a good job William had offered to drive the first leg, because he hadn't slept a wink.

'I love you and be safe,' Rachel said, turning his attempt at a delicate kiss into a sordid attack with her tongue. 'I'll be thinking of you,' she concluded, with a wink, smacking his bum as a final send off, watching him walk, a little bow legged, onto the top step of the bus, from where he glanced across at his fellow townsfolk. He opened his mouth to deliver a final rousing salvo, but shut it without uttering a word, a feeble wave their parting adieu, as the coach door closed behind him.

Morose. Funereal. The whole point of the tour was to rid them of their cup demons and yet here they were in the clutch of the moods they'd felt in those first post-match days. They sat at the tables staring at the cards as if they were foreign objects. Al had managed to light a woodbine, but the stick ate away at itself, un-puffed, hanging over the edge of the ashtray.

'Err, there's some growlers and a keg of Black underneath the tables, don't think you have to wait until after the yard arm,' Harold said, his voice, like the joke, falling flat.

'Shall I have us on our way Skipper?' Wise Owl called from the driver's chair, starting the ignition in anticipation of a positive response, which Harold gave him, as the voice of Skipperton radio's "Hard" Henry Smith blasted out over the engine. He was the sound of the airwaves from 8-8, a man so dedicated to his profession that the one time he'd suffered from a bout of laryngitis over a three day period back in '74 he'd done the shows in Morse code.

His nickname Hard had nothing to do with his prowess as a bully or his form in the boxing ring, but was due to the fact he was, at times, difficult to understand. This was because even after thirty years' constant service, he still hadn't realised that when he turned away from the microphone and continued to talk, people only caught half of his monologues.

All it would have taken was for someone to make a quick comment in his first couple of months, but now the town kept it a well guarded secret from him, both because it was reassuring to hear, and because games were created by inserting missing words.

'So now I want to bring us all up to date with a brand new piece...from Sheffield, they're called...Don't You Want Me?'

As the coach finally rolled off down the street, only three people breathed: Erik, William and Edward. The latter was far from subdued. He was smiling and showing genuine excitement. He had picked up the cards on the table occupied by himself, Harold and Richard II and was shuffling,

94

waiting for them to decide on the game.

'We're really going!' he exclaimed, bouncing in his seat, an attitude that could only be down to nerves.

'You might want to have a couple of sips of Black to settle yourself,' Harold suggested, pouring himself one at the same time, which Richard II clutched hold of before he could so much as mutter that there was plenty enough to go round.

'I'm sorry Skipper, I just really needed that,' Richard II gasped, wiping at the foam that had coated his moustache, making him resemble his dad to an even greater degree.

'No worries lad,' Harold muttered, as around him came the sound of slurps, sloshes and sighs of relief alongside the slamming of tankards.

Edward on the other hand waved off his share: 'I'm okay thanks. Oh just think, five more hours and we'll be near London!' he shrilled in delight.

It wasn't like they'd never travelled the country before. They'd gone as far south as Luton, as east as Norwich and west of Cardiff in a fleet of three cars, laughing, bantering, talking tactics or work, packed lunches in their bags and a spare canister of petrol in the boot, next to a flask, a packet of biscuits and a duvet in case of an emergency.

Now, however, even with a round or three of Black down them, their gaze roved tentatively out of the windscreen every couple of minutes, and on the brink of passing landmarks: the boundary of Skipperton, the border of Derbyshire, the Watford Gap, they held their breath as one, as if, when they attempted to suck air again, it would either be poisonous or devoid of oxygen and their bodies would explode.

'No doubt about it, we really are in Nigger Wog country now,' Al moaned, the third time he had emitted the same sentence, this time upon seeing a sign for Dover and the M20.

Harold was surprised he could see anything from where he was positioned due to the thick cloud of smoke being constantly added to in sharp, nervous puffs.

95

'Going to need to stop soon Skipper,' William called, 'we're low on petrol,' he added, Edward with him down at the front, switching over the radio channels. Harold didn't know what was worse, the music or the presenters' accents.

'Could do with a bite to eat as well,' Harold acknowledged, 'a breakfast and lunch of pork scratchings is fine, but something more substantial would be nice,' he admitted, the coach once again suddenly falling silent as the vehicle slowed down the slip road and into the service station car park.

'Oh. My. God!' Edward exclaimed, giddily through the vacuum, 'they're got a Little Chef and a Burger King!' he announced, his enthusiasm quelled by a gentle pat on his shoulder from his dad. 'But the quality, the exoticness,' he whispered, unable to contain himself. 'I've saved up for moments like this,' he added, fingering his wallet, loaded with every penny and note he owned.

'It's going to smell, and they're all going to be milling around thinking they own the place,' Al said, scowling at a child holding its mother's hand. It was a boy and there was pink in its shirt. Did these people's depravity know no bounds?

The coach came to a halt and Edward leapt from it.

'You'd have thought we were on a tour of the tea factory,' Wise Owl said, watching his son race into the building, blending in with the foreigners. Erik was off next, ducking to fit through the door, telling Harold he would grab them seats. Alan hesitated, stood, sat, stood, sat, before calling after Erik to wait and rushing out into the warm, southern air.

'I think I'll wait till I'm on the brink of starvation,' Al said, clutching a handful of scratchings, his skin to the wrist covered in a film of grease, which he used to wax the end of his moustache.

'Okay, well if you don't mind, you can go to the pump and fill her up.' Harold said, glancing around at the others. 'You lot ready then?' he asked, the remaining eight of them heading out, resembling a small section of Roman legionnaires, leaving Al at the wheel muttering about thieving southern wogs, mentally gunning down everyone who passed in front of the windscreen.

The service station wasn't busy. Erik was already sitting, staring straight ahead, enjoying his meal with Alan by his side, who checked suspiciously every which way.

'Going to have to go for a slash first Skipper,' Fred said, his motion chorused by three others and Alan, leaving them to split into two groups as if by mitosis.

Harold, Stuart, Richard II and Dereck made their way to the queue for canteen food, the "Special" advertised as a large Yorkshire pudding with mashed potatoes, gravy and sausages.

'See,' Harold said jovially, as each man received the same dish on his tray, 'it's like we've never left home,' he added.

The large woman at the till wearing a red and white hat and apron could have almost passed for Mel, except she only had one chin.

'Eight, ninety-nine,' she said to Harold, who removed his wallet.

'It's alright lads, I've got it,' he said, handing over a tenner, as the other three walked across to join Erik.

'Oh, you're paying for all four? In that case it's thirty-five, ninety-six.'

Harold gripped at his tray, knocking at his chest with his other hand to keep his heart from packing in.

'How bloody much?' he gasped.

'Thirty-five, ninety-six. You do each get a free cup of tea or coffee with it.'

'I'd be expecting a free night's accommodation at that price,' he spluttered, joined by Dereck, at the same time as the rallying cry of: 'How bloody much?' was heard bellowing from both the shop and all the way down at the petrol station.

'Here Skipper, you go sit down, let me handle this,' Dereck suggested, guiding a pale Harold over to the table. 'Right,' he said, turning back to the cashier, 'I tell you what love, since there's four of us, how about buy one get one free? There'll be twelve of us altogether see, think of all that extra cash.'

'Yes, in that case it will be one hundred and seven pounds and eighty-eight pence.'

Dereck stuck a finger in his ear and waggled it.

'But these aren't even sausages!' Stuart jumped in, both of the wieners speared on the end of his fork. 'They've less girth than a finger!'

'And what's this?' Richard II cried, spitting a piece of the alleged Yorkshire pudding onto his plate. 'Have you made it from cardboard? Plus it said large and this is bloody medium at best.'

Dereck shook his head in disappointment.

'Bet you're used to hearing disgruntled customers with these standards and prices all the time, so how about I do you a deal? We'll pay a pound per meal and come round to the kitchen to show you how to make some proper Yorkshires and sausages?'

He added a wink as if to seal the deal.

The cashier gave the people queuing behind (and enjoying the spectacle), a wave to signal she was sorry for the inconvenience and would be with them in a second, and then leaned in to whisper to Dereck.

'I tell you what, I'll make you a deal instead. You lot cough up the thirty-five pounds and ninety-six pence in the next twenty seconds and I won't call security.'

'Alright,' Dereck said, interlocking his fingers and extending them out in front of his chest to give them a crack, 'a bit of bartering, I can work with that.'

'Nineteen, eighteen, seventeen…'

'How about…'

The cashier's hand went to her walkie-talkie.

'…fourteen, thirteen…'

'No love, you see this isn't how bartering works, we're going to come to a mutual agreement somewhere in the middle.'

'…nine, eight…'

'Okay,' Dereck was beginning to sweat now, 'let's call it a nice, and I'm being generous here, even twenty quid.'

'...three, two...'

'Twenty-five?'

Security was already on the scene.

'Right, what seems to be the problem?'

'The problem,' Stuart said, rising from his seat, which he pushed back with such force it would have skittled a man to the floor had he carried on walking instead of staring dumbstruck at the thundering voice, 'is that these people are blatantly trying to rob us because we're not from around here.'

The security guards gave their fluorescent jackets a tug, keeping their hands on the bottom of the material above their waists, elbows out, under the assumption it made them appear more threatening and in control.

'Listen, we don't want any trouble here,' the smaller of the pair said, as from behind them, the second group, led by Fred, steamed across, all red faces.

'You won't believe it, not only do they not sell Woodbines, but do you know how much a packet of cigs costs? The same as my weekly bloody grocery bill!'

The security were now back to back and pressing down on the emergency button for back up, when Al, pushing a couple of Aryan children out of the way with the words: 'be gone with you little wops,' staggered into the group.

'Petrol is one pound thirty a litre. Do you hear me? One litre is one pound and thirty pence. I didn't say three pints of black for one thirty, I didn't say a gallon was one thirty, I said a litre. What the bloody hell is going on? Are all these southern Pakis millionaires?'

'Wait till you see how much they want for food,' Richard II said, frothing at the mouth. Wasn't his dad always right? Always.

The taller, and slightly more intellectual of the security guards, the one who could understand what was being said a little better because his mum heralded from Scarborough, saw there was only one way to have the team foot the bill for what they owed and leave in relative peace.

'Okay, unfortunately guys, the way this dispute is going, I can only see it being solved one way and that's by me calling the police. Now I don't know if you're aware of how much bail would be, but you're looking at roughly...'

The money was handed to the cashier, and the change that was returned was counted by each player with the same attention they gave the ball on the way back to the bowler, before it was placed into Harold's hands.

'Right, back on the coach lads,' he said, the four men with food picking up their plates, the security looking unimpressed once again.

'What? We'll bring them back, it's not like the cutlery's bloody stainless steel now is it?'

A glance down showed that actually it was.

'Bloody toffs.'

'Told you they were millionaires.'

'Well, we'll have it to bloody go then.'

Despite the irate mood, there was only Al who made the suggestion they turn around and head home before it was too late. The rest were of the consensus that they had found their way into a tussle and to turn back now without some sort of fight would be as bad as taking a beating on the pitch.

'Right,' Harold said, as his players shared the meals between them, his composure regained, feeling a little ashamed at how he had lost his cool. 'First, grab the tube and give it to Alan, Stuart you go with him and back him up,' he ordered, his bachelor batter able to siphon a full tank of petrol in under a minute. There wasn't another man in Skipperton who could suck like him, though every man, woman and child was experienced in the art of petrol dredging. It meant the area surrounding Skipperton had been given the name "The North Yorkshire Triangle", as tourists would come for day trips from across the globe and find that when they restarted their car, a quarter of the tank had disappeared.

A little under five minutes later, with Alan hoping his

ability to siphon had impressed some more than others, they were full again, petrol wise at least, but their stomachs still rumbled.

'On that front lads you'll just have to hold your horses till we get off the motorway and spot a supermarket for some bread and butter.'

'Bread? But we can't eat bread, it's special lent remember,' Stuart said.

'Right, aye, for some crumpets, pikelets or muffins then,' Harold replied, twisting round to face them from the driver's seat, suddenly noticing now that everything had settled down, that it was a little too settled.

'William, where the bloody hell's your lad?'

His assistant immediately looked down between his legs and under the table as if Edward had still been six. John bolted upstairs, but nobody had been sleeping in the beds.

'Not up here,' he cried down, as the team spilled cautiously out of the door into the car park.

Gallantly, Erik headed across to check inside the main buildings, while the rest of the team stared suspiciously at those who passed by. It didn't have anything to do with Edward's age (he was fourteen and had started looking into buying his own property during the past year), it was the stories they'd heard in the "rest of the country" section on the wireless that painted a darker picture.

'Hey up lads, think I've found something,' Dereck said, reaching for a scrap of paper that had been shoved underneath one of the wipers. 'Can't read it though, it's all in that fancy joined up style.'

'Southern,' Al spat, retreating into the coach, surprised it hadn't been typed up and printed out.

Harold took hold of it and read it aloud.

'Dear Team, I am really sorry for leaving you in the lurch like this, but I've been dreaming about this opportunity since I learned to read. I've caught a bus heading to London. I know it will be hard for some of you to understand, but that's where I see my future. I wish all of you great success on the tour, and Dad, I promise I'll write home and let mum

know what I'm up to. Edward.'

Bewilderment reigned. None of the players dared to look in Wise Owl's direction. Such a statement amounted to treason. Everyone shivered in shame and disgust as they imagined how it would feel for a relative of theirs to desert them in such a fashion and to flee to London, a place second only to Lancashire in the league table of hate.

'Does this letter mean,' Paul said, in a whisper, 'that he's been kidnapped and forced to write at gun point?'

'Are you…'

'I believe it does,' Harold answered, talking down the others. 'Either that or the kidnapper has written on his behalf. Those are the only possible explanations.'

'Only explanations! What are you talking about?' Stuart fumed, already thinking about calling or writing to his wife so she could remove Stephen from school before it was too late.

'The handwriting,' Paul said.

'Aye,' Harold added. 'Southern like Al said, and judging by the loops and flicks, a girl's too.'

'Well then, shouldn't we go to the police?'

It was a comment which was greeted by a round of "pahs".

'Come on now, you saw how the security treated us in there. You don't have to ask whose side they're on. No, listen, he's a big lad is Edward and he can take care of himself, and I'm sure he'll be able to battle his own way home eventually. Wouldn't you agree William? Wise Owl?'

William appeared on the top step, drinking and smoking simultaneously.

'I do Harold, I do,' he puffed and gargled, his eyes red. 'Don't mind if I take a lie down do you? I feel shattered from all that driving.'

The Tape

Cuthbert sat at his desk and checked his watch. He had expected a phone call from the police by now informing him of twelve mangled bodies involved in a horrendous car crash as they'd been driving their coach on the wrong side of the road. He had prayed for this not to be the case, but he was still prepared to rush round with the disastrous news and a box of tissues: 'A travesty…what a difficult time this is…I feel partially responsible…I would be happy to stay the night.'

He drummed his fingers on the papers in front of him. Each one was open at the page listing real jobs. The problem with them all, however, was that they wanted experience, none of which he had. Though this closed off an avenue of escape, Cuthbert found he was actually happy that this was an aspect of life he'd never had to deal with: interviews and salaries, hourly rates and sales expectations. Plus, he guessed if all else failed he'd just emigrate to America since they were masters of hiding church leaders in times of controversy.

Pushing the papers to the side and picking up the phone to check there was a dial tone, Cuthbert then made his way into the kitchen. While he waited for a legitimate excuse to run across town to Rachel, who had been busy taking her new role as boss of Skipperton Tea factory very seriously, he had decided that one of the ways to steal her heart would be by becoming a master of all cuisines.

His first few attempts had proven quite disastrous, what with him being a single man who had once survived on supermarket ready meals and instant noodles, and for the past nine months, since it was so cheap and if not nutritious, at least filling, the menu of The Caf, but his confidence hadn't been completely destroyed.

His expectations had been that by purchasing and reading six hefty cookbooks with celebrity faces on the front (that appeared so gleeful it wouldn't have surprised him to discover they were receiving oral sex from underneath the work surface), he would transform into an instant genius. The words after all only had to be followed, not thought through and separated into allegorical and literal sections. Nor did they require you to keep a dictionary to discover what such and such a word translated to into English. However, the parts where two or three things needed to be done at once had nearly killed him and he'd ended on one occasion, four hours later, sweating and famished, shovelling pieces of un-melted cheese and burnt toast down his throat.

Considering now that he may have set his sights too high with coq au vin and sweet and sour chicken, he was attempting an easier tuna pasta bake. But who was to say that was something Rachel enjoyed? What he should have done was found out what her favourite meal was - an assorted phallic shaped vegetable salad he assumed. The answer couldn't be that difficult to attain though, he would find some way to slip in the question when she next visited for confession, which, with the weekend starting at five that evening, would likely be tomorrow morning.

Cuthbert checked his watch again as he set the timer on the cooker. By his calculations, if everything had gone to plan, the team would be close to lunch on the inaugural game of the tour in Bruges.

Had his original schedule taken place it would have long been over, since it had seemed logical to stage the first game in Calais or another northern French city. However the response Cuthbert had received from the French was that they didn't want to play any games of cricket unless it was French cricket, which they were the best in the world at, and anyway, playing against foreign teams would only entice floods more immigrants. This all seemed a bit of a shame now, because having had that sentiment spat down the phone at him three or four times, Cuthbert had thought the Skipperton players would have found they had much in common and gained their first twinned town.

The team's avoidance of if not death for themselves, then certainly for others, only came about because a couple from their neck of the woods passed by the coach just before they were due to disembark onto the Calais roads. The woman was reminding her husband Fred that: 'these foreigners drive on the wrong side of the road. Remember what you did to that poor onion seller last time? At least that's one less of them on the road. So what do you need to do?'

'Keep as right as Thatcher,' Fred mumbled, bashing the door of his Skoda to force it open.

'Did you hear that?' Paul said, watching as the cars indeed switched to the right side of the road. 'You'd have thought Father Johnson would have mentioned something that important.'

'Now, now,' Harold said, backing The Vicar up, 'he can't do everything for us can he? We're not babies.'

The driving to Belgium was shared by Richard II and Erik, while everyone else took turns sleeping, playing cards, drinking and eating, since a toaster had been bought and put on a rota with the kettle beside the driver.

When they eventually arrived at their destination, they were delighted to find the city walls intact and cobbled roads. All in all there was a very homely atmosphere about it.

'Suppose it's a bit like York,' Al grumbled, 'except shitter of course because these Spics won't even speak English proper,' he added, stepping into the fresh air, which immediately made him gag, what with wogs being everywhere.

Harold stretched his back with mini-twists, feeling fresh, his only worry complacency: 'lads, I know you're all thinking this promises to be an easy game, like a cup draw against those spastics and infirm from out by Scarborough who try to eat the ball as much as bowl it, but we don't take pity on them do we? No, we quite rightly put them to the sword, have the game sewn up as quickly as possible and go and enjoy a nice cup of Skipperton. And you know, not that anyone needs extra incentive, and some of you may well disagree with me deep down, but on this tour we're not just representing Skipperton and Yorkshire, but also England as well.'

'Apart from Lancashire.'

Everyone stepped back so their shoes and trousers weren't coated.

'And London,' Stuart said.

'Well that goes without saying,' Harold replied. 'So Wise Owl, we'll let you go and do the talking while we go loosen up,' he added, allowing William past, the opposition standing around still in their suits, no youth, all experience.

'They look more like they're ready for a game of bowls,' John remarked, drawing a laugh, as they stared at their competition, whilst remaining close to the safety of the bus. It was strange, the Skipperton players had thought the people abroad would look a lot different, and yet, here they were, almost like cousins if you muted their voices.

'*Bonjower!*' William said, greeting the opposition captain, who possibly wasn't aware what a smile was, certainly there were no creases or wrinkles around his eyes and lips to suggest that was the case. 'Err, *Jee mapple William Egbert. Comment tu tapple?*'

The problem William had was that having only ever seen the words written, he pronounced them as he would have done in English. The Belgium skipper, completely grey, despite having just turned thirty-five, gazed back at William showing no sign of any emotion.

'Do you speak English?' he asked.

'Why, do you?' William replied, grateful for the reprieve since his next step would have been to divulge his age and tell the man his favourite colour was green, when actually it wasn't, it was more of a turquoise, but the book didn't have turquoise. He guessed he could have said blue green if he really wanted to be more specific.

'Of course. My name is Bruno, I am the one Cuthbert Johnson contacted about the game,' the man said, his accent flawless. He stretched out his hand, which William shook, the rest of the players watching on hoping he'd covered his skin with his sleeve before doing so. 'The problem we have at the moment is that we are not entirely certain of all the rules. Yes, a few of us have played friendly

106

games in the park and we watch the World Cup on television, but there are aspects we would like to go over, bowling action for instance and the fact you can bowl under arm if you please.'

'Aye, no problems I'll just go n't grab Skipper. He cn talk 'ind leg off a donkey ova t' rules.'

The Belgians, who were gathered around Bruno, looked at one another.

'I thought you said they were from England,' one of them muttered.

Bruno remained stoic: 'perhaps you have someone who can translate?' he asked.

By tea a ball still hadn't been bowled. Question after question arose. Points of the game Harold didn't even know existed were brought up, the boundary size the hottest topic of discussion, with the Belgians unable to reach a consensus of which model would suite their style of play better.

It was all so dull that most of the Skipperton players had gone back to the coach and dozed, though they had been lured out by the smell of lunch, the unfamiliar sight of the waffle greeting them, the bastard offspring of the crumpet or a lot of mini Yorkshires sewn together. Looking at them with suspicion, waiting for the Belgians to eat them to prove they weren't poisoned, each of the players then treated theirs in a different way.

Erik topped his with the conventional choice of cream. Stuart, Frank and John picked up two slices and grabbed meat and cheese from nearby plates, transforming them into sandwiches, which weren't that different from the ones now being served in Skipperton; apple and chutney cream turnovers, sausage and tripe finger doughnuts, jam and pork roly poly.

Dereck, meanwhile, having foreseen the cuisine on the road to be different to what he was used to, had brought along a stash of gravy granules, creating a small vat, which the rest of the players dunked into.

'So what happens now?' Bruno enquired, pointing to

the sun dipping low on the horizon. 'The umpire stops the game for bad light, but without either of us batting, the Duckworth Lewis method doesn't come in to play. Instead we have a bowl off at the stumps, correct?'

Harold nodded. He'd had one of his waffles with strawberry jam and the other with melted chocolate, which had tasted so good he'd secretly spooned on more next to the gravy pot hoping that no one would spot the difference.

Having won the toss, Bruno elected to bowl first. The player he chose was tall and rangy, his old skin sagging on his arms so it appeared on the verge of being shed. None of the Skipperton players had seen Da Vinci's *Virtuatian Man*, but if they had, that was the analogy they would have drawn regarding his bowling technique. He stood, side on, as though ready to embark on the world's most rigid cartwheel, and tossed the ball high, an effort Stuart would have sent down the motorway to Ghent, which bounced once and rolled centimetres wide of off stump. Altering his position a couple of degrees for his next attempt did nothing to change the end result.

Harold suspected he could win the tie for them, but he handed the ball to Frank, who bowled a couple of looseners into his son's hands, before steaming in and ripping out middle stump. His effort was applauded by the home team, who gathered round to shake hands, dignity in defeat a strange concept for the away players, who were all hoping there would be more waffles for tea.

'That is the bowling standard we must strive for,' Bruno said, his handshake firm. 'We do have a couple of indoor practice nets if you have a couple of hours to spare. Food would be served.'

'Waffles?'

'Cheese, pâté, salmon.'

'Waffles?'

'Yes, more waffles if you would care for them,' Bruno replied, unable to understand the obsession, having previously thought that in the modern age of globalisation they were everywhere. He'd certainly seen them on his last trip to London for a conference. 'Oh and Stella Artois of course,' he added with a grin.

'Oh well, not for me, I'm married,' Harold said, assuming she must be some pin up of Bruges. 'But I'm sure Alan will be delighted, I've been trying to hook him up for a while, though he's a little shy around our own ladies, so she might have to do most of the talking. However, back to the point of the cricket Bruno, as God's own ambassadors of the game, we shall willingly give your team a two hour lesson,' Harold said, ready to round up his players, when William, who had overheard the discussion, whispered in his ear.

'Oh aye, good point Wise Owl,' Harold acknowledged. 'Yes Mr. Bruno we were also wondering where we might buy some new tapes for the coach? Since we left England all we can pick up on the radio is this incomprehensible foreign bollocks, and since we've only one tape, that of a bootleg recording of the Skipperton Male Voice Choir Christmas 1986, which though bloody fantastic is known to everyone off by heart, we thought we could do with a couple more numbers.'

Despite straining with all his might, and having in his vice-captain Franc someone who had earned a first class degree in English, they couldn't quite understand what was being asked of them. What did tape have to do with music?

Harold shook his head, it was his fault, these foreigners only knew a few words of the mother tongue.

'Tape cassettes, you know,' he said, making the motion of inserting the object. 'The thing you put in the tape deck.'

'I think their CD player is broken,' Franc said in Flemish. 'Why don't you ask if we can take a look?'

Harold led them to the coach, while the rest of the players, keeping a respectable distance from their opposite number, had already begun in the last light of dusk to show ghost strokes or finger holds on the ball. The Belgian spinner had been forced to join with John, however, because not everyone was being as noble.

'There's no way they're coming on my bus,' Al spat,

standing in the doorway.

'It isn't your bus Al, I paid for it,' Harold said, 'and they're coming to see the tape deck to tell me where *I* can buy more.'

'They're here to sabotage it more like. These niggers were in cahoots with the Lancastrians during the war.'

Bruno and Franc had no idea what was being said, the strength of the accents meant the words reached their ears with as much clarity as grunts.

'Have you any evidence for that?' Harold asked.

'Have you?' Al responded, undecided whether he wanted to be upstairs or round the back so he didn't have to bear witness to the wogs stepping aboard their property. Lord knew what they spread.

'Books,' Harold replied, moving forward.

'Written by the winners,' Al said, 'and according to them it was probably one Lancastrian who took down thousands of us,' he added, retreating quickly to hide in a bed.

'I'm sorry about that,' Harold said, apologising to Bruno and Franc, who had no idea they'd been slighted.

'It is okay,' Bruno said, thinking Harold was excusing the coach, which resembled a pub at closing time. He and Franc monitored the front of the coach, impressed with the kettle and toaster, but their amazement was saved for the tape deck.

'This must be an antique!' Bruno said, pushing at the huge eject button to force the tape out. 'Is it possible to buy these anymore?' he asked his compatriot, who being an electrician was happy to insert a CD player in exchange for some help with his reverse sweep.

'In a specialist shop perhaps,' Franc replied, before turning to Harold. 'I'll go to my house and collect what's needed while you enjoy dinner.'

'Oh that's grand,' Harold said, feeling rather pleased with himself. 'Thank you very much indeed lads.'

'Okay, what the bloody hell has happened to our tape deck?'

110

William asked, gawping at the new shiny and sleek device in its place. The buttons glowed red and the slot where the tapes went in had been flattened to the extent it would take no more than a postcard.

'Sabotage, I told you!' Al shouted, almost triumphantly. 'They've put something in to spy on us!'

William, his fingers fumbling over the buttons, as the rest of the team edged closer, hit the play button, and thanks to Franc's generosity, a CD spun, and through the speakers came the voice of Freddie Mercury.

'It's worse than that!' Paul said, shoving his hands over his ears, 'they're trying to turn us queer.'

Punching the eject button, the CD slowly emerged and, like some hot potato, it was thrown around until it fell into the hands of Alan. He stared at the red writing on the black disc. He owned the very same recording on tape, though he had made labels to stick over the top that said *Northern Rugby Songs Side A and B*. When the music had blasted from the coach's speakers, he'd almost sang in delight with Freddie, but he'd caught himself and now, asking for the great man's forgiveness, he flung it like a Frisbee out of the window to a collective sigh of relief from the rest of the team.

'I say we smash the thing to pieces,' Al said, his suggestion gaining a few nods, but Alan, almost in a whisper, spoke out against it.

'Maybe it might be easier for us to find some more of those discs, but with Pulp or The Human League on?'

'Aye,' Harold said. 'Alan's got a point there. We'll see if we can find any in Amsterdam, and if we can't, then we'll smash it.'

'Might be better to dismantle it,' Dereck said, taking a closer look, 'looks like it's worth a few bob.'

The Muffins

While the rest of the team continued to concern themselves with the snazzy new CD player, talking about it as though it were the only interesting thing that had happened, drawn to it like a pack of moths, mesmerized by the way writing ran across its cover, Harold turned his attention to the up-coming game. It was the only date in the whole list where he'd thought there was the chance of an upset, what with the Dutch national team's recent improvements in the World Cups. What worried him the most, though he didn't like to admit it, was what if they did lose a game? Once their unbeaten run was ended, then there would be no further cause to carry on to India and he kind of liked his role of leading his players into unknown lands, it made him feel like Skipperton himself.

'We're here,' Erik announced, bringing the bus to a halt with the same amount of accuracy he showed on the pitch, the tyres on both sides set an equidistant length from the white lines. The hotel they were staying at was one Harold had chosen from a large purple book Father Johnson had given him, which had lots of details missing, or at least that's what he assumed, since it didn't have a single line dedicated to Skipperton in the Great Britain section.

Everyone stood with their bags, apart from Al, who made it easier to sort out roommates by declaring he would sleep on the bus to stop it from being tampered with any further. The pair of Richard II and John, meanwhile, offered to go in search of new music disks.

'Right,' Harold said, pretending that the note he was handing them was missing a zero, 'we're due to eat at seven, so make sure you're back in the hotel lobby by then. No playing funny buggers, we don't need any more controversy than we've already had in the past few days.'

With John checking the map every couple of steps, he and Richard II didn't converse much, rather they took it in turns to give observations as they strolled into the city centre.

'Very flat round here.'

'Lots of people use bikes.'

'Seem to be quite tall.'

'Sound like they've a mouth full of phlegm when they talk.'

Once they reached the music shop, they both nudged each other forward, until eventually they were both pressed against the cash desk. Since he wasn't going to be pushed until his body was bent at a right angle over the desk, Richard II ceded defeat and spoke.

'Alright lad, do you have The Human League and Pulp on a music disk that isn't vinyl?' he asked, taking the cashier by surprise, since the man had assumed they were a couple of shy first time gays who'd mistaken his store for one further down the street that sold DVDs.

'Oh, okay, so you like your Sheffield bands, hey?' he said, jovially.

'Whole of Yorkshire actually,' Richard II replied, a little aggressively, as he was handed copies of *Dare, Different Class* and *This is Hardcore.*

'So you like The Kaiser Chiefs too?' the cashier asked.

'Sound a bit foreign to me,' John muttered.

'No, they're from Leeds,' the cashier responded. 'I thought they were huge in England?'

The Yorkshiremen shrugged.

'With the toffee noses probably,' John said.

'So you want something a bit more punk? Well, what about The Cribs?'

'The Crips? Like a spastic band? How do they play their instruments?'

'It'll be one of those charity single things,' Richard II concluded, weighing the three albums up, guessing it was a start. He handed them back to the cashier and moved his hand down to his stomach as it rumbled in hunger.

'Aye,' John said, 'don't think I can make it till seven to eat either.'

'Pretty certain The Skipper won't mind us grabbing

something, we have put in this extra work after all,' Richard II said, as he was handed back a large stash of change.

'Not too much, just something to keep us going like,' John replied, leaving Richard II to yet again make the enquiry.

'Thanks for the music. Now we were wondering if there's anywhere that does a nice, I don't know, say muffin?'

'Of course, there are plenty of places that serve them. You just need to head down the street and stop in any coffee shop.'

The street the pair were instructed to head down was split in two by a canal. The buildings on either side of it didn't match, some were thin, others lurched out. Height wise it appeared some were ducking, while others were standing on tiptoe.

'Could have done with a spirit level,' John remarked.

'Difficult with the way this road slopes admittedly,' Richard II observed.

They made it another twenty metres up and then ceased to move any further. Their bodies, their whole bodies, had suddenly turned to rock. There were numerous comments or observations to be made, but they were too spellbound. It wasn't like either of them hadn't seen a naked or almost naked girl before, they both had fiancées, but their fiancées didn't look like this. Richard II's would only take her clothes off when the lights were out and John's, having only just turned fourteen, didn't have a fully developed chest.

The closest comparison they could draw was to pictures in a magazine that was stored inside a hole in a tree about a mile east of Charlton Road. Nobody knew how long the publication had been there for since the front cover had long since gone, and if you asked anyone in the town how it had come to be there, they'd have drawn a blank too. It was one of those mysteries of life and had surely been deposited by some tourist, because that type of smut couldn't be found in Philip Egbert's newsagents no matter how discreetly you went about asking. What was certain was that every boy over the age of ten in the town had laid eyes on it. The only

114

problem for those coming to it in recent years was that it was so badly worn it was near impossible to tell the difference between a crease and a vagina.

Fifteen minutes very soon became fifty. There were snails clinging to the inner wall of the canal overtaking them. The pair analysed what lay behind every window in such detail that had someone asked them for differences between woman two and woman twenty, they would have been able to give at least ten. They had constructed mental catalogues that they hoped, unlike the magazine, would never fade.

Richard II guessed that what they were standing in was some mini version of heaven. After all, Father Johnson had planned their route because of what The Lord had told him, and so God must therefore have intended them to witness this as some sort of advertisement. Richard II had never been one to go to church as religiously as his parents would have liked. In fact he'd only ever gone on alternative Sundays because of them, but he would go willingly at the end of each week now if this was a future he had to look forward to. Hell, he'd even put five pence on the collection plate so the big man could maintain the standards.

To his side, raising his arm so that when he checked his watch he could still keep the women in view, John, who had been hoping time had miraculously started moving backwards, discovered they were going to have to make a run for it if they didn't want the team thinking they'd also turned into deserters.

'You sure The Skipper didn't mean seven in the morning?' Richard II said, almost able to believe it himself.

'No,' John replied, 'but let's pick up those muffins anyway, then if we are late we've an excuse.'

Richard II said nothing. What they'd been doing was surely excuse enough.

The coffee shop café they entered was nothing like The Caf. For one it didn't smell of grease. Two - the people were speaking in hushed tones and slouching rather than leaning in and shouting over each other. Three - the menu was double sided and four - the cigarettes people were

115

smoking didn't smell like cigarettes. There was something almost sweet about them, and they were sharing them too, which wasn't a surprise considering how much they cost.

'Hi love,' John said, his confidence up what with all the beautiful girls that had been waving at him. 'Could we have eleven...'

'And a couple for now,' Richard II interjected, finding it strange the punters weren't staring at him in the same way he'd have been doing at some foreigner who'd entered The Caf, which he guessed was down to bad parenting.

'Sorry, thirteen muffins to take away, ta,' John said, accepting a box, each of the muffins coming individually wrapped. The pair tore off the plastic as they moved at a brisker pace back to the hotel.

'It's a bit dry,' Richard II remarked. 'Not quite as chocolatey as I expected either.'

'There's a taste I can't quite place,' John admitted, with his mouth full. 'Could definitely do with a dollop of cream or ice-cream as well.'

'Nice sized portion though.'

'Aye, lovely and big.'

They'd finished them by the time they reached Harold, who let them know in no uncertain terms that they were late (by ninety seconds, but still that was late.)

'But we...'

'No buts lads. Bloody hell, what do you think everyone's going to be thinking since we lost Edward?'

'Well we didn't actually lose Edward,' Richard II pointed out, 'and the reason we're late is...'

'Do I look like I'm interested in your reasons? How do you think your old man's feeling?' he asked John. 'I let you two out on faith, but if you act like that again I'll be locking you both in a windowless room. Is that clear?'

'Aye Skipper,' the pair muttered, staring down at the floor.

'Right, well go and put the music disks in the room and get yourselves back down here sharpish.'

As soon as they were out of ear shot, the pair lifted

their heads. It wasn't shame that had forced them to look at their feet, but the fact they had been on the verge of laughter. It was all so hilarious that they suddenly peeled into fits of it.

'Ah ha ha! We're late because we were looking at breasts,' John chortled, keeling over.

'So many boobies,' Richard II admitted, tears of joy streaming down his face.

They found it so hilarious they couldn't open the door at the first attempt and then once inside, the fact they were both going to take the bed nearest the door was side-splitting. But above all else, what made them struggle for breath, was that skipper rhymed with kipper.

Such antics would have had the rest of the team on high alert what with such good-humoured antics matching Edward's mood before he'd disappeared. Not only that, but being the youngest they were the most susceptible to be led astray, and the fact they'd been let out on their own would have been a decision that was questioned by everybody. Thankfully, however, they peaked before exiting the room. They still wore grins down to the lobby and let out little chuckles over the fact they'd forgotten to bring the desserts down, but they merely sniggered when pointing out each other's reflections in the glass covering old Dutch portraits.

Coming into view of the rest of the players sat round two large tables for dinner, their expressions waned to simple smiles, which they claimed they wore because they were pleased with their work in securing the music disks (though really they had no idea why they'd been delighted), and by the time Harold was talking about his expectations for the following day's game, they were as serious as ever.

'I expect,' Harold said, bringing his preliminary team talk to a conclusion, 'that everyone will have no trouble in sleeping tonight. It's been a long couple of days, been stressful too, but a good night's kip and some bacon and eggs for brekky tomorrow and we'll be ready to do what we do best!'

'Aye,' came a chorus of replies, 'nice one Skipper!'

117

John and Richard II remained downstairs for a nightcap with Frank and Paul, forced to drink Guinness since it was the closest product the hotel served to Black, and by close it meant they sipped it through gritted teeth as if it were a sour medicine being forced upon them, all of which meant that by the time they'd retired to their room, they'd forgotten all about the muffins.

'Oh yes!' John said, jumping onto the bed. 'I'd been thinking a snack before sleep would go down a treat,' he added, bowling a loosener into Richard II's hands, which barely saw the muffin before it was wolfed down.

'Could still do with something to give them a bit more moisture,' he said, chewing hard, licking at his molars, saliva glands working overtime.

'Should have bought a few more,' John commented, eyeing up the box, counting and re-counting the baked goods.

'Well it's not like we can hand them out now, you heard The Skipper's orders. The hall's silent, one step into it and he'll be out.'

'Aye, I know, and if they're already dry now, even with these plastic wrappers they'll have turned to rocks by tomorrow.'

'You know, thinking about what people buy from us, I'm not sure if everybody likes chocolate anyway, certainly not this type.'

'The Skipper keeps telling me I need to put on more weight so that I'm the same size as my old man, and dinner tonight wasn't the biggest.'

'Tiny.'

By the time they'd finished their seconds they were both slouched against the walls of their respective beds.

'You know I take it back about what I said earlier, and no disrespect to your mum here, but these are the best muffins I've ever tasted.'

'Oh none taken,' John said, his hands cupped behind his head, not feeling tired in the slightest anymore. 'These muffins are,' he sought for a word to articulate a valid description, and he didn't know where it came from, but it was, 'wicked.'

Richard II nodded in agreement.

'Wicked,' he mused. 'You know there's seven left now and nobody ever buys cakes in sevens do they?'

'Half dozens or singles,' John admitted, lazily leaning forward to grab one and split it in half.

'You know between me and you, I'm really starting to enjoy being abroad. It's err…wicked.'

'Yeah, boobs and those waffles. It's not as bad as I thought.'

'And these muffins.'

'Yeah, these muffins.'

'We should go see if they've ice cream in the kitchen.'

'Can't let The Skipper see us out.'

'Oh yeah.'

'Yeah.'

The conversation drifted, with both shuffling into an even more comfortable position until eventually they were horizontal. What they found really strange, and utterly hilarious, was the fact the more they ate, the hungrier they became.

'It must be magic.'

'Magic muffins.'

They laughed and then found they were happy to stare at the ceiling for three-quarters of an hour, thinking about nothing and everything. Ten minutes before their wake up call was due, they breakfasted on a final muffin each, the lack of any sleep not a problem.

'I can't wait to play cricket,' Richard II said dreamily, floating between the beds, bowling at what felt like normal speed, though any outside observer would have queried why he was moving in slow motion.

'Right lads, this is it, first game of the tour proper. This is a team that'll be able to play, so every one of you needs to be at your best.'

Under his breath, from his position leaning against his

roommate's shoulder, John whispered: 'at our breasts,' and the pair, to keep themselves from peeling into raucous laughter, coughed overdramatically.

'Are you two okay?' Harold enquired. He had monitored them all morning, because they appeared far more relaxed than the rest of the players.

'Aye Skipper, just think we need a couple of Woodbines to clear our lungs is all.'

'You sure there's nothing else?' Harold asked, as the rest of the team, bar Erik, let the sense of occasion show. Stuart was gnawing on his nails, Paul couldn't control his legs, Dereck kept bouncing in his seat.

'Well,' Richard II said, clearing his throat. 'As you know I'm not usually one for speeches, but you know cricket is cool, I'm not sure if I prefer bowling or batting, you can't really have one without the other see, but that's the beauty of the game. So what I want to say lads is go out and live through the bat and the ball, love it all, don't panic, don't tense up, just chill and become one with the object.'

'Deep,' John responded, too lethargic to bring his hands together for applause.

'He's turning queer,' Paul said.

'He'll be out picking flowers next,' Frank remarked.

There were others ready to pass comment too, but before they could open their mouths the umpires arrived and they filed out onto the pitch.

Richard II and John yearned to sit and make daisy chains, but there were no daises growing. Out in the field they sort of resembled the flower though, flopping forward in the sun, and yet despite this malaise, they still collected the first three Dutch wickets.

The first two came off the bowling of Richard II. Taking almost no run up, making the batsman think he was a spinner and the rest of his teammates think he was about to have a word with the umpire, he looped the ball so it had more vertical than horizontal distance on it. This compelled the batsman to come halfway down the pitch, picturing an easy six, but as the ball had so little pace on it and was falling at around 88°, when he connected with it, he more or less sent it back where it had come from, as if it had hit a trampoline. Down at long on, walking in, Dereck, watching the ball for an extremely long time, took an easy catch.

The second wicket taking delivery, though no flatter, this time had enough pace and distance on it to reach the stumps. Its high arc forced the batsman to stare straight into the sun, lose sight of the ball, swing wildly at it a couple of times like a sword fighter, only for it to end up crashing down on the bails as if it were a cherry being forcefully plonked on a cake.

Well aware these wickets were a novelty fluke, Harold withdrew his bowler after a single over and decided against bringing John into the attack, since the wicket he had taken had come in a tortoise and hare fashion. The Dutch batsmen had been caught exhausted in the middle of running 16 runs with John standing and staring at the ball, turning it over slowly in his hands, before finally snapping out of whatever spell he'd been put under and throwing directly at the stumps.

Fortunately neither was required to bat since Erik was in a formidable mood, which was a good job, because they had both been sleeping in the pavilion rather than putting their pads on. Harold gave them a slap awake once he'd made his way off the field with an unbeaten 28.

'What the bloody hell were you two doing last night? That's the last time you share a room. I'll tell you that for certain.'

'Bummer,' the pair admitted, before dozing back off.

The Nobs

There were faint murmurs, as they left Holland and entered Germany, barely audible, but still whispered by half the team, that though you could fault the Europeans for a lot of things: haircuts, clothes, food, drink, prices, TV shows, preferring coffee, you couldn't fault their hospitality or service. The Dutch players had handed over a pair of clogs as a souvenir, and in return Harold had, reluctantly whilst nobody else was watching, presented them with a box of tea, which the Dutch captain had been forced to prize from his grasp.

Their crossing into Germany was only noticed by Dereck, who followed the motorway signs for Hamburg, taking them within fifty kilometres of the city, before handing over the driving responsibility to Erik, who required only a single glance at the map in order to take them to their destination.

'So the place we're going to is called Hamburger?' Paul asked, lifting the lid off the teapot on his table to check if the bags had stewed for long enough.

'Bet they won't be like real bloody hamburgers,' Stuart said, his 82 runs having come off just fifty balls. He should have gone on to make his first century of the tour, but he'd gone swinging wildly and edged to second slip.

Whether it was a gift or a curse, he wasn't one to replay the shot and think about what he should have done; once it was gone it was almost as if it had never happened.

'They'll be the size of beer mats and they'll taste the same too. I've already lost a couple of pounds,' he said, forcing his thumb inside his waist band. 'Another month and I'll be looking like...' He'd been about to say Richard II, but the all rounder was, if anything, looking a little bloated.

'One of these Nazi niggers,' Al said, thinking his friend required help with his analogy. 'All...' he continued, checking behind the curtain to see what characteristics the new folks shared, only to find himself viewing a bus with seemingly every demographic on the planet in it. '...all faces and hair,' he added, in disgust, buttoning the curtain back to keep

122

further sights from invading his personal space.

Once they'd reached their hotel, food was quickly back on the agenda with many calls for waffles and the odd mention of muffins; the receptionist though, who lived up to the team's newfound stereotype of being extremely helpful and pleased to see them, suggested they go outside where there was a beer garden that served sausages.

'Sausages that'll never have seen an eyeball or gristle in their lives,' Stuart remarked once they were outside. 'Sausages that might as well have been made by Waddingtons, ones that'll have those Little Chef cocktail sticks looking like those candles Paul makes for the church.'

'They're bloody massive! Took me and the missus to carry the one we bought,' William said, 'and it's still going strong two years later.'

'Try my best,' Paul said modestly, as the smell of fried goods and the chinking of glasses greeted them. Even if the food wasn't great, the people still sounded like they were enjoying themselves.

'And you see,' Stuart said, as a group of Germans broke into song, 'that's the problem with all these places. Nobody is trying their best, nobody cares about their craft, they're happy to just churn out any old thing and idiots all over the place are willing to accept it.'

They rounded the corner to find a garden complete with custom made tables and chairs. On top of the tables stood mugs that held far more than a pint's worth of beer.

'Ah!' said one of the German men with a thick moustache, who had been singing and hugging two others, 'we have guests,' he added, breaking from the chain, keeping hold of his tankard. His shorts were like the ones Skipperton school boys wore, except these were green. He also had on knitted knee length beige socks and a pair of open toed sandals, which, judging by the rest of the crowd, was some sort of uniform.

'You have come for beer and sausage all the way from?'

'Skipperton. Yorkshire. England.'

'Ah yes, England, you love the beer and sausage as much as us, so come,' the German man said, ordering the barman to pull eleven pints of Beck's.

'Whoa, hang on there,' Frank said, spotting the steiners being lined up and an amber liquid being poured into them. 'Haven't you got any…'

'What? You would prefer soft drinks? I would say that you can have what the ladies are drinking, but they are also drinking lager.'

Without another word, the team grappled for a drink.

'If you also need someone to help cut your sausage into tiny, little pieces, just ask,' the man added, as foot long wursts were revealed.

'Blimey!'

'You know they might be even bigger than the ones at home.'

'It's about quality as well,' Stuart blurted, blushing, clutching hold of the beast, wielding it like some floppy truncheon. He could tell by its appearance, by its texture, that he was going to enjoy it. He was going to have another couple of lagers too, because it was refreshing. It didn't taste like watered down piss.

Paul tried to hide a sausage he was handed that had been coiled like a snake and had to be at least fifteen inches, but Stuart had seen it, and a lump formed in his throat as he chomped down the last morsel of his own beast. This was no laughing matter, his reputation, his family name, they were both at stake. He could see the rest of the team looking at him and he knew what they were thinking, because he was thinking it himself. What was required was something to elevate him, take their minds off the facts and restore both his self-esteem and their estimation of him.

'Alright,' he bellowed, bringing the festivities to a momentary halt. 'I challenge every one of you to a sausage eating and beer drinking competition.'

There was an almighty roar from the German contingent.

'Time for repayment for sixty-six on home soil!' one

man cried.

'Yes, yes, someone bring forth Heinz,' the man who had invited them in said, clapping his hands as a table was carried by men using only one hand so as to keep their beers aloft in the other.

The singing had now taken on a football ground mentality, with the Skipperton players raising a cry of: 'Yorkshire, Yorkshire,' against the swell of support rising in fervour for the home favourite, who appeared from beyond a cloth as if summoned from guarding the gates of Hell.

Stuart tried his best to look unfazed, but it was like being in the presence of four Eriks; a pair standing shoulder to shoulder, with another two balanced on top. Heinz's blonde hair didn't rustle in the wind, his muscles didn't move when he took steps forward, he was a piece of rock, his white socks, pulled tight around his calves, able to double at night as pillow cases. He offered out his hand.

'May the man who loves sausage most vin,' he said, the table rising off the ground to accommodate his knees, as he sat on his side of the bench, holding his hands aloft in salute to the support, as the rules of the competition were laid out - one sausage weighing 1lb to be eaten, then a steiner drunk, ad infinitum, until one man could take no more.

Stuart, elbows out in an attempt to make himself appear as imposing as possible, tried not to think of the consequences a defeat would cost him. He wouldn't be able to return home, that was for certain. He'd face exile. He'd have to ask to be let out in the depths of Barnsley on return, from where he'd write to Susan, who would have every right to move on without him.

'So one, two, three, let the contest begin!' came the call, as those in the crowd who hadn't been brave enough to step up to the challenge, attempted to match the pair of gladiators, both of whose tactics appeared to be route one, the opening sausages disappearing like they'd been tossed into a tunnel.

Though at first the rest of the team had remained tight as a single faction, with more beer and sausage to be ordered and the toilet to be visited, they quickly started to filter out into smaller pockets. Not that they seemed to notice, because each man was lost in his own world of zeal for Stuart, who put on such an impressive performance, even some of the natives began to join in with the songs sung by the Yorkshiremen, including a rendition of *The Dambusters*.

Down near the front, hands in his pockets, looking a little lost, stood Alan, who was actually studying the impressive, sturdy craftsmanship of the table at the centre of the duel.

'Ah!' their host said, sidling up to him, holding out a fresh steiner of beer, which he practically forced Alan into accepting and downing, 'these two men certainly do love their sausage. I am most impressed how they can fit such a big item so easily into their mouths,' he added, the jostle of the crowd forcing him to rub shoulders with Alan, who said nothing. 'I am Steffen by the way, I did not get the chance to fully introduce myself earlier,' he continued.

'Alan,' Alan replied, feeling his skin growing hot. He checked around him for the rest of the team to find they were either, in Al's case, screaming both patriotic slogans and threats in Stuart's ear, in Richard II and John's, edging gradually closer to the section of the bar being served by a woman with blonde pigtails. The rest were caught up in the general revelry.

'You know Alan, I like many kinds of sausage; long, thick, short, thin, it doesn't matter to me, a sausage is a sausage and the taste is like nothing else in the world. At night I lay in bed and dream of sausage; about the next time I can get my hands on a sausage and what I will do once I have it in my hands. I think you are also a fan of sausage, correct?'

Alan said nothing. The sausages he watched going into people's mouths were no longer just sausages. His mouth was dry. He wanted to lick his lips, but his tongue wouldn't work.

'Alan, *mein Freund*,' Steffen said, looking like he'd just shoved one of those coiled slabs of meat down the front of his shorts, 'do you want to break free from this crowd?'

It was bad enough to fraternise with the opposition the day before a game, but to wake up in their rivals' shirts having swapped them at the end of the sausage and beer competition was another thing (and waking full of their sausage an entirely different…anyway.)

Harold found his face plastered to his pillow and almost gave a shriek when he rubbed at his chest to find his shirt had been replaced with a vest advertising lager. He went to quickly and stealthily remove it before William noticed it, but since William was in the same predicament and opened his eyes at the strange noise his Skipper had made, they looked at each other and made a silent pact that news of what had gone on wasn't to leave their hotel room.

It was hard to tell what time they'd stumbled into their room after the enthralling draw between Stuart and Heinz, neither man able to finish their fourteenth lager, their handshake celebrated by all except for Al, who had to be dragged by Dereck and Paul to the coach, as he screamed at the top of his voice that Stuart had let his town and county down. It was a statement ridiculed by an English couple who had been caught up in the melee, with the man proclaiming that Stuart had done his country proud, and from somewhere a Union Jack had been tossed his way and like an athlete (a hammer or a shot putt thrower perhaps) Stuart had posed for pictures draped in the flag and had still been talking to Heinz when Harold had retired to bed.

It was behaviour none of them could be proud of, except for the result of course, because deep down, at the first glimpse of Heinz, no one had given Stuart a chance.

By the time Harold and William reached the lounge for breakfast, the rest of the players were already down, on their third or fourth tea, picking at breakfast, which Stuart wasn't touching since it was only meat.

'Don't want to see another sausage or slice of salami till lunch,' he muttered, slouched in his chair, a position aped by the rest of the team; nursing headaches, groaning, smelling of smoke, reminding Harold of the team he had adopted when he had taken the reins. He would have been a damn sight more worried about this lack of professionalism were it not for the fact his concern turned to the whereabouts of Alan. If he kept losing players at this rate, by the time he reached Russia he'd be on his own.

Now it wasn't a surprise nobody else had noticed his lack of presence, but Erik might have said something. Only Erik had swapped roommates because Harold had given him Richard II to take care of, and John had gone with his dad…Harold's head was starting to spin, but before he could say: 'who is sharing…' he first heard, and then saw Alan, shimmying and shuffling their way. Everyone fell silent as he glided over the floor.

'What's gotten into The Gnome?' someone whispered.

'Could still be drunk.'

'Hey,' Harold called, bringing Alan to attention. 'Where the bloody hell have you been?'

'I've been out, and I tell you I feel better than ever! I'm ready to knock balls all over the park. I don't feel any tension at all, I'm raring to go Skipper.'

As it dawned on Harold that The Gnome had got lucky with a lady, it also became clear to Al, who let out a scream and tried to force up some vomit as he imagined such an indiscretion.

'Ah right I see, well that's fine,' Harold said, 'just make sure you let me or William know next time,' he continued. 'Oh, and what was that you were singing?'

If the truth was told, Alan hadn't even realised he'd been singing, but if that was the case, there was only one song it could have been.

'I was singing, *I want some brekky*.'

'Oh that's alright then, because there's plenty of cold cuts. But you know I'm sure I've heard that tune somewhere else,' Harold replied, tapping his chin.

'Some old rugby league ditty my dad used to sing,' Alan said, beginning to hum randomly.

The ground they were playing at was round the back of a swimming pool/leisure complex. The sky overhead was cloudy, though the receptionist had assured them rain was not forecast. As with their previous encounters, William had been pushed to the front to make the initial greetings.

'*Bonjour*,' he announced. 'We are here to play cricket,' he added, altering his accent to change his language, as the team shuffled in behind him, their whites gleaming in the centre's strong artificial light.

The receptionist pointed them in the direction they needed to take, which passed through a changing room that had a man and a woman in it undressing side by side.

'I want to go on tour for the rest of my life,' John whispered in the ear of Richard II, as the team stood transfixed, their eyes glued on the woman as she and her partner slipped towels round themselves and headed through the door smiling.

'Are we in someone's house?'

'Did they just…'

'Where were her, you know?'

'God bless Father Johnson.'

'Size seems to come as standard.'

'She was like twenty-five, she must have hit puberty.'

'Lads, I'm not sure what we've just witnessed,' Harold said, reminded by the wax job that he hadn't yet written to Rachel, 'but you need to put whatever it was to the back of your minds, because behind that door is a team waiting to exact revenge not just for 1918, 1945 and 1966, but also for Stuart's brave showing last night. What we've just seen is probably part of some dirty tactics, but we can rise above it can't we?'

Any jokes about that being more than possible if the lass lost her towel again were held internally, as Harold pushed the door back to reveal an Eden, except with a bounty of men and women, and not a fig leaf in sight. He was about to slam the door closed, thinking maybe the sausage had been poisoned and they were having some team hallucination, but Heinz of all people spotted them and waved them over.

'The English are here for cricket! Welcome, come in, we play over here,' he said, pointing to where the rest of his teammates were warming up.

'What the bloody hell is this?'

'A sick joke, a sick joke is what this is.'

'Father Johnson couldn't have arranged this, he's a man of the cloth not a man of no cloth!'

'No chance I'm playing.'

'How are we supposed to know which ball to look at?'

'Heinz, we're going to need a minute,' Harold said, closing the door on the multitude of body parts flapping around.

'Just not right this Gaffa, this is not what I signed up for.'

'I didn't know what bringing the game into disrepute meant, but now I do.'

'Lads, lads, settle down. Do you think I knew this was scheduled? Bloody well would have skipped it if I had, but I'll tell you now, there's no way I'm bloody forfeiting this match.'

'But.'

'No buts.'

'Lots of butts actually.'

'Hey, this is not the time to be joking.'

'If it wasn't the time to be joking, they'd be wearing clothes.'

'I say we have a vote,' Al declared, such an idea met by a consensus of shallow nods, which was when Alan stepped in, itching to be out on the pitch.

'Lads, what's going on?' he asked, shaking his head in disappointment at them. 'Do you think when the Germans tried the same tactic at The Battle of Britain our lads refused to take to their planes? I'm pretty sure Churchill never said: "We'll fight them on the beaches, but only if they're wearing trousers", did he?'

'No,' came a couple of ashamed replies.

'So are we going to let everyone down or are we going

130

to go and show them what we're made of?'

'When you say show them you mean...right that's okay.'

'In that case I'll play,' grumbled Al, 'but don't think for one minute that I'm opening my eyes when I'm out on the field.'

With Stuart still feeling under the weather, Alan even offered to open the batting with Erik, and since he'd saved the game, Harold had no problem in pushing him up the order for a performance that was (if only you could have just kept your eyes on his bat and not followed the flight of the ball) a pleasure to watch.

While the wickets skittled around him, Alan racked up a score at a pace Stuart would have been proud of. If only it hadn't come off so many shots clipped over the fielders, making them jump in vain. He hardly hit a boundary, every stroke kept the fielders running tirelessly in their socks and sandals. Heinz, the team's captain, fared worse than the rest of his players, with his inner thighs badly bruised by the twentieth over.

After his ton came up with a couple of runs off a sweep down to third man, Alan held his bat aloft in the direction of his fellow teammates, who momentarily withdrew their hands from the cupped, blinkered, position either side of their eyes, to applaud the only player to make it past the teens.

'Tell you what, don't know what's got into him, but he's full of it.'

'We'll have to make sure we have what he's had before the next match.'

'He just looks full of life.'

He added a further four singles to finish the game unbeaten and take the team total to 166, which left the bowlers with an uphill task. Fortunately the batsmen took to the field with boxes attached to G-strings, which was a much more welcoming sight, except of course for Paul or anyone unfortunate enough to be rotated into the slips, especially when the batter decided to stretch their hamstrings.

Overall it resulted in a whole host of detrimental fielding records being set under Harold's reign. Eight dropped catches, three over throws and a ten ball over from Al, whose day ended in a worse state than his career low figures of a batting duck and one over for 15 that included four extras. He finished with a badly bruised body, not because of any opponent's knocks, but thanks to his own players throwing the ball to him during his over, only figuring the more sensible option was to place it into his hand four balls in. Then, hobbling and wincing in pain at the end of the game, which Skipperton had somehow scraped to victory by a margin of six runs, he went to grab one of the bails, only to find it wasn't hard, at least not at first.

The Mobs

Cuthbert couldn't recall ever being happier. He'd taken up jogging and found that even after a couple of days he could feel the benefits. There was a bounce in his step, he wasn't as tired of an evening and his skin felt fresher, more youthful. It probably helped that his diet had only included a variety of salads, since that was what Rachel had stated was her favourite meal. He had originally thought it sounded boring, that there wasn't much scope for creativity, but there appeared to be as many varieties of salad as there were branches of the church, and there was no doubt he was now a master when it came to the Nicoise, Garden and Waldorf. It was simply a matter of time before she came round to sample these delights. He was just waiting for the right moment to make the offer, which would be right after his Calvin Klein boxer shorts had arrived.

He whistled as he swept the stone floor of the church, gliding round his domain, which was beginning to look palatial. Every surface gleamed, the lighting appeared both grand and foreboding, and he'd even been down to see Barry Smith about acquiring a new stained glass window to form a huge centrepiece above the door.

Such a visit was part of his daily rounds that took him across town. He made a point of checking on the team's businesses with an even greater regularity, and had thus far found that it appeared that nobody was missing the twelve men. Susan had been laughing away heartily in the butcher's, the post office didn't have any queues, the bakery was writing a new rule book on cuisine and the candle business was ticking over like clockwork.

Of all the businesses though, he seemed to be pulling in the largest crowds with his Sunday service, since people had realised they could use the church as a spacious meeting place to have a good natter after he had finished. As obvious as this was, Cuthbert chose to believe that the continuing swell of people through the doors on those clear

Sunday mornings was due to the vigour he put into his work as the town grew with him.

Whilst Cuthbert was musing on his successes, Rachel came in unannounced, in her work attire. Had Cuthbert not known what her job was, he would have suspected she was earning her money by illicit means. How tea was still being boxed and placed on the shelves of the markets could only be due to a strong female workforce, because if he'd been at the factory he would have kept his hands free to catch her globes, as they forever appeared on the verge of popping out. They were under so much pressure they looked like they were on the brink of bursting.

The broom fell from Cuthbert's hands and clattered loudly, echoing out.

'Here, let me grab that for you.'

'Oh no, it's okay. If you insist,' Cuthbert remarked, sounding like a teenager teetering on puberty.

'Umm, you know I like sweeping too, so much more natural than a vacuum,' Rachel said, handing him the broom, continuing to fondle an imaginary broom after it had left her hand.

'I've been eating salads,' Cuthbert replied. No, that wasn't what he'd wanted to say. 'A vacuum? How? The extra appliances are serving the purpose of...?' Neither was that. 'Shall we go to the confession booths?' he spluttered, almost running into his booth, making threats against his own mind, which quickly laid the blame on his mouth.

'You know why I'm usually here Father,' Rachel said, dispensing with the formalities, 'and today's no different. It's been three weeks since Harold went and I've been through every household item you could imagine (Cuthbert was still having trouble with the vacuum) and I know there's just no way that I can last another five months without some real cock. I just need it the same way you need Jesus, the way the rest of the town needs tea and Yorkshires. Now don't get me wrong, there isn't anyone in Skipperton I'd do it with.'

'No one at all?' Cuthbert blurted, his face pressed against the section of gauze separating them.

134

'Well Erik would have done, but even if there was anyone else, you touch someone's fiancé or husband here and they'll burn you as a witch.'

'But there are single men that you know, ones who would be more, and I mean more spelt in giant capital letters, than happy to help you.'

'Like who?'

Cuthbert's: 'like me!' was drowned out by some extra loud banging at the door. It came again very quickly, a disgruntled banging, one that was made up of many fists collaborating, making it clear the people demanded to be heard immediately, but Cuthbert was too busy fuming about a missed opportunity to consider the reason why a multitude of people would be hammering on his door.

'Alright, alright, I'm coming,' he shouted, unable to hear his own voice, 'there's no need to...' His voice trailed off as he found himself face to face with a mob of thirty people, who, despite the fact that it was eleven in the morning, carried three burning torches.

'What's going on?' Rachel asked, her appearance at Cuthbert's side drawing a collective gasp from the mob.

'The foreigners, they're conspiring!' someone yelled, as in the distance another, larger mob, could also been seen making its way along the path to the church, as heavily armed as if Cuthbert were a hundred acre field ready for ploughing.

'We were not conspiring and I'm a vicar I'll have you all know, not a priest, I can have sex and get married and have more sex, but that wouldn't be something we were talking about obviously, no, Rachel was merely here confessing.'

'Confessing to a plot to tear this town limb from limb!'

'No,' Cuthbert said, certain half the town was heading his way. What on earth could have possibly happened? He knew he should have dug himself a trapdoor tunnel. 'She was just confessing how much she missed Harold's.'

'Harold's what?'

'His love, strength and care.'

135

'Well she better start asking herself if he's ever coming home, because my boy ain't,' Wilma Egbert said, stepping forward to thrust a piece of paper into Cuthbert's face. 'This is all your doing is this! You're responsible,' she cried, as Cuthbert took hold and read the letter.

Dear Mum,

I'm writing to you from our great capital, and by great I mean truly amazing! There's so much here, it's like living in the future. There's so much to tell you, but I can't all fit it in this letter! Really I was just writing to let you know where I am and that everything is fine. Dad and the rest of the team know where I am and I'm very happy. Will make sure I write again soon, and when I have a job and somewhere permanent to stay I'll send you my address too. In the meantime I hope everything's okay, hugs and kisses,
Edward

The note was snatched from Cuthbert's hands by Rachel, who seemed unfazed by the amount of people standing before her holding trowels and spades, hoes and dusters, rolling pins and branding irons.

'Mrs. Egbert,' Cuthbert said, met by at least a dozen replies of 'yes?'. 'I mean Mrs. Wilma Egbert. Is it not possible to discuss this matter alone maybe, without such backing?' he asked, now able to see that Mayor Keith was at the front of the second mob, which had nearly descended upon them.

'Oh aye, like she's going to be alone with you so that you can work your voodoo on her,' a member of the mob shouted to a host of jeers, which died down in time for Keith to be fully heard, pushing through the mass of bodies to the front.

'Has he not been banished yet?'

'Banished?' Cuthbert choked. 'This isn't fair Verona, you can't banish me,' he added, not stopping to consider that out of all the possible options they had in mind, it might well have been the most pleasant.

'I can do what I bloody well want because I'm the Mayor and I speak on behalf of the people of this glorious town. Now you've caused enough damage already, I shouldn't have let you get away with sending the lads off, but putting a spell on Edward isn't something I can stand by and accept.'

'But he sounds ecstatic about being there!' Cuthbert pointed out, 'and surely the rest of the team must have been happy with his decision or else they wouldn't have let him go.'

'Oh no, you can stop your mind games right there,' Keith said, as a couple of mutters started about how such a desertion to the capital had been possible. 'Those lads would do anything for each other, not like you and your God, out here doing what's best for yourself.'

'For myself? All I do all day is go round town checking on people and helping, ask Mrs. Barker, any number of them.'

'Yeah, well it's no good asking those people who we can see are happy and safe inside the town walls is it? They're not the ones who need help. How about I go and ask Edward about your qualities? Oh, I can't because I haven't even got a piddling address, because you haven't been tending to your flock properly Father.'

'Oh, so now the people of Skipperton are, "my flock" are they? Now that one of them's decided he'd prefer to live somewhere else, which actually can only be because of you and how you run it, but no, okay, it's all my fault. Well in that case, with God as my witness, I shall have Edward back here in "my flock" within a week,' Cuthbert said in bluster, not quite sure what had gotten into him. His macho posture came with a puffed chest and jabbing finger. He glanced over his shoulder to check how impressed Rachel looked, but she appeared to have taken the opportunity to flee to the safety of her home. No worries, he would go round and check on her later. This xenophobia could only bring them closer together.

'Yeah well, we'll see,' Keith said, as the mob began to disperse with neither a showdown nor lynching no longer looking likely, and plus, it was almost lunch time. 'But if he's not here by then, you'd better not be either,' he added,

137

turning on his heel and marching back into town.

Cuthbert didn't waste another second. He bolted the doors, ran to his room, turned on his computer, twiddled his thumbs as the connection laboriously kicked in, and then typed "private detectives in London," into Google. He didn't consider the cost of the operation. Even with all the luxuries he'd been surrounding himself with, he'd still been saving half his wage every month, and though Edward's return wouldn't bring any financial reward as reimbursement, he was certain the gains would be greater than any fiscal remuneration. He held one finger underneath the number as he dialled with his other hand.

'Hello, Gordon Shanks Private Detective, how may I help?'

'Hello, my name is Cuthbert Johnson and well I was wondering if you would be able to...well you see...I...'

'Don't worry Mr. Johnson, spit it out, where can I find her bonking?'

'What? No it's not like that. Why would you think that?' Cuthbert asked, staring into the phone, trying to see the look he was being given.

'Oh well that's just the usual request from a timid voice like yours, tend to be unsure if you want to know the truth or not, better if you do if you ask my opinion, some people even find they like it when the facts are revealed, might be up your alley.'

'It's certainly not up my alley!' Cuthbert fumed, 'and anyway it's not a woman I want you to find, it's a boy.'

'Right.'

'He's called Edward Egbert. He's from Skipperton, but he's run away from home.'

'And you're his father?' Gordon enquired, the sound of his pen and paper rustling up the line to Cuthbert.

'No, I'm his Vicar.'

'Oh I see, one of those jobs is it? Well it'll cost you a couple of grand more, because disposal's just not what it was twenty years ago.'

'What? No, I don't want him killed.'

138

'Right, just silenced.'

'No, I didn't do anything to him, I'm his Vicar, not his Priest. Why is it so hard for people to understand? Do I need a t-shirt with 'I love Martin Luther' on it?'

'The black guy?'

Fearing his grip was going to crush the phone into a mangled mess of plastic and wires, Cuthbert gritted his teeth and snarled down the line.

'I just want the boy kidnapping and returning is all. Can you do that?'

'Of course, none of my business what's gone on, apologies. Now where did you say he was from again?'

'Skipperton.'

'Err, you sure about that? I'm looking on Google Maps, but I don't see anything.'

Having finalised all the details and received a promise Edward would be delivered in one piece within the week, Cuthbert found himself gasping for a drink, which was no surprise since his clothes were so excessively wet from sweat, it looked as though he'd been standing in the rain.

He dropped his robes in the washing bin and ran the shower. He had a range of cosmetics now rather than a single all in one bottle from the supermarket standing next to a Bic razor. There was a balm to keep his skin fresh, a type of pen to remove any bags from under his eyes and a gruff scented shower cream, since Rachel had once mentioned she liked her men to smell manly. He ran his hand against his cheek, guessing that 'masculine' also required a layer of stubble grazing against the inside of her thighs. Although if it was as fine as his own, wasn't it more likely to tickle? Cuthbert interlocked his fingers in front of his face and nuzzled his chin inside his palms, then proceeded to lick at the gaps in his fingers, while opening and closing his jaw in the manner of a goldfish until he'd satisfied himself there was nothing humorous about it.

Once he'd towelled himself dry, he stood in front of his mirror and ran a finger underneath his pectorals, where there were definite signs of definition forming. So pleased was he by the state of his, if not ripped, then certainly rippling upper torso, he gave a roar at his reflection and strutted into the bedroom.

Ignoring the fact he'd been saving his new attire until the arrival of his boxer shorts (that had a pouch at the front to make it look all the more impressive), Cuthbert undid the wrapping of his new polo shirt and unfolded his jeans. In his fantasies, which usually contained not just the main focus of the event, but all the hours of preliminary build up, he envisioned himself removing the items one at a time, slowly, not just so Rachel could take her time to admire him, but also because being brand new, he didn't want to ruin them.

The jeans were blue, plain blue. They didn't flare, they didn't cut in at the ankle, they were as straight and stiff as The Bible. They made him feel secure and, he wasn't afraid to admit, sexy. He sprayed deodorant on until he choked, doused his neck and wrists in aftershave until his eyes watered, carefully lifted his shirt to take one final gaze at his blossoming chest and left for Rachel's house.

Despite the fact that members of the mobs still littered the streets en-route to the town's grandest abode, none of them paid Cuthbert much heed, having more pressing matters to attend to, though he did catch snippets of gossip mentioning his and The Mayor's names, with it sounding for all the world like a duel was imminent.

Cuthbert hadn't really ever had any fights; he'd been harassed a couple of times at high school, but even the bullies had tended to attack children who at least looked like they might offer a quip in return for further punishment.

He stopped to check his reflection in the window of a Robin Reliant, smoothing his eyebrows before knocking firmly on Rachel's front door, practising his greeting in his head; *hi, hey* or *hello*? The words never sounded like they'd held so much meaning before. Upon the door's opening, however, he merely grinned.

'Oh hello Father,' Rachel said, after a double take. 'I

didn't recognise you there. Do you want to come in?'

'Please,' Cuthbert replied, greeted once inside by a life size portrait of Harold staring back at him, a cricket bat held aloft in his right hand and a box of Skipperton cradled in his left, a painting he'd commissioned Jerry Smith to produce before his trip. Yet because he'd had such little time to pose for the piece, Jerry had drawn most of his inspiration from a fifty pence piece he'd had in his pocket, including a lion in profile by Harold's feet.

'So what brings you here Father?' Rachel asked, pouring him a cup of tea, adding a couple of biscuits to the side of his saucer, not a Yorkshire pudding in sight.

'Well I thought I'd come by and see if you were alright after this morning's rather shocking shenanigans,' Cuthbert replied, dipping a biscuit in his tea. Rachel opted for a fig roll.

'Oh that, I'd almost forgotten about it,' Rachel replied flippantly, feeling peckish for something more substantial.

'But there was a mob of more than two hundred at the end, they were threatening to banish me, and well, they seem to think we're on the same side,' Cuthbert remarked, heavily emphasising the final clause of the sentence.

'So that's why you're in disguise!' Rachel exclaimed, almost laughing as she removed a knife from its slot in the rack.

'No, this isn't a disguise, I'm not afraid of anyone, these are my casual clothes, the robes are just my work attire. It's like you don't see a chef in their white apron when they're out doing everyday things do you? Well except for Mel and Jonesy, but they're an exception, everyone in this town's an exception,' Cuthbert said, halting, feeling like he was losing track of the crux of the matter, not that anything he'd said seemed to have convinced Rachel otherwise.

'Listen, I know these people know how to hold a grudge, but really that's just if you're from Lancashire or the South.'

'But I am from the South, and anyway, people here consider anything below the town walls to be The South!' Cuthbert exclaimed, watching her deftly go about her duties, dicing and slicing with ease. When he tried to chop vegetables in fast forward like the chefs did on TV, he found most of the food flew onto the floor and he barely had any worktop left.

'When I married Harold,' Rachel said, apparently oblivious to anything Cuthbert had to say, even if they were stone cold facts, 'there were a lot of people against it because I wasn't a local girl, because they didn't know how to spell my surname, because I'm taller than 5'2", but they treat me as one of their own now.'

'But someone in that first mob claimed: "the foreigners are conspiring",' Cuthbert said, losing all hope of Rachel falling into a panic and running crying into his arms. It was more likely to happen vice versa at the present and that was the antithesis of manly.

'That was said in the heat of the moment. Honestly, I've enough experience of this town to know what the outcome will be, and once you've brought Edward home, you'll probably be inked into the birth section of the registry.'

Cuthbert didn't bother to respond this time, he simply watched her as she put the finishing touches to their plates and topped up their teas. Experience. That one word summed it all up, she had lots of it and he had none. He'd come into her home hoping to act suave and ended up flapping like a humming bird at the Chelsea Flower Show. She'd prepared a meal that would have taken him at least double that time and yet he'd had it in his head that when she eventually slid into bed with him she'd be hooked, unable to see any other future except one with him and ten children.

What was he thinking? She wouldn't have seen premature ejaculation since the start of her teens. Oh, he didn't doubt that he could go all night, but it would be more stop start than a game of American Football, with touchdowns a completely one sided affair. But where was he going to find the practice? There was no way he was going to pay for it, he wasn't ready to stoop that low yet. There was the internet he supposed, he'd happened to stumble onto some sites when he'd mistakenly typed "church swinging" instead of "church singing", the most shocking part of it being that there were as many hits for the misspelling. Yes, a great tool the internet, he'd find something on it to help.

'Umm, this is very tasty,' he said, composing himself. 'I really must repay the favour. You should come over to mine sometime in the forthcoming week.'

'Oh,' Rachel said, nibbling on a carrot, 'that would be lovely.'

The Letters

Hello Love,

Been thinking about you a lot, as always, hoping you're okay and everyone's behaving themselves at the Factory. To be honest I think we should have brought double the amount of Skipperton with us, since we're already being very economical. There's times when one of the lads will get everyone depressed by announcing that the stock's going to run out and it'll be like the war with rationing and all, but fortunately most of the time we're so busy it's not something we think about. That might be hard to believe I know, but every day's a new adventure and we're coping well. On the pitch we haven't been put under real threat, there's been a couple of nifty players here and there, but mainly it's been about teaching the game, sharing the love of it. To tell you the truth, by the time we're finished, I suspect it'll have overtaken football as the world's leading sport.

A recent highlight was when we played a game in a place called Zdiar in Slovakia. Well we were staying in Zdiar, lovely mountain town, everything run properly by families and such, very quiet since it's mainly a ski resort and it was out of season. So we were scheduled to play on Sunday, but everything was shut, and with only one bus in the morning and one in the evening, the start was delayed because half their team missed the first bus and had to hitch one or two at a time. We didn't need our allotted 50 overs for bowling as per usual though, and that's even giving Stuart an over to bowl! I tell you, it's a good job he attacks the meat in his cellar with his cleaver in hand and doesn't throw it or else the carcasses wouldn't see the slightest nick on them.

I've rotated the batting order too, keep changing it so everyone keeps their eye in. Been good for William, he's been able to put his feet up, smoke his pipe and read his books, while Paul, Fred and John have lifted their averages into the high twenties and are starting to call themselves all-rounders.

So anyway, after we'd batted in this game their team would have been forced to sit around and wait for the evening bus for another three hours, so I told them we were heading back towards Zdiar and dropped most of them off along the way. They were all full of praise for my generosity, as they should have been, but as we arrived back into Zdiar, I thought they'd gone and overdone it slightly by having music blasted out of these speakers lined up for miles along the road in our honour. Turns out, so the lad in our hotel said, that this music plays every Sunday for a couple of hours to sort of get everyone in a patriotic mood, and you know I'm thinking something like that could really work at home, but for the original reason I had in mind, to announce triumphs, let everyone know the lads have won again and put everyone in a good mood. What do you think? Can't wait to hear you tell me, I'm marking off the days.
Love Harold

Dear Dad,
I have to tell you this now or else I never will, but thank you for declining to go on this tour because I'm having the best time of my life. That's right, better than ever before, being out of Skipperton, out of Yorkshire, because there's a huge world out there, more than just the school, more than just our house, hell, even more than cricket even.

Yesterday, for example, after we'd beaten this side in Trencin, Slovakia, we had a day off from driving and I went down to this water park. It was outside because it was so blazing hot and there were so many pretty girls I thought I'd be happy to live there. They were wearing bikinis, not bathing suits, playing ball games instead of knitting by the side of the pool. These are the types of things that should be happening at home dad, we need to start making changes in Skipperton, we have to move forward, that's what this trip is teaching me. It's no use being in a constant comfort zone, we have to push the boundaries, learn new skills, like Slovakian. The time to do it is now, because you have to realise that we're not just from Skipperton, Yorkshire and England, we're from Europe too.

Don't shut me out for this. Even if it wasn't the right decision for you, it is for me. Give all my love to mum and I'll see you soon for a plateful of Yorkshires, waffles and croissants.
Richard II

Dear Erik,
I hope that before you read this I have already found the courage to tell you how I feel, but if not, now you know. I don't expect you to do anything, I understand that you are a God among men and will no doubt one day find a beautiful Goddess, but should you yearn for another God, alas I fear I've said too much, but now I have no choice but to continue, to write down all that I have longed to scream out at the top of my lungs so that the whole world can hear.

Remember when we walked round that castle at Neuschwanstein and rowed across that lake behind it? For me, walking through that castle, seeing how everything, from the skirting boards to the chair legs, had been designed and carved, slaved over, made me realise that although marvels can be created, something I strive for with every task, nothing is more perfect than you: rowing topless, symmetrical, unblemished. Your hair, your smile, they make my heart sing joyous songs. That day is one I will take with me to the grave. If only I'd have been braver then, opened up my heart to you...

Understand that I expect nothing, I just need you to know.
All my love, Alan

Alright Love,
Know I said I wasn't going to write, but since Harold's given us all a free stamp, thought I might as well put it to use. Between me and you I think he's losing it a little bit. Not only did he give away the stamps, but he let a Slovakian team ride back on our coach without paying a fair and then the other day he said we were all entitled to dessert having won

our tenth game of the tour.

Took a splendid catch in that match, probably one of the best in my life in fact, their player got a really fine edge to a quicker ball of Frank's and I tell you, everyone thought it was going for four since we had no one out at third man, but I back peddled and I leapt like never before, like a bomb had gone off beneath my feet. I managed to get an inch of glove on it, which knocked it forward and then I sort of dived and fell forward to claim it, bloody superb it was.

That's not the only piece of amazing fielding to my name obviously, but if I went on about all my performances I doubt I'd have very much room left on the paper for anything else.

Anyway, my main reason for writing was to tell you how much I miss you and the workshop. Today you see we played this team from a town called Egger in Hungary and after we'd beaten them by seven wickets, one of them told us that we were all welcome to come to his wine cellar for a drink. Well I nearly wept when we went in and saw the whole place was lit by candles, such a variety of them too! I couldn't stop myself from reaching out and touching them as I walked across his *stone* floor. When I started talking to him about them he told me how much they cost and I almost choked, told him I could do them for half the price and so he said he'd look into postage and packaging costs and gave me his business card. Would be a great bit of trade during the summer months, but I know what you're thinking, you're not bothered about the candles and the money, you're worried about us going to a wine cellar, but I tell you, that's another thing I've learned, wine's not just for women and puffs.

The lad called his red wine "Bull's Blood" and he made us tip out the water in our bottles to fill them to the brim so we didn't have to drink out of those glasses that look like they'll snap when you grab them. Right nice it was and a good alternative now that we've been forced to ration the tea and Black.

Well, hope everything's okay with the business and yourself,

147

Paul.

How do everyone at Post Office HQ,
Hope business is running smoothly, I'm sure it is, you've learned from the best after all! Remember what I told you about selling those extras though, don't want to come back finding a load of old stock left in the back, someone always needs a new cosy or an umbrella, but as I said, I left the place in capable hands, so what about me and the lads you may be asking?

Well we've made it all the way down to Albania, unbeaten of course, everyone's looking relaxed with bat and ball, not too much, not complacent like, just very natural. Not enough space on this postcard to go into the finer details of innings so I'll tell you a couple of other things that have happened where I've come good for the team.

First time was in Czechoslovakia in Prague, we'd just arrived and we were off out for a bite (nice grub out here, though don't tell anyone I told you) and we crossed this road and when we reached the other side these three police officers, all about Stuart's size, stood in our way.

'Why don't you respect the red man?' the one at the front asked.

Now Harold was leading our group and he didn't think the bobby meant the traffic light, because why would that matter? Whoever pays attention to the traffic lights? Harold thought the lad was talking about the commies, so he starts going on about Stalin and the Second World War and the way the Soviets behave in Rocky IV, which all goes on for a while, until the bobby points at the traffic lights and explains it's illegal to cross on a red man. Now I could see what these three were doing, I knew their game because it's something I might have played myself, and they start telling us the fine's twenty quid each! Well there was no chance of us paying that, so I jump in and start talking as a distraction to let a few of the lads sneak off. By the time I'd finished you could see the looks of confusion on the bobbys' faces because there was only five of us left, and though we ended up still having to pay £2.50 each, when I pointed out to Harold we'd made a saving of £207.50 he wasn't fuming for too long.

Alright, not really enough space for any more tales, but I have to write one final thing. So they're crazy about their car washes here in Albania, must be one per car on the road. This team we played in the south near Butrint were utterly disgusted by how much dust our coach had collected, so I managed to barter down one guy to wash us at the same price as a motorbike. Beautiful dealing it was,
Dereck.

Dear diary,
Now I know what Hell's like. Macedonia and Bulgaria should be called the land of wops, slit eyes and wogs. Bloody Pakis are out there collaborating, speaking English so that they can bloody well swarm into the country and take all our jobs and money.

Make sure I check under the bus and every sodding bed sheet for one of the buggers sneaking aboard for a safe passage back. And I'll tell you another reason why I know that's their plan, because they're all trying to look like us, sound like us, become us. The lads reckon it's hard to tell who's English and not sometimes, but that's bloody ridiculous!

I tell you, there are people around me who are starting to lose it massively, thinking of us as being from England first and not Skipperton, Yorkshire. They're drinking lager, for example, and at first the excuse we were running low on Black was fair enough, but now some are opting for it out of choice and pleasure. I swear, someone's going to order a bloody coffee soon and nobody'll bat a bloody eyelid. It's going to be down to me to put a stop to it all, because Harold's gone insane. He lets the lads go off in small groups in their spare time and they all come back, happy, filled with kebabs made by dirty hands in dirty establishments. Those brown folk, how do you know if they've washed their hands or if they're not just covered in dirt? One big abomination all of it, but what can I do? If I try and leave now I'll end up

149

raped and dead in a ditch at the hands of these wogs. Oh they can all smile and put on a nice front, but I know what they're really thinking about, forging my bloody passport, but they can't fool me.
Al

Hello Darling,
Everything's going absolutely fine out here, no problems at all, whatsoever. Every member of the team's really very happy, including our son. He isn't writing you a postcard because I am, but he sends his love. He's up in his room reading his books as per usual, nothing's changed, everything's as it should be. I think the only worry is that some of us are enjoying it so much there's talk of staying out a little longer would you believe!

The games have all been relatively easy, which means I've been able to use my skills as sparingly as I, and Harold, would have liked, but I've chipped in with a fair few wickets when I've been called upon. Just the other day, up here in the Polish version of the Lake District, I took 2 for 7; one that cut back in to clip the bails of off and the other a fine catch from Paul that their batter had gone flapping at.

After the game, as has been customary thus far, we gave them an hour's coaching and in return they took us out. Sometimes it's been to do something and at other times to see something. Only last week we were walking round one of Dracula's castles and today we took a stroll round Adolf Hitler's lair, Wolfschanze, which if I'm being honest was far creepier than the castles. Wolf Lair's is what it's called in English, a very derelict place out in the woods, very atmospheric. All the buildings are sort of half crushed with stamps on the outside in four different languages, telling you not to go inside them.

Oh, there's Edward calling out that he sends hugs! I would have let him write, but I'm not sure the posties around here would be able to read his scrawl.

One final note then, all these stays in hotels have given me plenty of ideas on how to renovate our place and make the experience for the guests more enjoyable, because they've all been so nice out here, offering hot water twenty-four hours a day and such.

Right, must be off, I'm driving to Druskiniki in Lithuania,
Much love, William. And Edward of course x

Dear Mum,
I'm writing to you from just outside the capital of Latvia. Yesterday I took my first hat-trick of the tour against the Riga XI. First one was an outswinger, second I almost broke middle, and the third I had this guy trapped plumb. Talking of plums, how's the ham and plum roll doing? Best seller no doubt.

Food's been plentiful out here, they love their soups and stews in this part of the world, all good to keep us nice and warm since it's started to turn a little chilly in the past couple of days, not freezing or anything, just a bit nippy.

Oh, I just remembered about catching our own food in Poland! Honestly, there's so much going on out here that it's hard to recall all the great stuff that's happened. Me, Dad, Paul and Richard II went to this huge indoor water park yesterday for example and it was bloody amazing. Love their water parks out in Europe I tell you, and I can see why. We should definitely build one on the outskirts of the town so it can be super huge with loads of slides and lasses wearing bikinis.

But where was I? Fishing out in Poland on the lakes I caught a two footer and we had a right nice barbecue that the family who owned the guesthouse put on for us. They had a lovely pet dog, think I'll buy a dog when we return, and a mobile phone, it's a phone you carry around with you everywhere without any wire attached, amazing device. Honestly mum, I wish you could see it all. We're treated so well by everyone.
See you later,
John.

Of course since every postcard or envelope had a stamp with a silhouette of her majesty Queen Elizabeth II on a gold background in the top right corner, every sorting officer turned it over, read it if they could overcome the spelling mistakes and/or handwriting, and then posted it into the bin, shaking their heads at the fact that some British citizens still believed they had an Empire.

The Pud

Every head was solemnly bowed. Those at the front who could see the coffin kept their eyes fixed on it as it was slowly lowered into the open ground, a used teabag staining the MDF lid.

Cuthbert stood at the front of the grave, Bible open, his voice sounding strange in his ears. When he found he'd reached the bottom of the page, he realised he had no recollection of saying anything.

Soil began to rain down, a few people blew their noses, sobs could be heard from some of the women, but it all felt so surreal, like it was on some television soap set.

'Ashes to ashes, dust to dust,' Cuthbert muttered, making the sign of the cross as the widow watched him, hanging on his every word. He was almost ready to laugh; after all, they did say that if a week was a long time in politics, then a fortnight was a lifetime.

It all started on the day of rest with the town coming en-masse to church expecting some sort of showdown, despite the fact it was only four days into the allotted seven Cuthbert had been given. Not that Cuthbert felt like he had another seventy-two hours on his side. Each new morning with no Edward on his doorstep had led to him immediately picking up the phone to call down to London after his alarm clock had gone off. On the first couple of occasions Gordon had assured him progress was being made, but since then he hadn't answered a call, leaving Cuthbert to lie awake at night, his suitcases packed beside the bed, forever rising to go to his desk to write another letter to Rachel, which he then added to a bulging envelope that also contained a silver bracelet Tony Thompson the jeweller had engraved. It read *Cuthbert and Rachel Forever*, though it possibly wasn't as silver as had been claimed.

Although most of his thoughts were negative, there were moments when Cuthbert dreamt he was confronting

Keith and driving his cross through the mayor's heart. Unfortunately, these positive visions were rare, and when they did occur, the scenarios usually ended with him dodging pitchforks hurled like javelins at his back.

The story Cuthbert had opted to retell on this particular Sunday was Jesus' miracle of the loaves and fishes up by the Sea of Galilee. The tale was usually as firm a favourite with the people as bangers and mash in front of the TV or wireless on a Saturday evening. On this occasion, however, Keith, possibly feeling the weight of the people's expectations to witness something other than a usual Sunday morning pre-lunch story, began to heckle.

In comparison to the abuse Cuthbert had suffered in Birmingham (including enquires about whether God loved all Johnsons - a slang term Cuthbert hadn't been acquainted with) it was pretty tame. Keith simply questioned whether or not the event with the loaves had been real and even if it had been, why should anyone be concerned with it now, with it having happened so far in the past? (Cuthbert had raised his eyebrows, but it was apparent the irony had bypassed everyone else). Miracles didn't occur in the modern day, Keith went on, they were just fairytales for people who were afraid to put in hard graft.

They were arguments easy to nullify, though Cuthbert had learned the hard way not to talk about the "miracle of birth and life". Instead, he gave examples of people who'd survived aeroplane crashes, feats of strength where parents had lifted cars (ones with four wheels) off their children trapped underneath, people who'd been rescued from under rubble days after they should have been dead. There were countless instances of superhuman feats occurring all the time across the globe, and if they were "superhuman", then who else could be involved other than someone of a constant superhuman nature?

A more sophisticated comeback would have been to question whether it had been an entirely fair divine intervention to kill the earthquake victims' families and to destroy their environment in the first place; furthermore, an intelligent counterargument would have also explained the scientific rationale behind so-called superhuman feats in times of desperation.

Instead Keith offered God a fight. Since he didn't happen to be around, however, and Cuthbert seemed to do all his work for him anyway, the offer reverted to Cuthbert.

The animated reaction from the congregation transformed the church into an arena, and from his position high above them all, his shins level with Keith's bald head, which was scarred from the rigours of his early life as a prop forward (though the marks were now difficult to distinguish from the wrinkles), Cuthbert fancied his chances. The Bible, the power of God, was between his hands and its weight could render an opponent unconscious with one almighty blow.

Keith rolled his sleeves to the elbows, as Cuthbert glanced down at his fair maiden, his actions giving away no clue as to what he intended to do next, when all of a sudden the doors burst open with a tremendous clattering.

Excluding Cuthbert, who assumed the dark storm clouds that had been brewing on the horizon had finally reached them, everyone else turned in hushed reverence, expecting to see the big man himself, a pair of boxer's shorts underneath his open white robe, dukes up. What greeted them all, however, was a body moaning and groaning on the floor, one which Keith couldn't see since he had taken cover in the trench of his pew.

'Oh my Lord it's Edward!' someone shouted, as the boy uncurled himself from the ball position he'd been squashed into, after being removed from the car boot and hurled into the church doors.

'He's back, just like Father Johnson promised,' Wilma cried, rushing across to help her son up, though he managed to make it to his feet unaided. Judging by his face, Gordon had been unable to resist roughing him up, though that was no doubt because Edward had resisted his kidnapping. Now the boy stared up at Cuthbert and pointed an accusing finger, a far more vicious and volatile proposition than Keith.

'You,' he growled, 'you're the one who brought me back here,' he added, his steps towards the altar halted as streams of family, uncles, aunts, cousins, second cousins, third cousins, rushed forward to greet him.

'Oh he's done exactly like he said he would!' Wilma shouted out again, walking towards Cuthbert, her arms wide to embrace him, as The Vicar struggled to take it all in. Calls rose up from across the church asking him to perform other duties, tears were shed, there were people enquiring whether this constituted a miracle, and down at the front, Rachel sat with a smile that said, *I told you so.*

'I don't know what happened. One moment I was in London and the next minute everything went black and then I was back here. I know it was him, because I heard his name like it was in a dream, Cuthbert Johnson,' Edward said, his vitriol mistaken, somehow or another, for euphoria, the mystique surrounding the vagueness of his answer only increasing Cuthbert's stock, which Cuthbert could see was something he should do everything in his powers to protect. News that it was chloroform, and not divine providence responsible for Edward's return, wasn't a truth anyone would be better off hearing.

'Ladies and Gentlemen,' Cuthbert announced, raising his hands and his voice. 'I promised that with the help of God I would bring Edward back to *my* flock and here he is before our very eyes. He has returned to this great town because it was mine and God's will, but right now he is tired and weary from such a journey and I think it is only fair to allow him to eat and drink in the quiet of my abode.'

As if they were under mass hypnosis, the congregation rose and, nodding in agreement with all Cuthbert had said, filtered out, eventually leaving only Edward, who still looked ready to charge.

'I want you to know,' Cuthbert said, retaining his vantage point, 'that it wasn't my idea to bring you back and as soon as I can move you down to London again I will do.'

'You had me bundled into the boot of a car!'

'You sold out your teammates to escape to London,

156

then wrote a stupid letter to your mum. How do you think all that news was going to be received? I did what I had to do for my own sake, but like I said, I'm willing to play fairly. I know all the joys that London has to offer and believe me, I don't plan to stay in this town for the rest of my life either.'

'But why did you have to drag me back? They have trains that don't run on coal down there, food sourced from across the globe, colourful clothes, thousands of different haircuts and types of shoes!'

'I brought you back because I haven't got what I want from this town yet, and by that I mean I haven't given this town my all and well...listen you can't simply arrive at a place and then leave again within a year, people will think you're running away or you've something to hide.'

'I was both running away from this and running to a place far greater and cosmopolitan, and as for you, you're a Vicar, people think you're only doing your job because you have something to hide,' Edward said, almost calm, not wanting to admit that he was excited at the prospect of a cup of tea having not had a proper, decent cuppa since he'd walked off the coach.

'What might I have to hide?' Cuthbert asked, certain he was always giving signs away regarding his true feelings.

'Erection problems.'

'What! What do you mean by problems?'

Edward curled his finger and Cuthbert laughed.

'Ha! It's not crooked at all, it's as straight as an arrow. In fact if I did something with the hair it would look exactly like an arrow.'

Edward took a step back so his rear was firmly up against the wood of the pew.

'Oh no, it's not like that, I didn't have you kidnapped for that reason. I'm a lady's man. Well, more of a lady man really or soon to be lady man hopefully.'

'Err, I think I'd like to go home and see my mum now,' Edward said, not wanting to discover what the glazed over look on Cuthbert's face was all about.

'Okay course, run along my child,' Cuthbert said, 'but

don't stray too far. Remember, God is watching you every step of the way.'

It began to feel very quickly as if that final statement had been broadcast over a megaphone throughout the town. There was a fervour in the hours after Edward had rolled into church, which was stoked at every turn. Jesus' face was found in a bowl of porridge, a fried egg, several clouds, sheep's wool and at the bottom of most tea cups. Miracles were seen across town as cats made it down from trees on their own, a bus narrowly missed striking Trevor Barker after he'd slipped walking on White Rose Lane, and the statue of Henry Skipperton wept during a heavy shower. Everyone knew it was all God's doing, but since he wasn't around to accept the plaudits, they were pushed onto Cuthbert.

Over the next few days he received a constant merry-go-round of townsfolk there to either congratulate him and explain just what a wonderful duty God had performed for them, or else to ask him how they too could go about acquiring what they wanted, desperate for his personal blessing to enhance their chances of success.

It was merely a passing fad is what Keith told himself, watching the hoards of people walking to and from the church as though they were on some conveyor belt, the majority of them smiling. They spoke about how knowledgeable Cuthbert was, how The Lord worked in mysterious ways, how those up by the gas works had been having strange visions for a while, but could now finally attribute their insightful dreams to someone.

It was a craze that would be gone quicker than a perm in a storm, but each day Keith awoke it appeared that, if anything, the number of people seeking the wisdom of Cuthbert's words was increasing, until eventually it reached the stage that every minute during daylight hours there was a queue outside the church doors.

This wouldn't have been the final straw for The Mayor were it not for him catching wind of the fact that there were people going in their pairs not just to listen to The Vicar's opinion, but to take his word over matters of a civil nature. At this point Keith removed his handkerchief, polished his mayoral medallion until it gleamed like a brand new penny, dusted off his jacket, removed a scroll of the town's constitution from his desk, finished his cup of tea, popped on his flat cap, took a walking stick from the coat rack and set off at a stroll, shaking his head and making a "tsk, tsk" noise every time he heard someone mention Father Johnson or God. Ignoring the queue, he barged straight into the church.

'Do you know who has jurisdiction over this place?' he announced, swinging his walking stick menacingly. 'I do. That's right, me, The Mayor of Skipperton,' he added, drawing Cuthbert from his confession booth, still apologising to Deborah Egbert, who had decided to declare her menacing history of murdering spiders. She had admitted, in great detail, killing other insects and bugs too, but it was the fact she felt joy from taking the lives of spiders that had made her come to him, because if she was capable of such an act on a regular basis, who was to say she wouldn't eventually work her way up to larger animals in time without help?

'Mayor,' Cuthbert said, watching Keith twirl the stick, reminding Cuthbert of the female Olympic gymnasts with their batons. 'As you can see I'm rather busy with *my* flock right now, but since you are one of them, then please join the back of the queue and I'll see you in good time,' he added, power sourcing through his veins. He felt like Robert De Niro in *The Godfather II*. Sure he hadn't been given anything for free, but his lunch at The Caf had come with a 50% discount since he had cured Mel's dandruff with a special potion (Head & Shoulders), and the soles of his shoes had been cobbled for a couple of pence, there on the spot, thanks to his effort of making it rain continuously for a twenty-four hour period that had brought Harold Baker a whole lot of business.

'Oh no lad, you don't get to talk to me like that. I told you, I own you and I'm not impressed by whatever spells you're casting over the good people of my town. This church operates under my office, not side by side, and certainly not above it.'

159

'I'm sorry, what happened to me not tending? And now all of a sudden I'm tending too much?'

'You're stepping on my toes and you're well aware of it!' Keith growled, pounding the tip of the stick against the floor. 'It's not your place to tell these people how to deal with a dandelion pushing across the other's fence, that's a matter for me. And now you are too. Don't think I don't know full well Edward returning was just a fluke. You see I've been telling your God he's a bender ever since and that I'm bloody well going to drive the pair of you out of here and knock this place down before you can cause any more problems, but unless he's gone deaf, he doesn't seem to care.'

With that Keith discarded his walking stick and stuck twos up at the ceiling. When no retribution was forthcoming, he began to spin very slowly in a circle making wanking gestures, and as a finale to his ritual he shouted: 'Lancashire,' prompting a flood of phlegm.

'You see,' he said to Cuthbert. 'I'm the one with the real power in this town and now I'm going to make my way back to my office and draw up a piece of legislation calling for this building to be turned into a memorial for all those who gave their lives at Bosworth.'

Cuthbert could see, out of the corner of his eye, half the queue beginning to sneak off. The exodus had started. Did this mean he had thirty-eight years in the wilderness on the horizon? If it was a euphemism, he'd already suffered thirty-eight years, he couldn't double that, whoever lost their virginity at seventy-six?

His shoulders slumped as those that hadn't originally been moved by Keith's theatrics were swayed by those leaving either side of them, meaning the only person who was left was Edward, and he'd only come because Cuthbert had promised him use of the internet.

'Err, well since it seems he doesn't mind what we do,' Deborah said, ringing her hands, sliding past him, 'I'm off to the garden to slaughter a few more,' she added with glee, passing Edward, who gave Cuthbert a conciliatory pat on the back.

'Shall I book two tickets on the next National Express?' he asked, not waiting for an answer, leaving Cuthbert to traipse off to the store cupboard for the mop and bucket, cursing his boss. Why bother to tease him like that? Everything had started pointing to his actual existence, to a grand remuneration for the hours slaved and toiled over in Birmingham, and now he was going to have to go and see his Bishop and explain why he'd failed in his duties yet again. There was only one way he could console himself and that was with his Rachel practice. She was someone who was understanding; she hadn't moaned once about his recent busy schedule and the fact that the last couple of nights, when he'd returned home late in the evening with the stars twinkling, he'd literally fallen asleep on her.

'Edward, don't forget to lock up will you, and post the key through my door when you've finished,' Cuthbert called, not caring if he was loud enough to be heard. Why should he care if someone came in and vandalised the place now? 'Oh Rachel,' he mumbled, feeling like a leper, as he made the short walk to his living quarters, hanging up his coat with such little enthusiasm it fell in a crumpled heap on the floor. He stared at it dejectedly, the inner lining of Yorkshire tartan; white, yellow and blue, disgusting him so much he gave it a kick. Rachel's understudy was certainly going to get it tonight. Dinner first and then he'd have her, unleash all his frustrations like a lion. Though he wasn't the alpha animal was he, he was more like a cheetah. He began to roll a montage in his mind, out in the savannah, on all fours beneath thick elephant grass, his sights set on his mate, the deep voice-over explaining how the mating ritual was going to unfold, when there came a pounding at the door. It was relentless, and as he'd found out earlier in the week, relentless meant bad news. It had to be bloody terrible in fact, because it came at an even quicker rate than it had the other day. Why couldn't they just leave him alone? He would go willingly, he didn't need to be harassed and harangued out of the town. Unless the dissolution of the church meant they were returning to paganism.

161

Cuthbert threw his coat back on, certain the banging had grown louder, and headed for his rear window. No time for any items to be clutched, there wasn't anything he couldn't replace, and any objects would only slow him down.

'Ah, Father Johnson, there you are!' Edward said, watching Cuthbert, who hesitated, his body half in and half out of the window. 'Father it's... what are you doing?'

'Climbing out of the window,' Cuthbert answered assuredly, checking there were no torches burning round the corner, before falling the rest of the way out.

Edward made no attempt to assist him to his feet.

'But why?' he asked, as Cuthbert dusted himself down, showing no signs that he'd badly bashed his knee, which he could tell was bleeding.

'Because it's special lent,' he said, glancing this way and that, 'and I've given up doors,' he continued.

'But I've seen you go through the one at church,' Edward said, forgetting why he'd dashed round in the first place.

'Haven't seen me exit through it though have you?' Cuthbert replied, trying to think of the lowest escape point. 'Anyway that doesn't really matter. What is the reason you're here knocking my door off its hinges? Come to warn me we need to make a rapid escape to the capital?'

'Oh no, no, not at all,' Edward said, his enthusiasm growing again, 'just the opposite. I came to tell you that God exists. It's been proven.'

Cuthbert shook his head. He doubted the kid had been reading Descartes or Aquinas.

'It's been proven? What are you on about? How?' he asked, as the cries of mobs could once again be heard growing in volume as they made their way churchwards, except this time each rallying cry ended with a rapturous: 'Amen!'

'Keith,' Edward said, forced to raise his voice as more and more of the town took to the streets upon hearing the news, 'he's dead. He choked on a bloody Yorkshire.'

The Stud

John and Richard II stood side by side on the gym's running machines. Their workout had begun at two after their lunch had settled, and it was now six. By John's side, Erik, acting as their chaperone, was jogging at a steady pace of 16KPH like he'd been working out for four minutes rather than hours. He wasn't even sweating, but then since when did stone perspire?

At first the two lads had been disappointed by the fact he had been ordered to follow them everywhere until they returned to the hotel, but now they were delighted to have him around. The girls, who were decked out in lycra and nothing but lycra, gravitated towards him as though he were the sun, and there wasn't a single one of them in the room that wasn't stunning. The only thing frustrating the pair was that they weren't by the canal in Amsterdam or in a water park in Slovakia to appreciate even more of them, though the way the material stuck to their bodies left little to vivid imaginations.

'We could do...an Edward,' John panted, happy to chase after the carrots dangling in front of his eyes forever.

'We could ask them to marry us. Al's always saying how everyone's after a passport,' Richard II replied, his water loss coming in equal parts sweat and saliva.

'He also said he'd rather drink his own piss than a bottle of lager and that masturbating over a foreign girl would turn your hand into a stump,' John said, flexing all ten of the extremities on his hands.

'To be fair I reckon that if that really did happen I'd just have myself fixed with a prosthetic one,' Richard II said, not sure if he could cope with a fifth round of weights.

Without saying a word, Erik slowed his machine to a walk and allowed himself to be rolled off the rear of the machine. He had checked behind before doing so, but having anticipated what he planned to do, a woman had run halfway across the room and thrown herself into an accidental collision with him. No sooner had they made contact than Erik had swivelled round to hold her steady in his arms.

'Sorry about that,' he said in Estonian, her body quivering at his touch.

'It's okay,' she managed, as John and Richard II followed their team mate's lead, only to find themselves bumping and entangling with each other rather than a five foot five blonde with snow white skin and nipples practically slicing through their top. Erik threw out his left hand to steady them while their jellied legs composed themselves.

'Thanks.'

'Yeah, thanks John,' they said, separating from each other quickly to join either side of Erik, so close to him they appeared as if they were trying to merge into his body.

'You're not Estonian?' the girl asked Erik, who shook his head. 'And these two are your friends?' she added switching back to Estonian, making him nod. 'Well I'm Katja and I was planning to meet two of my friends in the centre for a drink, would you care to join me?'

'Yes, I think we probably would.'

Upon explaining where they were heading once they were changed and ready, Erik retired to his cubicle, while John and Richard II, finding a new lease of life, ran round the changing room high fiving everyone and leaping onto the benches like they were inside a large playpen. Their excitement died down, however, when they found that what remained of their weekly wage (a new system Harold had implemented that allowed him to keep a better track of his finances) was a few feeble Euros.

'I don't think they want to go out for a drink of tap water,' John said, despondently, recounting the shrapnel. 'Don't think they're like our girls at home, can't impress them with a slice of lemon and a few ice cubes,' he added.

'You know I haven't seen a single bike shed to get behind, and from what I've seen none of them would be interested in sharing a woodbine,' Richard II muttered, shaking the almost empty packet, which didn't cause him too much despair since Dereck had picked up some unfiltered gems wholesale for a price that would have constituted a bargain at home.

'So what are we going to do, impress them with our conversation?'

'Sorry, but you're not coming in.'

'What? Why? It's because I'm foreign isn't it?' John said, face to chest with a bouncer outside of a bar, which looked like it would even charge for tap water.

'No, it's not because you're foreign or else I wouldn't have let your friends in.'

'I don't get it, you ask for ID and I show you it and now you won't let me in. There is a lass in there waiting for me and she hasn't a scrap of acrylic on her,' John said, pointing to the girl standing in the middle of Erik and Richard II's dates, all five of them lingering in the porch way.

'I asked for ID because you have to be eighteen to come in, you know that,' the bouncer replied, sweet whispers in his ear from Erik's girl and Erik's imposing presence doing nothing to soften his stance.

'Eighteen! A third of your life gone before you can go for a drink. How about instead if you give me my passport back and I run my pen over the date, hey?'

'I'm sorry John, the rule is plain, no minors,' the bouncer responded, shoving the passport back into his hand.

'But I've never been down the mines in my life! Thatcher had them all closed down, but you knew that didn't you. You're trying to be funny and get personal. Well I can see that The Soviets shaped your head using the tools on your flag,' John said, drawing an imaginary square with his fingers, which had the Estonian girls laughing and joining the three players as they scarpered down the street to safety.

'I told you that the British sense of humour was the best,' Katja panted.

'Just listening to their voices makes me giggle. It's like hearing Shakespeare,' Richard II's girl said, taking a deep breath, clinging to his arm, as they finally stopped when they were certain they were out of danger.

'Ah, this is more like it, Saturday night in a park,' Richard II said, unable to pronounce his date's name, though whatever it was, he was sure it suited Egbert.

All six of them looked around at the benches and the set of swings, the scenery making the girls laugh even harder.

'It's like we're sixteen again!' John's girl laughed, as Erik was dragged behind the bushes and Richard II's girl said that meant they had to grab bottles of vodka, leaving John and Elena to take a seat on the bench.

'When I used to come here in my youth I would spend so much time kissing that when I left my lips would be all broken and sore,' Elena said, licking the corners of her mouth like a big cat.

'We should definitely see if that still happens,' John remarked, sliding across so they were squeezed tight to each other, ready to embrace, when a loud rustling startled Elena.

'Oh don't worry,' John said, his lips dangling where hers should have been, 'it'll just be Erik.'

'But Katja took him that way,' Elena pointed out, wriggling this way and that, a set of shadowy shapes making her jump into John's lap.

'Amazing,' John muttered, his hands roving, ignoring the looming shadows until one of them spoke, and the voice belonged to neither Erik nor Richard II.

'Alright there kidder, you've had your fun here and now it's time to let someone else have a turn. Don't worry like, me and the boys won't be here next week so you'll have even more wimmin to choose from.'

Elena's look of bewilderment was nothing compared to the shock shown by John.

'He's not speaking Estonian,' she whispered.

'I know,' John said, straining as he put on his most neutral accent. 'He's from Lancashire.'

'Where?'

'Where? Lancashire love, greatest county in the world; winner of Bosworth field, home to the red rose,

Freddie Flintoff (the greatest cricketer of the past decade), the hotpot and the only tower that really matters. And where are you from kid?' he asked, eyeing John with suspicion, as two more Lancastrians appeared with their arms wrapped around local women.

'I'm from Derbyshire,' John replied, squinting at one of the men who looked a lot like Erik.

'Yeah? Whereabouts?' the main man asked, passing over his bottle of cider to his girl to hold.

'Smalley,' John said, the town of a recently beaten team springing straight to mind.

'Oh yeah, you play cricket for them?'

'No,' John said, shaking his head, the whole confrontation too hard for the girls to follow, and so they started to speak to each other in whispers, admitting that though it was all very exciting, it was a tad strange that British men appeared to have a penchant for parks.

'No you don't do you, because I'd have recognised you straight away since we played your lot in the cup a couple of months ago. Gave you a right hammering too,' the man said, high fiving his compatriots.

'Wouldn't know, don't really care,' John said, ready to make a run for it if back up hadn't arrived within the next minute, since he doubted he could hold his tongue for much longer. 'But if you're cricket players, what are you doing out here?' he added, buying time, wondering just what could be taking Erik and Richard II so long? Surely Richard II would have been finished by now.

'Happens that we're out on tour as recompense for the actions of our previous manager,' the leader said. 'According to our priest, a hard slog around the world teaching heathens the nature of the game will atone for our sin of having won a cup semi through bribery four years ago against this team from Yorkshire...' At this word the three Lancastrians, despite the close female contingent, scrunched their faces, squeezed with all their might, and broke wind loudly. 'Ridiculous thing is that not only can I not recall the name of the team, but we didn't require any help to beat those lowly sheep shaggers anyway.'

'Oh yes you bloody well did!' John proclaimed, jumping to his feet. 'And sure we might shag a few sheep, but it's you lot who end up eating them in your crappy hotpots.'

'You what?!'

'Aye up, what's going on here,' Richard II shouted, suddenly appearing and rushing to John's side. He immediately recognised the faces of their legendary foes, having been the twelfth man on that fateful day: 'You!'

'You!'

The Lancastrians grouped closer together, their numerical superiority pegged level in an instant by Erik metamorphosing from out of the bushes, looking untroubled, while Katja, hair all over the place, mouth hanging open, staggered bow legged to the group of girls, who the five men had all but forgotten.

'They cheated us out of the semis! They bribed the umpire,' John shouted, remembering all those nights during the past four years when he'd woken in the middle of the night to rekindle the fire and found his dad at the table staring into an empty cup, the tea in it as cold as the emotion in his heart.

'No we didn't, you pudding eating nancy, our old manager did. Don't start crying now, like you have been doing for the past four years, trembling on the other side of The Pennines, too scared to step across.'

'Scared? We were in the division below and *you* bribed the umpire you pudding (a black or white one this would be) eating queer.'

Thus ensued a ten minute slanging match between two-thirds of the six, with Erik and his doppelgänger remaining silent, exchanging icy glares, all of which was so boring for the girls that they gave a shrug and wandered off. They'd been absent for a good while before anyone noticed.

'Hey, they've gone! That's your fault that.'

'You wouldn't have scored now that we're here anyway.'

168

'None of them were woolly so what would you care?'

'It wasn't a relative so you wouldn't have been able to perform.'

'Pot, kettle.'

'You carrying a glossy photo of a whippet to stick on her face to help you rise to the occasion?'

'Right, that's it, this could go on forever and we all know there's only one way to settle this,' Richard II shouted, cracking his knuckles, 'and that's with a game of cricket.'

'What, here? Now?' the leader of the Lancastrians asked, laughing.

'Sounds like you're scared? Of course you would be with no umpire around.'

'Oh let's have it kidder.'

'That's more like it, Kwick cricket it is then. That bin over there is the stumps and err,' Richard II gave a forage in the bushes and removed a rather large branch, 'this here's the bat,' he added, yanking off the leaves and smaller twigs.

'And I have a tennis ball,' Erik chipped in, producing by magic a brand new ball from his trouser pocket.

'Two innings a piece?' the Lancastrians asked.

'Aye,' Richard II grunted, firmly handing the bat across after winning the toss, leaving John to measure out the distance to the bowler's end, tossing up what he hoped was dried mud and not dog turd to test the strength and direction of the wind.

Despite a large tailwind, poor light and the narrow width of the branch, Erik's lookalike showed that it was more than a physical resemblance they shared, piling on the runs, frustrating John and Richard II to the point they were in danger of exhausting themselves so badly they would have been unable to run their singles when it came to batting. Eventually, however, coming down the wicket to attack a tired, medium paced delivery from John, the Lancashire version of Erik threw a little too much behind the shot and ended up playing a towering drive that went over the fence into the nearby basketball court.

'That's a six and out,' Richard II said, raising his finger

as Erik found a hole through which to sneak in order to retrieve it.'

'Six 'n out? I don't think so kidder,' the Lancastrian captain said, gesticulating to his batsman to continue running.

'I do, we're playing in a park, so park rules apply. It's six and out,' John chipped in, swapping ball for bat, hoping Erik didn't see this game's score as having any effect on his overall average.

Thankfully, the performance he turned in would have had people questioning whether he wasn't nocturnal. The ball was stroked carefully in all directions across the concrete, tens scored off every few balls (the highest amount of runs off a single shot since it would often be lost in the undergrowth and require his hawk like sight to retrieve it) until he too finally succumbed, slugging a huge stroke that found its way into the pond. Such heroics from the two lookalikes meant that after the first innings, with Skipperton leading by a slender two runs, it was approaching one in the morning.

'We can't carry on like this,' the Lancastrian captain said, 'we've a game in seven hours.'

'Aye, so have we,' Richard II said with a yawn. 'So how are we going to speed it up, give them both twigs?'

'Do you think that would make the slightest bit of difference?'

'No, probably not, just spur them on.'

'What about if we loaded them up on booze?' the captain said, pointing to an un-touched vodka and a three-quarters full bottle of cider.

'Never seems to affect Erik, but we can give it a try,' Richard II said with a shrug, his mouth feeling pretty parched. 'Might wet my own whistle first,' he concluded, reaching across to grab the vodka, from which he took a hearty swig. 'Oh,' he gasped, eyes watering as his throat was engulfed by flames, 'that bloody...' he saw Kevin about to comment through his tears, '...hits the spot,' he added, forcing it into the Lancastrian's hand, ready to tilt the bottle up if the gulp his opposite number took wasn't of an equal measure, but bravado saw the captain tipping the bottle high until he almost choked, forced to bend double to suck in cold air.

'Bugger me, it's not very strong,' he whispered hoarsely, 'could almost mistake it for water,' he continued, handing it back, picking up the cider to wash away the sharp taste as John, taking a few practice bowls, was handed the vodka, which continued its hot potato antics until a couple of minutes later it was empty.

'Okay,' John announced, swaying, unable to feel his tongue, 'lunch is over, let's begin the afternoon session,' he added, poking a finger in his mouth to make sure it was still there, while the opening Lancastrian batsman staggered towards the wicket bin. Wobbling in front of it, he held the branch in both hands and asked for middle, leading the captain to close one eye and order him left, then right, then left again, until he tripped over his feet and everyone burst out laughing.

'Again, do that again,' Richard II chortled, putting on a demonstration performance that also received guffaws of joy from all players, which would have lasted a fair while longer were it not for the sound of sirens and the flashing of red and blue lights.

'The Bizzies!' the Lancashire captain cried, the commotion suddenly sobering him and his two players in an instant. Their survival techniques in such circumstances were second to none, and just as they had appeared from the ether, so they vanished into it, tucking their trousers inside their socks for extra speed, as police officers stormed from their vehicles yelling: 'no ball games,' and wielding truncheons (which Richard II would later point out would have made far superior bats) over the triumphant claims of John that Skipperton had won the match by default, as he chased after the heels of Erik to safety.

To say that Harold and the team felt unnerved and angry that the dinner curfew hadn't been met, would have been an understatement akin to telling someone Al wasn't fond of anyone with colour in their skin. Not only had they been toying with the idea of contacting the police, they'd also gone out and bought a couple of manacles, again thanks to the advice of a helpful receptionist.

'It's no use trying any of these soft modern techniques, they won't work, they need discipline. They need to feel shame for their actions. We should throw them in the stocks.'

There were nods of agreement and a shiver of excitement at the prospect of hurling buckets of peelings, having not done so for so long.

'Easiest way to stop their behaviour is to take away their wage. No wonder they're running riot. Why when I was John's age I didn't see that kind of sum in a month. Going to the gym meant lifting sacks of spuds.'

This comment was also met with a positive consensus, as quietly, at the back, Paul ordered another bowl of olives and William a couple of after dinner mints. Chocolates on guest's pillows, would it work with a cream bun?

'John Smith though, what are we going to do with him? I mean he never asks for money, it just appears endlessly from his pockets, and he's due a couple of centuries.'

Harold gave the manacles a shake. Why did a couple of people have to go and spoil it for everyone else? He didn't want to have to keep a constant check and have meetings on the hour throughout the day. He'd been enjoying his free leisure time as cricket's ambassador. He'd bought himself a suit, one that didn't scratch and itch, to frequent the homes and be taken to bars by his opposite numbers as a gesture of goodwill. He'd not only discovered pasta, but a pasta made from potatoes. There wasn't a chance of him unearthing more gems of such ilk if he was going to be pressurised into babysitting. He was considering putting forward some motions for a vote, when Erik, John and Richard II burst through the retractable doors in unison.

'Redillian are here!' Richard II yelled, his fraught shout

making the rest of the team, who'd already been on the verge of standing to confront the trio, jump and scramble, laying hands on knives, forks and, in Paul's case, a toothpick.

'Where?' came the cry, as the players grouped into an attacking position, gazing over the shoulders of the trio, fully expecting their nemesis to come charging in behind them.

'How? How did they make it here?' Harold asked, still on alert, turning the knife over in his hand.

'Don't know, there were three of them. One looked and played like Erik.'

'Kieran,' Dereck said, a player none of those who had played in that semi-final had forgotten.

'We were two runs up in a game of Kwick cricket too. I'm sure we'd have annihilated them in the second innings.'

'No doubt lads,' Harold said, everyone beginning to replace their cutlery, the manacles surreptitiously hidden on a chair.

'But what were they doing? Why are they here?'

'Well they said that,' John paused to weigh up the options, sharing a glance with Richard II, whose hand was buried inside his trouser pocket clutching hold of the paper on which his Estonian girl had written her number. 'They said they were touring because they were the greatest side in the world and that we couldn't even cheat or bribe our way to victory against them.'

The Train

There was a lot of pent up aggression to take out the following morning and Harold was determined to win the toss so each of his players could pretend one of those Lancastrians was the ball and knock it into oblivion. In a lucid daydream, he actually envisioned himself playing a forward defensive in order to kill the ball dead in front of him and proceed to club it into the ground until the umpires pulled him off.

Every single Skipperton player's mouth was dry. The only way in which they would have been able to satisfactorily replenish their saliva glands was by being hooked up to an IV tea drip. If only Fred's bright idea of phoning all the hotels in the city had occurred to him when they'd been lying awake fuming and thrashing at their pillows instead of on the coach minutes from the ground, a showdown would have certainly made headline news.

The catharsis was not to come in the Lahemaa National Park, however, due to the fact that the playing pitch was a bog. Any plans to club the ball constantly over the boundary were quickly dispelled as the openers took to the field and promptly sank to their knees. Whether these conditions favoured the fielding side, though, it was difficult to tell.

From a batting perspective running came at the expense of burning lungs and, should a misplacement of step occur, a fall to the ground that required something closer to a swim to make it to the safety of the crease. A generous full toss was the only delivery that could be counted upon as a scoring opportunity and only then if the batter hadn't unconsciously brought his bat down as a defensive precautionary against his feet before the ball was bowled to then discover he couldn't lift it back out of the mud.

As for the bowlers, they had to pause to catch their breath mid-way through their run ups, meaning that they were rotated after a single over, except that by the time they had made their way over to their outfield position, they would often find themselves being recalled without a second of rest having been achieved. Finally, the fielders were possibly in the riskiest position, since every time they fell for a catch they were putting their lives at risk, often ending encased in mud, head first in the bog, unable to fight their way out of it with one hand, what with the other remaining above the ground clutching the ball.

All in all it meant it was the first game the Skipperton lads had played since their school days where they'd won with, and were thoroughly impressed by, a score of 24.

'Gutsy,' Stuart remarked in the shower after, as four players at a time stood, fully clothed, trying to scrub their whites back to something resembling their name.

'All about graft. Only a performance that could have been put in by a Yorkshire team that. Wouldn't have seen it from them queers the other side of The Pennines, they'd have been crying into their hotpots,' Fred chipped in, proud of his son, who had re-told the story so many times that the whole team now felt like they'd been there in the thick of the action. Little did they know that five miles away, on the other side of the bog, in conditions slightly better and against an inferior team, Redillian had only managed a two wicket victory with a total of 23.

'So where to next Skipper?' Paul asked Harold, who was drying his hair with a towel so heavily caked in mud that the action was doing more harm than good. He dropped it to the floor and withdrew his chunky purple guidebook, turning to the Estonian section to find a folded post-it note from Cuthbert stuck to the back page.

You have finished this book. Please see - Trans Siberian Railway - for your next destination.

'You'll have to bear with me there lads, we require a new book,' Harold said, more than a little excited about laying his hands on a piece of literature for new, exotic lands. 'Oh and once you're ready, if you make your way over to the clubhouse, well that tent type thing they've erected, they said they're laying on a spread for us,' he added.

175

'Make sure you bring across some bloody Black,' Al called after him, the cleanest of the team having desperately scrubbed his skin with his nails not just to remove the foreign germs, but mainly in an attempt to scrape off the golden colour his exposed skin had begun to acquire. 'Be mistaking myself for a bloody monkey soon,' he mumbled, his arms pink and sore, but then hold up! the Estonians hadn't used a rope for the boundary, they'd painted it in. 'See you over by the wog tent,' he said begrudgingly, sliding past Dereck, who was in the midst of finalising a deal for a batch of woollen tops he'd brought with him.

'All I'm saying is that what you're buying here is the top product, the best in the business. I can vouch for every sheep this wool came from, well not personally, but my nephew can, only eleven see, not really into girls yet. What I'm saying is this wool has been cared for, caressed and not only that, but they've all been dyed in the proper traditional manner too, none of that modified crap, just look at this yellow. Hang on a sec, hey Gaffa, is everything alright?' he said, as he spotted Harold, a little white in the gills. He kept his eye on his boss and held out his hand, which remained horizontal until he felt the correct weight of notes placed into his palm. 'Nice doing business with you. Gaffa, hey Harold, what's up?'

'This is our final trip on the coach,' Harold said, staring out across the horizon, wondering how he was going to bring up the subject with Al.

'We're going to India all the way from here?' Dereck said, scratching his head.

'No, we're going to Russia, but we're going to have to start taking the train once we're in, it's the only way to cover the distance in time.'

'But we only had it washed a fortnight ago in Tirana and it does sixty miles an hour on a flat, sixty-five when we're motoring down a hill!'

'Hopefully those specifications and the new wax job'll push its resale value up,' Harold said, with a shrug, guessing it was best to start talking commission and exchange rates before they found a potential buyer. Before he could take another breath, Dereck's pencil was out from behind his ear and sums were being scrawled across the pad.

'Leave it with me,' he said, walking off to take a stock check of the perishable items stored aboard, as the rest of the team made their way in drips from the showers.

Maybe hourly meetings would have to be introduced, because it didn't appear they could stick together for twenty minutes any more, let alone twenty hours; over by a tree, Richard II wasn't doing very well hiding the fact he'd borrowed a mobile phone from one of the opposition, since his shouts of: 'I love you' were so loud the birds were flocking from their nests. Paul was picking through the sandwiches enquiring if there were any with pâté and Stuart was visibly excited at the proposition of going to hunt some deer with an Estonian butcher, who'd gone as far as to withdraw knives the length of his forearm from the boot of his car.

Surveying the whole panorama of activity, Harold guessed that in terms of forgetting the past and wiping clean the ghastly memories of that fateful quarter-final, they were achieving well beyond what could have been imagined. Twelve hours ago they'd heard news of an insult large enough to advocate another war, but instead of still being in The Arms talking destructive tactics whilst Henry Baker the blacksmith bypassed sleep to forge an arsenal of weapons, they looked like they were part of some gigantic picnic festival. Such a peaceful, pleasant scene was suddenly destroyed by screams from a pair of Estonians.

'A ghost!'

'No, The Bog Monster! The legend is true,' they shouted, backing off, pointing in the direction of a bright white entity staggering across the grass emitting mumbled groans with its arms flailing haphazardly. There definitely wasn't any chance it was a ghost, because instead of walking through the trees it ricocheted off them, disorientating it even more. This also ruled out The Bog Monster since it would surely have been at its most adept in such conditions. Pointing this fact out, the Estonian butcher delved back into the boot of his car and removed a dart rifle.

'It must be a crazed, escaped mime from the circus,' he concluded. 'One who is trying to smash the imaginary box he is trapped inside,' he added.

'No, hang on, I think that's...' Harold wasn't able to finish his sentence, as in that split second, a tranquiliser dart embedded itself into Al's neck. Before the spinner had the chance to remove it, he was a crumpled heap.

'Now that's the type of accuracy I was talking about earlier,' Stuart said, congratulating his contemporary with a pat on the back, as everyone flooded across to see the fallen being. 'Straight out of the middle of the bat,' he continued, making an imaginary cover drive, while the first Estonian on the scene kneeled to check for a pulse.

'Is he dead?' Harold asked, wondering how Al had managed to run the paint roller over his back so effectively. There really wasn't a single speck of him that wasn't chalky white.

'No, he's alive, but he'll be sleeping for a while,' the Estonian said, too polite to ask for a reason for the post match guise, aware that you never did learn the most interesting cultural traditions of a country at school.

'A while as in two hours, or a while as in twenty-four?' Harold enquired.

'I'd say at least five,' the butcher answered, testing Al's weight with a gentle prod of his foot to the ribs.

'Right,' Harold said, 'in that case could we have another couple of those darts? Ta.'

As Harold had expected, the news that they would have to spend the remainder of the trip travelling via public transport was met with little more than a few shrugs of disappointment, mainly due to the fact that they would be forced to lug their bags around with them. The coach had served them well, but if it was now obsolete, what were they to do? Though concerned by his players' ability to forgo an object so easily when two months prior they had been clinging to the same set of cutlery that had been in the family for six generations and was welded together every Christmas, Harold had no complaints in disposing with the vehicle either since even with Dereck's slice of commission, he made double on what he'd originally paid for it. Still, even with his new windfall, rather than purchase the second class private cabins that held four on the train from St. Petersburg to Moscow, he opted for the third class platskartney; or at least he did eventually when they found the one person in the queue that spoke English, having been shocked by the revelation that the po faced woman at the counter didn't understand the first one hundred phrases of French (Yorkshire edition).

'Feel a little useless,' William admitted, as the student booked their tickets for them.

'Nonsense, she's probably hard of hearing. Look at her, she must be in her early fifties,' Harold replied, handing in all their passports.

'To be honest I thought she was a statue, I thought they all were,' William whispered, looking from one ticket window to the next to see uniformed women staring sternly at the person on the other side of the glass. One of the cashiers, halfway through a transaction, rose from her seat, pointed to the large hall clock running on Moscow time, and promptly brought her blind down to signal her fifteen minute break had started, and that was that.

'The whole country looks like it was built from stone,' Alan joined in with admiration.

'Guess when there's so many people around there's no time to stop for a chat, just have to be professional, process the tickets and be on to the next customer,' Harold concluded, thanking the student.

'That's fair enough, but they could do everyone a bloody favour by using the real alphabet instead of a made up one. Looks like they went straight from chisels to the printing press without ever discovering the quill,' Richard II said, struggling under the weight of two bags, since Stuart had Al, who now resembled a large piece of road kill with a serious skin disease, slung over his shoulder.

'Do you think we should let him wake up for at least a

few minutes?' Stuart enquired, shuffling Al's body around so the arms draped over one side of his neck and the legs the other.

'Reckon we could flog him as a shawl if we cleaned him up a bit first,' said Dereck, as they lined up along the platform in front of their carriage.

'Ticket and passport,' the attendant manning their door said, checking each member on individually then following on behind them, shoving her way past when it became apparent the experience was new for them.

'The seats are beds!' John exclaimed, spinning this way and that, forcing people to dodge, as his bag swung with him, an action that didn't impress the attendant, who snatched it off him and threw it under one of the bottom bunks.

'Bet she'd have been handy in the shot putt,' Stuart whispered, as the woman proceeded to push and shove the team into their correct numbered beds, which were set six to a compartment, two on the side in line with the corridor and four in the main section, two up, two down.

They were stared at by the other travellers in the carriage who, being more experienced, had begun to change into their pyjamas, if indeed they hadn't already boarded in their leisurewear. Most began to pull food and drink out of plastic bags, with a few already crowding round tables to play cards.

'It's almost like we haven't left the coach at all. I even saw a hot water boiler at the front,' William said with glee, as he was hustled along by the attendant, who broke off only to return with a small brush as she tried to set about creating order.

'She looks like a brick version of Mel,' Paul pointed out, rubbing the tricep he'd been gripped on, the train now in motion, leaving the very second it had been scheduled to.

'Wouldn't like to meet the Jonesy version,' Fred responded, finding himself alone, at least in terms of teammates, three compartments down. His roommates for the evening looked at him, as he edged cautiously away from

180

them as soon as the attendant had turned her back. Making eye contact, and without saying a word, one of the men reached into his holdall, removed a bottle of vodka and offered it to Fred.

'You need this,' he said, digging back inside for another couple of bottles, which were hastily screwed open and, with a brief lift to act as a toast, sipped at and passed round.

'What's the catch?' Fred asked, looking down the train for some support, which came in the form of a curt nod by Harold, who was perched on the lip of his bed, recounting his team.

'Catch?' the vodka supplier repeated, unfamiliar with the phrase. 'No catch. Drink, play cards, eat, come sit,' he said, shuffling along so all six members of the compartment occupied the bottom berths, still in the process of making introductions to one another. 'My name is Nikolai,' the man said, raising his bottle, 'salut.'

'My name is Fred,' Fred replied, following suit, 'salut.'

'Welcome Fred, so this game we are about to play is called Durak. Salut,' Nikolai said, as his wife shuffled the deck in a fashion far fancier than Fred was used to witnessing.

'Sounds good. Salut?'

'Salut,' Nikolai said with a nod.

Back down in the middle section of the carriage, Harold wasn't being offered any alcohol, instead he was holding a large chunk of bread with half an inch of mayonnaise layering its surface and a slab of ham crowning it.

'Ta,' he said, accepting it from a rather attractive woman, who had remained in her tight black jeans and jumper. She pointed above them at the top bunks, where Erik and Alan were laying down, the only members of the team who had made their beds without having to be shown what to do by the carriage attendant.

'I'm sure they'd love a bite too, very kind of you,' Harold said, nodding and smiling, withdrawing some tea bags since Dereck had discovered that they could borrow glass mugs, most of the Russians using theirs to make what appeared to be a thick mud rather than coffee. A silt lined mug already adorned the table between himself and Vasilisa.

'Care for a cuppa?' he asked, waving a tea bag like some excited hypnotist, drawing a shrug from Vasilisa, who guessed she might as well give it a try. If it was unappetising she had enough mayonnaise to take the taste away. She watched Harold, who had barely made it to his feet, before being forced to squeeze to the side to allow a large woman dressed in a red jumper suit with a pattern of miniature polar bears to pass down the aisle; she was heading towards the toilets, where Dereck was engaged in an argument with the attendant.

'No toilet,' the attendant said, waving her mini sweeping brush in her marigold covered hands.

'But you cleaned them last time we stopped. You don't need to clean them every time, it means they'll be closed for longer than they're open.'

'No toilet.'

'It's not a number two lass, just a number one. I'll be fifteen seconds, possibly less now that it's been building for so long.'

Wondering how else she could possibly convey her message, the attendant was about to enter into a game of charades, when Fred, who had overheard the conversation, just, above the din of his compartment's revelries, decided to help his teammate out since he considered his Russian had to be close to perfect due to how much he was enjoying himself.

'Dereck, Dereck lad,' he said, waving his vodka bottle, which had to be thrown to his lips yet again as Nikolai toasted his latest card move. 'She's telling you that you can't go to the lav at the moment. You'll have to wait. Don't worry, it's one of those lingo things, I think I must just have it, naturally, like baking you know? What, is it my go? Salut to that,' he said, holding his cards so loosely they were on show for all to see, his attention to them meaning he missed the

182

look shared by the rest of the table.

'I think we have the rules good,' Nikolai said, chewing on the end of a Kabana sausage, 'so now we play for money?' he added.

'Aye, absolutely,' Fred remarked. 'Did you hear that Dereck, money involved.'

'Fifty point sixty-five Rubles to the Pound,' Dereck replied.

'Right you are. Can you go and ask Harold if I can have an advance when you're done then?' Fred asked, his smirk dropping when he swivelled back to face the other five card players.

Dereck wasn't keen on moving at all, since there were people with toothbrushes ready, and vacating his spot would leave him at the back of the queue during the ten minute window the toilets were open. Thankfully, he wasn't required to summon Harold, because news of the game had spread fast, and was attracting a large gathering.

'Your friend plays cards,' Vasilisa informed The Skipper, as they craned their necks to see what the fuss was about.

'Right,' Harold said, standing, waiting for her to join him, thinking that if her hair hadn't been cut all the way round with a leveller and her skin been a shade darker, she could have passed for Rachel's younger sister. He was almost glad they couldn't share a proper conversation, though that hadn't stopped him constantly looking over at her and smiling. Could he be blamed when she polished off the cuppa and asked if she could have another?

They walked side by side to where the action was happening, money trading hands freely, as Dereck stood with a slate board covered in chalk, the benefit of numbers being that they made sense everywhere.

'Skipper,' Fred called, waving Harold over to a table of confused and disgruntled looking Russians. 'Need a few more bob,' he continued, swigging liberally on the vodka. 'I'm a whole five pounds up and I think I can go into double figures,' he added, waving his winnings, which could have been far greater had he bet more than forty pence at a time. 'This lot here thought I was too drunk to play, else they believed I didn't know the game properly, but let me tell you all that I've been playing down at The Arms since I was four years old. We play round the dinner table too for the last bag of scratchings, and as for this stuff, it tastes like milk compared to the brew we made in that terrible summer of '95 when the Black factory ran dry for three weeks because of that squirrel problem. It wasn't a moonshine we produced, called it sunshine instead, because just looking at it would make you go temporarily blind.'

'Aye, I recall that,' Stuart said, 'had a yellow tinge to it. Susan used it as disinfectant for all the cleavers as well. Mind you, had to rinse them after or else they'd have collapsed quicker than the middle order under Atherton's captaincy.'

'Atherton, Michael Atherton?' Vasilisa enquired.

'Aye, Michael Atherton, biggest joke of an England captain ever. Holds the record for the most test ducks. Hey up, how do you know who Michael Atherton is?' Harold asked, telling himself it wasn't love he was feeling, just a bit of heartburn from the mayonnaise, which he was sure was supposed to be a spread, not the main ingredient, as a rapturous cry of "Yorkshire, Yorkshire" was started by Fred, now five pounds sixty to the good.

Vasilisa held her finger up signalling she required a minute, during which time the natives ploughed more money into Dereck's pockets as they backed their comrades rather than Fred.

'Haven't lost a competitive card game at The Arms since the turn of the century. Let me guard down a couple of times with my lad at home, but that's only to keep his spirits up. As soon as there's so much as a Yorkshire up for grabs you can bank on me winning,' he announced with great satisfaction, trying hard not to let his mind wander onto what he could splash his riches on, though a new pair of thick insoles would do wonders for his feet.

Harold took the opportunity to place a hundred

Rubles on his bowler before Vasilisa re-appeared, not with a stranger to act as an interpreter, but a mobile phone in her hand. She finished tapping away and handed it over, a robotic voice translating what she had written.

'I know Michael Atherton, because my boyfriend loves cricket. He is the best player in Moscow. I think he is going to play you next if you are Skipperton of Yorkshire.'

'Bloody hell, this thing's amazing,' Harold said, his finger slipping, setting the robotic voice off again. 'Yes we're Skipperton alright. You're boyfriend's not...' he stopped, realising she didn't understand a word, finding himself simultaneously pleased and disappointed by the news of a boyfriend, but what had he expected? She was gorgeous and she was twenty. If the lad had any sense he'd have snapped her straight up instead of just deciding to court her.

'Right, let's see,' he mumbled, checking the screen, pushing here and there until it started vibrating in his hands, making him throw it back as if it had stung him. Vasilisa briskly typed away: *You don't have Google translate on your phone?*

Harold visualised the large white cube with the finger holes over the numbers sitting on top of The Yellow Pages in his hallway. It had an orange sticker on the front with the number of the emergency services.

'Oh aye, of course we do, just not used to this particular version, but I know someone who is, just let me grab Richard II for you. Hang on...oh bugger, William! Wise Owl! Where did I put that other dart?'

Without a flicker of panic, Richard II slid into Harold's place, his hair slicked up into a quiff, as close a match to Erik's as was physically possible: 'It's alright, you go and sort that Skipper, I'll take over here. Come, let's move out of the way a bit,' he added, as Harold positioned himself in the middle of the corridor like a nervous gunslinger. 'Can I just say,' Richard II added, 'there's something very Estonian about you Vasilisa, your name for one. Do you like parks?'

Distracted by the thing that was unfurling itself on a top bunk with pained groans of anguish, she pointed to the phone.

'Ah, I see. Haven't got a number myself out here, but that doesn't mean I'm not interested, I'm very interested. Whoa there, no need to snatch.'

Vasilisa held the phone to Richard II's ear, but Al's moans had now grown into comprehensible ravings and he couldn't hear a word.

'Think we better take this into the smoking section,' Richard II said, as Al, losing his balance, crashed to the floor.

'I'm in Hell!' he screamed, clutching his knee. 'Oh God, coffee, it's all I can smell,' he gagged, his antics cutting short the card game, waking those who had been slumbering, and alerting the carriage attendant, who had been trying to catch five minutes rest in her cubby hole at the front of the carriage.

'A train, I'm on a train and I don't smell coal. We're moving too fast and oh the wogs,' Al wept. 'How have I ended up here after all I've done?'

A boy, not yet in his teens, offered out what he assumed, from the life he had led so far, was the cure to all adult problems, but Al recoiled at the sight of him and the vodka.

'They've been touching me haven't they? All these spics and pakis, look what they've done to my arms, they've burnt them!'

'Stuart that dart's in the bag under my bed. You're going to have to take him out so I can get to it,' Harold said, watching the distorted figure of Al, as he cowered into a ball and then sprang large, jabbing his finger at every sight he beheld.

'You. Stop,' came the command from the carriage attendant. She prodded Al on the shoulder, the action releasing a caterwaul.

'The plague, they'll give me the plague and AIDS! Stop you bloody monkeys, stop.'

'I wouldn't touch him if I were you lass, honest, we'll have it sorted in a second.'

'Take him down how? Like with a rugby tackle or a

punch?'

'Sit or I throw you out.'

'Just do something quick or we're going to be out in the middle of nowhere and English doesn't seem to be something they use round here.'

'Listen here lass, you tell the driver to slow down a notch and I'll happily throw myself from this window.'

'We can't keep knocking him out and waking him up for games.'

'We could.'

'I not say again.'

'You know what love, I didn't catch any of that bloody crap because I don't speak wop. I'm from Skipperton, Yorkshire, not some hole filled with talking rubbish, you little Nazi.'

'You mean take him out like that?'

'Aye, exactly,' Harold said, as they watched the carriage attendant flex her hand, before hauling the once again unconscious Al onto an empty bed.

'Talk again, off,' she called down the carriage, hoiking a thumb in the direction of the window.

'No worries love,' Harold replied, waiting for her to retreat to her office, 'you won't hear another peep from any of us.'

Despite the fact that most of the players hardly slept during what remained of the eight hour journey to Moscow, they all made a sprightly exit from the carriage when they arrived and bowed low to the attendant as they passed her.

Much to the disappointment of Richard II, Vasilisa's boyfriend Dimar was already standing on the platform, his arms wide open, not just for his girlfriend, but the whole team.

'Pleasure to meet you...So nice to meet real cricketers...This is an honour...Darren Gough is my favourite ever player.'

'Like this lad, bit touchy feely, but he speaks a lot of sense.'

187

'Aye,' Harold said, in complete agreement. 'Hey, do you remember that fifth test of 98/99 when Goughy took that hat-trick against the Aussies in their first innings? He'd have bloody gone and won the game for us with his batting too had the other bloody pillocks not left him stranded on seven not out.'

'So where are you staying?'

'Err, not really sure. Why, do you have a recommendation?' Harold said, having not taken the time to check through the guide-book since he'd taken responsibility of watching over Al, dart in hand.

'You should stay with me,' Dimar replied.

'In the same bed?' Richard II enquired.

'Ha, of course not. Some of you can stay at my flat and some at my parents', they are in the same block. Come, it will be fine, you must be hungry and thirsty and I can see one of you is still very tired.'

The lure of free accommodation meant that the team followed the young skipper of their forthcoming opponents to a housing complex that took up more space than Skipperton town centre. There were some broken swings and slides in the middle of a court, with cars parked at all angles.

'A Lada, consistent quality,' Fred remarked, stroking the faded ochre bonnet of a vehicle half mounting the curb.

'Proper good prices,' Dereck acknowledged, as they made their way up the dank stairwell to the top floor.

'My parents aren't in yet, but we can all squeeze into here until they return,' Dimar said, unveiling an open floor plan flat that would just about hold everyone if they remained vertical.

'There's no way we can sleep here,' Stuart whispered, 'and since Al can't say it himself, I think it might be a ploy,' he added, as Harold shuffled into a kitchen comprising a couple of high chairs, a kettle, a microwave and an oven. Adorning every wall of it were pictures of the world's greatest bowlers of the past quarter of a century: Warne, McGrath, Akram, Younis, Gough, Muralitharan, Walsh, Ambrose, Vass, Pollock, Botham and some fat guy. Harold chose to ignore this last photo since the lad obviously led a sheltered life.

'You don't need to worry about space, because me and my parents will stay at my grandma's.'

'And Vasilisa?'

'Of course she will stay with me,' Dimar said, laughing at what he assumed was Richard II's joke.

'Sounds grand,' Harold acknowledged, feeling like he could sleep standing up. 'I'll let William sort out the details with you while I put the kettle on.'

With most of the players opting for a constant re-fill of their tea, happy to be away from the foreigners for a while, Alan took the time to ask Erik whether he would join him not just for a stroll around the city, but also for a trip to a banya. It was a type of sauna he had read about in the guide-book, one that had played an integral role in his daydreams ever since; a collage of Greco-Roman wrestling tournaments, a naval training exercise and a Hitler Youth adult weekend camp.

'Sure,' Erik answered, after hearing a very brief synopsis of what it entailed. 'Let me go and grab my trunks and towel,' he added, his answer in the affirmative fuelling Alan's enthusiasm once they were on their own and heading towards the Metro.

'You're not going to be disappointed. In the book it claims it's one of the must do activities in Russia. It'll be such a unique experience. I could have chosen anyone to go with, but I wanted, I mean I thought you'd appreciate it the most. I don't think some of the others would understand.'

So constant was Alan's nattering that he didn't have time to contemplate the craftsmanship that had gone into the Metro system, which was as lavish in scope as anything above ground. Scenery didn't matter, there was no backdrop or moment that was better than any other in which to announce his true feelings. Now was as good a time as any, but would that spoil the hours he had planned for them together? Would it make Erik change his mind when he found out exactly what was in store? The banya was too great an opportunity to miss, and so The Gnome satisfied himself with a daydream in which stood an Alan bolder than he, one who wasn't preparing to act as if he were shocked when the exact workings of the banya were revealed...

'Naked! Bloody hell, what's the world coming to? They're all at it. Honestly, if I'd have known I'd have never made the suggestion,' Alan muttered, standing in the middle of a locker room, which was filled with men standing and chatting, lounging on chairs drinking what they claimed was tea or being massaged on a table underneath a TV showing boxing. At most they had a towel wrapped round their waists, but those with such an item were in the minority.

'I mean it was a fair distance to make it here and it seems a shame to miss out, but you know it's not really what I expected I can tell you that,' Alan added, as he unbuttoned his shirt, the sentence not a complete lie, because there was far more hair and fat on show than his mind had conjured.

A man opened a door leading to a separate chamber and announced everything was ready, starting an exodus from the changing room into a tiled shower and plunge pool area, where large buckets of water stood containing bundles of branches from different trees.

'If you'd rather we went somewhere for a bite to eat instead I totally understand, but you...' Alan stopped. Not only was there no need to go on any further, there were no superlatives to describe what was on view. Erik folded his clothes into a pile above his brogues and strolled after the other men sounding like a metronome, leaving Alan to tear off his attire in order to both marvel and cherish what was on show.

Unlike a sauna, a banya didn't have coals, rather a furnace into which buckets of water were thrown. One man, wearing a hat borrowed from a Smurf, sat in the middle of a ring spread around him. These men would have usually been laying on their front, waiting for the ring leader to waft the air and lightly slap their skin with the bundled branches, but they were also too busy staring at Erik. Their descriptions of what they saw would range from lamppost to vase, bottle to dustpan, but what it really resembled, as Alan joined the contingent mesmerised by such a shapely member, was a cricket bat. There was no mistaking it for any other item. It couldn't be real. It had to have been grafted between his legs or been the result of some freak accident. Yet there was something undeniably beautiful about it, the sturdy square edge of the base, the roll of foreskin, which curved over the top of the handle (or bell end depending on how you wanted to view it), a shade darker than the thick willow shaft.

There were curt glances to check if it was a package all foreigners brought with them, but discovering Alan to be normal, and with the heat rising, the men lay face down, curious as to whether women just took the normal "handle" or tried to make it down the middle. Alan, meanwhile, too busy trying to measure the dimensions of his mouth with his fingers, didn't follow their lead, and wanting to make sure he didn't miss anything, placed his back against the pine boards instead, as the heat began to singe hair and fingernails, all of which was painful, but no way near as agonising as when the ring leader, having reached him on his way round the circle, didn't even pause, before striking him not once, but thrice.

'Perhaps,' one of the regular members would suggest later, as he discussed the incident with a friend over a beer, 'that is what they do, beat it until it swells?'

'In that case, the blonde man must strike his with a nuclear weapon,' his friend mused.

'We have to do something Skipper or we're going to be fielding half a team soon,' William said, his arm so stiff it had locked into place, forcing him to drink his tea through a straw, after having been forced into five overs of bowling and a rise up the batting order due to Al's concussion.

'We've a day and a half's rest now, and we wouldn't be so depleted if we still had twelve players, would we?' Harold grunted, his frustration really aimed at his own performance, having been bowled clean by Dimar for 8. The opposition skipper had finished the game with the most impressive bowling figures of either side, and had it not been for the wicket keeper dropping Stuart on 6 and some horrendous fielding on the boundary by the Muscovites, there would have been a nail biting climax. Such tight results were becoming far too much of a regular occurrence.

Not that anyone else appeared worried by the trend, for there was always a strong sense that despite the circumstances, just like with the staff team on quiz night at The Arms, they'd win regardless. They had become like Gregory West and his annual prize winning turnips. No matter what was wrong: bad weather, rat infestation, part time scarecrows, lads using them in an attempt to show off, they'd be on top of the podium come the end, because they'd made winning a habit. That was one of the lines from Gregory's annual speech, which every child above the age of six could recite. In fact there was probably only Gregory himself who didn't know it word for word and relied on the piece of paper he pulled from his trouser pocket, which thanked the natural elements first, before moving on to his tools, which he praised individually, saving his trowel for last, an object that really should have been retired a decade ago. But he couldn't trust another one, could he?

'Apologies,' Harold said to his deputy, who had gone and bought his own treatment; a bag of frozen peas, which had sufficed as a cure for all three injured players. He and Alan clutched them to their sore sections, while Al, whose book *Herbs and Remedies 1743* didn't include concussion as an ailment, instead treated himself for a headache with the placement of peas in all his orifices and a drink of cold tea without milk.

Harold had allowed them, and anyone else who felt under the weather, to remain in Dimar's flat to recuperate, rather than join him for supper round at Grandma's. Since they had a kitchen at their disposal and Stuart had offered to make a fry up, only Richard II, William and Erik had accompanied Harold to what they expected to be a mayonnaise mezze. At lunch the hot dogs and pizza had been covered in the gunk, and it had actually been a surprise to find it absent from their water at the drink's break.

'Ah, the great cricket players have arrived! Come in please, welcome. The top batsman,' Dimar said, never low on enthusiasm. 'Is there any chance you can show me how to play that reverse sweep?' he added, bending to mimic Erik's shot. 'You hit four boundaries off it, and you,' he continued, shaking hands with Richard II, who was busy surveying who else had come for grub, 'you were the one who bowled me with the full toss. Just how was it you gripped the ball?' he asked, ignoring the previous five deliveries which had been either beamers or bouncers attempting to knock him out cold. 'And Skipper, what tactics to win with only nine players batting, very impressive,' he concluded, as they headed into the living room, which didn't look unlike Richard II's own. The colour scheme was brown and green, the furniture was at least forty years old and the carpet was thick with dust. There were candles lined along the window frame, but the light came from a dim bulb emitting its energy from beneath a lamp shade that was swamped in its own dangly string.

'This is where we shall eat,' Dimar explained, 'but come to the kitchen to collect your plate and drink. We are having stuffed pepper,' he said, drawing blank stares from the Skipperton players, who crossed their fingers in the hope that Stuart had gone overboard with his purchase of sausage and bacon.

'Evening,' Harold said, extending his hand to Dimar's dad, who was busy helping his mother spoon in the rice and mushrooms, between swigs of whiskey.

'Drink?' he asked, his hand moving blindly to seek out tumblers, leading Harold's gaze over to the display mounted on the wall. It was a vast collection of silver spoons, some of them in cases, all of them with an emblem on the handle to show where they had come from. He didn't understand it personally, decent spoons should have been making decent cuppas, not leaning useless against the wall, but Rachel's parents had a similar collection of cups they kept out of the reach of liquids, brought back from countries they'd visited, and as he absentmindedly thought that he should have perhaps bought his wife a gift by now, he checked the names on the spoons to see if there were any from places they'd passed through.

'Checking my Grandma's spoons? They're gifts from foreign teams we've played in chronological order. She's the treasurer of the club you see and everyone sends her one once they've returned home,' Dimar said, passing the glasses of whiskey along. 'I believe Cuthbert, the man who organised this game, has her address,' he added, moving away from the wall so as to unveil the latest edition.

Harold's plate was placed into his hands, but as he stared back up from what looked more like a creation from someone's stomach lining, it dropped, smashing to the floor.

'What the bloody nora? It can't be! This is not happening,' he shouted, stomping on the remnants of the pepper to eyeball the spoon, which unlike the rest of the collection didn't sparkle, as it had previously been used.

The three players moved to form a protective semi circle around The Skipper, as the Russians stood, stunned into silence.

'Bloody hell.'

'This is bloody outrageous.'

'What is this?' Harold muttered hoarsely, unable to touch the tippex writing and red felt tip colouring. LANCS. Where was the bleach?

'They're following us.'

'They've already bloody been here! When was this?' Harold demanded, his body itching with the violation it had received; where they'd slept, where they'd played, where they'd eaten.

'Two days before you,' Dimar mumbled, muttering to his dad to hold off any violent reaction until they'd heard a full explanation.

'And where are they now? Where are they off to next?'

'I don't know. Why would I know? What is going on?' Dimar asked, as William, spotting the knife twisting in their host's father's hand, began to pick up what had been spilt on the floor, leaving Harold to begin a history lesson, his head still shaking long after he'd started.

'...and so you can see why I'm so bloody mad,' he eventually concluded, a good while after everyone except Dimar had taken themselves off to bed.

'My word. I never knew. In that case,' Dimar announced, moved into bending the Lancastrian spoon double in response to Harold's rhetoric, 'I will come with you. I will aid your quest and become an all round player.'

'Well, I don't know about that lad, the thing is...' Harold stopped. What had Wise Owl said a couple of hours ago? Were they likely to come across anyone with as much zeal and talent? Plus Kevin Pieterson and Jonathon Trott hadn't been born in England, but they still played for the Three Lions. No way near as good as Bresnan like, but there were certain things only breeding could give you.

'You know what lad, bugger it. I'm The Skipper and I'm going to say that you're in. Might have to pass an initiation, but as far as I'm concerned start packing. Just leave the queer hugging business at home though.'

The Result

'Oh yes that's it. That is it. Let me kiss those lips again.'

Rachel wheezed as Cuthbert pressed his lips against hers, his tongue flailing away like it was drunk at a disco, while his hands explored her body, squeezing, fingering every nook again and again.

He broke off the tryst slowly, their mouths covered in saliva. Rachel stared blankly back at him as he ran a finger over the smooth surface of her lips, glistening in the candlelight.

'It's alright, you don't need to say a word,' Cuthbert cooed, moving her hand onto his penis. 'Ready to go again?' he purred, watching her hand fall back to the side of her open legs. They'd gone through a whole box of baby wipes in the past week. They were going to have to buy wholesale, the pace was relentless, and best of all, the pleasure was mutual. There hadn't been a single argument. It had been bliss, every second of it.

'I think before we get rampant again I'm going to grab myself a water to replenish the juices. Do you want one? No, okay then my little saucepan, I'll be two seconds,' Cuthbert said, springing from the bed. The grin he wore was a constant one, for presently he was King of the world, and there was little to suggest that would be changing any time soon.

The ice fell into the tumbler with a clink from its plastic tray.

'Did you hear that ice? Ice baby,' Cuthbert sang, growing further pleased with himself. At present there wasn't anything he couldn't do, and as proof, he threw out his arms at all kinds of strange angles to indulge his rhythmic side, as the cold water drummed hard and fast against the glass.

'Oh Rachel baby, I'm ready for another double blow,' he announced, shaking his hips into the hallway, where Rachel stood.

'What the Lord? Frucking hell!' Cuthbert blurted,

throwing the water everywhere, as he bent to cover the erection his boxer shorts were doing little to hide. 'What are you doing?' he asked, watching Rachel watch him, apparently unconcerned about the liquid splashed on her skirt and legs.

'You told me that your door was always open and that if it wasn't there was a key under the mat,' she said, holding it out to return it.

'But why now? Couldn't you have knocked?' Cuthbert whimpered, the sight of her sticky pink lip gloss doing nothing to help him deflate.

'I had been trying to call you, but your phone was off. I see why now. Isn't what you're doing...illegal?'

'It certainly is not.'

'I mean since you're a vicar and all.'

'Vicars can have sex! It's priests that can't,' Cuthbert said, side stepping round to the coat rack.

'Oh,' Rachel said, shrugging. 'So she's called Rachel too? It's not Rachel Barker is it?'

'No it's not Rachel Barker,' Cuthbert replied, wrapping his coat around his waist at the same time as arching his back to keep in the picture his triumphant bulge.

'Well it can't be Rachel Smith, because that would be illegal. Mind you, she should keep her school uniform because it will come in handy in a few years. I used to love wearing my uniform at college even though we didn't have to. My mum said it helped my marks. But if it's not either of those, then who is she?' Rachel enquired, craning her neck, forcing Cuthbert to move between her and the bedroom door.

'She's just a friend.'

'Oh it's like that,' Rachel said, approvingly. 'Can I see her?'

'I don't think so, she's very shy.'

'Well surely she'll be coming with us to the mayoral candidacy debate?' Rachel said, wanting to compare. A woman from out of town might be able to tell her about the up to date trends she was missing out on, provide gossip that didn't include someone she knew.

197

'Ah yes, the mayoral debates. Well she could come I suppose, but it might raise unwanted questions and definitely won't help me with the image I've been creating. Also, she isn't able to vote so it will probably bore her,' Cuthbert said, leading Rachel into the kitchen.

'Oh of course, she's from out of town. You're right, there would be uproar as to how she made it inside the walls without anyone knowing,' Rachel said, taking a seat, her skirt rising high on her thigh. If only Cuthbert knew what she was thinking he'd have passed out from all the blood running to his second head. 'Where is she from exactly?'

'Somewhere in China,' Cuthbert replied, knowing the best lies always contained part truths.

'I say, that's exotic,' Rachel said, raising her eyebrows, wanting to warm her hands on herself rather than the cup of tea placed before her. 'Are you sure she doesn't want to talk while you change?'

Cuthbert gave a vigorous shake of his head: 'I'm afraid she doesn't speak any English,' he said.

It was Cuthbert's intention to speak all the way to the Town Hall so as not to be asked any tricky questions about his new squeeze, but the way Rachel was walking, almost hip to hip with him, had him in a stuttering mess and concluding that it might be wise to invest in a pair of clown's trousers to stop the embarrassing hunch he was forced into performing.

Before nipping out he had gone and checked on other Rachel (Rachel Johnson incidentally, as he often referred to her), to find her a little deflated, but he had given her a quick squeeze and assured her that, unless some miracle occurred, he would be back to go at it again later.

'Evening Father.'

'Wonderful day again Father, great work.'

'Not too much to ask for a little sprinkling of rain tomorrow Father?'

The greetings came thick and fast once they merged with the rest of the crowd milling down to the Town Hall. Since Cuthbert no longer opened around the clock as he had before Keith's demise (he now called it a day at five to make dinner for himself and Rachel), appointment times were scarce and his presence out on the street now drew a similar response to Harold's. There was an unspoken need for the people to be close to him, yet even those in the coveted positions flanking his sides maintained an almost regal distance.

'Lovely to see everyone,' Cuthbert acknowledged. 'God bless you all,' he added, making the sign of the cross in front of his chest out of expectation, forced to repeat the action every fifteen or so steps when new people emerged who'd failed to see his last blessing and kept staring at him until he'd done it.

Once they stepped inside the Town Hall, there were arguments on the front row as to who gave up their seats to him and Rachel, with most having arrived early just to produce such a favour.

'Ooh, it's like we're David and Victoria! That's what I used to call me and Harold,' Rachel said, her choice of the words "used to" sticking like Yorkshire Pudding batter in Cuthbert's head. "Used to" like when she first arrived into his world of constant adulation? Or "used to" as in he was gone and forgotten? Because David and Victoria Beckham were a couple and they did all the things couples did together. They had four children last time Cuthbert had heard, but that number could be as high as a dozen by now.

So caught up in imagining their new lives as the town's Beckhams, Cuthbert didn't tune in to the opening lines spoken by the acting Mayor Gary Smith, who had served as the Deputy Mayor under the previous two leaders and made it clear that he liked his role and had no intention of running for the hot seat. In fact the sooner they voted in a replacement, the better.

'As you all know, Keith never sired an heir, so this is the time for those candidates who have put their names forward to step up and deliver a speech to promote themselves. According to Town Hall regulation 3.19, they have three minutes to make their address once I've flipped over the timer. The first man up is Jonathon James "Timmy" Baker.'

Watching the former miner shuffle onto the platform fumbling his cards, the lenses of his glasses finishing an inch beyond his nose, Cuthbert once again turned his concentration inward, knowing as well as everyone else the only agenda would be coal, the mining of it and its price.

He let his hand slide off his knee and brush against Rachel's skirt as it dropped down between the chairs. All the way from the church they'd been touching, there was a closeness and it was growing. Sure everyone in town wanted to be his best friend since Keith had met his grisly fate, but tonight he felt that Rachel's friendship was not based on fear, as it was with the others.

The prospect of another "miracle" occurring had been something Cuthbert had been contemplating ever since. Nothing in the immediate future, but another event would have to occur eventually to dismiss the whispers of Keith's death being a coincidence.

There was a loud, hearty applause from the East End congregation somewhere toward the rear of the room. Cuthbert found himself delivering a much more liberal applause in time with those around him, though it actually started to grow as Richard Egbert strode from the rear to the front of the stage.

'Ladies and gentlemen, I have decided to put myself forward for the position of Mayor. I think there are incidents that have gone off in this town over the past few months that have seen us lose sight of who we are, and I feel that unless the right man is elected, we could lose our way as a town and a community...'

There were mutterings from some of the female contingent about how tall he looked, how he appeared as though he could protect the town with his bare hands (strangle it more like, from his opening statement, Cuthbert thought), but the women didn't listen to the words. What they heard was the reassuring deep voice. Cuthbert cast a sideways glance at Rachel and found she too was captivated. Power, it was that simple. How else would Hitler have got laid? A touch of facial hair would give Cuthbert an air of dignity too, but as he stroked the smooth space above his top lip, he knew there was no time to wait for a moustache of Richard's calibre, the iron was hot, in fact it was scolding. He had naively thought himself a king earlier, when in fact he was still only a prince.

He stood, as the resounding cheers for Richard Egbert made it clear the headmaster was the firm favourite to be installed as the new Mayor, and after a prolonged glance skywards, Cuthbert cast up his hands as he turned to face the room. 'I shall also be nominated,' he proclaimed

There was a brief respite as everyone craned to see what Cuthbert had been looking at. It appeared to them, to be a patch of damp coming through the roof, which would have to be seen to soon or would cause structural damage, but it was clear that the anointed one saw beyond such earthly matters.

'Aye, Father Johnson for Mayor,' came a shout from Arthur Thompson, a man who, through the service of God, had recently found two pounds and three pence hidden down the back of his armchair, which he knew must have been placed there by a higher power, because it hadn't been there when his great granddad had bought it.

The remark started an avalanche, and from the din, it didn't sound as though there was a single person who wasn't backing The Vicar.

Gary Smith's attempts on the stage to restore calm were laughable. He moved across the wooden boards waving his arms like a falling Icarus, explaining the illegitimacy of it all, and by the time Cuthbert raised his hand to bring about immediate order, he was bent double and out of breath.

'What is the next step?' Cuthbert enquired, seeking out adoring female gazes. Rachel was beaming at him and that was all that mattered. This was ground breaking. The church and the state brought back together. It was like him and The Big Man were competing in a one-upmanship gift

201

giving session.

'Well,' Gary panted, 'firstly you missed the closing date for the applications, so this is all completely illegitimate...'

He was drowned out by a chorus of boos and a cry of: 'You calling the Father a bastard?'

'No, what I'm saying is...' Gary started, knowing full well that his words were useless against the mob. But he had to perform his duty as it should be carried out, because that was what mayoral integrity was about. Keith had known that, he'd always stood up for what was right, except when he'd been squirming and kicking, clutching at his throat as he turned purple on that fateful night...

'To the Mayor's office!' Gary declared, raising his finger to triumphant: 'Ayes!' leading the short procession to the adjacent building, with Cuthbert walking on air, literally. He was carried forward by the mob, who loved him. Not his job, not his uniform, but him personally. Chants of his name were still ringing out when he reached The Mayor's desk.

'You need to sign here and here,' Gary said, holding down the parchment, after handing over the inked quill, the pair maintaining the pose while Stanley Smith, The Gazette's photographer, hauled in his equipment and scurried under the black cloak trailing from the camera box.

'Say tea!' he said, as Cuthbert placed quill to parchment, the first man born outside of the town walls to be named Mayor since the great founder himself. That would require some sort of landmark, a statue shoulder to shoulder in the centre perhaps? *The Saviour*. Was it too much to call himself "The Saviour"? Maybe if he started with "Reformer" it could lead to "Saviour" later? Then there was the question of his seal, did he amalgamate the cross and the white rose? So many details to consider, but of course his main priority was working closely with the business that made the town tick. There would have to be daily meetings.

Exhausted by the number of schemes milling through his head, Cuthbert slumped into the large, leather covered chair after the last person had vacated his new office. The

Mayor, who said God didn't work in mysterious ways?

'Oh, come in,' he called, when he finally registered the knocking was coming at his door. It was pushed open by blonde Barbara Thompson. Her hair was large and it bounced as she walked. It wasn't the only part of her that did so either. She wore half an inch of make-up more than was necessary and her fingernails looked like they belonged to a cat. All her efforts detracted from her natural beauties. Cuthbert sat up straight.

'Can I help you?'

'Oh no Father, Mr. Johnson, Mayor, it's about how I can help you. I'm your personal secretary see,' Barbara said, perching herself on the edge of his desk, propping up her ample chest with her clipboard. 'Been doing this job since I was fourteen. Well I was assistant assistant for a couple of years, but I've taken care of The Mayor ever since.'

She brought her thickly caked eyelashes together in a wink.

'Err.'

'Let's just say that I know what's required in this role,' she added, licking her lips, making Cuthbert wriggle. He knew what was coming and he gawped, caught like a rabbit in the headlights, as Barbara slid to her knees, her dark roots on show, her hands fumbling under his cossack to locate what she was looking for.

Cuthbert closed his eyes and rested his hand on top of Barbara's head in the same fashion he would have sworn on The Bible when taking an oath.

'Oh Rachel, oh Rachel,' he mumbled, his words not deterring Barbara, who had no sooner glimpsed what she sought than she was blinking as her face was covered.

'Usually gives me a longer break from the paperwork than that,' she grumbled, reaching for the conveniently placed tissues. 'And I'm Barbara, not Rachel. Who is Rachel anyway?' she asked, standing, as Cuthbert considered how he went about asking for her to try again.

'Oh Rachel, it's a bit like saying "Jesus" except not as blasphemous. She was one of his forgotten disciples. It's a

Vicar thing,' he said, wondering if by technical definition he had lost at least a percentage of his virginity?

'Oh,' Barbara said, her gaze drawn back to Cuthbert's still bulging crotch. Something told her it was a good job the carpet was heavily padded.

The Cult

The matriculation of Dimar was considered delusional, dangerous and in the words of Al, bloody apple, Apollo, the start of the end of the world, for approximately five minutes. It wasn't just his linguistic ability that won the players over and guided them safely across the vast country that had him considered one of the team. Nor was it the mammoth pack lunch his mum and gran had prepared, which kept them heartily filled for two days. What won the team over without any doubts left lingering, was his worldly knowledge that put them in touch with home. An international phone code, who'd have guessed?

When they were told Cuthbert had been elected as Mayor they had all balked, ranted and definitely failed to mention the new addition to the team. William had almost gone into cardiac arrest when Edward answered the phone. Thankfully Wilma hadn't been able to make it to the phone, but had promised, through Edward, that they could have a good long discussion about everything as soon as he returned home.

Harold had expressed his surprise to Rachel about the anointment of Father Johnson to the town's hot seat, especially with Richard Egbert having been in the running, but she had reassured him that the people had elected the best man for the job.

All the while, as the news unravelled, Al stared at the sky, ready for the four horsemen. Once it became clear Dimar was with them for the long haul, he tried to promote an apartheid system, but since John wanted to play on his phone all the time, Richard II look at the pictures stored on it and everyone else use him as a translator every hour of the day, such an idea became implausible.

'Just not right, nothing worse than impurity,' was his remark, in a private meeting with Harold, aboard a train somewhere outside of Kazan.

'Al, he's proud to be a member not just of the team,

but of Skipperton,' Harold replied, more relaxed than ever having had jobs taken off his hands by the capable Russian, whose knowledge had enabled him to indulge in private phone calls with Rachel from the confines of his bedroom. He'd been relatively shy about what to say and had she required stimulation from his phrases, she would have been left frustrated with his low mumblings. Thankfully, however, she had turned in a rather detailed and theatrical story for both their benefits.

'And who wouldn't be? But if we take one, then every wog, nigger, wop, spico, Jew will be in and we won't know what Skipperton is anymore and nobody will understand each other, and all us proper, hard-working Skippertonites will be out of a job.'

'But we do have new Skippertonites, Rachel's one, she married into it. Didn't mean her whole family and friends moved with her did it?'

'So you're telling me he's a woofter who wants to marry one of us!' Al exclaimed, feeling light headed, quickly covering his arsehole with his hands.

'No, no, not at all, he has a girlfriend remember. Look, what I mean is Rachel's part of the town, and Dimar's part of this team. Perhaps you could give him one of those citizenship type tests the government uses to try and keep all the darkies out down south?' Harold suggested.

'Aye, it might go some way to showing the rest of the lads he's not like us, and when he doesn't pass, we can call him a mercenary and maybe he could wear something to show he's different and not really with us,' Al agreed happily.

To his utter disbelief and dismay, however, his forty question test was completed with the pass percentage of 100% and Dimar's name was changed to Dave Baker. There was mild confusion as to how he had passed, but it could easily be attributed to two people. One of those was Cuthbert, who had decided that if he was going to be Mayor of a town, it would be one people outside of a twenty mile radius knew about, and the other was Edward, who he had commissioned to create a Wikipedia page, one which turned out to be so comprehensive, it even had who lived at number thirteen Stew Lane and the price of a roast beef tea cake at The Caf.

'No, it's luv-er-lee luk-in lass,' Wise Owl said, trading language tips with Dave, who was still on the lookout for a flat cap.

'Yes, that's better,' William said, after Dimar had given the sentence another go, adding a wolf whistle.

'And what does this say?' Dimar asked, pointing at the Cyrillic on the bag slung over his shoulder.

'It says Mongolia,' William replied, as they made their way on to the minivan, which chugged out plumes of black smoke from its exhaust, already crammed full with the rest of the team. The driver of the vehicle, Irkmey, was a thick set, jovial, round faced gentleman for whom the van was an extension of himself. Had it been in the hands of anyone else, it would have long since been resigned to the scrap heap. He checked in the rear view mirror as he flexed his fingers inside his gloves.

'Go? he asked Harold, whose legs, like everyone else's, were hidden under a blanket.

'Aye Ian, go,' The Skipper replied, his hands curled into fists inside his batting gloves for extra warmth, another useful tip provided by Dimar.

The van's heaters kicked in a couple of hours after they had left behind the bustle and sprawl of Ulaanbaatar, by which time the roads and people had vanished, as they made their way south into The Gobi, the landscape a barren ochre filled with divots and potholes that kept any of them from drifting off for too long.

'Whoa!' Dereck called suddenly from the front, making everyone jolt forward. 'Look, it's them things with humps in the school copy of *Funny Foreign Animals*,' he added, as the whole van peered through the windscreen for a closer stare at the selection of camels.

'Photo?' Irkmey enquired.

'Yes, they will be good to post home, add to the ones

stood next to all the Lenin statues and Motherland Calls,' Dimar said, stepping out of the car with his phone ready, while the rest of the team took tentative steps towards the creatures.

'They're bloody bigger than they are in the book,' Stuart commented.

'And where are the guys with the table cloths on their heads minding them?' Alan enquired, now almost able to take a whole 500ml bottle of mouthwash without gagging.

'They stink,' said Al, 'though maybe it's not just them,' he muttered, under his breath, raising his hand to cover his face when he saw Dimar point the camera his way. He retreated to the rear of the van a good quarter of an hour before the rest of the team, who gradually moved as close to the animals as they could without scaring them into bolting off.

'Shame we haven't a pair of shears, there's enough wool on one of them to make gloves and scarves for us all,' Dereck said, re-boarding the van, which, having been re-fuelled from a canister, continued to roll on its way down through the desert scrub. Eventually, on the cusp of dusk, it came to a stop next to a line of gers and a giant herd of sheep, horses and goats. The people that appeared from the largest of the circular mobile homes did not look anything like Harold had been expecting.

'Welcome to Gerdland,' a six foot tall Messiah Doppelgänger said, hand outstretched, as his equally tall and Caucasian wife went and opened the doors to the team's evening's accommodation.

'You're not Mongolian,' Harold said, peeking inside the ger to see five beds set in a circle against the felt walls, all covered with thick blankets, while a stove stood in the middle, its thin chimney sticking out of the rooftop.

'Well now I guess we are, although this is actually a semi-autonomous region. Anyway, originally we were Austrian,' the man said, his beard a sort of orange that matched the steppe that surrounded them.

'Did you move here because you're a Nazi?' Frank

asked, as the wife shovelled dried sheep manure on top of some coal to start a fire.

'Ha! Funny! English humour, it is the best. Mr Bean is the greatest comedy ever, and then cricket, the reason you are here, that is the most wonderful game ever created.'

'If you like England so much, why not move there instead of here?' Dimar asked, watching one of the actual native Mongolian women, dressed in just a short sleeved vest and a piece of cloth acting as a skirt, milk a camel.

'Because, well,' the Messiah lookalike said, casting glances, as if someone was suddenly going to appear from beneath the steppe in a cartoon fashion. 'It's too long a story to tell. How about instead we all squeeze inside my ger, drink some vodka, talk cricket, and I'll have Urgum prepare dinner,' he added, retracting a large knife from a hip holster, as he shouted orders in Mongolian and pointed at one of the sheep.

'Well, you can't say they don't know their butchering,' Stuart said, ten minutes later, having watched the animal be sliced into segments as though it were a block of warm butter. Its head was now resting on one side of the ger, its organs were in a plastic bowl, and its body had been carved up, with chunks of meat (fat and bone) thrown into a pan of boiling water. It wouldn't be long before its wool was being worn as a jacket either. 'But what,' he added, holding up a small, plastic cup, 'the bloody hell is this I've been given?'

'Milk tea,' Irkmey said, a whole flask of it by his side.

'No Ian, no everyone else living in these tents either. Stop what you're doing and listen, this is not tea,' Stuart continued, as the Skipperton players looked into their cups of murky liquid with disgust. 'Giving it the name tea is blasphemous. It's never seen a bloody tea bag in its life.'

'It's milk, salt and water,' said Gerd, the Austrian/Mongolian Messiah. (It may be noted that this is what 11/12 of the Skipperton team thought of him as, while the one with more worldly knowledge considered the resemblance closer to Charles Manson).

'Salt lad? How many screws have you loose? You

trying to poison us all? No wonder you still live in bloody tents. Now where's the nearest shop?'

'An hour and a half that way.'

'An hour and a half?! But biscuits and...' Stuart trailed off. 'How many boxes of Skipperton do we have left?'

'Fifteen,' Dereck immediately replied.

'But, oh, it's not going to be like this for another three months is it?' Stuart said, shaking slightly. 'I think I need a lie down,' he added, retiring to his ger, where the beds felt like they were made of stone and were only long enough to fully accommodate Alan.

'Err, just before we all go and get our heads down for the night, what should one do if one requires a number two?' Paul enquired, the sight of the sheep in all its guts and glory stirring a strange feeling of repulsion in him. Was this what it felt like when you were turning queer? He side stepped deftly to catch the wet wipes thrown at him by Michaela, the Messiah's wife.

'And I go?'

'Somewhere to the left,' she answered, lifting the lid on the boiling mutton soup. 'But be quick, dinner's almost ready.'

Those not sulking about the state of the food and drink or downright refusing to go into a woggy tent filled with many wogs, stayed up drinking vodka and playing cards or jacks (with bits of bone and a piece of rusted bike chain), under the candlelight, the air around them a hazy blue as more manure was shovelled on (dried only of course).

As had become a recent habit, Harold and Dimar gave a few coaching tips and lessons prior to the game, so as to help the opposition keep the away team on their toes. They highlighted player's strengths and weaknesses to Gerd, who wrote them down on any space available in a mammoth, leather bound, book filled with miscellaneous allsorts. There were photographs, maps, doodles, scribbling in at least five languages and fragments of cloth.

'A travelling book?' Dimar enquired, on the brink of

retiring for the evening. His friendly rivalry for wickets with John and Richard II had certainly raised the bowling standards, and his batting was improving visibly with every game. Harold gave him a pat on the shoulder and snuck out of the ger into the brisk night air. He stood, hands in his pockets, his body warm with vodka, gaze tilted at the sky. There were millions of stars. It must have been similar to how the sky looked at the beginning of time. He tried to guess which one of the silver twinkles was his dad watching down on him. There wasn't any doubt his old man would be proud. This whole journey had taken everything to another level and they weren't even half way. Sure, there were moments when he wished he was in front of the wireless with his slippers on and a pot of tea sitting cosily between him and Rachel, but being on this non-stop merry-go-round of touring meant he'd be back before you could say the names of great Lancastrians, and once he was, he'd broaden Rachel's horizons like he had done with the tea, by whisking her off on holiday to somewhere that wasn't the caravan in Filey.

The Skipperton players woke to the sound of half dressed Mongolian women stoking the fires of their gers, dung in one hand, a packet of biscuits and large flask of boiling water in the other. By the time the tents were warm enough for the players to slip out from underneath their sleeping bags and blankets, there was already a small crowd gathered out on the steppe, with camels, horses and motorbikes parked beside them. They were cheering the Mongolian team's warm up, which consisted of not only the usual strokes, throws and bowling looseners, but also a jog over to a mound of rocks covered in blue tape, which they danced around, flapping their arms like birds.

'You know it's like Father Johnson just picked the queerest places he could find. I mean what the bloody hell is that? If that Austrian, Mongolian, Jesus guy tries to tell me they're Maypole Dancing, then I'm going to shove,' Stuart stopped, for there were no poles or trees on the horizon to be grabbed. 'I'll shove his bloody bat up his arse. From the look of things, though, I think he'd bloody enjoy it,' he added, his comment giving Alan some interesting ideas.

'Now let's not get worked up, could be some sort of black magic scheme they're trying to pull,' Harold said, considering himself for a few overs with the ball at some stage, as he lead his team forward for the toss, unable to see where the pitch was. 'Morning,' he said to Gerd, whose all white attire made him appear even more spiritual. 'So where exactly are we playing?' he asked, scouting the horizon for something, anything, resembling a boundary.

'We play here,' Gerd said, pointing to his feet, adorned in some sturdy sport sandals. 'But you see we haven't been able to paint in the boundary because we had to use the brushes for culinary purposes.'

'So?'

'So no fours or sixes?'

'Right,' Harold replied, by now finding that he was more surprised if everything was as it should be at the start of a game. 'Sounds fair enough I guess, so let's get on with the toss then.'

'We have no toss. There are no coins in Mongolian currency,' Gerd pointed out, a little sheepishly.

'Joke this Harold.'

'Need to teach these a lot more than cricket.'

'Wogs. Niggers. Spics.'

'Wouldn't have bloody well happened in Europe this.'

'So how do we decide who bats first then?' Harold asked, unfazed by the mumblings from a section of his team.

'It's the Mongolian custom to wrestle.'

'Seriously? Your biggest versus my biggest?'

'No, all players wrestle at once and the team with the most victors decides what they want to do first,' Gerd said. 'And since you are the guests, you can choose who your players wrestle,' he added, calling over his team, who though may have had far more experience, were giving away quite a bit in reach and weight.

'It's the first person on their back that loses?' Harold asked, confident of an overall victory, matching himself with

Gerd, whose every move was monitored by the small band of supporters.

'That's correct,' the opposing skipper said, flapping his arms to cheers of support. A couple of the crowd were waving pictures of him, their zeal making Harold a little jealous that his captaincy wasn't shown as much appreciation. The most he was rewarded with was a large "woo-hoo" from Rachel when he went out to bat, and that was only if she hadn't nipped inside for tea and biscuits.

'They're my followers,' Gerd explained, grabbing hold of Harold's chunky knit blazer by the shoulders to signal the start of the bout. 'That's the reason I'm here. I'm still not quite sure what they believe exactly, even after four years,' he continued, his balance and poise not faltering as Harold dragged him this way and that, not really knowing what to do. He'd never been in any sort of scrap in his life. 'What I am sure of is that I'm their cult leader. They bring me offerings and I don't seem to have to do anything except be myself. It's all very strange, but it certainly beats the office I used to work in,' Gerd concluded, bringing in a leg sweep to send Harold tumbling onto dried manure, much to the delight of the followers, who cared little that Skipperton claimed an overall victory of 8-4.

'Your cult? I can think of another word beginning with C,' Harold muttered, wiping off the sheep droppings, as he was helped to his feet by Dimar, since Gerd was too busy allowing his faithful to touch his beard and hair. He signalled with a twist of his finger, on his return to the "pitch", that they were all crazy. 'Oh, and I forgot to add, as you can see we have no wickets either, so we usually just use a pile of rocks,' he added, rolling his shoulders.

'We're batting first, so you can put feathers down if you want, because they won't be moving,' Harold said, promoting himself to opener.

Despite the fact The Skipper kept his promise and he and Erik completed the innings on their own, the whole team arrived back in Ulaanbaatar exhausted. They'd been forced to bring in runners for runners, with sixes and sevens common and tens not out of the ordinary.

As a treat for helping him achieve his highest score of the tour and a team total of 418, Harold bought everyone a chocolate brownie from a bakery called *Wendy's* at a price and standard that would have made The Caf balk.

'You know, while we're here, it'd probably be a good idea to buy presents for home and that,' Dereck said, having done many calculations. 'Ian said something about a black market,' he added, rubbing his hands with glee. 'And I know everyone's knackered and we've a mammoth train journey tomorrow, so I don't mind making purchases on behalf of people,' he continued, removing his paper and pencil. 'Wise Owl, let's start with you, because we all know you'll be needing something to sweeten the missus,' he practically sang, wetting the end of the pencil with his tongue, signalling to Irkmay that he should go and start the engine, scribbling down items he knew were being thought of, but not suggested.

'Be back soon,' he concluded, trotting to the van.

But he wasn't.

'What do you bloody well mean "Dereck stay black market"?' Harold asked Irkmey, who had dumped a mountin of items on three tables. The Mongolian driver stared back at Harold in confusion. He knew his English wasn't great, but he really didn't think it needed any more of an explanation.

'Dereck stay black market sell,' he replied, rummaging through the goods he'd returned with for a fox fur scarf. 'Present,' he added, the item almost batted out of his hands in anger, except seeing how soft and warm it looked, Harold grabbed hold of it instead. After all, it was seven below outside.

'Take me to him,' Harold demanded, his neck suddenly feeling like he'd thrown a hot water bottle round it. 'And pass me that matching hat too.'

The market was gargantuan. It had to hold every object that had ever been created. It was impossible to tell where it started and where it ended. The alleys within it sprawled down rabbit warrens like *Alice in Wonderland*, and yet Harold didn't need to ask Irkmey where he'd left Dereck, he simply followed the bulk of the crowd and sure enough, within minutes, he was standing before a Yorkshire foghorn.

'Honestly, it's like I'm giving blood it's such a deal.'

'No, you don't want two, you'll want three of those.'

'Matching, you have to have the matching set or else there's no point in having any of it at all.'

In Dereck's hands, a flurry of money flowed. He looked like one of those strange God statues they'd come across with loads of eyes, except their smiles had been serene, while his was wild.

'Dereck, Oi!' Harold shouted, confusing his player, since in his new attire he blended in with the rest of the crowd.

'Ah Gaffa,' Dereck said finally, unable to shove his roll of notes into one pocket. Even when he'd shared them between two, he could still feel the stitches straining. 'See you like the new gear I bought you.'

'That's beside the point,' Harold said, having decided from a passing glance in a mirror that he looked like some ancient king, around the time when the capital had been in its proper place, York, Yorkshire. 'What are you doing telling Ian that you're staying? Have you lost the plot?'

'Exact opposite actually Gaffa. One second. No refunds lad, I saw how you were yanking it. Can do you another for a third off, but that's the best you're going to get. Lovely, see you around. I think I've found my plot, my own piece of land, this spot, right here.'

Harold looked at his player like he was deranged.

'But we don't belong here, we're European,' Harold said, watching Dereck's hands work of their own accord.

'Oh by all means Gaffa, I don't plan to stay here forever, but for now, this is my calling. I can't explain it, well I can, I've just earned more in three hours than I would in a week at the post office, but it's not just about the money.'

Harold raised an eyebrow.

'Not just about it, honest. I feel free. I feel happy. And

I'm teaching the heathens, passing on my wisdom. I know it's not cricket, but it feels like my purpose is here. We came away to banish the ghosts and teach the world, and I haven't thought about Redillian since Volgograd.'

'But they're still out there!' Harold exclaimed, experiencing déjà vu, knowing this conversation was going to end in the same way it had done in Richard Egbert's office.

'Aye, somewhere,' Dereck said, waving his hands, 'and they always will be. Do you think beating this Indian team will really be the end of it all?'

'So that's it, you're deserting us?' Harold said, ignoring the question, unable to describe his feelings towards Dereck's decision. Shame? Anger? Guilt? None of them fit like they should have done. It was strange, but he almost felt a twinge of pride.

'Not deserting no. I know the itinerary and I wouldn't be taking a "holiday" if we hadn't recruited Dave. He's a player Gaffa, and he deserves more game time, all of us can see that. Honestly, everything will be alright, you know that.'

Harold stared down at his feet. His toes were starting to freeze. He gave a little stamp. Was there such a thing as fur inner soles?

'You know what? I don't know what I know anymore,' he mumbled.

The Bishop

It was amazing how rapidly a town could be transformed under the right leadership. A job boom had been created, mainly in the public sector admittedly (did one man really require eighteen secretaries? He did if his title was The Lord Mayor and Overseer of All), but there was also a construction crew working round the clock on a new building grand enough to combine both church and state, while artisans were picking up their minimum wage crafting statues of the man who was going to make the town a city.

     Cuthbert had yet to divulge the full extent of his plans, which were drawn neatly on a large mind map, items ticked off and new ones added every part of the day as the scope of his project grew. How was he financing all these endeavours? By exporting goods; expertly crafted hand made goods were being sold on across the country at a price that would have had their creators dreaming of early retirement.

     Since this was his secret, however, there was a happy buzz around the town as everyone thrived and felt the benefits of the economic boom. Even better was the fact that everyone had been in contact with the team (which Cuthbert had of course been given credit for). Yes, at the present time, had any one of the citizens (except the headmaster of the school) been asked, they would have said that nothing could go wrong.

Cuthbert reclined in his chair, stroking the foundations of a moustache that ran the length of his lip. The hairs were fine, thin and smooth. He reminded himself of Clark Gable in *Gone with the Wind*. He checked the second hand on his watch: one minute seven seconds. He tried to focus on his agenda for the rest of the morning, on the boring details, there had to be some boring details, it couldn't all be...

'Oh yes!' he grunted, as the lower part of his body spasmed. 'One minute seventeen, a new record!' he added, grinning proudly, his goal of two minutes coming into focus. With his current rate of progress, it meant he was a fortnight away from making his final move on Rachel, who he had dined with at lunch or dinner every day, to the point that they now chose two meals and shared. The first time she handed over her fork with her plate, he had pretended to drop it so as to lap at her dried saliva like a rabid dog. She was going to become The Lord Mayoress and Overseer of all, and the consummation would be fireworks for them both. That was an idea: fireworks for the opening of the Overseer's Church, huge bombastic ones for the people and The Lord.

'I need a hundred, no a thousand fireworks! The biggest anyone can make,' Cuthbert said, zipping himself up before reaching for the phone. 'Oh and tell Lucy Thompson I'll require her in five,' he added. He waited for Gemma Baker to give a nod of understanding and close the door behind her, before dialling Tesco's Yorkshire Development Office to see if the manager had received his email detailing Morrison's counter offer to set up a supermarket where the Town Hall presently stood. Progress: every single day he moved the town forward, all for the good of his people. This was the age of enlightenment and he was Hobbes, Locke and Smith. From the number of hits accumulated on travel websites – thanks to Edward's computer skills, he was going to have to set up a tourist board soon, and he'd already had enquiries about being twinned with Tehran.

'Listen, it's simple,' he said, barely above a whisper, as he heard footsteps come to a halt at the door, 'you raise your bid beyond that and it's yours. We can sign the contract next week,' he concluded, placing the phone carefully back in its cradle.

'Okay then you sexy little lynx, you know what you need to do to please The Lord,' he called, thinking it might be simpler if he simply abandoned his trousers of a morning once he'd set foot inside the office.

The door opened slowly.

'Tell me, what does one need to do to please The Lord?' the voice boomed, coming not from a five foot brunette in a micro skirt and pigtails (the official public service uniform), but a six foot two inch man filling the door frame.

'Bishop Basher, I mean Bishop Bashir, what a delightful surprise,' Cuthbert said, catching his trousers on the slide as he jumped up. 'Just had a huge breakfast,' he continued, patting his stomach, 'wanted to sample all of the great ingredients The Lord has supplied us with. I can have something rustled up for you now if you like? You look like the type that would appreciate it. Ah Lucy Sekserlinks, yes Lucy, I'm talking to you. Could you go and grab us a 'The Caf' from The Caf? Thank you,' he added, giving The Bishop a roll of his eyes that said: "staff these days".

'Strange attire for a curate,' The Bishop said, moving around the office.

'Yes,' Cuthbert replied, standing by his desk. 'Unfortunately she hung it out on the line last night only for it to rain. Had to borrow what she could from her younger sister.'

'Hmm,' The Bishop mumbled, halting by an enlarged framed copy of the front page of The Gazette, celebrating Cuthbert's appointment as Mayor, which, to increase its value, Cuthbert had signed. 'Of course you know as well as I do that a curate works in a church, and this is not a church. I went to the church earlier, but all I found was a young boy on Google Maps trying to locate the nearest McDonalds.'

'Ah yes, we've temporarily located here while restoration work is completed. There was some asbestos in the tiles you see,' Cuthbert said, opening the drinks cabinet, as The Bishop finally seated himself, his vast weight forcing a creak from the chair.

'You know Cuthbert, when I started in this line of service as a boy, I always thought I could make the world right, return it to a glorious state of harmony, where people believed again, had faith in God and the good,' The Bishop said, placing his hands above the glass to stop Cuthbert from pouring any whiskey into it. 'But as the years went by, I began to realise that it is a job like any other. Sadly people have more faith in money than they do in everything else,' he continued, extracting a hip flask: 'It's strange how people think our line of work and business can't mix, as if making a living from the truth is somehow contradictory. Oh, it's okay to keep afloat charities, each one of them out for their own single minded cause, but us, the ones who are looking at the bigger picture, trying to save everyone, not just those stuck unjustly in prison or a couple of old dogs, no, apparently we are expected to survive outside the world that has been manufactured. And one day we will, we will be up in the Heaven that was made. You understand don't you?'

Cuthbert didn't have a clue, but he nodded sagely as he sipped his single malt.

'Well then, you can see the upsetting predicament I now find myself in,' The Bishop continued, forced to pause at the arrival of his breakfast, which Lucy had to cradle, the polystyrene box transparent from grease.

'Doesn't get healthier,' Cuthbert remarked, sourcing a fork.

'I'll bet,' The Bishop replied, having seen the life expectancy stats on Wikipedia. Still, he stabbed into a sausage as he returned to his spiel.

'Yes, awkward and delicate is how I'd describe it, and it's society in general that's tying my hands, but you see the church can't afford anymore bad press, and having a megalomaniac take over a town isn't going to have people singing our praises.'

The Bishop looked Cuthbert dead in the eyes.

'The megalomaniac is you, Mr. Johnson.'

'But they voted me in!' Cuthbert protested. 'I didn't ask for it, I was chosen.'

'Ah, the why's and the how's, you know as well as I do Cuthbert that it's only the results that matter. There'll be people all across the country calling you a fraud, claiming you manipulated the masses through hypnosis or some such other hocus pocus.'

'I've done no such thing,' Cuthbert balked, 'it's all down to good old fashioned charisma.'

The Bishop cast a doubtful stare, as he wrapped a piece of bacon around his fork that was so thick he wondered if it wasn't a piece of steak.

'I'll cut to the chase shall I? You're going to step down from your position of vicar, and the money you're using to create three metre statues of yourself is going to be funnelled discretely and directly into the church's coffers. If you don't you'll be looking at time for embezzlement and money laundering and I think you know how they treat men like you in the slammer.'

'But my power over them comes through the uniform! They fear me. They fear Him. I can't just be The Mayor,' Cuthbert said, picturing himself surrounded by twenty stone plus topless men snorting as they asked for the love of God.

'But Vicar, you just told me you were elected thanks to your charisma. I'm sure you'll be able to think of something,' The Bishop said with a grin, topping himself up from his hip flask.

'And what if...what if I refuse?' Cuthbert said.

The Bishop gave a small shrug of his shoulders, allowing the gravy to soak into every pore of the fried bread.

'I wouldn't like to give the exact details, but let's put it this way, there won't be anyone around to protect you. The Lord can't be on both our sides can he? I'll give you twelve hours before I start making calls and sending e-mails.' The Bishop stood. 'Don't worry, I know where the exit is. Been a pleasure Cuthbert, splendid breakfast. I look forward to hearing from you,' he added, moving across to the drink cabinet to top himself up, before turning on his heel to leave Cuthbert alone and dejected.

'Err, are you ready for me now?' Lucy Thompson asked, peeping round the door.

Cuthbert really should have ordered them all in for a final flourish, claim his money's worth, but he needed to think without distractions.

'Maybe later,' he sighed, already asking himself the question that had plagued humanity since Eve had passed away: was he better to have loved and lost? Did any of it really constitute love? And he wasn't losing it, it was being taken away. So was it better to lose it or have it snatched away? He guessed the latter since that meant he could hate someone else rather than himself. What was he doing? He wasn't going to come up with an ingenious plan, and he would have plenty of time to mope and moan later, eternity in fact.

'Actually Lucy,' he shouted, running to the door. 'You're required! As for everyone else in this office, expect to put in a large shift of overtime.'

Collapsing on his bed with ten minutes of the deadline remaining, Cuthbert was surprised he hadn't turned to a pile of ash, since he doubted there was any juice left in his body. He rolled over, raising his hand, feeling the muscles around his ribs strain. It felt like he'd cracked his pelvis too, but he'd battled on through every available second. His finger lazily spun the dial. His decision was neither of those The Bishop had offered. He was going to resign completely, disappear in the dead of night, and start afresh abroad with the bundle of money he'd removed from the safe. He'd contemplated leaving without the call, but he had to let The Bishop think he had him scared, he didn't want the police arresting him at the airport. As for Rachel, she would remain an incomplete piece of the puzzle; like the gold leaf finishing on his statues, the Great Overseer building, and the design of his new uniform (a slender white fitted jump suit, with a gossamer cape that billowed at a whisper of wind.)

'Hello.'

'Hello,' Cuthbert said, 'I need to speak to Bishop

Bashir.'

'Bishop Bashir no longer works here,' the person said coldly.

'What do you mean he no longer works here? Has he been promoted?'

'I cannot comment on that. Can I ask the purpose of your call?'

'Is this some kind of joke?' Cuthbert asked, listening for the click of a tape running in the background that would capture his confession and be used against him in court. 'The Bishop gave me this number on a church visit this morning and told me, The Lor...Vicar Johnson, to call him this evening, which I am now doing. What is going on exactly?'

'Ah Vicar,' the person said, going down to a whisper, 'my apologies. It's just that there's been a lot of calls from the press trying to get a story, when there's no story to get. He's innocent.'

'Innocent of what?' Cuthbert asked, too tired to think ahead of what he was being told.

'Of it all,' the person replied. 'They've tried to frame him, charged him with drink driving and then planted all the other material on him. It's another of The Lord's tests for us, trying to see if we desert The Bishop in his hour of need, which I mean we have, because he's been sacked pending the trial, but everyone's confident that forensics won't find a scrap of DNA evidence on all the stuff that was hidden in the boot of his car. If anything you know, his only crime is caring about them all too much.'

'He's going to jail?' Cuthbert blurted.

'If that is what The Lord wills.'

'For how long?'

'He'd be looking at a stretch of ten to fifteen.'

'Ha!' Cuthbert exclaimed, almost yanking the phone from its socket as he jumped from the bed, one finger raised to the sky. 'You know what this means don't you?'

'More people asking for money. It's like they think a few thousand pounds can restore their virginity. Makes them sound like a bunch of prostitutes to me. Sinners.'

'It means Cuthbert Johnson is the chosen one. He can do whatever he pleases. God is on his side. He really does exist.'

Without waiting for a response, Cuthbert hung up. He could feel the aura of protection pulsing around him. This was for real; the cape, the title, Rachel. He wanted him to have them all.

The Tea

If only life was all about statistics, the members of Skipperton cricket club would have been content as the Harlem Globetrotters. Each player had scored over five hundred runs, with Stuart and Harold both notching over two thousand plus apiece. The bowlers had collected so many five-wicket hauls they had more balls than apples in an orchard. Most importantly, they were still unbeaten, untouchable, a class apart from their competitors.

The problem was that there was more to life than results and runs, and after four months on the road, every player was feeling it. The three weeks across the many plains of China had come with several low points. The fact that they hadn't been able to call home had been the start of the downward spiral. One minute their loved ones were a finger-punch away and the next there was a female voice informing them that the number they were dialling no longer existed. Dimar couldn't explain it and informed them that the web page he'd collected all his information from had been shut down too. It was as if the town had vanished. Instinct told the older players Thatcher and her power cuts were back, but apparently the Iron Lady was nowhere near Downing Street.

The second source of frustration had been their inability to read or speak to anyone. Everything had been written in an infant's squiggle, which Al claimed meant that Dimar was now useless and could bugger off back to where he'd come from. The rest of the team were quick to show their support for him, however, having no problems with someone who showed such loyalty and determination to the cause. What they did want to debate was whether Dereck should be allowed to simply re-join the team after he turned up ten minutes before the game against Labrang Monastery Monks without any explanation, luggage or money.

Harold no longer seemed to be manager and skipper, but head of customer relations. All he heard were complaints and conflicts. Wise Owl constantly moaned his back was stiff from the beds on the Chinese trains and refused to take one on the highest bunk. Al wanted his money back after an excursion to the Great Wall since: 'it wasn't any bloody better than Skipperton's' and was: 'yet another sign of wog culture being thought of as more spectacular just because it was impressive they'd managed to slot some stones together at all.'

Stuart and Frank had fallen out with Paul, taking offence at his willingness to sample dog and cat as cuisine, since how were they supposed to trust him around their terriers now? The wicket keeper had tried to assure them it was a one off and he would be sticking to turtle, as the meat of man's closest allies was a little rough and stringy, but it hadn't stopped Frank drawing up plans for some reinforced partitioning.

Alan hadn't actually vocalised what was depressing him, but he'd looked the epitome of glum for longer than most. He was at his worst around the time Erik had chaperoned Dimar, Richard II and John to a "karaoke bar" in Shanghai. It was possible that he didn't approve of that type of activity, but Harold couldn't blame those lads. He'd have snuck off himself if it wasn't for the thought that if he did anything untoward, his actions would be mirrored by Rachel.

Alongside all these issues, there was also the problem of the Chinese themselves, who matched every pro, with a greater con.

Pro: they dressed properly, wearing hand stitched black trousers and plain black shoes constructed of five parts that made them look like they'd walked straight out of Skipperton market. Con: they would eat God knew what (every living creature on God's Earth it appeared) and chuck the bones/remnants/peelings on the floor instead of in a bin.

Pro: they were all for smoking anywhere and everywhere, good old fashioned cigarettes too without the long filters. Con: they were more inclined to hawk up everything that the cigarettes had cleaned from their lungs and deposit it amongst the duck bones and black egg shells.

Pro: their food was bloody reasonable. Rice and noodles were a snip. In one restaurant they'd paid twenty pence for a bucket of rice that had sufficed for half a team, and out in the west they'd discovered cheap flat breads cooked in outdoor stoves called naans, which had intrigued Frank and John no end. Con: their attitude to queuing was downright hideous, especially when it came to trains. Not wise to the fact that there was limited space for bags and that most people carried their homes with them, it meant that on the first train from Beijing to Datong they were forced to sit with their bags piled high on their knees.

However, that all seemed like a free roast dinner with a mountain of trimmings in comparison to their journey from deep in the west at Urumqi to Leshan. Finding the train practically full when purchasing tickets the same day they were due to leave, they had been forced to split the journey between six beds and six standing allocations.

'Hell.' 'A bloody zoo.' 'On par with a day trip to Wigan.' were just a selection of comments muttered by the shell shocked players following their twelve hour stint in a carriage so crammed full with bags that they were also packed floor to ceiling in one of the two available toilets. (The toilets across the country were, incidentally, the worst sight any of the players had ever seen, and Wise Owl had once accidentally driven down Manchester high street). Those spending the night leg of the journey shin deep in the bones of chicken feet, phlegm, cigarette butts, empty pot noodles and baby's urine, were also locked inside the carriage, since it was apparent the Chinese guards suspected that the lowest class would try to sneak out and steal a bed or a chair.

A little light relief did come a day after the nightmarish journey during the warm up against The Red Communist Men's Athletic and Culture League XI of Emei Shan when, out of the blue, Al suddenly yelled: 'a monkey's got our ball, a bloody monkey's grabbed our ball!'

Since it wasn't unusual for a side to be without full equipment and have items loaned to them, the rest of the team ignored the cry, expecting Al to walk to the kit bag to grab an antiseptic wet wipe, but instead he raised his cry again, as audibly distressed as if it were himself and not the ball that was being touched by one of the opposition.

'No lads, you don't understand, a real bloody monkey's making off with our ball,' Al cried, finally grabbing the attention of the rest of the team in time for them to witness a rather aggressive Tibetan Macaque wave the ball manically, having failed in its attempt to eat it.

Over the next couple of days, the jokes were incessant, revolving around Harold's desire to sign the monkey since he could speak another language and was lightning in the field. There were also witty suggestions that no-one would notice if The Skipper traded in Alan for the monkey, since the pair were the same size and equally hairy, due to the fact that the depressed Gnome had forsaken shaving.

Suddenly, happier days looked like they were on the horizon, and for thirty-six hours nothing but laughter was emitted, but that was all, for in Chengdu, disaster struck.

Frank stared into the empty box of Skipperton. He tipped it upside down and patted it. Everyone searched through their bags and pockets. They eyed any bulges with suspicion, they removed clothes, they reached inside gloves, but the fact remained that they had run out of tea.

Stuart sat on a chair in the changing room shaking his head in disbelief. No one knew what to say. What could be said in such a situation to make anyone feel better? Paul took the box from Frank's trembling hands and took it apart until it was flat. He flipped it over, checked underneath it. Huddled in a corner, knees tucked into his chest, Al wept. Harold looked across hopefully at Erik, expecting him to perform some kind of miracle, but when the batter removed his hands from his pockets, he held phone numbers, poems and other souvenirs, not tea bags.

There wasn't one of them who could say they hadn't known it was inevitable. Each player had woken with a start, haunted by the prospect, having dreamt the nightmare scenario, but for it to actually happen, to be in *that* moment, you couldn't prepare yourself for it.

'What are we going to...?'

'How will we...?'

Half mumbled questions lingered in the air.

The only person who wasn't going through the grieving process was Dimar, though by looking at him it would have been impossible to tell. He knew what was required to stay on the tour, which is why he drank coffee in secret, and then licked the end of a cigarette to mask the smell. With heavy hands, he flicked through the guide-book.

'Wait a second lads!' he blurted, jumping from his seat. 'Chengdu is the tea capital of China! There are tea houses galore!' he announced, to wild cheers and a scramble for the subway station.

The quaint, peaceful, practically sedate atmosphere of Jin's teahouse, was destroyed as the players fought their way through the front door, calling out for their beloved drink, their arms outstretched in an attempt to let the vapours diffuse through their pores. What was brought to them, however, was not what they were expecting.

'That's not bloody tea.'

'That lad is some grass in hot water.'

'Jia? Jia? No sunshine, tea, tea.'

'It's gone off. Look, the mould's taken over completely.'

'Excuse gentlemen,' a Chinese man said, rising from his squatted position. 'Jia is Chinese word for tea.'

'Oh is it now?' Stuart said, unable to stop his body from shaking. 'Because it looks to me like it's the word for bollocks. Don't think we don't know what tea looks like, Mr Foreigner. I was drinking it before you were born, and never, ever has it been a clump of green sticks. So tell the lad serving that we can't be fobbed off with this bloody nonsense and we'll have the same as everybody else is having, real bloody tea with milk and half a sugar.'

The Chinese man picked up his glass and passed it over for inspection, making players dart to other tables to open pots and swill customers' cups in despair.

'You see, Jia, green tea,' the man said, his drink thrust back at him, as some players sobbed and others swayed.

'Honestly Harold, I don't think I can take any more of this country,' William said, unable to control his shivers. 'Just when you think it's going to do you a favour, it ends up slapping you in the face.'

'But what about our double header in Hong Kong?' Harold said.

'Do we still own it?'

'No, we handed it back for some reason.'

'Then it'll just be more of the bloody same.'

'Aye,' came the chorus. 'No more of this. Let's move on to the next country. Surely they'll have tea.'

In terms of naive mistakes, it ranked up there with Oedipus'. Although Hong Kong was no longer British owned, it still bore strong resemblances to its former controlling nation, and though they wouldn't have picked up boxes of Skipperton, they could certainly have stocked up on lesser quality, household name brands they were familiar with. Instead, they entered the north of Vietnam.

The five men in front of them at the border showed their passports and walked through into the country. It was hard to tell their nationality, but what was certain was that no money had changed hands at the counters.

'One dollar,' came the chorus from the row of border guards, sitting behind a wall of Perspex, their uniforms shiny from the collars to the buttons.

'No, we've already paid for our visas. V-I-S-A-S,' Harold said, prodding the Perspex.

'One dollar,' erupted the guards again, in a slightly higher pitch.

'For what?' Dimar enquired.

The level of vocabulary of the guards was limited.

'But those five lads didn't pay anything,' Dereck said, pointing to the men currently boarding a bus.

The guards weren't interested.

'Thieving bastards,' Stuart muttered, as Harold forked over twelve dollars, the players moving forward at a reserved pace, energy levels low. They'd managed to buy three tea bags from an English woman on a train who'd been storing them in her glasses case and aside from that had opted for hot chocolate as a temporary replacement.

Once fully into their seventeenth country, they were greeted by a swarm of money changers and other hawkers offering drinks, sweets, rides and tours.

'This is how a cow pat must feel,' Richard II remarked, as the constant shaking of his head was ignored.

'Do not come any closer,' Al warned, from within the midst of the players, trying to shut all his senses down, three packets worth of wet wipes covering the un-clothed sections of his body.

'Yes, but how much for twelve?' Wise Owl asked, attempting to sort out tickets to Hanoi, as Harold sought to exchange his Yuan, the pair of them liaising with Dave, who had both the guide-book and a currency convertor application on his phone. Admiring the natives' aggressive selling techniques, Dereck cast an eye on all the money changing hands, listened to the numbers being touted, then shook his head.

'I don't bloody well think so,' he said, to the touts. 'Those tickets cost twenty thousand Dong. I've just seen that lad pay over there by the bus,' he added, pointing to a local. 'That's a mark up of three hundred percent you're charging. That's bloody outrageous. And as for you,' he added, picking out a begging child alternating between the words "dollar" and "money", whilst tugging at the players' arms, 'bugger off and go and earn a living.'

The child's reaction was to spit on the floor, stick up his middle finger and announce: 'fuck off foreigners.'

'Foreigners!' Al balked, taking a step forward, then sharply retreating. 'We're not foreigners. You're the bloody foreigner, you little Spic Jew,' he added, as the rest of the players stood perplexed.

'Think you've said enough for now Al,' Harold whispered, sensing the rising tension, as he acknowledged there was no way out for them except to go with one of the ticket sellers.

'American scum.'

'You what?' Richard II asked, as insults flew in their direction over the top of Al's sermon.

'You pay now. Pay.'

It was all rather dizzying. At least in China they'd never felt unwelcome.

'Foreigners?! Have you lost what tiny minds you have? How dare you treat us like this!'

Arguments and insults erupted all over, but at least it meant everyone was sticking together. It wasn't the type of team bonding session Harold had been contemplating, but uniting against a common enemy was cheaper than a knees up and cards night.

'I tell you what Gaffa,' Dereck huffed, red with rage. 'Once we get home we need to start charging one price for us and one for the foreigners.'

'We already do,' Harold pointed out, watching Al attempt to shake off the word foreigner.

'No, I mean real foreigners,' Dereck said, turning back to the ticket seller.

'Hey,' John commented, waggling two fingers on each hand in every direction. 'I thought that German guy in the karaoke bar said the Vietnamese were nice?'

He received a shake of the head from Dimar.

'No, he said everyone in South East Asia apart from the North Vietnamese were pleasant. He claimed the ones up here were sly, money grabbing bandits,' he replied.

'A dollar each? Sunshine, you should be paying us to come into your poxy hole of a country.'

The Vietnamese were suddenly throwing insults at the back of Yorkshire heads, as on either side of the border, the two groups of players huddled tight into their respective teams.

'You can't put this charge on everyone, because

232

there's no way they'd have paid in,' shouted Kevin, the Redillian skipper.

'What's the problem? Don't they accept giros?' Richard II yelled.

'On second thoughts, now we've seen what you let into your country, I think we'll bypass.'

'Hey look lads, China's still full of filth. Must be a lot of people with hideous diseases to cough that lot up.'

'Aye,' John piped up. 'But should we really be surprised to see them bribing officials so things go their way?'

'You what?' asked the Skipperton players, not privy to this information.

'Ah,' John mumbled sheepishly, as Richard II shook his head and stared down at his feet. 'I forgot to tell you, the only reason they beat us, is because they paid off the umpire.'

What was said during the next fifteen minutes was heard only by the individual, and had it not been for police intervention, there was no telling when it might have ended.

What the Skipperton players found strange was that although they felt better, they weren't filled with a sense of euphoria. All that pain and bitterness they'd been carrying inside them didn't suddenly disappear. Some of it had depleted during the tour, and a little more had evaporated at that official announcement they'd been cheated. But they'd always told themselves that was the case anyway, and the result still remained. Even if someone went back and re-wrote the history books, what good would it do? They couldn't go to the final, couldn't alter the decision they'd made not to play in the third round at Bolton and forfeit the chance to create history.

If anything, coming now, without a cup of tea in sight, it incensed Harold even further.

'Not that we'd accept any apologies from you bunch of cheating bloody queers,' he said, nose to nose with his opposite number, the pair agreeing to do all the talking. 'But you didn't have to follow us all the way out here to give it, so you can bugger off back home now.'

'Us follow you? How's that possible when we were at Russian traitor boy's house before you?'

'Most likely because you bottled out of a few harder ties, didn't have the right currency on you to match fix.'

'More like we didn't stop by at every farm on the way that had sheep. And we're not bothered about quantity, only teams that make it competitive. Why else do you think we skipped Yorkshire?'

'Because you wanted to avoid humiliation. We're good to go right here, right bloody now.'

'Oh, if only we had the time to spare for a morale boosting knock about and to barter a few pence off our bus tickets, but we've a game tomorrow and a flight to catch after that.'

'A flight?'

'That's right, on a plane, you know? Actually you wouldn't would you? Too tight to fork out for anything more than a walk. Still sending your air mail by pigeon?'

'Air mail?' Harold chuckled, glad he'd listened in to his younger players' conversations with Dimar. 'E-mails nowadays lad, though I suppose you still send postcards back so your families can wallpaper their council houses.'

'You know what sunshine, once we're back from India and you've swam across the channel, a re-match is on.'

'India?' Harold asked.

'Yeah, Darjeeling. Off to beat a side that haven't lost a game in four years,' Kevin said, cracking his knuckles to cheers from his team.

'No you're not,' Harold said, almost choking.

'I think you'll find we are, day after tomorrow.'

Silence fell upon The Skipper. The grail, the conquest, the reason they'd braved squat toilets, a day without tea, months without a Yorkshire, was about to be snatched away from them by what could only be described as The Plague. Well it wasn't going to happen.

'Right then, well good luck, we'll see you at our place in a couple of months, assuming you don't pay a better team

234

to take your place,' he said, backing away, twisting his head to whisper in Dimar's ear: 'I want tickets booked on a flight to India tonight.'

'But that'll cost a fortune!'

Harold took a deep breath: 'I don't care,' he said. 'Just do it.'

The Free

Having taken time for contemplation, Cuthbert had decided that although The Bishop had been wrong about a lot of things (allegedly), he had been right to be concerned about questions from the rest of the country regarding the legality of his regime. In a dream, Cuthbert had not only been hounded by photographers and reporters jabbing their microphones in his face (it was a good job there wasn't a psychologist in town for him to see), but the people of his town had deserted him en masse. They had believed the rumours, they had asked questions, and they had emigrated to local hamlets. Not one of them had stood up at his trial as a character witness and in his dream he had been dragged out of the courtroom kicking and screaming.

Upon waking, his solution had been to place men on the north and south entrances of the town walls. He had cameras fixed above the gates to scan the horizon, and those wishing to visit the town for a spot of lunch, or wanting to break their journey by stretching their legs, were informed that there had been an outbreak of foot-and-mouth disease and the area was quarantined. Of course had they come for some local jam, a knitted garment or a highly crafted wooden ornament, there were stalls outside the city walls that they could browse.

As for those on the inside wishing to go out, a permit had to be obtained. Only four were applied for in the first fortnight, and out of those, only Alan Timothy Thompson pushed for his to be granted. This was due to the fact that the line of questioning regarding the purpose for vacating the town (however briefly) led to the other three applicants believing they would be labelled as traitors and would face excommunication from the town.

To make certain the farmer wasn't meeting a national reporter, Edward had been sent along on the drive up to The Dales for the collection of specialized chemical agents. To ensure that Edward wasn't in league with Alan, Edward had worn a wire so Cuthbert could listen to all that was divulged. So happy was he with the three hours' surveillance of the pair, that Cuthbert introduced further secret programmes to keep the town safe from intrusion by the media. Blocking off all routes from the outside world was the priority, and he did it by re-directing all external post to the Mayoral/Overseer office and scrapping all planned internet connections, except the one leading to his office. He also told the inhabitants that he was going to change their telephone numbers, and that this was a job that required a maintenance man to visit every house: a ruse so a bug could be planted and activated when key words were spoken.

During one of his newly arranged bi-nightly sermons, he praised the concerns voiced by Richard Egbert and agreed that the fabric of their society could not be allowed to change. He explained that only last week he had fended off a lucrative offer from a supermarket chain, in order to keep the town free from the modern ills and inconveniences that multi-national corporations brought with them. Freedom, Cuthbert claimed, was what made Skipperton special and unique, the gateway to its own world.

Where else were people free to attend evening meetings in an Overseer building to discuss whatever they wanted? How good did it feel to be to free to eat and drink as much produce as they wanted that was sold by companies within the town walls? Each person was free to donate any sum in excess of ten percent of their weekly wage to the construction of the Overseer building and other town related monuments being erected. They were free to come and pray, to confess not only their sins, but the sins of others. They were free to sing his praises and those of The Lord in public, and of course free to denounce the teachings of Darwinism.

Such a wealth of freedoms and yet, for the majority of the town, life remained the same. They were sure they hadn't walked past vast statues of Cuthbert a couple of months ago, and the ten percent donation had caused a few grumbles, but having seen The Lord was serious about this matter, some had even chosen to grease the plate with ten point one percent of their wage. And was that such a heavy price to pay knowing The Lord was keeping a watchful eye on them? His smite, after all, had been plain for everyone to see, when the biggest dissenters of the donation law, Ron and Jane Baker of 3 Yorkshire Pudding Lane, had woken one morning to find their chicken coop and all ten chickens burnt to dust.

With such a constant workload of monitoring and analysis to keep the town free and safe, it might be assumed that The Lord Mayor and Overseer of All had been forced to forsake time for life's frivolities, but no, Cuthbert took the title Overseer of *All* seriously. Draped in his gossamer white cape, moustache no longer or thicker than it had been a week ago, he sat at one end of a table laden with goose, rabbit, veal, and a side salad for the lady. He swilled his red wine round the glass until a large amount spilled down the side. Fortunately Rachel didn't notice. He wiped his hand on a towel embroidered with the initials of his title, and stared at Rachel's hidden bosom. The top she was wearing was awful, it was like a sack, without even a hint of nipple protruding. And jeans, she'd worn jeans! Not tight, skinny ones that looked like she'd been forced to butter herself prior to squeezing them on, but a pair that had apparently been donated by an old lesbian.

'So, I thought I'd invite you round since you haven't been to confession for a while,' Cuthbert said, in his haughtiest tone, as he carved himself some goose. 'You know it's not good to keep all your feelings locked away, The Lord and I should hear them. It's for your own good, and I know you must be desperate by now,' he added, rolling his hips suggestively, 'clawing at the walls for some action. We have needs, natural needs that have to be taken care of and The Lord understands that. He wants us to follow them, all the way, until orgasm.'

Cuthbert was surprised she wasn't already on top of him, because he'd made himself hard.

Rachel sighed. Speared on the end of her fork was a crouton. Harold hadn't known the difference between a

238

crouton and a futon before he'd left and yet when they'd spoken last, he'd mentioned borsch and scuba diving.

'The reason I haven't been to see you is because I haven't felt like doing anything naughty. I haven't had one thought that's made me drop my knickers. I'm cured. You and The Lord have done your job. I love my husband and I can't wait for him to return.'

'What?' Cuthbert asked, aghast. 'You mean you're not in the mood right now? Not ready to go at it against the door, on the table, in the chair, on the floor?'

Rachel shook her head. Her hair was unwashed, her legs were unshaved.

'To be honest, if it wasn't you, I think I'd feel guilty just being alone with another man.'

'Oh enough of that nonsense once and for all! I am a man like any other, more so in fact. I have carnal desires and The Lord wishes me to fulfil them. The reason you don't feel guilty is because us being here together is right. The Lord wants me to be with the woman of my dreams, and you are her. This is destiny. This is what we were put on earth for,' Cuthbert said, looking to Rachel in his costume like an oversized child ready to go trick or treating.

'But what about *till death do us part*?' she asked.

'I'm not sure people even say that any more do they? Let me tell you Rachel, there are parts of The Bible you should take literally and others figuratively. It doesn't mean until actual death, it means until the relationship dies for one of you.'

'But it's not dead. I love Harold more now than ever. I spend all of my time staring at the calendar in the kitchen willing the phone to ring, and I know he's thinking of me too, I can feel it. It's like you said in the team's leaving ceremony - *God can help us communicate across the divide*.'

Cuthbert's left hand covered half his forehead and his eyes.

'Rachel, honestly...'

'I'm sorry Father or whatever it is you're called nowadays, but I have to go home. If he calls and I miss it,

239

then I shan't forgive myself.'

'But he can't call because I...' Cuthbert trailed off, '...don't think they have phones in China or Vietnam or wherever it is they're at this very minute.'

'Vinh. They're playing Hochiminhxi. It's the second game of their south-east Asian section. They go to Law-os after it.'

'Yes, yes, I know their itinerary, I came up with it,' Cuthbert grumbled, pouring himself more wine. 'I am The Lord Mayor and Overseer of All you know,' he added, as Rachel rose once she'd drained the last drop of tea. 'And I get everything I want. I am chosen,' he continued, though Rachel was obviously no longer listening.

'That's nice. I'll see you for your evening speech tomorrow,' she said, putting on a coat a size too big for her. 'Sleep well.'

Sleep well! How was he supposed to sleep at all on a bed of roses? He'd laid them from pillow to foot for her. He'd have to put on his gardening gloves to remove them, and to think he'd gone round practising (for what he could only assume was some kinky pleasure/pain activity many women apparently found "romantic") by jabbing himself in the back and bum with a drawing pin.

Aggressively he shoved his chair under the table and went in search of something to take his mind off the rebuttal. He stomped into the study and collected the transcripts of recent phone calls containing key words. Nearly all of them were boring. Sometimes someone was saying what a good job he was doing, but ninety-nine times out of a hundred it was a conversation about Nathan's day at school, the dog eating some furniture or a tea afternoon being arranged. Cuthbert began to bin the sheets. How had she refused him? No one refused him. Everyone loved him, listened to his every word. Unless they were onto him and scheming behind his back, in code? Oh, how could he have been so naïve? Where was that sheet?

'...father's grave this Sunday. After it we'll all go for ice-cream.'

An assassination attempt at Mass by the widow of James Egbert might as well have been posted around town: now he could see it clearly! But what would she use as a weapon? A gun? A knife? There were plenty of knives in people's kitchens. He was practically taking his life into his hands every time he left the Overseer building. He needed Kevlar and a law banning knives. Hang on, didn't she knit? Knitting needles too, they could be used as javelins.

Any thoughts of constitutional changes were placed on hold, however, at the sound of feet hurrying in his direction, accompanied by the noise of someone attempting not to cry. Cuthbert glanced round for something to arm himself with, his nerves on edge. He rolled the Skipperton Gazette into a cylinder, the best weapon he could concoct, as he shuffled behind the door, holding his breath.

'Earthquake! There's been an earthquake! Overseer.'

Cuthbert lowered his hands, which had been alternating between a jabbing and clubbing action, at the sound of Edward's voice.

'Earthquake?' he said, walking back into the dining room, making fencing jabs with the newspaper, the other hand behind his back. 'Nonsense, I didn't feel a thing.'

'Not here, in the Indian Ocean, 7.8 on the Richter Scale,' Edward said, his eyes wide and moist, his hands trembling, stains under his lip from where he'd failed to wipe away snot. 'It caused a tidal wave and it's taken out Vinh. I saw pictures; cars, people, they just disappear. Houses, no more. They're dead, I...why? How could it happen? You said they, we, a quest for Him,' Edward mumbled, continuing to ramble, as Cuthbert led them back to the computer.

The footage was shaky. The wave simply wiped out everything in its path, flattening the terrain. Cuthbert scanned the text below the video; the flood reached ten miles inland, shrapnel was washed even further ashore, at least eighty thousand dead, a hotline number. As quickly as his hands would allow, he pulled up the address for the venue the team had been playing at and pasted it into Google Maps. He zoomed out, one click and then another. Three miles inland.

'They could have had time to run,' Edward spluttered, falling to his knees.

Cuthbert shook his head.

'But we can't just sit here, we have to do something. Call the line. Pray. Ask Him for a favour.'

'It's already happened Edward, I can't ask him to recall what's done.'

'But why? You said he'd protect them, and I should have been there. How could it happen?' Edward asked, looking somewhat pathetic, Cuthbert thought.

'How should I know what they've been doing out there? All sorts of hideous crimes no doubt. The Lord didn't place the Ring of Fire in that area because God fearing people lived there, he did it because it's full of heathens and savages. The Lord doesn't make mistakes remember, he helps the righteous and smites the sinners. He has chosen to spare you, and he has shown beyond all doubt that Rachel must give herself to me.'

'Rachel Baker?' Edward gasped, finding himself sinking to a whole new level of shock he hadn't believed existed. 'But she's The Skipper's wife, and, and...'

'He's dead,' Cuthbert said, rising like a piece of marshmallow. '*Till death do us part.* She said it herself just now. It was she who wanted proof that I always get what I want, and here it is.'

'I can't let you do that, Harold is...'

'Harold was,' Cuthbert corrected him. 'And you're free to do as you please Edward. As was the deceased Mayor, the ex-Bishop and your former team.'

242

The End

The team wasn't aware of the disaster that had struck the Vietnamese coast, for they had managed to exit the country the same day they had arrived, just as Harold had wished.

Thinking a bus would be too slow, they had opted to travel by motorbike from the border, requiring just four vehicles to transport all twelve of them. Lightning wouldn't have moved quicker, especially once they were inside Hanoi, where there was no such thing as a correct side of the road; streets and pavements were a state of mind, and right of way went to who was biggest. When they encountered a police officer who jumped out to try and stop them to exact a bribe, they merely swerved round him, yelling and waving their arms. The only surprising aspect of the journey, or so the Vietnamese motorists thought, was that the players had spread themselves over four bikes and not three.

Having reached the check-in desk with minutes to spare, the players hadn't had time to think about their inaugural flight. They dashed into the line to have their boarding cards inspected and rushed aboard, desperate to make every second count so as to reach Darjeeling before their arch enemies.

Due to a limited number of seats having been available, they once again found themselves sharing the time spent between club and economy class, though on this occasion the cheap seats didn't come with a crying child being slapped around by a parent and people spitting on their shoes. The members of the team in first class had the added bonus of being entitled to an unlimited amount of tea, at least unlimited until the cabin ran out of tea bags.

If they weren't drinking, or queuing for the lavatory, then they were listening to a song Richard II had accidentally discovered on the plane's audio system called *Dreadlock Holiday*, having glanced at the name 10CC and connected it with YCCC. Even Al found himself taken by the opening chorus of the song.

'Can't argue with that line, truer words are rarely

243

spoken by darkies. But you know the rest of it would be a thousand times better if it were sung by white northern folk rather than wogs,' he said, his finger constantly hovering over the rewind button.

What they alighted into was a hotter, more crowded version of China, which seemed even worse than its predecessor, thanks to the luxuries they'd been afforded during the nine hour plane journey.

'It smells funny,' Stuart complained, as they waited for their bags.

'Everyone looks like they've just been let out of a prison that couldn't afford to paint stripes on the uniform,' William remarked.

Harold, meanwhile, only had eyes for his watch. As they hadn't been able to fly directly to their destination, they needed to take a train from Calcutta station.

'Now I know why all the women cover their faces - to avoid breathing in the stench of these countries,' Al said, covering his face with his handkerchief.

'The guide book says we can take a bus to the train station,' Dimar said, needing both hands to hold the hefty item.

'No way can we travel on a bus,' Paul said, not thinking of speed, but his distaste for mixing with people beneath them.

'But it's only ten miles, so if we weren't short of time we could walk to save cash,' Dimar said.

'Aye, you're right lad, as per usual,' Harold replied. 'But as it is, we're best to go in taxis,' he added, the second part of his sentence picked up by everyone in the terminal.

Bundling into two taxis, they found it might have been quicker to walk, as thousands of people were doing, weaving through the traffic, carrying giant knapsacks on their heads, their sandals kicking up dust, making way only for cows and bulls, which had right of way over absolutely everything.

Off to the side of the road, in any spaces available, groups of children were playing cricket. Cardboard boxes and corrugated sheets substituted for wickets, and though the bat and ball were usually in good shape, one group were playing with a spherical object made of rubber bands.

Erik reached into his pocket and tossed them a tennis ball, Richard II shouted to a bowler to split his grip and John signalled that an lbw appeal had indeed trapped the batter plum. For the first time since leaving Yorkshire, here were people who knew exactly what the sport was about. Inside the taxis a sense of excitement and trepidation built. Every player knew that they were no longer on holiday, that there would be no more teaching techniques and exhibition matches, this was business.

Frank visualised his grip on the slower delivery. Stuart was desperate to see the length of the boundaries. Alan thought about how much concentration would be required against the spin. Harold recalled David Gower's 1984-85 side that took the series 2-1. This was a similar situation as then, when there had been no room on the plane for quacks, coaches and all the other hocus pocus interferers who gave themselves fancy titles so they could have a free holiday. He was still daydreaming about the fourth test in Madras, which he had listened to on the BBC World Service, one England won thanks to a pair of double centuries from Fowler and Gatting, when Paul tapped him on the shoulder.

'Err, what is that?'

Out across the tracks, there appeared to be a train made out of people.

'The train to New Jalpaiguri?' enquired Harold, squinting, as if his eyes were deceiving him.

'Yes, leaves in forty minutes,' the driver replied.

'Perhaps it works like Fred Flintstone's car,' William suggested.

'I'm surprised there's enough people left to do such a job. Thought this place would be empty with them all moving over to take our work,' Al said. 'Can tell they come from monkeys the way they hang off the frame with such ease. Wogs.'

'No, don't worry, no wogs around here,' the driver

said, catching only part of Al's ramble. 'We don't like the Africans either, they have no heart.'

'You what?' spluttered Al.

'No decent black cricketers that's for sure,' the driver replied, shaking his head.

'Hang on,' Dimar said, leaning forward. 'What about Ambrose, Walsh, Richards and Sobers? And Brian Lara has the biggest test innings score ever,' he added, supported by nods from Erik and Harold, while Al muttered: 'but, but,' over and over again.

The driver shook his head dismissively: 'No heart, no soul, no hard work. They're lazy,' he said, applying the handbrake.

'Lara scored 400 not out. He scored centuries against every test playing nation. He scored nine double centuries. He's scored the most runs off a single over,' Dimar protested, as they piled out of the car.

'Luck,' the driver said, counting his money. 'And The Devil,' he added, managing to shake hands with a stupefied Al who, when he finally came round, went in search of a bottle of bleach.

Forced to upgrade to first class so they had space to breathe, the players found the twelve hour journey flew by. Due to the availability of such a vast variety of teas, they had lengthy blind taste tests and competitions with well to do locals, who provided so much discussion about the IPL, the 20/20 game and the state of test cricket, that the incessant chatter lasted until the train terminated four miles short of Darjeeling. Their favourite topic of conversation, however, was their local heroes, players who were going to destroy the English side they were due to play in forty-eight hours.

'Invincible throughout the order,' was one comment, spoken without a hint of hyperbole.

The four top order batters all had averages in the fifties, although when those statistics were narrowed down to games against touring teams, then two of them rose into the sixties. The wicket keeper, a part time snake charmer, was said to possess such elasticity that he had been the model for the Street Fighter character Dhalsim. One man claimed to have witnessed him make a stumping from two and a half metres away, which, when converted into feet and inches, had Paul pulling on his fingers. And those five weren't even the most revered by the fans. That accolade went to the spinners, two brothers who had never played for their country, simply because they had vowed to stay and take care of their dying mother, who claimed that only the touch of their fingers to her temples on an evening kept her alive for another twenty-four hours. These cricketers' techniques were so otherworldly that the ICC had been brought in on numerous occasions for inspections. They had bowling averages of 7.

'Impossible.'

'Can't be.'

'A pack of bloody lies. Surely?'

'Listen lads, what have I told you? These foreigners are full of mind games. They're just trying to get inside our heads,' Harold said, internally panicking as much as his players. After all, if they'd divulged they had a player with a batting average of 99.3, wouldn't the Indians have been saying the same thing? Now he found himself in two minds whether or not to press forward with the head to head tussle first.

'Tallying up the stats, we're heading for a six wicket loss,' Dereck quietly muttered, as they walked in a pack from the train station.

Only Erik didn't appear concerned, striding down the road with his head high, bag slung over his shoulder, looking liked it weighed nothing. He led the way to their hotel, which they entered on the cusp of dusk, drained, dusty and with sweaty clothes sticking to their skin.

They were greeted by a man dressed all in white.

'Please put your bags down and let me get you some tea,' he said.

While the tea was being prepared and Harold, Wise Owl and Dimar sorted the rooms, the other players draped

247

themselves over the sofas in the lobby.

'Hey look,' Frank said, chuckling, pointing to the huge poster behind a desk. 'They've named this palace or church or whatever it is after that restaurant on the pier in Scarborough.'

'You want to take tour to Taj Mahal? I can sort. Very good price: travel, accommodation, tickets all included,' the manager said.

'No, we've no time for tourism. We're here for one thing and one thing only and that's to play cricket,' Harold said.

'Ah yes, yes,' the manager replied. 'Of course, you have brought a miniature version of WG Grace along,' he added, pointing to Alan.

While everyone chuckled, The Gnome said nothing in response to the witty comparison, because he had been trying for quite some time to create a poem for Erik. He had accepted, from what he had seen and heard on the tour, that his love would remain unrequited, and so had chosen to close it with a lament. The problem was that nothing that rhymed with Erik was worth putting down on paper.

Better than Berwick/ You mean more to me than money does to Dereck/ Your smile makes me Merick/ I need you more than a curry does Turmeric.

Useless, bloody useless. He held out his hand for the cup of tea offered and took a sip.

'Hey! This is Skipperton!' he exclaimed, jumping from his chair, startling the room.

'Bloody hell, he's right you know,' Frank said.

'Skipperton, can't be,' the players murmured, the room suddenly buzzing, as the tea was sipped in astonishment. Even Dimar found himself comparing it to a drink and not dirty dish water.

'Skipperton? The name is familiar,' the manager said. 'Why of course, the biggest importer of Sar Mar's tea,' he added, with a nod.

'You mean Sar Mar Birk?' Harold gasped, amazed by such revelations.

248

'The one and only! You have heard of our captain?'

'He's the guy I pay every month for the tea. I'm Harold Baker.'

'A relation of Geoffrey Baker?'

'His son,' Harold beamed proudly.

'Well, why didn't you say so?' the manager cried. 'We need upgrades and more tea and some girls. I am honoured to have you here,' he continued, extending his hand to Harold with a bow.

'The pleasure is ours,' Harold said, as John, Dimar and Richard II checked themselves over in the mirror, only to find that when they turned around, the girls had come and gone in a harem with Erik.

'For the best,' Harold said. 'You three need time in the real nets, not fish nets,' he added, turning back to the manager, who was picking out CDs to play. 'So this Sar Mar is the Darjeeling skipper?' Harold asked.

'Oh yes. He is my favourite player. His nickname is "Superstar". He lives up in Puttapong. It's his uncle's business he runs. No son to take it over you see, real shame, but still family you know?' the manager said, his words resonating deep within Harold. 'There is a picture of him over there in action,' he added, pointing to a framed, sepia image.

The man was a behemoth. He had to be seven foot tall and eighteen stone. He was arranging his field, ball in hand ready to bowl, with a cigar of similar stature to his own frame between his teeth.

'Looks like a bit of a primadonna to me,' William said.

'Yes, but a man who has never lost a game he has captained has that right.'

'We haven't been beaten in four years either, but you don't see our Harold prancing around like a tart,' Stuart commented.

'Four years? Really? Hmmm, interesting. Well enough of that for now. I'm going to guess you've had a long journey and are now hungry, so let me call to the kitchen for you.'

If he had stood out before the disaster that had struck Vinh, Cuthbert really was now the diamond in the coal face. Despite having been granted a day of mourning, not one person had changed out of black clothing since the death of the team had been announced. Even the sky was perpetually dark, casting heavy rain inside the town walls.

When he was out on the street, shining like the only star in the sky, Cuthbert kept a solemn air, passing blessings, assuring everyone the team had gone to a better place. Inside the nearly completed Overseer building, however, he danced, he laughed, he ate pheasant for breakfast. He upped the weekly tax to fifteen percent to speed up developments. He spoke of unity and the importance of moving on. When asked about what would happen at the bakery at the end of special lent and how they would replenish the decreasing supply of candles, he assured his people that no one would go hungry or without light, that the Overseer office would take control, while the wives of the deceased worked there on a wage. No one was certain who or where the applause started from during the evening ceremonies, but it never ended in anything less than a rapturous standing ovation.

Having briefly attempted a moonwalk, Cuthbert strolled into his office after watching his people disperse.

'Second night in a row Richard Egbert hasn't been down and you weren't there either,' he added, narrowing his eyes as he spoke to Edward.

'You told me to stay here and translate the transcripts,' Edward blurted hurriedly. 'And Mr. Egbert's taken the news pretty hard. He's locked himself inside his headmaster's office and won't speak to anyone. Apparently.'

'Hmm,' Cuthbert said, placing his hands on his hips as he stared at his reflection. *'Sounds legitimate. I'll give him until the end of the week,'* he added to himself, as an internal afterthought. Then, without another word, he gave Edward a firm pat on the back and left for the house of his fiancé.

Their engagement hadn't been announced, because Cuthbert hadn't yet proposed, but he had set a wedding date for three days' time as part of the grand opening of the Overseer building, which had every spare body working on it around the clock.

He knocked on Rachel's door and let himself in, leading with a giant bouquet of flowers.

'Good evening Sugar Pumpkin,' he announced, kissing her cheek, which did nothing to stir her.

He found the vase he'd deposited yesterday's bouquet in now empty.

'Surely they didn't die already?' he asked, running the tap.

'I took them down to the team's grave at the cemetery,' Rachel said, her gaze on the phone.

'Well they are yours to do whatever you want with I suppose Baby Duck, but I think these should be kept here to lighten your mood and all that,' Cuthbert replied, taking the box of matches from the mantelpiece to light some candles. 'Shall I run a bath for you?'

Rachel shook her head.

'I think what you meant to do is nod,' Cuthbert said, throwing a couple of logs on the fire. 'You know it's natural to feel how you do at the present, but time will heal and the town will move forward. You're not alone, everyone in Skipperton lost a relative.'

'But it's all my fault. I was the one who said till death do us part and you said...' Rachel whispered, lips trembling.

'Yes, it's true that you have to shoulder the blame and should the people ever find out they would drown you as a witch, but you also have the ability to give the town something to get excited about, take their mind off all the gloom. There's nothing like a wedding to spread joy, well except maybe Christmas and that is imminent too,' Cuthbert beamed.

'But isn't it a bit soon? Won't they think I'm some kind of harlot?'

'I'm pretty sure they think that already, and there will be as much free tea and Black as they can drink.'

'Couldn't we just have that as a sort of wake?' Rachel

asked, as Cuthbert held the cast iron poker between his legs to stoke the fire.

'Err...no, no I don't think we could. I've set the date for us, so all you have to do is get on the phone and call your parents and I'll make a grand announcement tomorrow, future Mrs. Johnson.'

Due to the fact that the following morning the majority of the team was bed(pan) ridden, it was left to Erik to go along to the cricket club. When he reached it, he found his Redillian doppelgänger Kieran already in conversation with Sar Mar, who stood at six and a half feet, not seven. It transpired that with most of the Redillian players in a similar state to the Skipperton ones, the Lancastrians were asking for a postponement.

'The tickets have already been sold,' Sar Mar said.

'But we won't be able to field a team.'

'Nonsense, here's another one of your players now looking as fit as yourself,' Sar Mar beamed, as the Englishmen glared at each other.

'I'm not his teammate,' Erik said. 'I'm here representing Skipperton.'

Sar Mar checked his watch: 'aren't you a couple of months early?'

'We heard about what this lot were up to and changed our plans. We want the right to break your record. Then you can play them,' Erik said, calmly.

'Break our record?' Sar Mar spluttered. 'I'm afraid you'll have to wait to become another of our victims until after we've played your fellow countrymen.'

Erik shook his head: 'us first, then them. They owe us.'

'We owe you nothing,' Kieran responded, casually.

'Of course Mr. Harold Baker says he is aware there are other tea plantations in the area.'

Sar Mar twitched: 'gentlemen, gentlemen, I do believe the fairest way to settle this is by playing a round robin. If you compete against each other first, then the winner will play us.

252

How does that sound?'

'Like we end up getting what we want,' Erik replied, already walking away.

In the state they were in, the rest of the team didn't share Erik's confidence when he returned to explain what had been arranged, but sticking to a diet of tea made with bottled water - the purity of which allowed for an even clearer taste - they arrived at the ground the following day with twelve players.

Despite the state of the pitch, both captains were keen to bat first so the majority of the team could continue to lie down, and with the toss going Redillian's way, they immediately started as favourites in spite of having the less impressive recent form.

The Darjeeling players, who sat in the stands to make scouting reports, found themselves switching off after five overs, with amateur cricket in England looking to have dropped behind that of Bangladesh. Not only were the players weak (too weary to even muster an occasional sledge); but they also shuffled instead of ran, lacked the power to hit boundaries or bowl quicker than medium pace, and their techniques were also rusty. The only smooth displays came from a solid 75 struck by Kieran and the overs of Al, who had refused to consume any of the food or drink he'd been offered.

During the early overs, Skipperton had worked the rolling substitute well, and for large chunks of the game they managed to field with their allotted number of players. However, at other times they were decimated to such an extent that Erik, the vice-captain for the game, took Paul's gloves behind the stumps and directed the two fielders to stand square of the wicket so that alongside the bowler (only Stuart and Paul didn't take on the responsibility) they formed a diamond. At the end of the allotted fifty overs, the score was a clumsy 189/7.

'I can't lift my arms, let alone swing a bat.'

'Can't we extend lunch for a day?'

'Where's the rain?'

'Lads they're in the dressing room right now saying exactly the same thing,' Harold said, lying on a bench, others in a matching position on the floor, as Erik helped Stuart with his pads. 'So let's make this as easy for ourselves as possible. Keep Erik on strike and if we all manage a knock into double figures, then the game is ours.'

Until Erik went sweeping, walking from the pitch while the ball was in the air, for 89, any sane bet was in favour of a Skipperton victory. With their talisman out, however, and the batting order depending on who felt well enough to take to the field at the time, Redillian were quickly given the upper hand, their bowling so slow and measured that they hadn't given away a single extra.

Each Skipperton player though, bound by the duty Harold had bestowed upon them, struggled into double figures, so that when he hauled himself up to bat seventh, with Richard II, Frank, John and Dereck remaining, they were 149/5. A ball later and it was 149/6. With five overs remaining, they were heading for a loss by a few runs.

'Need a few more than ten,' Harold said, touching gloves with Richard II: 'but there's no one to cheat us out of this time, so let's go and bloody do it.'

They scored eight off the over, the same again the following six balls, but it wasn't until they'd taken their partnership to 24 with 12 balls remaining and 17 required to win that the fielders grew shaky.

'Just keep it going,' Harold said, sweating profusely despite the cool evening air.

Courtesy of a clutch of good Yorkers in the penultimate over, they only managed seven from it.

'Right, got them where we wanted. A couple of boundaries and revenge is complete,' Harold said, his body feeling like it was made of lead, his stomach rumbling ominously.

Richard II started the over with a single, then Harold added another. Richard II struck a double and on the fourth ball, hurling himself, glad for every inch of his height, squeezed home for a single. 5 needed off 2 balls. A trademark drive down the ground from The Skipper and another single and that was it.

With eyes only for the ball, Harold stepped onto his tiptoes ready to take a step down the crease, his bat straight, his intent clear. But as he pulled back, his stomach went into such convulsions that he lost control of his bat, tilted it skywards and chipped the ball into the air down the throat of the man running round from long on. Somehow, as he collapsed forward, he stumbled far enough down the crease to cross with Richard II, putting Egbert Jnr on strike for the final delivery.

'Do it for your dad,' Harold whispered, as he was carried off by Erik.

The neutrals in the ground were in throes of ecstasy with excitement, while on the field Richard II scanned to see which of the players covering the boundary were going to collapse rather than stagger after the ball. An image of his dad's long face came into view, but it didn't offer any advice or support, just stared at him. Not once had his dad spoken about that cup over, but Richard II had heard him scream out in his nightmares. Was it possible to vanquish everyone's demons in a single delivery? In a trance he launched himself, clubbing at the ball like he'd watched Stuart do on many an occasion, and sent the ball of cork sailing towards deep mid-wicket. The fielder watched it, unable to move into its flight path. The umpire lifted his hands, ready for the signal, but he required only one limb, as the ball lodged itself under the boundary rope.

'Game drawn,' he announced.

At the bottom of a mine, either side of a candle stub, two boys stood conversing.

'Thanks for agreeing to meet.'

'It's okay, I've been wanting to talk to someone about the team for a while.'

'We both should have been there.'

'I know.'

The depths of the mine had been chosen out of fear

and for protection. The consensus being that if The Devil ruled Hell, then they were currently closer to him, and out of reach of God and The Overseer's spheres of influence.

'What do you think is going to happen?'

'After the wedding? I don't know. He doesn't speak to me as much as he did. He shreds all his memos too, even his grocery list in case someone notices a pattern and poisons those vegetables.'

'Any scope in it?'

'Not with me as his food taster there's not!' Edward said, his raised voice drawing footsteps on the surface. He stepped back and crouched down in a subsidiary shaft, as a torch was shone down from the entrance.

'Who are you talking to?'

'No one dad. Just thinking out loud,' Jamie said, shielding his eyes with a hand.

'Yeah? Well thinking's for break times and you're five hours from one, so put some elbow grease into your labour instead,' David Baker ordered.

The boys waited until they heard the back door close with a bang.

'Looks like we both need to get out of here,' Edward whispered. 'And the sad thing is, I honestly thought Cuthbert was going to move us in the right direction, but this last week, and his reaction to the team's death...You know he doesn't have anyone coming to the wedding from his side of the family. Not a single friend either. I'm his best man and my speech has been written for me. He had Rachel's family strip searched and their car taken apart by Phil, Stanley and Jim pretending to be MI6 operatives half an hour from the walls. Every single flower for the ceremony has been fitted with a microphone. If only it wasn't for the fact he's the chosen one I'd have done something by now I swear, but you saw what happened to Keith.'

'Oh, there's no doubt he's protected by his God,' Jamie said: 'but you know I don't think it's the same God for everyone. I'm beginning to think this one only understands a southern accent, because I've spoken, prayed, done everything The Overseer has told me, but I never get answers and I'm still down here every day doing sixteen hour shifts. But the other night, after I'd heard the news about the lads, I closed my eyes and talked to them and they all replied and had helpful advice. They must have been made saints.'

'Aye?'

'Oh aye, I wouldn't bloody lie about that would I?'

'I believe you,' Edward said, picturing the team, each member with a crown, beard and long white robe playing cricket on clouds. His heart suddenly filled with hope. 'Others will want to join when they hear about it,' he said.

'But how do we spread such a message? We can't have people meeting down here, and if we mention it up there we'll be run over by a bus or drown in the bath.'

'We need a symbol, something inconspicuous.'

'How about this?' Jamie said, carving into the floor a set of wickets with a bat resting horizontally on top.

'Perfect,' Edward said.

And so, The Church of the Latter Day Team was born.

With the match drawn and no bowlers willing to raise their arms in a bowl off, Erik won on the toss of a coin to set Skipperton up with Darjeeling first. Their luck didn't end there either, because the following day it rained from dawn to dusk, giving them both an extra day's rest and greasing the outfield, which with no heat in sight, would make it disadvantageous for the spinners.

Eating only pre-packaged goods and drinking tea with their usual intensity, the players gathered for meetings to discuss where they'd gone wrong in the battle against Redillian, who had stated that they didn't care about breaking Darjeeling's record, only winning the mini-tournament outright.

As they had achieved such a heroic fight back in the final overs and had come within millimetres of a winning six, however, the Skipperton players actually felt like they'd won the game and didn't dwell on the negatives. Considering the state they'd been in, and batting second, well it all went to prove just how great a team they were. They were relaxed. They spent the evening laughing, joking and reminiscing about the tour, which Harold described as a well crafted Yorkshire, all ready for its crowning gravy.

The noise from the stadium was deafening half a mile out, and inside it was like nothing the players had ever seen. Every seat was taken. The spaces between seats were accounted for. The stadium wall was being clung to. Flags of the region and country were held aloft in every row, leaving the Skipperton players standing in the field feeling like insignificant ingredients in a cauldron of stew.

Inside the dressing room, Harold resorted to writing on cards to deliver his team speech, buoyed by the winning of the toss and his election to bat first. **This is what we came for. This will secure our immortality. Don't be scared by their stories. They haven't played a team from Yorkshire. And once we've finished with them they won't again. A lifetime's supply of free Skipperton awaits.**

With the outfield still greasy (bottles of water had accidentally been spilled during the warm up) batting first was the correct decision. The spinners couldn't gain a proper grip of the ball and they quickly became demoralised by the stroke play of Erik, who left them bewildered as to the line and length they should bowl.

Unaccustomed to seeing batters remain at the crease, the crowd quickly grew disgruntled, which in turn transferred onto the Darjeeling players. They started bickering, lost concentration, began making fielding errors and, alongside some bad calls from their captain, as well as solid performances down the order from the away team, they found themselves at the end of the fifty overs with a game on their hands.

Batting Scorecard -

		Runs	Balls
E M Larsson	lbw A S Prasad	127	120
S J Barker	c Delsim b Sar Mar	39	24
H G Baker	b S S Prasad	45	41
R Egbert II	not out	36	38
A E Smith	c&b A S Prasad	18	18
D M Baker	c Delsim b A S Prasad	27	30
P D Barker	not out	31	29
Extras		12	
Total		335/5	

'Right then lads,' Harold said, in a far quieter setting. 'What I said yesterday was that whoever was on first had to make sure the second act had a fighting chance of victory. Well we've just blown cannonballs all across their deck, so arm yourselves, because it's time to board and plunder. I want wickets, and I want them now.'

Unfortunately, unlike the Darjeeling bowlers, the home team's batsmen showed more spirit to hold onto their impressive figures. The top four all made it into their fifties, though they did it at a rate shy of the 6.72 an over required to win. Still, needing 78 to win off 42 balls with six wickets in hand, they held the upper hand as the floodlights were turned on.

It was at this stage, however, that nerves started to gain the upper hand. In the space of two overs the score went from 258/4 to 276/6. Three overs later it was 299/7. Two runs a ball off the last three overs, meant the stadium was vibrating.

Up on the balcony, Wise Owl was so tense he simply yelled whatever words came into his head and pointed as if he was being controlled by a puppet master constantly scratching their nose. A few Skipperton players tried to kid themselves that even if the result didn't go their way, they'd been part of something so epic it didn't matter. But then they told themselves to stop thinking like a southern pansy, wiped away the sweat on their foreheads and focused on the ball, which the Indians slugged at, bringing the result closer to their favour with a series of boundaries at the loss of one precious wicket.

Bowling figures after 49 overs —

	O	M	R	W	Econ.
F J Barker	10	1	58	1	5.80
J J Barker	10	0	67	3	6.70
R Egbert II	10	0	65	2	6.50
Al Smith	8	1	50	1	6.25
D M Martenyenkov	8	0	56	1	7.00
H G Baker	3	0	19	0	6.33
Extras	11				

Harold held the ball. The only person he really wanted to entrust it to was thousands of miles away in a dark room staring at a blackboard. He glanced up at the balcony to see what Wise Owl suggested and found his vice captain pointing at both Al and Dimar, and so he closed his eyes. The crowd was frenetic, the energy pulsed and they were being urged to grow louder by the Darjeeling players watching on. Al had bowled one stunning wicket maiden in his second over, but since then he'd been more expensive. But could Harold honestly place the result in the hands of a foreigner? Four years ago it wouldn't have mattered who he'd handed the ball to, but now...He opened his eyes and stared at his bowlers: *'go with your gut lad,'* a voice inside his head said.

'Aye,' Harold replied, and into the hands of Al the ball went.

A ball later and it seemed like his gut was suffering the after effects of the past couple of days, as his spinner was driven to the boundary. The second ball, however, beat the batter looking to deliver the winning runs in style and gave Paul an easy stumping. 330/9.

A light spit of rain started to fall. Al, for Skipperton, for Yorkshire, came around the wicket and bowled his third of the over. It was too short of a length and he could only watch in despair as the batter got everything on it, straight out of the middle, sending it high into the air.

From its trajectory, everyone could see it was clearing the boundary by a good ten metres. The Skipperton players slumped, the Redillian players rejoiced with the rest of the crowd, some of whom had already begun to invade the pitch. The umpire held his hands aloft, and Erik ran.

He hurdled the boarding, jumped onto the chairs, parting the supporters (who had readied themselves to challenge each other to claim the ball as a souvenir) in disbelief. Steadying himself, he leapt forward and pushed the ball in a volleyball style back inside the boundary, chasing after it as jaws dropped, making a final dive back over the rope to cradle it before it struck the ground. Casually, tossing the ball into the air over his shoulder, he announced: 'how's that?'

Despite being utterly shocked by the fielding miracle, the Skipperton players, used to Erik's superhuman antics, grabbed the wickets and bails and dashed into the changing room, while the rest of the stadium neither moved nor made a sound.

'Bloody amazing.'
'Bloody fantastic.'
'Bloody brilliant.'
'Bloody unbelievable.'
'Bloody superb.'
'Bloody terrific.'

The players shook hands with each other, the younger ones exchanged hugs. The sense of elation was akin to being put on a drip of Black in The Arms, while the commentator on the wireless spoke of a successful invasion into Lancashire from the newly appointed Prime Minister, Darren Gough. The magnitude of their achievement was still sinking in, when Kevin and Kieran appeared at the door. Bewilderingly, they were smiling.

'Leave your congratulations at the door and bugger off.'

'Coming round to make a collection for the umpires

tomorrow?'

'Don't worry, you can make history by being the first team to start their new winning streak rather than being the last in their previous one.'

'You're like a pack of dogs licking your own bollocks, and I'm pleased for you,' Kevin started, 'but there's a big shiny trophy to be collected tomorrow and the chaps out there are already draping red and white ribbons on it. You see ladies, it's Kieran here's thirtieth birthday today and he isn't the only one in this dressing room celebrating his big three-O today.'

Erik stood: 'so?'

'You should have told us JS. That means even bigger celebrations are called for!'

'Oh yes, John Smith. Cute, give the foreigner a name to help him fit in.'

'You what?' the players said in unison, rising to defend their star. 'Erik's Skipperton through and through, born and bred.'

'Hang on a second, you don't think it's a coincidence two people who look almost identical are having their thirtieth birthday on the same day?' Kevin asked.

'As much of a coincidence as your wife and sister looking alike.'

'Well, you're on the right line sheep shaggers. You see Kieran was given this letter by the postal service just before we came out. It was posted from someone he thought was dead and who ordered him not to open it until his birthday. Just be thankful he chose to do it after the game and not before it. Go ahead, read it to them.'

'*Dear Kieran, please don't be angry or cross. I'm sorry for a lot of things and wish I could explain it all, and maybe one day I will, but for now I want you to know that you have a twin brother. Whether he is still alive I don't know, because I was forced to hide him when you were born or else your father, a man I'm glad you never knew, would have slain him. I took him into Yorkshire in the dead of night, and before I left him to fate, I did like I did to you and scored an L on his left buttock and a cross on his right. He didn't cry, and as I kissed him goodbye, I'm sure he nodded to let me know everything would be alright. I left a note inside his blanket asking whoever took him in to name him Erik. I hope that will give you a start.'*

At the news of the markings, Alan broke down. He wailed in anguish and suddenly it was the Skipperton players who took on the role of gawping dummies.

'Well,' Harold said. 'We knew you lads were fruity, but coming up with such a tale to see one of our player's arses. Get out of here.'

'But the markings are...true,' Erik said, feeling them. 'I...I have a brother,' he continued. 'And he may have answers I've been searching for my whole life.'

Kieran opened his arms: 'brother.'

'But...but...' the players mumbled.

'Oh come now,' Kevin jested, 'you couldn't honestly have believed someone with such ability could be a Yorkshireman could you? He's got Lancashire coursing through his veins. The pride of Bosworth.'

'Erik, wait!' Alan cried, watching Erik embrace his brother as he had longed to. 'You can't go, I love you.'

'Aye,' Harold said, 'we all love you.'

'I'd give up Yorkshires for you to remain on our team,' Richard II said.

'I love you like a good keg of Black,' Stuart added.

'You're Yorkshire here lad, and that's what counts,' Dereck said, drumming his fist against his stomach.

'You're everything. It's not just the cricket, it's who you are, I love everything about you. I've wanted to tell you for so long,' Alan said, finding it difficult to breathe.

'Err...aye, we should tell you more often how much we appreciate you I think is what Alan's trying to say,' John chipped in.

'No, no, no, you don't understand!' Alan heaved, 'I love you like a man loves a man.'

'A man loves a man? No it's a man loves a...oh.'

It was like the fabric of time and space had opened up

and slapped them. There were words that came close to describing their feelings; bewilderment, astonishment, shock, but none could capture the exact essence.

With his hands covering his face, Alan fled in tears. Kieran pulled his brother out of harm's way of a potential bumming, and so as to show Erik's future now lay without them, Kevin slammed the dressing room door shut.

'A queer and a Lancastrian!' Al said, turning on Harold. 'You've been harbouring a bloody gay and a traitor! I could have been touched up in my sleep!'

'Which one turned the other?' Frank asked. 'Oi, Skipper I'm talking to you! I want answers now.'

Harold was staring at the door. It was all a nightmare, it would end soon and he'd come round on the pitch having been dropped during the celebrations.

The door swung open.

'Amazing guys, absolutely amazing!'

It was a lightly coloured Asian man.

'Oi!' Al blurted. 'It says away team, not gay team or a wog team. Get out.'

The man, whose spirits had been as high as the team's when they'd left the pitch, stopped dancing and glanced around at the despair on the faces of the Skipperton players.

'Guys, what's going on? You were awesome. That was unbelievable. Oh to beat my cousin like that. You guys are my heroes. Seriously, come and let me take you all out for a beef burger to really insult those bastards.'

Looking up from his feet, Dimar did a double take: 'Err, who are you exactly?' he asked.

'I am Akabar, the rightful heir to the Puttapong tea plantation.'

Now it was Wise Owl's turn to stare in shock at Akabar, his skin tone far lighter than it should have been: 'But our receptionist said Harpal didn't have a son.'

'In a way I guess not,' Akabar said. 'You see my parents went to visit your home town when the great Geoffrey Baker invited them over to discuss trade and how to

264

set up and develop the Skipperton Tea factory. They stayed for five days and it was during that time that I was conceived. If I am honest, I not only came here to celebrate, but see if it was possible for you to take a strand of my hair to do some DNA testing. You see my mum was killed on the hospital bed and my father, though he couldn't kill me, never spoke to me my whole life.'

Having heard his father's name, Harold looked up: 'Bloody Hell lad,' he blurted, unable to control himself. 'There's no need for any DNA testing. Err Al, I think you need to see this.'

The scream emitted from the dressing room reached the streets surrounding the stadium and sent a chill down the spines of everyone who heard it.

Cuthbert stood in the middle of The Overseer building and marvelled at its design. It made the rest of Skipperton look like a toy town and it would continue to grow; spires and turrets would be added, until it finally resembled the wedding cake he had commissioned. It was a cake that stood two metres high and had crowning it a bride and groom (both in white) with an excessive bulge in the groom's trouser department.

Cuthbert stopped to admire the quality of the flowers, which were so plentiful that a random visitor could have been excused for thinking The Hanging Gardens had re-located. He had decided that Rachel would wear a wreath of new white roses shaped into a crown, her old wedding dress, earrings she had borrowed from her mum, and the blue would start the very second they were alone after the conclusion of the ceremony.

He had explained to her that a honeymoon to an exotic location would have to be postponed what with all his new business duties; a portfolio that now included Skipperton Tea. His first order of business there had been to reduce the price of a box by five pence in order to dirty his dead predecessor's name, for he had heard people whispering Harold's name with a reverence only he should have been granted. Were it to persist, there was a doctored photograph of the team wearing jumpers emblazoned with red roses all ready for circulation.

Above him, the bell tower began to strike its first nine tolls of the day.

'Well Overseer,' Cuthbert purred, rubbing his hands together. 'Best go and get yourself ready.'

As things stood, there was no longer a Skipperton cricket team. They had unofficially disbanded. Without any real idea as to what they should do, however, all eleven "members" were watching the Redillian versus Darjeeling game, scattered around the stadium in groups no bigger than three. Even those who sat together, like Harold and William, did so in silence, while the crowd, growing steadily more sedated as the game ticked over, tried their best to rally their team from slumping to a second defeat in a row against a bunch of dirty colonial upstarts.

With Redillian batting first though, all they could do was admire the brilliance of the new opening partnership, for Erik and Kieran matched each other run for run, congratulating each other with hugs as they both brought up fifties and centuries, their first wicket partnership 207 off 190 balls.

Harold watched on like Julius Caesar on the senate steps, every boundary another knife wound delivered by Brutus, until he could eventually take no more and raised his t-shirt over his eyes.

With the twins having laid such a solid foundation and left the bowling attacked tired and in disarray, even when they had both walked back to the pavilion the runs kept piling up, and at the end of their innings, Redillian had surpassed the target Skipperton had set the day before, with a whopping 365/7.

Down at the cemetery with her mother, father and brother beside her, Rachel lay her final flower beside the team's gravestone.

Either side of it were wreaths in the shape of wickets with a bat resting on top where the bails should have been. It was an image she'd seen two or three times around the town over the past twenty-four hours; chalked on a pavement, sprayed on a wall. She had found herself doodling it on a piece of paper before bed. It spoke to her, it was a lovely tribute, she guessed.

'We're best to start getting ready,' she said, as the chimes of the Overseer bell reached out from wall to wall.

'It's your day darling, we're here to do what you want,' her mum said, linking arms with her daughter, as she cast a glance back at her husband.

'You know Rachey darling,' her dad started, nodding at his wife. 'We all loved Harold. We thought he was a bit old fashioned and we didn't know if you'd made the right choice at first, but we trusted you and could see that you were happy.'

'I was extremely happy,' Rachel replied, remembering how she had been carried over the threshold on that warm summer's day.

'We know, and we also know that sometimes, in moments of grief, we can make rash and rather strange decisions,' her dad continued.

'What we're trying to say,' her brother said, taking over, 'is that this Cuthbert guy's weird and we think you're making a mistake.'

Rachel shrugged: 'I don't know. But I do know that there's no way out if it.'

'No way out? Of course there's a way out. Run inside the house and pack and we'll drive out of here now. I'll even start the engine. In fact, don't even bother packing,' her brother added, his hand reaching into his pocket for the car keys.

'And how are we going to drive with four flat tyres?' Rachel asked, pointing to the deflated vehicle.

'Four flats! Seriously? Right that's it, I'll piggy back you then. Come on. Argh! Bloody Hell, what the...' her brother cried, grabbing at his calf, which felt like it had been given a large nip and was very quickly going numb.

'I told you all, no way out of it. It's what The Lord wants. I'm going to put my dress on. I'll see you downstairs in twenty minutes,' she sighed.

'You know South Africa once chased down 435 against Australia at home,' Dimar said, tucking into a curry alongside Richard II and John.

'Erik once scored 200 off 120 balls when we chased down White Leodis' total of 380,' John said, as the sides re-emerged onto the field.

'I don't think he looks as happy with them,' Dimar pointed out.

'Who in their right minds bloody would?' Richard II sighed. 'You know they even steal from their own dressing room? It's true, no one ever has the same clothes or equipment two matches in a row.'

'Well there certainly won't be any stealing of the turd variety in our dressing room anymore,' John said, making the three of them cast glances at the sad sight of Alan, more gnome-like than ever. He hadn't moved all day, just sat there, with his head in his hands.

'Who would have thought it?' Richard II said, their attention turning back to the game, as the opening batters made their intent clear by smashing boundaries in the opening over. 'The whole time Harold's been in charge, we've lost one game with a Lancastrian *and* a queer in the team.'

'I didn't think he should have had the strength to lift a bat,' John said, shaking his head.

'It's just not cricket,' Dimar added, the rhythm of the sentence leading them into a half hearted first verse of *Dreadlock Holiday*.

'You know the strangest thing about it all?' Richard II mused. 'Is that you're told at school they're both really easy to spot, and yet not one of us knew.'

The people of Skipperton, dressed in their Sunday best, filed into the Overseer Church to find Cuthbert at the head of the altar, ready to preside over the service since there was nobody else acquainted with the performance of an Overseer wedding. They sat in their pews, packed tight together, hoping it wasn't a long ceremony, since they'd only come for the free Skipperton and Black they'd been promised at the evening do.

'And where is your son?' Cuthbert asked Rachel's mum, as she took a seat alone on the front row. 'Does he think it's okay to miss his sister's special day?'

'He's been struck down by something. Couldn't even walk to the front door,' she replied, nervously.

'Ah well, no worries, I can have a couple of my men carry him here. Wouldn't want him to miss out on this would we?' Cuthbert said, signalling to someone in the wings.

'Excellent,' he added to himself with a smile, watching the final rows fill to their capacity. There was still no sign of Richard Egbert though, the man could well have died inside his office by now, and if he hadn't, then by next week Cuthbert would make sure he, along with others who had strong loyalties to the team, had been discredited and disposed of.

'Do you have the rings with you Edward?' he asked, his question producing two platinum bands engraved with the same message - *The Overseers Forever and Ever*. 'Then I do believe we may start.'

He nodded to Polly Thompson that she could begin the wedding march on the organ, bringing the guests to their feet. They turned to face the bride, who looked more stunning than ever. Having hardly eaten during the last week, she had dropped the pounds gained in the past few months from iced cream eclair sandwiches, though importantly this weight had not left her chest. With the wreath crowning her black, unkempt hair, which flowed naturally past her shoulders, she could have been mistaken for a goddess.

'Oh she is going to get it tonight,' Cuthbert mumbled, winking down at Edward, who was wearing, beneath his top hat and tails, a vest with the symbol of The Church of the

Latter Day Team drawn in charcoal.

Rachel kept her head still, staring down the aisle at her future husband, while her dad glanced nervously around them and had to be prized from his daughter by Edward and ushered to his seat.

'Dearly beloved of the great town of Skipperton, we are gathered here today to celebrate the union of Rachel Clough and The Overseer of All. We shall start the service with the song - *The Overseer Bright and Beautiful*.'

As it came to its conclusion, Cuthbert, who had made his way into the groom's position for the song, jumped back up into his Overseer role.

'Rachel Sarah Clough, repeat after me. I, Rachel Clough, take you, Overseer of All, to be my husband and Love God. I promise to be true to you in good times and in bad, in sickness and in health, and to do you at least once a night. I will love you, honour you and have many babies with you for the rest of my life.'

'Now Overseer, you don't need to repeat, because you're already talking. So do you accept Rachel's vows? Well of course you do or you wouldn't be standing here now would you!

'So I now pronounce you husband and wife. You may tongue each other senseless.'

'Oh no you don't!' Richard Egbert said, his frame filling up the doorway, his shoulders stooped, his body ashen. 'You missed out the part where anyone with a reason why it shouldn't go ahead should speak up,' he added, his moustache twitching, now part of a larger, scraggly beard. Dressed all in black, he looked like one of the dead, as though he'd just stepped out of his coffin. And that was how he felt, that was where he should have been, resting under the ground, in place of his son. He should have been amongst his fallen friends. All Harold had wanted to do was help the team, make them better, heal the wound that he had opened and now they were gone. He had sat in his head teacher's office thinking that there was nothing he could do to help them or himself, but his town was a different matter.

Why else had he refused to go were it not for the love of the town?

'I'm afraid you're a little late, traitor,' Cuthbert shouted. 'Yes, that's right people, Richard Egbert is a traitor. Not only did he desert our team when they needed him, but he never came to their funeral and never forked out a penny for a flower to lay upon their graves.'

'They shouldn't bloody well be in a grave. You said you and God would look after them.'

'You sent your son to die in your place.'

'I didn't send my lad, he's a big boy and he made his own decision and so did Harold and the rest of the lads, and just because I didn't agree with it, doesn't mean we stopped being pals. I'd have been the first to greet them when they returned and I haven't been to their graves, because they're not there. Once their bodies have been brought back, then I'll go and pay my respects.'

'Well why not volunteer to go out and find them? I'll pay for your flight.'

'Oh aye! By the time I came back there'd be no town left. You're destroying this place day by day. My new jumper's all frayed and fuzzy, because Dorothy has to use sticks instead of knitting needles, and do you have any idea how hard it is to carve a Sunday roast with a spoon? People are having to start on a Saturday night, by which time the meat's gone dry. And the worst insult of all, the one that shows you're not fit to be The Mayor of this town is the fact you claimed the team have gone to a "better place". If that were true, why don't you go and join them?'

'Hmmm,' Cuthbert nodded, ready to signal he wanted Richard clipped by a poisoned pellet. 'If, a big word that. *If* you'd have bowled properly, none of this would ever have happened right? *If* you hadn't choked in that final over, the team would still be alive.'

As Cuthbert continued, Richard only heard certain words (some of which weren't even spoken), and at each insult his rage grew, his eyes narrowed and his mouth twitched.

'...WIDE of the mark...people now have EXTRAS...there will be NO BALL...but we should let LEG BYE gones be BYE gones...'

'We were bloody cheated out of that game and everyone knows it!' Richard Egbert raged, coming out of his trance. 'And I'll bloody show you about bowling extras, you southern nancy.'

Cuthbert raised both arms, but it did not bring Richard Egbert to his knees.

'Now is the time,' he bellowed, as Richard produced a shiny, new corky from his pocket.

'The Lord will strike you down,' Cuthbert blurted, taking a step back, as Richard brought his hand down and began his run up.

'You will...oh Jesus!' Cuthbert screamed, as an 80mph beamer flew into his shoulder, knocking him to the ground in a daze of excruciating pain. It shattered his collar bone, but he had no time to cry with Richard re-pacing his run up with a new ball in hand. Cuthbert took one last look at Rachel, glanced up to the sky, and started to run, with the sound of Richard's feet pounding against the stone floor filling his ears.

The game progressed in a similar fashion as it had done the previous day, with the Darjeeling top four piling on runs, but none of them managed to push on to make a score as significant as Erik's.

As more wickets began to fall, the Skipperton players, in their little pockets around the ground, tried to become the twelfth man.

'His wrist's so limp he can't bowl faster than a two legged dog. Go and smash him to the boundary!' Stuart bellowed, with Frank beside him waving his boundary sheet manically to try and put off the fielders out in the deep.

'He's been bowling off stump all day, he can't bowl any different line,' Harold yelled, pushing at the shot for the batters, as the scoreboard ticked over. If Redillian won and they held aloft the trophy in front of thousands of spectators, what was he to do then? Go off into the jungle for two years to start up tea factories? His time as captain was over that was for sure. One defeat in five years and it was going to end on a low note, how was that even possible?

'No you moron! The middle of your bat. I'll go and buy you one twice the size if you need it,' Dereck bawled, as he was handed a Coca-Cola by Paul, which he stared at for a second, before sipping it and passing it back.

Dimar, Richard II and John, who had made their way round to be closer to Frank and John, paused to cheer a misfield, allowing Darjeeling to claim an extra run.

'They're going to do this, they're going to win,' John said, jumping with a hand on a shoulder of each of his companions. 'This trophy's going to be ours. Just keep it steady now, nothing silly.'

Alan's focus remained on Erik. It hadn't budged from him for a second. He hadn't blinked. He hadn't missed a movement. This would be his final chance to watch him and he couldn't miss any of it. He hated him in the Lancashire top, despised him for deserting the team, but as much as he wanted to watch him fail, he couldn't help but will him to succeed.

The score stood at 361/9 with Sar Mar on strike. The series had already been dubbed "The Greatest Ever" by the local newspapers. People tried to rack their brains to recall if they'd ever seen such back to back tension and they concluded only in the movies, or possibly English Premiership football were storylines written to such an improbable degree. This was it, the final delivery.

And so up in the air the ball went. It was all air, coming down a good five meters inside the boundary, and more importantly, Erik stood beneath it. Compared to the catch he had pulled off yesterday, this one could have been made blindfolded with his feet nailed into the grass. It was coming right down his throat. His hands were cupped by his waist, but they did not rise up to the ball. As it started its downward trajectory, they reached for the bottom of his shirt instead, and in one movement, he pulled his top over his head and walked towards the boundary, turning his back to the crowd to point at the surname on the top of his shirt-*Smith. J.* The ball bounced and rolled, but nobody was watching its path to the boundary, they were trying to read what it said on the front of his t-shirt. *Skipperton - World Tour* ran the header, with the lower font listing the team, their runs scored and wickets taken. The Skipperton players, shedding tears, struggling for comprehensible words, ran, arms wide, as the crowd parted for their batter, clearing a path up to Harold.

'Yorkshire here, here and here,' Erik said, batting his head, heart and stomach.

'I know lad, I know,' Harold replied, giving up on the pretence that they weren't tears streaming down his face, as a bouncing team circle emerged in the stands. Chants rose up of both Yorkshire and Europe, as the jubilant players clutched on to one another's tops.

'Hey!' Harold said, peering out through a chink at Alan, who stood on the periphery, hands in his pockets. 'What do you think you're doing?'

'I...I...'

'It says your name on this shirt as well lad. Just watch where your hands go is all I ask,' Harold added, creating a space to welcome in The Gnome.

'We're the champs lads. Unbeaten, still, invincible I'd say, and we've a bloody big trophy to bring back home too,' Stuart said, from the middle of the scrum.

'Home?' Richard II asked, bringing his head up. 'But we're supposed to be out here for another two months.'

'Aye,' John piped up, 'we haven't visited Thailand, The Philippines or Bali.'

'And err, we heard that they really need help with their cricket,' Dimar added.

'Lads, what we need first and foremost is a victory parade. But I promise you now that anyone who wants to take a holiday to exotic locations before the season re-starts can do so with the money that would have been spent in the extra sixty days. For now though, I can think of nothing I'd rather do than sit down in the armchair beside the Mrs next to the fire, with a huge pot of Skipperton and a plate of Yorkshires piled high in my lap.'

'Aye, I'll do the same after I've set up camp at The Arms for a week,' Frank chirped.

'Wonder if they can get some export?' thought Stuart.

'What chances are there of some hors d'oeuvres?' pondered Paul.

'Would a range of cocktails attract a more refined girl?' considered John.

There was a second's silence, as they all felt that there was something missing, something gone unsaid.

'Err, where's Al?' William asked.

The players checked around them, shielding their eyes from the floodlights to see into the distance, but he couldn't be spotted.

'Owes me a fiver too,' Dereck said. 'And he didn't come back to the hotel last night.'

'He was still rocking on the bench, letting out little whimpers when I finally left the dressing room,' Harold said.

'Well, when he hears about this, he'll surely be back this evening,' William commented, as they made their way onto the pitch for the presentation.

Up in the stand, meanwhile, way, way up at the back, two men sat together, one with his arm around the other.

'You won bro! Your team has won! Don't you want to go and collect the trophy with them?' Akabar asked, squeezing the shoulders of his half brother. He had covered Al's head with a scarf in the morning to stave off sun stroke and now he brought out a handkerchief to wipe away the dribble that was running from his brother's mouth.

'Can't even bear to leave my side for one minute hey bro? Well the feelings are mutual, and you know it's easy to get lost in this country. You'll be as dark as me in no time and I'll look after you forever and ever, because we're family,' he added, cuddling Al tight, as his brother emitted a low gurgle. 'Oh and bro, I've decided if your old team can beat Darjeeling, then we can bring our cousin's empire down, the empire that by all rights belongs to us. Yes bro, we're going to start a fashion trend, we're going to open a coffee shop.'

Also by the Author

Great Relocation

'Reduce, Reuse, Recycle, Replenish, Restructure, Reform.'
With seven weeks until the 15th year anniversary celebrations of The People's Party rise to power, Charles Piltdown is still struggling to come to terms with a world far removed from that of his youth. Beset by internal conflict, he is unable to decide on the best way to raise his daughter and follow his own desires. When he discovers there are people able to show him a life reminiscent of his past, he has to decide how much he is willing to risk in his attempts to regain a life of truth and reality.

'A fresh take on 1984, this is a disturbing and compelling read.'

'There are questions which I'm still debating...This is not disposable fiction.'

www.ingramcontent.com/pod-product-compliance
Lightning Source LLC
Chambersburg PA
CBHW071453170626
46811CB00007B/2563